CITY OF SINNERS

www.penguin.co.uk

Also by A. A. Dhand

STREETS OF DARKNESS
GIRL ZERO

For more information on A. A. Dhand
and his books, see his website at www.aadhand.com

CITY OF SINNERS

A. A. Dhand

BANTAM PRESS

LONDON · NEW YORK · TORONTO · SYDNEY · AUCKLAND

TRANSWORLD PUBLISHERS
61–63 Uxbridge Road, London W5 5SA
www.penguin.co.uk

Transworld is part of the Penguin Random House group of companies
whose addresses can be found at global.penguinrandomhouse.com

Penguin
Random House
UK

First published in Great Britain in 2018 by Bantam Press
an imprint of Transworld Publishers

A CIP catalogue record for this book
is available from the British Library.

ISBN 9780593080498

Typeset in 11.5/14.5 pt Aldus by Jouve (UK), Milton Keynes
Printed and bound in Great Britain by Clays Ltd, Elcograf S.p.A.

Penguin Random House is committed to a sustainable
future for our business, our readers and our planet. This book
is made from Forest Stewardship Council® certified paper.

MIX
Paper from
responsible sources
FSC® C018179

1 3 5 7 9 10 8 6 4 2

For Sam

PROLOGUE

HE'LL NEVER BE THE same again, I'm going to make sure of it.

Once he steps under the yellow police cordon, to enter a nightmare entirely of his own making.

Detective Harry Virdee. The papers say there isn't a case he can't solve. But he won't have seen a murder like this.

Never like this.

I'm going to drag him to the darkest corners of my mind, a place where nothing pure exists any more.

I can still feel it, my hand clasped over her mouth, as her life slipped away. I felt powerful then.

Like I mattered.

Sitting here, in City Park, the bench cold under me, dried blood lingering in the creases of my palms, the world carries on around me. No one knows what I have done. The passers-by are attached to their phones, lost in their own worlds. They don't see me here. But I see them. Even in the bitter cold, the girls dress to show off their figures, tight-fitting coats, bare legs, expensive heels and immaculate make-up. They think these things are important.

They should know better.

I like being this close, seeing the flashing blue lights of police cars as they park outside Bradford Waterstones.

This is my doing. I created this anarchy. It excites me.

As the forensic vans arrive, men in white suits organize themselves outside the shop window; they're too professional to whisper but I know what they're thinking.

Who could do this?

Why?

Looking around City Park, it is quite clear to me.

We're all numb. We have become so used to violence and trauma on our TV screens that we just don't care any more.

We are unshockable.

We don't listen. And we never learn.

Today, the start of Bradford's darkest week begins.

By the end of this, people will listen.

They will learn.

Most importantly, they will never forget.

Detective Virdee is about to discover this is merely the start.

I am surrounded by sin, this is a city of sinners, a city that is about to learn an important lesson. And I am the one to deliver it.

The time for ignorance is over.

ONE

DCI HARRY VIRDEE STARED up at the body. Suspended high in the air by a noose around her neck, she hung from the rafters of Bradford's most beautiful bookshop. She was naked except for a red headscarf wrapped around her face, the decorative detail glistening in the early morning gloom. The quiet was marred only by the stifled cries of the manager, who had already identified the body as one of her members of staff, Usma Khan.

It was an impressive building. It had once been the Wool Exchange, back when Bradford had been one of the richest cities in Europe.

Those times were long gone.

Harry couldn't help but think the dramatic setting perfectly complemented the macabre image of the girl floating in the air. She looked like a banished angel. The dome-shaped ceiling was over a hundred feet high, gloomily lit by the weak sun streaming through ornate glass windows.

One window had been smashed, the Star of David at its centre destroyed.

*

Harry had been with HMET, the Homicide Major Enquiry Team, in Bradford for over a decade. He was a difficult man to shock but he'd never seen anything quite like this. Nor had his team. Scenes of crime officers stood beside him, trying to figure out how they were going to search the area, awaiting Harry's orders. Forensics looked equally uncertain. Sweeping the space was going to be a logistical nightmare, the bookshop would be full of DNA, it'd be impossible to tell the killer apart from the customers.

'What a shit Monday morning,' DI Simon Palmer said, looking up to the ceiling. Harry could smell bacon on his breath. Whereas Harry was athletic, his suit fitting snugly across his broad shoulders, Palmer's hung clumsily from his rounded frame.

He waited expectantly.

As Senior Investigating Officer, everyone's eyes were on Harry. A dead Asian girl, in such theatrical circumstances, was a new one for Harry, yet in the cauldron of Bradford nothing really surprised him any more.

'If the killer got up there, Simon, we can too,' he said. 'We're not dealing with Spider-Man.'

Harry left the team standing among the bookshelves as he approached the ornately carved stone staircase and walked slowly up to the mezzanine floor, which housed a café.

From here he had a closer view of the victim; she was fair for an Asian girl and slight. Her long black hair was visible despite the red veil across her face. No tattoos, no defining features. Harry felt a familiar sense of unease. *What was he missing?*

The noose; not a rope but barbed wire.

Harry winced.

Usma had been responsible for locking up the shop at the end of her Sunday shift. She'd have been alone here for at least half an hour. Suicide couldn't be ruled out.

But cries for help were seldom this sensationally staged. Harry felt it in his gut: this was a murder scene.

Palmer joined him at the top of the stairs.

'Is that barbed wire?' he asked.

'Looks it.'

'Christ.'

Palmer dangled a set of keys at Harry. 'There's a passage that leads up to the dome. Before we go up, we'll have to do a risk assess—'

Harry took the keys from him.

The second staircase looped around the main floor space of the bookshop. A narrow enclosed walkway, with a claustrophobic feel. Harry and Palmer kept to one side, placing their feet carefully, their white SOCO suits bright in the dim light.

At the top, a stone path circled the domed ceiling, giving access to each of the beautiful old windows. Under the broken one, among the shattered glass, Harry could see a scattering of pink rose petals and what looked like a bloody print. He released a breath he didn't know he'd been holding. They might get lucky there.

Harry inched closer, peering out through the broken window.

Hell of a drop.

The barbed wire suspending the victim's body had been fed out through the window and was tied around something Harry couldn't quite make out. But the sight of more rose petals decorating the barbed wire brought bunting fleetingly to mind.

'Turning out to be a proper house of horror, this one,' said Harry. 'Question is, how to get her down?'

They couldn't pull her body up. The barbed wire would shred the skin around her neck and they needed to preserve her body exactly as they had found it.

Harry turned to Palmer. 'Get the fire brigade down here and tell them we're going to need a crane.'

TWO

HARRY CLEARED THE AREA as the body was brought down by the fire brigade. Just his core team remained, awkward and expectant, standing among the rows of neatly organized bookcases. In the silence, he heard a pair of high heels clicking on the stone floor behind him. His boss had arrived.

The sound stopped just behind Harry, who had crouched by the victim. Detective Superintendent Clare Conway wasn't there to babysit Harry, far from it; but a murder like this was sure to have everyone on edge, from uniformed officers on the street to the top of the political hierarchy.

This was no spur-of-the-moment killing.

Somebody had taken their time.

Somebody wanted to make an impression.

Harry took in the detail he hadn't been able to see before. Usma's pale skin was spotted with deep purple hives, and she looked swollen somehow. She wore a gold ring on each index finger and decorative red henna mehndi on her hands. It reminded Harry of an Asian bride on her wedding day. Most bizarrely, she wore false nails vividly decorated in red, orange and green with a three-dimensional rose on one nail of each hand.

How much of this was Usma and how much was the killer?

Harry nodded for a forensic officer to remove the red veil from across the girl's face. It was unravelled three times, gently pulled free and immediately placed in an evidence bag.

Harry heard a collective intake of breath from his team.

He remained motionless. The girl's eyes had been sewn shut.

There was a note secured around her neck.

The forensic officer gently raised the victim's head, removed the note and handed it to Harry, who shifted on to one knee. He sensed Clare Conway moving in closer behind him, her black heels now in his peripheral view.

Harry unfolded the note. His eyes narrowed, his brow creased.

He read it again.

And a third time.

One simple word.

SINNER.

As Harry stood up, the note in his hand, his boss grabbed him by the shoulder hard enough to startle him.

'Jesus,' she said, 'look at her eyes.'

Harry turned back to face the victim.

'Did they just—?' he started.

Clare stepped closer, her hand tightening nervously on Harry's arm.

He was seeing things, surely.

Harry crouched down again, his heart racing, sweat prickling on his temples. He leaned forward and waited.

Nothing.

He reached out a hand and double-checked.

No pulse.

Skin cold to the touch.

He removed a pen from his pocket, paused, then tapped the victim's left eye.

Harry flinched as her eye twitched.

He heard his boss whisper something in disbelief.

Harry's hand was shaking, nothing in his experience had prepared him for this. He tapped the girl's other eye and when the same thing happened, he got quickly to his feet.

'Mortuary,' he said to the lead forensic officer. '*Now.*'

THREE

THE SCREEN ABOVE SAIMA Virdee's desk showed the A&E waiting times. Most of the text was red. Officially, patients were still being told to expect a four-hour wait. In reality it was closer to six.

Monday morning and already the department was an endless cacophony of chatter. Patients lay on gurneys that lined the corridors by the wards. Ambulances were backed up outside, unable to leave their patients until they had been accepted by a department which had run out of beds hours ago. Bradford's emergency unit, like every other in the country, was buckling under the strain of this winter's flu virus, a far more virulent strain than previous years. And on top of that, a bitter snap of arctic, winter air seemingly had every asthmatic in the city rushing towards A&E. This week, the forecast was for snow. Flu would give way to broken bones. Waiting times weren't about to improve.

In the waiting room, a security guard was attempting to calm a drunk who was convinced a glass-cut on his arm was turning septic.

The start of the week and already Saima was dealing with drunks.

'Why do I do this?' she whispered to herself.

As the man's behaviour grew worse and his voice louder, a

junior doctor approached the nursing desk, requesting that Saima call the police. She waved him away. Security would decide if and when the police were needed.

Saima rubbed her bloodshot eyes. She hadn't slept well, Aaron had woken up at four a.m. and refused to go back to sleep until she took him into bed with her. Her three-year-old was adept at the art of toddler manipulation. She knew she needed to be firmer but she loved sleeping next to him, his innocent breath on her face.

Sharp footsteps interrupted her thoughts.

Auburn pigtails bobbing on her shoulders, her colleague Linda, known in the department as the 'pocket-rocket', marched up to the desk and thrust a coat into Saima's arms.

'We've got manual handling, Nurse Virdee. We miss training again and Matron's going to shit a brick. There's more than enough nurses off sick with bad backs because they lifted a patient incorrectly whilst wiping their arse.'

'Linda, it's my neck on the line, not yours,' replied Saima, pointing up at the screen. 'If I can't get this sorted then—'

'Look at that beautiful red screen, like a menstrual cycle for the department.'

Saima frowned. 'Do you always have to be so vulgar?'

'We're bleeding staff, beds and' – Linda pointed down the corridor where the drunk was still shouting – 'patience. Everyone's in a shitty mood. Feels like a perfect period to me.'

Linda placed her stethoscope on the counter and nudged Saima's jacket. 'Manual handling? Leave the headaches to someone else for a while.'

'You want to trade jobs?' asked Saima.

'Hell no. You're doing a band eight job on a band six wage.'

Saima shrugged. 'Charity begins at home.'

'This isn't home.'

'Might as well be. We spend more time here.'

Saima picked up her coffee cup, its contents now cold. 'Second one I've made this morning and not finished.'

'You had time to make *two* coffees?' said Linda, tapping her foot impatiently. 'Can't you find a cute doctor to make you another one?'

'They've not exactly taken a shine to me yet. All they've seen so far is a bossy bitch worried about waiting times,' said Saima.

'What, no love for the hot new sister in charge? Come on.'

Saima shot her friend a look.

'I've heard them talking, love. If your husband wasn't a copper, they'd all be trying it on.'

Linda picked up Saima's coat again. 'Come on, we need to go. Let's knock this training out. And since we're mates, you want to let me piss off early after?'

Saima smiled. 'Not a chance.'

Saima stood outside the A&E entrance, waiting for Linda. Manual handling was an hour's refresher course, held at St Luke's. Quicker to drive than wait for hospital transport. When they were done, Saima would return to A&E, back to the red computer screen, counting down the hours until she could collect Aaron from nursery at four o'clock.

She wondered what new words he would have picked up today. She and Harry had just the one child. They were talking about trying for another. They'd both come from big families, but since their own parents had cut them out, Aaron wouldn't grow up playing with his cousins in the way his parents had. Harry was Sikh and Saima Muslim; according to their parents, they had each married the devil.

Recently, Saima's sister, Nadia, had reconnected with her, but Saima didn't trust her family any more than she trusted Harry's; neither side was ever going to really accept their relationship.

At last Linda's clapped-out Toyota pulled into view, its horn beeping loudly.

'About time,' said Saima.

As she moved towards it, an ambulance pulled in, lights still flashing, and the back doors flew open. One paramedic leapt from the back while his colleague exited the driver's side and ran to help.

Saima stepped aside as they pulled a trolley out of the van, an elderly Asian man lying on it. One paramedic began chest compressions on him while the other steered the trolley towards the building.

The paramedics' voices were urgent. Both were too intent on getting their new patient inside to notice that, during their frantic dash, a wallet had fallen from the trolley to the floor.

Saima picked it up and followed the ambulance crew, waving away Linda's exaggerated gestures at her watch.

'One minute!' Saima called as she headed for resus.

As she entered, the paramedics were still performing chest compressions while a junior doctor stood looking petrified by their side, his hands visibly shaking.

The sister in charge shot Saima a look, flashing her eyes towards the junior doctor. Saima shared her dismay.

'Where's the registrar?' she asked.

The nurse shook her head. 'Trauma next door. Can you help?' She was desperate.

Saima's heart sank; she'd never get to training on time now.

Behind her, the paramedics were completing the handover.

Saima wheeled around, alarmed.

'Could you repeat that?'

'Ranjit-Singh Virdee, seventy, found collapsed at—'

Virdee.

Her shoulders fell as she looked more closely at the man on the trolley.

Saima Virdee was looking at her father-in-law.

A man she had never been allowed to meet.

A man who blamed her for taking Harry away and ruining his family.

A man whose life she now needed to save.

FOUR

STARTING AN AUTOPSY JUST before lunchtime had never been something Harry had understood. It took a certain type of stomach to push aside what was about to happen and proceed with the day as normal.

Harry watched in confusion as Dr Wendy Smith, the forensic pathologist, made her final checks before starting the autopsy. Usma Khan's eyes continued to twitch like a zombie from a bad eighties movie. Wendy appeared unperturbed.

Perhaps it wasn't the worst thing she'd seen in this room.

Harry often wondered how such a small, delicate woman as Wendy had found her calling working with the dead, trying to decipher what their bodies revealed about how they'd died. He'd asked her many times and never got a satisfactory response.

After leaving the murder scene, Harry had returned to HMET headquarters at Trafalgar House to organize his team. The first twenty-four hours of any investigation were critical, especially with a murder as disturbing as this. He'd split his team of twenty into two groups. The first would form an outside enquiry team which would gather statements from staff and try to locate Usma's belongings, including her mobile phone. They'd focus on CCTV footage inside the bookshop before expanding to the neighbouring area.

His other team would handle the victimology, gathering as much information on Usma as they could. They would be responsible for trying to establish the details of her life.

Which left Harry to deal with the autopsy; in his opinion, the worst part of the job.

It wasn't that he didn't have the stomach for it, but ever since he'd become a father, he'd been unable to see a lifeless body on the cold metal of the dissecting table without thinking of the parents whose child he was looking at. Parents who had lost the most precious thing they had. The thought never came to him at the murder scene, only ever in the harsh light of the lab . . .

Harry pushed his thoughts aside and focused on Usma Khan as Wendy dictated to her assistant.

'Swollen abdomen, severe hives, ligature marks on the neck exacerbated by the barbed wire, eyelids sewn shut . . .' Wendy moved around the body, gently touching each area that she mentioned, listing the most obvious external injuries before she reached for the scalpel.

In the background, a SOCO systematically took photographs of the body from every angle, capturing each detail as Wendy noted it for the recording. Another SOCO was bagging everything Usma had on her and passing carefully labelled items through a small hatch to the exhibits officer. They had removed Usma's false nails, Harry once again struck by their unique design. He'd taken a picture on his iPhone, recognizing that this was something that would need to be looked into.

Despite the meticulous work taking place, Harry could tell that everyone in the room was thinking one thing: *Why are her eyes twitching like that?*

'You sure you've never seen anything like this?' asked Harry.

'You can ask me as many times as you want, DCI Virdee, answer's still the same,' Wendy said mechanically.

DCI Virdee.

Wendy was all about procedure and didn't do casual. Her total focus was on the dead, something which unnerved Harry. He'd witnessed autopsies many times, yet the change in Wendy's face, the colour flooding into her usually pale skin as she approached the victim with a scalpel reminded him of a child approaching a sweet-counter. She had often pointed out that Harry had the same sickness with his cases.

Sickness.

Her choice of word set Harry wondering.

He shook the thoughts from his head.

'You know,' he said, staring at the clinical white walls, 'I've always wondered why you don't add a little colour to this place. I mean, it's basically your office. Would it kill you to brighten it up and make it a bit *less* morbid?'

Wendy kept her head bowed but shot a glance in his direction. 'Morbid is what we do, DCI Virdee.'

'Just trying to lighten the mood, Doc.'

While her assistant, Ingrid, arranged tools on a steel trolley and pushed them closer to the dissection table, Wendy stepped on to a small stool so her five-foot frame could easily reach the body. She leaned in to pull the girl's lower lip down and examine her mouth.

'Unlikely she died from asphyxiation.'

Harry saw what she had noticed.

'There are no burst blood vessels on the inside of her lips, a phenomenon consistent with strangulation or hanging,' Wendy commented, as if reading from a textbook.

'Right, so what did she die from?'

'First impression? The swelling tells us that it's likely to be some sort of massive allergic reaction.'

'Can you die from that?'

'You can.' Wendy grabbed a scalpel. 'Let's have a look.'

15

She tapped the girl's eyelids with the smooth side of the scalpel and didn't flinch when they twitched.

'How does a dead girl blink?' said Harry.

'There's something inside there,' replied Wendy.

With utmost precision, she used the scalpel to cut the first stitch from the girl's eyes, placing it into a plastic exhibits container which she handed to Ingrid, who in turn handed it to the exhibits officer.

In the uncomfortable quiet of the laboratory, Wendy took her time removing the other five stitches, each thread bagged separately.

Only then did Wendy peel back the girl's eyelid, and for the first time in their ten-year working relationship, Harry saw her recoil. Before he could react, she had jumped off the stool and dropped the scalpel to the floor as something flew out of the girl's eye.

Something fucking angry.

Wendy screamed, an alien sound in the mortuary.

Harry backed away hurriedly as a large black insect shot towards him.

'What the fuck is that?' he said, a note of panic in his voice.

Buzzing loudly, the insect made for the light directly above Usma's corpse, its body hammering against the glass.

'Damn thing's on steroids,' Harry said to himself. The room was frozen in mute chaos, everyone's eyes on the insect.

Wendy was the first to switch back to professional mode.

'Well, that was unexpected. Now, tell me you don't want that thing alive,' she said.

'God knows,' said Harry, his voice still shaky. This was unfamiliar territory. 'No way we're getting it alive. Guess I need to play hero?'

'Afraid of little insects?' asked Ingrid, the only one not to have shown any signs of panic. Harry saw her suppress a smile.

'Don't be stupid,' he lied. He hated bugs, especially, he realized, when they flew out of corpses.

Goddamn horror movie, he thought.

'I'll handle it,' he muttered, afraid that if it flew aggressively towards him he'd do a dance similar to the one Wendy had just done.

He moved to turn the overhead light off.

The insect flew away to rest beneath a light on the wall.

Sensing he was only going to get one shot at this, he tried to keep his cool while slowly, *very slowly*, removing his shoe and raising it above his head. It took him almost a minute to get his hand within a few inches of the insect.

Menacing-looking bastard. Black with a hint of blood on its wings.

He moved quickly and hammered his shoe firmly against it, hearing a satisfying crunch. The insect fell to the floor.

'Container,' barked Harry, 'and tweezers.'

One of the SOCOs hurried towards him and handed Harry both. He crouched by the insect and used the tweezers to place it into the container, relieved his hands were not shaking.

Damn thing looked dead, but Harry wasn't certain.

He brought the container closer to his face.

'Looks like some kind of freakish wasp. Only it's the wrong colour.'

He carried the container back to Wendy, wiping beads of sweat from his temple as he did so.

'Guess we know what's inside the other eye,' said Harry. He handed the plastic container through the hatch to the exhibits officer.

Wendy had stepped back to the body.

'The eyeball has been completely removed. Nothing surgical about it – butcher's job. Whoever did this isn't skilled,' she said.

Harry joined her, looking into the clear void where Usma's eye had been.

'Assuming we are going to find something similar in the other eye socket, can we get this one alive – since we know what we're dealing with?' asked Harry.

Wendy grabbed a larger plastic container, more of a lunchbox size this time. 'I'll make a clean cut above her eyelid. As I peel it back, you'll need to be quick. Hold this above the eye. The bug flies inside and you trap it, right?'

Harry didn't fancy the task but his ego wouldn't let him refuse.

Back beside the body, Wendy used the scalpel to tap the girl's other eye.

'You okay?' she asked.

'I don't like insects,' Harry replied coldly, 'that's all.'

'You want me to—' started Ingrid, stepping closer.

'No,' said Harry, refusing to let his pride take the blow.

Wendy sliced a fluid stroke above the girl's eyelid and held the blade there.

'Ready?' she whispered.

'As I'll ever be,' replied Harry, turning his feet slightly so that, if he missed, he would at least be ready to retreat. 'You mind?' he said to Ingrid, who was encroaching into his personal space. Harry brought the plastic container closer as Wendy used the blade to peel back the eyelid.

Nothing.

She peeled it further.

The insect crawled weakly out of the hollow socket, its wings clogged with blood, trying desperately to flap.

Harry moved the container on to its side, touching it to Usma's face, allowing the insect to crawl inside. As soon as it was in, he trapped it there and breathed a sigh of relief. Only then did he take a closer look.

'What do you think?' he asked the others in the room, all of whom had now closed in around him.

'I don't know,' said Wendy.

'Spider wasp,' called out the exhibits officer, holding his mobile phone through the hatch. The screen showed a picture he'd found on the Internet.

'There's something else here,' said Ingrid.

Harry watched as she removed a small piece of plastic from the hollow socket. She set it on the bench, gently pulling a scrap of folded paper from inside. She unfolded it and, for a moment, her tweezers obscured the words from Harry's view. Only once she'd stood back, her step faltering as she did so, could he read the words written on it:

This is only the beginning, Harry.

FIVE

I SEE HIM AS he leaves the mortuary, afternoon giving way to evening.

I'm hoping he found the note I left for him. By the look on his face, I'm guessing he found the wasps, at least.

Did everyone in the room scream? I wish I could have witnessed it.

I see you, Virdee – all of you, not just the parts you choose to show to the world.

I know you are not a good man. I know what you have done.

Did you think there would be no consequences for your actions?

Did you think nobody would find out? That I would take what you did to me lying down?

He starts to walk towards me as I push my hands deeper into my pockets, whistling as if I haven't a care in the world.

But I do care.

He's so close I can smell the stench of the dead girl's corpse on his clothes. But he doesn't look at me as he passes, eyes to the ground, brow furrowed.

I've caused that. And I'm not done yet.

In fact, this is only the beginning.

Soon, Virdee, I will be coming for you.

SIX

SAIMA WAS ALONE IN the A&E resus room, a few feet from her father-in-law's resting body. His orange turban was perched on a seat, Ranjit's long grey hair chaotically strewn across his chest. A cardiac monitor beeped rhythmically and a ventilator hummed continuously, every so often letting out a whisper of air.

Saima had picked Aaron up from nursery and returned here, awaiting her mother-in-law. She'd left him with Linda, not wanting him in the room near Ranjit. It just didn't feel right.

Alone, staring at a man who hated everything about her on principle, though he'd never even met her, Saima didn't know how to feel.

She turned away from Ranjit and closed her eyes. Her hand gripped her mobile phone tightly.

You've got to call Harry.

But Saima knew what had happened between father and son when Harry had broken the news that he intended to marry her.

Blood had been shed.

Ranjit had beaten his son. First with an open palm. Then the reverse side, his ring cutting Harry above the eye.

Finally, a fist.

When Harry hadn't backed down, Ranjit had come at Harry with his kirpan, the sacred sword carried by devout Sikhs.

Harry's mother, Joyti, had thrown herself between the men and dragged Harry from the room. She had led him outside where she had embraced him, removed her slippers and given them to Harry because, from that day forth, Harry would never be able to touch his mother's feet again, a traditional display of respect he had carried out every morning since he had been a boy.

Saima thought about those slippers. They sat on a table by their front door and Aaron would copy his father and touch them every morning.

'These are Grandma's slippers,' Harry would explain to their son. 'When I was a boy, I was taught to touch her feet every morning to show my respect. But I can't do that now, so instead I touch these slippers.' Aaron would look up at him and pretend to understand.

Saima let a tear fall.

She hated Ranjit.

The words of the junior doctor came back to her.

'Should we call it?'

Saima hadn't been able to stop the thought entering her mind:

If he died, would their problems be over?

But she hadn't allowed herself to hope for his death. Despite the pain he had caused, Saima had worked as if the devil were on her back. Looking over at him now, she saw a frail old man, bruised and vulnerable from the heart attack which had damn well nearly killed him.

Saima had his blood on her uniform.

Her thoughts were disturbed by a gentle knock on the door. Harry's mother, Joyti, and her daughter-in-law, Mundeep, walked in, the door closing softly behind them. Joyti had obviously been crying.

A painful silence.

The women had met before, but they were far from comfortable with each other.

Saima saw Joyti glance at the blood on her uniform before she looked over at her husband. Her mouth dropped open and she blinked away tears.

Joyti approached Ranjit, placed her wrinkled hands on his body and combed his hair away from his face.

Saima and Mandy shared a look.

And in that look, they also shared a memory.

A confession from two years previously, when, on another dark night for the Virdees, Mandy had confessed that she didn't resent Saima because of her faith but because Saima had taken the one thing from her which had given her happiness in her doomed marriage: her brother-in-law, Harry.

A brother-in-law Mandy had loved dearly, a man she had eventually fallen in love with, despite herself.

Saima didn't drop her gaze as Mandy looked away, her secret clearly as distressing now as if it had been confessed only the day before.

As Joyti approached, Saima stooped to touch her mother-in-law's feet.

'You don't need to do that, I know it is not a Muslim tradition,' said Joyti, trying to stop her.

'Your boy still does it every morning.' Saima paused, then added, 'And your grandson.'

Joyti grasped Saima's hands.

'Why,' said Joyti in Punjabi, 'must we always meet over a tragedy?'

The language was familiar to Saima, she had spoken it as a girl with her family.

The two women embraced, each trying hard not to cry.

'Kismet,' whispered Saima. *Fate.*

'They said you saved him. You didn't let him . . . go,' said Joyti.

'I only did my job.'

Joyti forced a smile. 'You didn't let him go,' she repeated, pulling a tissue from her pocket and wiping a tear from Saima's cheek.

24

Saima nodded once.

'And my Hardeep?

Saima shook her head.

Joyti whispered for God to give her strength.

She turned back to her husband, opened her mouth to say something, then reconsidered.

'Will he wake up?' she said, turning back to Saima.

'I don't know.'

'Is his condition very bad?'

Saima's eyes met her mother-in-law's. 'Yes.'

Mandy shuffled uncomfortably at the news.

'If I asked you for something, would you honour me the favour?' Joyti's eyes held Saima's gaze intently.

'Anything,' said Saima.

'Don't tell my Hardeep. Not yet. He will be pained to see him this way, knowing that even in this state, for his father, nothing has changed.'

'We don't keep secrets from each other,' Saima said firmly.

'I'm sure you don't,' said Joyti. 'But, my child, there can be no win for us here. Not like this. Let his father wake up. Let him build a little strength. Then,' Joyti paused, uncertain how to finish, 'we . . . will see.'

Saima was about to object when the resus doors opened and Aaron ran inside.

'I've got to go,' said Linda, looking apologetic. Saima nodded and mouthed 'thank you' just as Aaron reached her, grabbing her leg. She scooped him up.

'Oh, wet!' said Aaron, wiping a tear from Saima's face. 'Mamma wet?'

Saima smiled. 'Yes,' she said, wiping her face before kissing him.

'Mamma hurt?' he asked innocently.

'No.' She tried to laugh his concern away as Joyti stood beside her, face streaming with tears.

It was only the second time Joyti had met her grandson.

'He's my Hardeep,' whispered Joyti in amazement, putting her arms out to take hold of him, but Aaron shied away.

Saima hugged him tightly. 'I . . . I . . . can't do this,' she said to Joyti. 'Not here. Not like this. It's too much.'

'Please,' said Joyti. 'He . . . he looks just like my little Hardeep.'

'Why does it have to be like this?' said Saima, unable to hide her pain. 'Why can't you just let us be a part of your lives? We never wanted this. All we ever did was fall in love.'

She started to cry and held Aaron tighter so he couldn't see. 'I don't deserve this. I never asked for any of it.'

Joyti brought her face closer to Aaron's and kissed his head as he struggled free of Saima.

Saima put him down, wiping her face and allowing herself a sob as Joyti crouched to her knees and held Aaron's face reverentially in her hands. She watched as Joyti stroked his face, kissing his cheeks and letting her tears fall on to his head while Aaron shouted, 'Wet!'

'My Hardeep,' she whispered, and kept kissing Aaron, hugging him tightly in spite of his struggles to break free.

Saima crouched to her knees and allowed Aaron to scramble into her arms, watching as Mandy left the room, wiping her face as she went.

SEVEN

THE CLOCK ON THE dash nudged five o'clock as Harry exited his car and headed towards Usma Khan's house on Barkerend Road. She'd lived opposite the once vibrant St Mary's Church, now abandoned like so many other churches in Bradford.

Times had changed.

People had changed.

For Harry, walking past the dark shadow of the church, steeling himself to deliver the news no parent should have to hear, this felt about as far removed from God as he could get. An hour ago, standing in the mortuary with the stench of death clinging to every piece of his clothing, Harry had been wrong to think that was the worst part of the job.

This was.

Harry hated breaking this kind of news, but he had a feeling today would be harder than usual.

Inside the house, sitting beside the family liaison officer, DC Paula Kelly, Harry observed a now familiar kind of hurt. Usma's family were Muslim and when they'd learned they could not bury their daughter within twenty-four hours as their religion demanded, the pain seemed to deepen on their faces.

The living room was hot and muggy with incense, which didn't quite mask the smell of damp. Harry had first-hand experience of how warm Asian people kept their homes, but this was something else. The thermostat must have been close to thirty. DC Kelly looked ready to faint. An old gas heater in the corner continued to push punishing heat into the room, intensifying the suffering.

Usma's father, Mohammed, wearing loose, traditional Islamic clothing, took his seat next to his wife, Ameena, putting his arms around her. In spite of the heat, she was wearing a thick cardigan over her Asian suit, grey hairs creeping out from her headscarf. Their two grown-up sons lived nearby and had been at the house all day. They looked angrily at Harry, as if they could not believe what he had told them. Harry met their gaze and offered an apologetic nod of his head.

An hour later, with the family trying their hardest to answer Harry's questions, he had learned Usma had called Ameena the evening before and told her she was staying late at Waterstones to arrange a new window display.

Ameena was on morphine and sleeping tablets for chronic back pain and had gone to bed early. Her medication had knocked her out.

That morning when Usma had not woken for college, Ameena had gone into her room and been startled to see the bed unslept in and called the police.

It had been around the same time that Harry had been supervising the recovery of Usma's body from Waterstones.

Looking at Ameena now, Harry couldn't help but think of the look on his own mother's face when she had led him to the door of her house and handed him her slippers. Ameena's loss, though different from that of Harry's mother in one obvious regard, was too close for comfort.

Both had lost a child.

*

Harry stood staring into the gloomy shadow around St Mary's Church, the night air a welcome chill on his face. His eyes saw nothing, for his mind was still in the Khans' living room, the sorrow palpable. Even from here, Harry could hear the wailing; deep and unrelenting.

'Christ, I've never known heat like that,' said DC Kelly, stepping outside to join him.

'Tell me about it.'

'They've just turned that gas heater up again. Made me feel faint.'

'You're going to be with them a while.' Harry turned to face her. 'Best keep yourself hydrated.'

'I'll need an IV line at this rate.'

'Shittiest part of the job, this.'

'Sons are trying their best, but it's a mess.'

'Can they take them to theirs while we finish clearing Usma's room?'

'Doubtful, but I'll give it a try.'

Harry removed his tie and unfastened the top two buttons of his shirt, welcoming the breeze on his skin. 'That place ever used for anything?' he said, pointing towards the church.

'Don't think so. Certainly not for Mass. Think it's used as a storage facility for clothes and food for the homeless now.'

'Run by the council?'

'I guess so. Why do you ask?'

'Just interested,' replied Harry.

A SOCO exited the house, passed them on the steps carrying a large clear bag of Usma's belongings. Harry prepared to re-enter the house; he wanted to see her bedroom for himself.

Back inside the house, the family's grief was palpable, thick like the air. The phone rang almost constantly.

If you need a rumour spreading, tell the Asians, Harry thought.

On arriving upstairs he'd found Usma's name carved into her bedroom door in elegant calligraphy.

The bedroom was unremarkable. Magnolia walls, a couple of framed paintings of what appeared to be teachings from the Koran. Three SOCOs were working methodically through the cramped room.

One of them gave Harry an update. Usma's wardrobe had contained half a dozen traditional Islamic outfits, not quite burkas but not far off. They had found no make-up in her room, no perfume and the only western clothing was an old pair of jeans. Harry wasn't surprised, everything about the house and the family within it screamed traditional. But something didn't quite fit.

Usma's nails.

Harry thought of the immaculate pattern and the three-dimensional rose.

'Harry?' said a SOCO.

His attention was drawn to Usma's bed. The SOCOs had lifted the mattress and found five carrier bags neatly bundled under it. Harry moved closer and nodded for them to be examined.

'Don't think our girl was quite as straightforward as we thought,' he said.

EIGHT

SAIMA AND MANDY SAT in silence outside the resus room, leaving Joyti with her husband. They were away from the main A&E area and Saima had allowed Aaron to sit on the floor in front of them and play with a stethoscope and a truck.

As the voices of A&E staff echoed down the corridor, each woman waited patiently for the other to break the spell. Saima glanced at her watch, dismayed to see it had passed five thirty. She needed to get Aaron home.

'I'm sorry,' said Mandy, finally.

'For what?' replied Saima, focusing on Aaron and not looking at her.

'Saying what I said to you, last time we spoke. About Harry.'

'Was it not true?'

Mandy didn't reply.

'Mandy?' said Saima, a little more forcefully than she intended, looking at her now.

Mandy's continued silence said everything she could not.

'If you're unhappy with Ronnie, divorce him,' said Saima. 'But don't look at my husband as something I took from you. You never had him to start with.'

'I know that,' said Mandy, irritation clear on her face. 'You think it's easy to simply up and leave in that household? The shame that—'

'Don't talk to me about shame,' Saima snapped, turning her body towards Mandy so her next statement was delivered with full force: 'Screw the shame and screw the damn community. You want to be happy? Make it happen. Don't hide behind some out-of-touch idea of honour or shame. The only shame which still exists is people peddling those ideas which should have died with our parents' generation.'

Mandy was taken aback.

'You sound like Harry,' she said, her tone soft but her eyes cold.

Saima knew she couldn't trust her.

Not one bit.

'Are you going to tell Harry?' said Mandy.

'About what? His father? Or the fact his sister-in-law harbours secret feelings for him?'

Mandy looked uncomfortable. 'I don't,' she said.

Saima wasn't convinced.

'Two years ago, when we last spoke, I had lost a daughter, my marriage was unravelling and I was a mess. I . . . I . . . wasn't thinking clearly.'

'You were thinking just fine,' said Saima icily.

'Even if it were true, what's the point of dwelling on it? It doesn't change anything.'

'Because for years you made me think you hated me because of who I am.' Saima corrected herself: 'Because of *what* I am. Do you know how that made me feel? We'd never even met.'

'This isn't the time to talk about—'

'Yes it is. Look at him,' said Saima, pointing at Aaron. 'You all judged me. Judged him. When you know nothing about who we are.'

'I sided with the family. You would have done the same thing in my shoes.'

'Don't tell me what I would have done.'

'We can't all have a fairytale love story, Saima. I've endured living in that house with them,' she said, nodding towards the side room.

'I've endured an arranged marriage to an ex-convict alcoholic. So, I sought comfort in Harry's company. Can you blame me?'

She paused for breath, then went on:

'He was kind to me, he made me laugh. He gave me respite from a terrible situation. But I'm not in love with Harry. Perhaps, once upon a time, I fell in love with how free he was. But to hell with you if you think that was unnatural. I never acted on it, I never crossed any lines. And then one day you took him from me— from us all,' Mandy quickly corrected herself. 'And yet you can't see why I hated you?'

Saima sighed and looked away. She so wanted to hate this woman.

'You might have suffered,' whispered Mandy, 'but no more than I have.'

The women were interrupted by Aaron, who thrust a toy truck into Mandy's lap.

'Vroom vroom!' he said excitedly.

Mandy smiled, the first genuine smile Saima had seen on her face. 'What colour is the vroom-vroom?' she asked.

Aaron thought about his answer very solemnly before replying, 'Red?'

'Good boy.'

'Look,' said Aaron, pulling at his top, his confidence buoyed. 'Blue.'

Mandy clapped her hands. 'Aren't you clever!'

'Black,' said Aaron pointing at his trousers, before grabbing the truck and running down the corridor, driving it along the seats of empty chairs.

'He really is Harry's spitting image,' said Mandy.

'Same temper as well,' replied Saima.

'They're not the only ones.'

'Is Ronnie coming?'

Mandy nodded down the corridor where Ronnie was striding towards them in a smart grey suit, no tie. 'He's already here.'

*

Ronnie was standing by his father's bed, holding his hand, his back towards the women. He'd changed considerably since Saima had last seen him. Thinner, almost ill-looking. There was little colour in his face and his black hair was flecked with grey.

Saima had left Aaron with a friend in the staff room but she longed to hold him close for comfort. She felt like an outsider in this room, alone.

'What's the prognosis?' asked Ronnie clinically, glancing at the cardiac monitor which continued to beep rhythmically.

With any other patient, Saima would have given a well-rehearsed noncommittal response. But she couldn't mislead Harry's family.

'Fifty-fifty,' she replied.

'How long was he . . . flat?'

'Three minutes.'

Ronnie took a sharp intake of breath.

'Is Harry aware?'

'No.'

'Let's keep it that way.'

His tone irritated Saima, his attempt at control in a situation he was far from in charge of.

'You don't get to decide that,' she said to his back.

Ronnie turned his face to the side.

'What?'

'You heard me, Ronnie. This isn't one of your businesses, you're not in charge here.'

Ronnie replaced his father's hand on the bed but kept his back to Saima.

'Harry comes down here and sees the old man like this? What good can come of that? Or, better yet, he wakes up and the first thing he sees is Harry and it kicks off and sends the old man's heart over the edge.'

Ronnie turned around. He glanced at Mandy, then his mother.

'Look at this room. At the drama. The consequences of everything we've been through.'

Ronnie touched his father's body. 'Five broken people and you think we need a sixth?'

'Harry has a right to know,' Saima repeated, her voice uncertain now because she knew Ronnie had a point. If Ranjit saw Harry here, he might never recover.

'He does,' said Ronnie. 'Let the old man wake up, get out of here. Then he and Harry can do this on their terms.'

'And if he doesn't wake up?' said Saima, glancing at Ranjit's body.

'Then the situation will be as it always has been.'

'How can you be so cold?'

Ronnie simply shrugged.

Joyti took Saima's hands, grasping them tight and forcing a smile. 'Like always, it falls to the women to be strong in these times. If you keep this from Hardeep just until his father wakes up – and he *will* wake up – I will be in your debt. I'm asking you for this favour and I have never asked anything of you before except to be happy and keep my boy happy.'

'You are asking me to lie to Harry.'

Joyti shook her head. 'I am asking you not to tell him. Nobody is lying.'

There was silence as Saima struggled with a response.

'Please,' said Joyti, eyes welling up. She squeezed Saima's hands tightly. 'Please. For the sake of Ranjit's recovery?'

Saima nodded reluctantly. 'Okay,' she whispered.

'I'm in your debt.'

'We all are,' said Ronnie, finally looking Saima in the eye.

NINE

AT SEVEN O'CLOCK HARRY opened his front door, reaching automatically to touch his mother's slippers. Had his mother been there, she would have whispered a blessing, for God to protect her son. Incense was burning somewhere in the house, which meant Saima had suffered a hellish day at work.

This is only the beginning, Harry.

Hellish days all round.

He shook the thought of the killer's note from his mind, refusing to allow work to infect his home.

Upstairs, he heard the sound of the bath running and Aaron singing 'Wind the bobbin up', his current favourite nursery rhyme.

That crap drove Harry mental.

At least the wheels on the bus made sense.

Aaron appeared at the top of the stairs and grabbed hold of the baby gate.

'Daddy! Out. Want out.'

'That's what the prisoners at Daddy's work say,' said Harry, climbing the stairs and stopping on the top one. 'What crimes have you done today?'

'Up,' said Aaron, raising his hands.

'Please?'

'Peas.'

'Better.'

Harry scooped Aaron into his arms, held him close and pushed his face into Aaron's, searching for that smell.

Innocence.

Instead of innocence, he found what appeared to be jam all over Aaron's face.

'What have you been eating?'

'Jam. Toast. Want more.'

'No, he bloody doesn't,' said Saima, coming out of the bathroom. She looked harried, still in her uniform.

'Bad day?' he said, opening the baby gate and stepping through to plant a kiss on his wife's mouth.

'There are no good days in A&E, love.'

Aaron was busily licking his lips, trying to reach the jam he'd now found on his face.

'It's a good job you're cute, kid; there's not so much upstairs, is there?' said Harry, carrying Aaron into the bathroom and setting him down on the floor. Aaron started to remove his clothes, excited at the sound of the running bath.

This was father-and-son time.

For the next twenty minutes, Harry carried out his nightly routine of bathing his son, listening to Aaron's incoherent chatter and allowing his ghastly day to slowly be replaced by the only thing he really cared about.

His family.

'Are you staying home tonight?' called Saima from the kitchen. She'd seen that Harry had not changed out of his suit after putting

Aaron to bed. He hated to disappoint her, which was why he always tried to come home of an evening to bathe his son and have dinner with his wife, giving them a sense of normality even if he did have to go back out again afterwards.

Harry was setting the table in the living room. 'Not sure, yet. Bad case at work.'

'You're on HMET. Are there ever any good ones?'

'Sometimes we get a suicide.'

'*Harry*.' Saima frowned over at him.

The angry black wasp flashed in front of Harry's eyes.

'Anyway, you know we don't discuss work at home. Rule five, isn't it?' said Saima.

'Four.'

'Too many rules.'

'You can count them on one hand.'

'I'm sure it's rule five,' insisted Saima.

Harry walked over to a small frame on the mantelpiece.

1. No lies. Ever.
2. Family first. Everything else later.
3. Religious melodrama loses out to wedding rings.
4. Dinner together every night (unless working night shifts).
5. No police or hospital talk at home.

'You're right. Rule five it is,' said Harry. 'Four is having dinner together.'

'Are you honouring that?'

'I'm here, aren't I?'

'Are you *here*, here? Or am I having dinner with one-word answers while you obsess about whatever hit your desk today?'

Harry smiled, taking his jacket off and draping it over a chair. 'Cynic. Anyway, you look like you had a shittier day than me, which would be a bloody miracle.'

*

In the kitchen, Saima thought about Harry's father lying in hospital and the promise she had made her mother-in-law.

Rule number one: *No lies. Ever.*

She wasn't lying, *technically*.

Saima convinced herself it wasn't a lie not to mention the truth.

Her appetite now gone, she picked up the dinner plates loaded with chicken, rice and yoghurt, and brought them into the living room.

Putting the plates on the table, she pushed her chair back to sit down.

'What's this? You having an affair?' Harry muttered as he bent down beside her.

'What?' said Saima.

She stopped dead when she saw what Harry had picked up.

'This just fell out of your jacket,' said Harry, waving a man's wallet at her.

Harry's father's. The one Saima had picked up from the floor outside the ambulance.

'Who is it? Could I kick his ass?' Harry smiled.

Saima was momentarily lost for words. She adjusted her cutlery, racking her brains for something smart to say but finding only the truth.

'Fell out of a patient's pocket when they lifted him out of the ambulance. He was flatlining. I stuck it in my pocket. Totally forgot.'

Harry thumbed the wallet. 'Expensive leather.'

He started to open it, but Saima clicked her fingers sternly and held out her hand.

'Excuse me, mate,' she said. 'Patient confidentiality?'

'Hmmm . . . depends.'

'On what?'

'Did he make it? Do the dead benefit from patient confidentiality too?'

Saima nodded.

'If you open that, I'll have to report you,' she said. 'Call the police. Fill out forms. All that stuff you love.'

Harry smiled and handed it back. 'Nobody wants that.'

Saima returned the wallet to her jacket pocket, zipping it shut.

'Do you want to start without me?' she asked.

'Eh?'

'I just . . .' she said, shaking her head. 'I just want to pray before we eat.'

She saw Harry's eyes narrow.

'Wow. Really must have been some day,' he said.

Saima sighed. 'It was. But you know me, if I spend ten minutes praying, it'll clear my mind.'

'Take all the time you need. I'll wait.'

'Dinner will get cold.'

'We've got a microwave.'

She saw the way Harry was looking at her. 'You're too good to me, you know that?'

'Rule number four,' he replied, pointing to the chart on the wall. 'Dinner together every night. Or we'll end up like one of those cliché cop families who never spend any time together.'

With Saima upstairs, cleansing her mind and spirit, Harry turned on his laptop. Try as he might to forget about work for an hour or so, the discovery of ten thousand pounds in cash hidden under Usma's mattress was playing on his mind.

Harry hadn't asked the family about it, their grief was too raw. Besides, it was clear they knew nothing about it.

This was money Usma had hidden.

How did a twenty-year-old student land that kind of cash?

The search of Usma's room had also revealed a small bag filled with tiny brushes and nail varnishes, hidden underneath her bed behind boxes of books. Harry thought it likely the two hidden items were connected. He flicked through the photos on his iPhone, stopping when he reached one of Usma's false nails. At first he had thought that the pattern was printed but now he could see that it was artwork – painted by someone with a very steady hand. Usma's kit-bag had 'That Nail Girl' printed on the side in bold red letters.

Harry zoomed in on Usma's nails and saw a tiny 'TNG' logo on the side of one of them.

A quick Internet search revealed a polished website of a company based in the Tyersal area of Bradford. That Nail Girl was both a salon and an adjoining academy offering nail technician courses. Harry clicked on the Instagram link and saw the account had over seventy thousand followers.

Harry then accessed a Facebook link and was transferred to a group page for TNG students. The group administrator was listed as Kim Tu. Harry wrote the name down and also the address of her salon. Scrawling down a list of members he found an alias he assumed to be Usma Khan's, listed as UZI-K. Clicking on her name took Harry to a list of all the threads she had posted on.

It seemed Usma was Kim's most prolific nail technician and had moved into teaching as well.

Saima had her nails done every so often; nothing as fancy as this, but even something simple set his wife back forty quid, and the salons always wanted cash.

Suddenly the ten thousand pounds hidden under Usma's mattress didn't seem so out of place.

TEN

RONNIE VIRDEE CAME INTO the grand living room of his Victorian house to find his mother, Joyti, sitting by a roaring fire, flicking through an album of baby photographs of him and Harry. He closed the door, pleased Mandy was upstairs with their two children, Raj and Kirin, helping them with their homework before the children's bedtime. This was a sensitive conversation he needed to have with his mother.

'Where did you get that from?' asked Ronnie, sitting by his mother and pointing to the album in her lap. 'I thought we'd put them all in the loft?'

She didn't reply, instead trailing her hand down a photograph of Harry as a baby.

'They look identical,' she whispered. 'Took me back to when he used to fall asleep in my arms.'

'Did you let me do that?'

Joyti shook her head. 'I spoiled him, I know that, but he was the baby of the family.'

Ronnie squeezed her gently. 'Don't do this now, Mum.'

Joyti wiped her face. 'I do it every night,' she said, turning to look at him. 'Our family is cursed with loss. First Harry, then Tara.'

Ronnie hung his head; he missed his eldest daughter every day. He tried to take the album from her but she kept a firm hold.

'I cannot continue this way,' she said.

Ronnie sighed. He had known the moment he had seen her with Aaron this would happen. If he was being honest, he'd felt it too.

'You never told me why you and Harry stopped speaking. I used to be thankful that he at least had you.' She turned to face him, her cheeks red, a tear drifting down her skin.

Ronnie stared into the roaring fire, flames flirting with the air in the room. 'He wanted me to do something I couldn't,' he said quietly.

'Bring us all back together?'

Ronnie nodded. It wasn't so far from the truth.

Four years before, Harry had discovered that Ronnie didn't just own several cash-and-carries and a large network of convenience stores in Bradford, he also ran the largest distribution network of heroin in the city. The revelation had strained the brothers' relationship, each waging a constant battle to bring the other over to his side. After Tara had been murdered, Harry and Ronnie had finally given up. Parting ways had seemed the simplest solution. But it was still painful, for them both.

'He is so alone,' whispered Joyti, unable to keep her hand from stroking the photograph.

'He has his family. And he's strong, Mum. Like you.'

'I'm not strong any more,' said Joyti, removing the picture from the album and holding it close to her face. 'Same nose, lips, cheeks. With Saima's green eyes.' She closed her eyes, allowed the tears to run down her face.

Ronnie held her tightly. 'Mum, let's focus on Dad—'

'No!' she snapped, shaking her head and breaking free of his grip. She stood up, taking the photograph with her, and walked towards a framed portrait on the wall of her standing beside her husband.

'He made the choice for all of us,' she spat, pointing at Ranjit, 'and just like that, I lost a son.' Her words disappeared into the darkness, flickering silhouettes dancing off the walls. 'And now I don't get to watch Aaron grow up. I am forbidden because I have to follow your father's rules,' she said, turning back to Ronnie.

'You know Dad will never allow it.'

Ronnie narrowed his eyes. He saw his mother consider her response.

'He may not survive,' she said.

It was what she didn't say that unnerved Ronnie and set him wondering: *Does she want him not to survive? Have we really reached that point?*

'You need to be careful, Mum, if you grow closer to Aaron, it means bringing Saima and Harry back into this family. And as far as Dad's concerned, there is no room for manoeuvre on that.'

Joyti looked downcast.

'He still touches my slippers every morning. Saima told me.'

'And he will for ever.'

'I'm not dead that he cannot touch my feet,' she said fiercely.

Ronnie was surprised at the passion in her voice.

'He really got to you today, didn't he? Aaron?'

Joyti swallowed a lump in her throat and switched from English to Punjabi. 'Perhaps only a mother can understand what I felt today. It was like I had gone back in time. I was young again. I had energy in my bones and my heart felt full of life. When I felt Aaron's face on my lips, his body in my hands, I woke up from the pain of these past years. I cannot – I will not spend one more day isolated from Harry and his family.'

Joyti looked at the picture in her hands.

'My little Hardeep has come back to me and this time nothing will keep me from seeing him. Not you. Or Mundeep. *Or your father.*'

ELEVEN

HARRY ARRIVED AT TRAFALGAR House shortly after nine o'clock and saw that Conway's office door was open. He stuck his head inside, only to find it empty. The computer was still on, her mobile on the desk and her expensive-looking black heels on the floor next to the desk.

Harry found her in the kitchen, heating up a microwave dinner.

'Jesus, you made me jump,' she said.

Harry held his hands up apologetically.

'What are you doing here?' she asked him and placed two slices of bread in the toaster.

'Wanted to leaf through the witness statements we took from the staff at Waterstones. You heard about the autopsy?'

Conway nodded. 'There's messed up and then there's that.'

'Be thankful you weren't there to see it.'

Conway couldn't hide her smile. 'Heard it got you . . .'

Harry's eyes narrowed. He didn't like the smirk. 'Exhibits officer?'

She shook her head. 'Wendy.'

He shrugged. 'Last thing you expect to come out of a victim's eyes is a bloody wasp.'

'Any leads?' she asked.

'Give us a chance.'

'That why you're here?'

'Wanted to check out a few things that are bugging me. Didn't want to sleep on them.'

'Such as?'

'The note we found. It felt personal.'

'I'll say,' she replied. The microwave dinged and she pulled out her dinner. 'What are you thinking?'

'Worried this is the start of something major. This city has a history of serial killers and that's where my mind is going. We need to find this freak fast.'

Harry pointed to the toaster where smoke was rising.

'Shit!' snapped Conway. 'Bloody toaster!'

She tried to force the release button but it wouldn't move. Harry leaned past her and turned it off at the wall switch. Charred toast popped out.

'Every time,' he muttered. 'Open the purse strings would you and authorize a new one?'

Conway binned the toast and sighed at the sad crust left in the bread bag.

'You want me to pop to the 7-Eleven for you?' asked Harry.

'No, no, don't be silly. Shouldn't be having carbs after nine o'clock anyway.'

'How long are you around for?' he asked, handing her a plate to put her meal on.

'Thanks,' she replied, taking it from him. 'Cinderella clocks out at midnight.'

Harry pointed to her feet where red trainers had replaced her heels. 'If I don't come back to you before then, don't leave me one of those to find.'

At his desk, with only a lamp illuminating the space around it, Harry flicked through the witness statements his team had collected.

Amongst the usual mundane details, he was looking for one specific clue.

It took him half an hour but he found it. One of the part-time members of staff who had often shared a shift with Usma had said she thought Usma had a boyfriend. A white guy, no less, but she didn't know his name or any details.

Harry sighed.

Something had been niggling him ever since he had seen the note.

This is only the beginning, Harry.

He logged into the computer database and started to search through old cases he had been in charge of. Bradford had one of the highest incidences of homicide outside of Greater London. For a moment, Harry was surprised at just how many cases he had closed.

Most murderers were sloppy bastards, leaving enough clues to make his job easy. It wasn't often that he came across a killer like this one, who made the aftermath of the murder almost as bad as the crime itself.

This guy wanted an audience, and that rarely meant one murder. Harry was concerned more bodies would follow.

The planning it must have taken to have pulled this off.

Harry stopped at a case file.

He didn't need to click on it. It was ten years old but he knew the details as if it had only happened the day before.

Gurpal Singh had battered his wife, Inderjeet Kaur, and killed her boyfriend Tony Casper. He'd gone to jail for ABH and manslaughter.

He had been released on probation nine weeks ago.

'Shit,' he whispered.

Harry printed off a copy of the report and took it with him to Conway's office. He knocked and opened the door, finding his boss at her desk, the microwave dinner untouched on the plate.

'No good?' asked Harry, pointing towards it.

She turned her nose up at the cheesy mess. 'At least now I know why they were on offer at two for a fiver.'

Harry handed her the piece of paper he had brought with him. 'Remember this case?'

She stared at it. A moment passed before her eyes widened in recognition. 'Everyone remembers this case. It was a bloody mess.'

'No argument there.'

'He got off on murder, didn't he?'

Harry nodded. 'Travesty.'

'Said you'd set him up.'

'Don't they all.'

'This guy meant it, though, didn't he?' said Conway. There was no suspicion in her voice, merely the recollection of how vehemently Gurpal Singh had insisted that Harry had concealed evidence which would have proved his innocence.

'He's out on parole,' said Harry. 'Got out nine weeks ago.'

'What does this have to do with the Usma Khan case?'

'I'll pull the transcripts from Sheffield tomorrow, but in court, after he was sentenced, I remember what he screamed at me. Security had to hold him back.'

Conway put the piece of paper down. 'Go on,' she said.

'He told me it wasn't over. In fact, I think his precise words to me were, "This isn't over, Harry. This is the fucking beginning."'

TWELVE

IT IS DARK HERE. But the light from the wasp tanks creates a calming glow.

Inside one of them are Usma Khan's eyes, but the wasps haven't taken to them.

Eyes that knew sin.

It is time for the queen to lay her eggs. So I've lowered a beastly-looking tarantula into her tank.

It's no contest.

The spider knows, as soon as he senses her presence, that his time is over.

He retreats into a corner, raises two of his legs and bares his fangs as the wasp hovers, just out of reach.

The first time I saw this I was a boy, eleven years old.

Up until that point, I had believed that size and strength were all that mattered.

The wasp plays with the spider. She attacks him, panics him.

And just as the spider sees that there is no escape, she backs away.

The queen has my focus. Calm. Antennae twitching in front of her. Eyes dark.

Holding for the perfect moment.

Tormenting the spider.

The spider runs.

Charging for freedom.

Body lowered, sting primed, the queen swoops in and injects her venom into the abdomen of the spider with devastating accuracy. As quickly as she attacked, she retreats.

The venom is paralysing but it will not kill. It will simply allow her to lay her eggs in the spider's crippled body, where the eggs will consume the spider, growing until they are ready to hatch into fully grown adults.

Like the ones behind Usma's eyelids.

Difficult letting them go, after the time and effort I dedicated to them.

The detective won't understand.

Nobody will.

Did they fly out, proud and angry?

That would have been something to see.

Did Virdee scream when he saw them?

I'll ask him when we meet.

He's like the spider.

A predator, until something much more dangerous arrives. Something which really shouldn't be able to cause such paralysis.

But I can.

THIRTEEN

MIDNIGHT WAS APPROACHING AS Ronnie entered Undercliffe Cemetery, the ground treacherous with ice. It had once been a burial ground for the rich wool merchants of Bradford. The audacious tombs, some rising fifty feet in the air, a declaration of importance and wealth, made for a creepy walk through the darkness. The cemetery had long been opened up to public burials, no matter the wealth of the individual.

Ronnie was carrying a bunch of white lilies, a thick blanket and a flask of hot chocolate. He arrived at Tara's tomb, a modest granite stone which read:

Tara Kaur Virdee, beloved daughter,
granddaughter and sister, died aged 20.

He placed the flowers on her grave then laid the blanket next to it. He sat down, removed a packet of cigarettes and lit one. Keeping it in his mouth, he opened the flask, removed an extra plastic cup from his pocket and poured two cups. Ronnie placed one on Tara's grave.

'Cold tonight, kid. Brought your favourite. They keep promising it's going to snow. You'd have liked that, wouldn't you? Old man sitting here with his arse getting wet. Raj and Kirin were talking about you today. GCSE English homework. Your mother was trying to help them and making a mess of it.'

Ronnie removed the cigarette from his mouth, 'Yeah, yeah, I know. I'm down to five a day. Like fruit. Think your mother's on to me, mind.'

He leaned back, rested his head on the tombstone and stared at the sky.

No stars.

Just a crescent-shaped moon.

Ronnie lifted his cup of chocolate and took a sip.

'AA meeting tonight was good. I talked. Not about the stuff that would get me jail-time. Just about the drink. Felt I needed it after today.'

Ronnie told her what had happened with his father and how Joyti wanted to try and reunite with Harry.

'It's going to get messy, kid. Don't think the family can take another loss after you. But, I'm not here to talk about that,' he said.

Yesterday Ronnie had told Tara about the horrific incident in his father's corner shop, two decades before, when a teenager, Michael King, had tried to rob their store, brandishing a knife and slashing Ronnie's mother when she refused to hand over any money. She had fallen and been knocked unconscious. In that moment, Harry had intervened, grabbing a pair of scissors from the counter and stabbing them into Michael's neck.

Michael had died.

Ronnie had taken the scissors from Harry and assumed the blame. He'd gone to prison. It was the beginning of everything for Ronnie and until that night, only the brothers had known the truth of it. Ronnie had been glad to share it with Tara.

Ronnie removed a tattered notebook from inside his jacket. 'Where were we?'

He leafed through the pages until he came to a folded corner.

'Right, okay: 2005 and the trade. I said I'd be honest with you.'

Ronnie spoke quietly, reading from the diary he'd kept while in jail; recalling the rude awakening that, in prison, drugs were currency. Ronnie was smarter than most of those guys in the prison, he'd been on track for straight As at A-level, but those avenues would be closed to him now.

So he'd picked up the tricks of the trade from the dealers serving their sentences alongside him. He was a quick study, watching how the system worked and, crucially, the ways it didn't.

People.

It was always people who messed it up.

After his release, he'd drunk alcohol until it controlled him rather than the other way around. Harry, consumed with guilt over what Ronnie had become, serving time on his behalf, had helped him get sober.

As Ronnie gradually took control of his addiction, he had followed his father into the family business and bought a corner shop.

A year later, he'd bought another.

Within two years he'd acquired several more and decided to open a cash-and-carry. He was making decent money.

But it wasn't enough.

He was creating a cover, a viable, legal network, to help him enter the drug trade. He'd learned from the best in prison – it seemed a shame to waste the opportunity.

He'd started small.

Determined not to make the same mistakes that had landed others in prison.

Determined not to be greedy.

As he read that word, 'greedy', he paused.

'That didn't exactly work out, did it, kid?'

He looked down at his daughter's tombstone. No parent should have to bury a child, he knew that. But he also knew that he was being punished.

His guilt would never dissipate.

Shaking his head, he found his place and began to read again.

He told Tara that once he'd started to make contacts across Europe and Asia under the pretext of forging cash-and-carry distribution deals, he had quickly established a different kind of distribution deal, working with one product other cash-and-carry owners didn't touch.

Heroin.

He employed only ex-SAS operatives who had been injured in battle or turfed out for minor offences, usually to do with some bullshit procedure. They were bitter at not being looked after and proved to be perfect employees.

Disciplined.

Loyal.

Trained to kill.

Ultimately, he made them partners, meaning they had ownership for whichever area of Bradford they were in charge of. Buying their commitment.

Ronnie organized his business like the old mafia movies he had seen.

One family.

'It wasn't just the money, kid,' said Ronnie, lighting another cigarette. 'Sure, I wanted you guys to have the best of things in life, and having a record meant I was always behind in the game. But it was more than that. I realized drugs had always existed in Bradford and caused so much damage because these dealers kept cutting the drugs with all kinds of rubbish just to feed their own greed. Since drugs were always going to be part of society and always part of Bradford, I'd supply something clean. I felt like I could make a difference and earn a wage at the same time.'

Ronnie finished his cup of hot chocolate and checked his watch.

'You know, talking to you makes the time fly.'

He packed up his flask, gathered his blanket and neatened the area around Tara's grave. He left Tara's hot chocolate and wiped down the headstone.

'The meeting's on Barkerend Road tomorrow night. Smaller crowd, but it finishes early so I'll be here around eight.'

Ronnie looked to the skies. 'Snow tomorrow, I reckon. I'll bring more hot chocolate.'

Before he left, he smiled at the grave. 'You do learn something at those AA meetings; seems that sharing is the only way to take on the demons. And it's working, Tara. I promise. I've changed. I *am* changing. I'm going to get out of this game. Then and only then, will I ask you to forgive me for what I did. For what I became.'

FOURTEEN

'GET UP.'

Harry woke up to his usual 06:30 alarm of Aaron trying to pull off his duvet.

'Being a morning person isn't a Virdee trait,' grumbled Harry, getting out of bed and scooping his son into his arms.

'I brush teeth,' said Aaron.

'Already?'

'No, I want brush teeth, Daddy.'

Harry carried Aaron into the bathroom where Saima was perfecting her make-up. When she wasn't working nights, she had to leave before Harry. He squeezed her backside, making her jolt her lipstick.

'Hey!' she said.

'He did it,' said Harry, sitting Aaron on the cabinet by the side of the sink.

'Look at what you made me do! I look like the bloody Joker.'

'I saw it, I liked it, I squeezed it,' said Harry, trying it again. Saima moved out of the way and slapped his hand playfully away. Aaron thought it was a game and started to laugh.

'If you came home at a reasonable hour, you could squeeze whatever you wanted,' she said and wiped the lipstick smear from her face.

'That sounds like a promise to me,' said Harry, handing Aaron his toothbrush. When Harry tried to squeeze toothpaste on to it, Aaron started a familiar meltdown.

'Fine, fine,' said Harry, 'do it yourself.'

Harry watched as Aaron made as big a mess as he could before standing back and allowing Saima to take over. She brushed Aaron's teeth with military precision and as she lifted him to rinse his face, Aaron moved his head back sharply and butted it into Saima's nose.

'Ow!' she screamed and almost dropped him.

'Shit,' said Harry, seeing the blood.

Aaron started to cry.

'It's okay, it's okay,' said Saima, turning away from Aaron and pinching her nose at the bridge as blood streamed steadily over her top lip.

Harry picked up Aaron, carrying him out of the room as Saima tended to her nose.

'What a bloody way to start the morning,' he hissed as he returned to check she was okay, leaving Aaron in his room distracted with his mobile phone.

Saima was hunched over the sink, blood dripping into the basin, face streaming with tears.

'Definitely look like the Joker now,' said Harry.

After the nursery drop-off, Harry arrived at Trafalgar House fifteen minutes before the daily eight a.m. HMET briefing where all four DCIs in the team would update their boss, Detective Superintendent Conway.

Barely forty-five minutes later, briefing completed, Harry was sitting in front of a computer with his team. He'd briefed them about his hunch about Gurpal Singh and tasked a couple of DSs with finding his current address, the name of his probation officer and the court transcripts from the storage facility in Sheffield. Harry also asked them to locate Indy, Gurpal's ex-wife.

The team now turned their attention to the grainy CCTV footage from inside Waterstones, the first time they'd get to see what had happened on Sunday evening.

The quality was shit.

They could make out Usma Khan locking up. According to the manager, she should have had someone with her – they weren't supposed to lock up alone.

As she put the key in the door to close for the day, Harry saw a figure dressed in a burka approach from the street.

'Is that a weapon in the Burka's hand?' said Harry, leaning closer to the screen.

'Can't be sure,' replied DI Palmer, the smell of coffee strong on his breath. 'We've tried getting a close-up but these cameras have such low pixels the picture distorts.'

Usma stepped back to allow the Burka inside the store. She was clearly afraid, backing away and looking around uncertainly. The killer pushed Usma towards the rear of the store where the stone arches blocked them from CCTV view. Harry could just make out the swift movement of an arm raised high – a blow to the head.

'There's nothing now until eleven p.m.,' said Palmer.

'And what time is this?' Harry asked.

'Four forty.'

'There's nothing?'

'Nope.'

'What, the killer just sat in the shadows for six hours?'

'It's the only blind spot. He must have known that. Next time we see him, it's eleven p.m. and thereafter it's all about the staging.'

Palmer cut to another video file, this one in night-vision mode, giving the killer an eerie glow. He was still wearing a burka but now he was not at all perturbed by the cameras. He dragged Usma's body from under the arches through the store. At least the SOCOs now knew exactly where the murder site was.

As the killer started up the stairs, Palmer changed the video to another file, this one of a camera directly facing the windows in the upper dome above the shop.

'Shit,' said Harry as he watched the towering window shatter, the Star of David disintegrating as the killer smashed it with some sort of pole. Then, he quietly – methodically – went about the business of stringing up his victim.

'Twisted bastard,' spat Harry and turned to Palmer. 'This is what – midnight?'

Palmer nodded. There was more to come, Harry could see it on his DI's face.

'What time did the freak leave?'

'Better brace yourself for this, boss.'

Palmer changed the file again.

'But this is store opening,' said Harry. 'You've missed the killer leaving.'

'We haven't,' said Palmer, and suddenly Harry understood.

'He was still there?'

'Watch,' said Palmer and pointed to the screen.

At 07:55 on Monday morning, the store manager, Jane, could be seen opening up the front door. She turned the lights on and moved through the store, past a labyrinth of towering wooden bookshelves and tables piled high with new releases. It was only when she approached the stairs some eight minutes later that she saw the broken glass on the floor. Looking around for the cause of the mess, her head turned up and she found the body hanging from the ceiling.

Jane then ran swiftly to the counter, picked up the phone and dialled the police. Then, as any other person would have done, she ran outside to the only other store open at that time, a pastry shop around the corner.

Only now did the killer emerge, walking brazenly through the store, then pausing to give a jeering wave towards the camera before slipping outside.

'I've seen a lot of shit in my time but this is something else.'

Harry stood up and looked Palmer in the eye. 'Tell me we've got him outside?'

'Oh yeah, it gets even better.'

'*Good* better?' Harry grimaced, knowing the answer.

'Not exactly, Harry.'

Palmer brought up CCTV surveillance of Hustlergate, the area around the bookshop. The killer couldn't have picked a worse place to try to escape a murder scene, Bradford's city centre was covered by CCTV. Harry's team had a clear view of the killer as he walked calmly out of Waterstones towards City Park.

Past the fountains.

Across the road.

Into Bradford Interchange train station.

They'd have him in no time, the place was blanketed in surveillance. Looking at Palmer's face, Harry lost confidence.

They tracked the killer walking through the interchange into the ladies' toilets.

The time was 08:19.

He never came out.

At 08:30 the interchange swelled with commuters – workers and students alike. There were hundreds of Burkas and dozens of them entered the ladies' toilets. Some came out as they had gone in but the vast majority emerged in western clothing. It was a sight Harry was well accustomed to; Asian girls would leave their homes in traditional attire, then change into western clothing as soon as they could.

'How many girls we got?'

'We've got the footage for the whole day. So far, one hundred and thirty girls enter those toilets in burkas. Forty-two leave with them on. Impossible to tell where our guy is or even if it is a guy.'

'I want officers there every morning at eight a.m. Canvass the girls – they must use those toilets every day. Start a log. Eliminate them from the footage. See what it leaves us.'

'Already on it, boss.'

'You're telling me we've got no clue which of these people is the killer?'

'Harry, even the girls who came out in western clothing were wearing heavy coats, scarves and hats. It was minus two out there yesterday morning, not much warmer today. It's going to take us time.'

'Shit,' said Harry, sighing heavily. 'This guy's no fool, is he?'

'He's a brazen son of a bitch, I'll give him that.'

With the CCTV looking like a dead-end or at least one which was going to consume hundreds of man-hours, Harry was forced to look at what else they had at their disposal.

Usma's phone hadn't been found at the crime scene or her home. The outside enquiry team had used cell-site data to determine that it was last switched on in the vicinity of Waterstones. It was probable the killer had taken it.

Harry punched Usma's number into his phone and stored it.

Harry had read the witness statements from staff at Waterstones the night before. They all said similar things: quiet girl, kept herself to herself and loved drawing, especially nail-art. Harry instructed Palmer to interview the family members, now that they'd had twenty-four hours to process. They couldn't afford to wait any longer. He also requested the tech guys to analyse the Waterstones footage and compare it to known footage they had of Gurpal Singh. Compare the two for height, build and gait.

'There was a bloody footprint at the scene. Right?' asked Harry.

Palmer nodded.

'See what shoe size we've got recorded for Gurpal and if it's the same size as the print.'

Palmer made a note of everything Harry had asked for.

'Take DC Farooqi with you when you go to see Usma's parents.'

'Why?' Palmer asked, looking a bit offended.

'He speaks the lingo. You might need some translation help if they get emotional,' Harry said with a shrug.

Palmer made a move for the door.

'Oh, and Simon,' Harry stood tall to make sure his voice carried across the office, 'make sure you get all you can on what they know about that money, I want to make sure there was nothing else dodgy going on there.'

'Right you are, boss.'

In the meantime, Harry left Trafalgar House, still reeling from the way the killer had simply walked out of the front door when Jane had opened up.

This was a different type of murderer – calm, calculating and well organized.

And Harry had the distinct feeling his next victim was already in the planning.

FIFTEEN

GOOGLE MAPS SHOWED That Nail Girl boutique nail salon was only three miles from Trafalgar House. Harry found it nestled in the middle of a parade of shops with a large forecourt. He pulled up next to the only car parked out front, a sleek black Range Rover with the registration plate, 'Kim2TNG'.

The parade of shops housed a suntan parlour, Indian takeaway, pharmacy, nail salon, sandwich shop and a large triple-fronted convenience store. He took a walk around the parade and saw nothing out of place. Harry entered the boutique and was immediately assaulted by the strong smell of something chemical in the air and a radio playing nineties boyband music.

It was compact, to say the least. The walls were a glossy red with the TNG logo painted on each one. Three technicians were working at three small workstations down one side of the room. Each of the customers was part way through what looked like a complicated manicure of some kind that Harry couldn't get his head around. Shelves on the far wall stocked glitters and polishes in every colour Harry had ever seen. A framed certificate on the wall by the reception desk caught Harry's eye.

Kim Tu

Star of Fame, UK Nail Awards

*Awarded for innovation in 3-D nail design with special
commendation to Kim's signature Blood Rose design*

Beside it were other awards. Seemed Kim was no ordinary nail artist.

A petite blonde receptionist tapping away on a laptop gave Harry a cursory glance and asked if he needed any help.

'I'm looking for Kim Tu,' he said.

'That's me,' said a girl sitting behind the furthest workstation. Brunette. Late twenties. Attractive. She didn't look up, her focus remained intently set on her customer's nails.

Harry approached her and told her who he was, offering his identification.

Kim didn't take her eyes off her work, she'd completed a graphic design on her customer's nails – one hand had been set aside to dry under the glare of an ultraviolet lamp while she applied finishing touches to the other.

'I need to speak with you,' said Harry.

'What about?'

'It's delicate. Here's not really the place.'

'I finish at six.'

'That's not going to work for me.'

'This is intricate work. Do you mind?' she said, her voice sharpening.

Harry crouched beside her, leaving only a few inches between them. He changed his tone. 'Kim, this is a conversation we're going to have.'

She glanced at Harry. 'You're going to have to tell me what it's about. If I cancel a client? That's forty quid, minimum.'

'It's about Usma Khan,' replied Harry.

A shift in Kim's eyes. Discreet, but Harry clocked it. She focused back on her client. 'I've got another ten minutes on these nails. Okay?'

'Missed my breakfast. Sandwich shop next door any good?'
Kim nodded.

L'Kitchen was a cosy little café rather than a sandwich shop. Harry ordered a fried egg sandwich and a milky coffee.

He quickly learned the owner was called Lena, she had a one-year-old girl and she was very willing to talk.

Harry asked if she knew Usma Khan.

'Asian girl with the rich boyfriend?' said Lena, putting some milk in the microwave for Harry's coffee.

'Rich boyfriend?'

'She's always being picked up by a different sports car. I'm a *Top Gear* fan, I know my cars.'

'What kind of motors?'

'Porsche. Bentley.' She nodded towards Kim's Range Rover. 'Think that used to be one of his until Kim bought it off him.'

'Know who he is?'

'Why the interest, mate?'

The microwave stopped and Lena finished making Harry's coffee, handing him the mug. 'I'll bring your sandwich over.'

'Cheers. The boyfriend then. You were saying?'

'What are you, a cop?'

Harry nodded.

Lena looked suddenly uncertain.

'Relax. It's just routine enquiries.'

'Police don't make routine enquiries.'

Harry waited for an answer to his question.

'If we're talking about the same Asian girl, then her fella owns a second-hand garage on Sticker Lane.'

'Cheers,' said Harry. 'I'll take a window seat over there.'

The sandwich was generous, the bread roll soft as butter and the yolk perfectly runny. The coffee wasn't bad either. Harry made a note to visit again.

He used his phone to google second-hand car garages on Sticker Lane and found three companies. Checking their stock, he found only one with the types of cars Lena had spoken of. The owner, Xavier Cross, was a white guy with a shaved head and tattoos – the picture of him on the site showed him standing next to a Bentley. Harry noted its location, that'd be his next stop.

With the sandwich finished and the coffee mug empty, Harry was about to go back into the nail salon when Kim came in and marched straight over to him.

'So?' she said, looking more exasperated than Harry expected.

'Easy, kid. Get yourself a coffee. A fry-up if you want.'

'I'm on a clock.'

'What? You don't eat breakfast?'

'It's almost lunch. Besides, I've got a client in twenty.'

Harry called out for Lena to make him another coffee and waited for Kim.

'I'll have a latte,' she said to Lena and sat down.

'So?'

'Can we start over? Maybe lose the attitude?' said Harry.

'I'm busy. Got clients.'

'I can see.'

Harry nodded towards the Range Rover. 'Business must be good.'

'It is.'

'Didn't think nail salons made so much money.'

'They don't. I do.'

Lena brought over the coffees and left the bill on the table.

'Usma Khan. She used to work for you?'

Harry regretted the slip of the tongue.

Kim frowned. 'Used to?'

Harry dropped his voice and told her what had happened, omitting some of the finer details. Blood drained from Kim's face and her whole demeanour changed. She looked genuinely devastated.

'I'm sorry,' said Harry. 'That wasn't how I intended to tell you the news.'

Kim looked away, blinking hard.

'Christ,' she said. 'Usma? You're sure?'

Harry handed her a napkin and gave her a few minutes.

'Can we do this another time?' said Kim.

'I'm afraid not. First twenty-four hours after something like this are critical. I really need to know a few things about her. I'm guessing there are some secrets maybe only you know about.'

Kim looked at him, perplexed.

'Come on, Kim, I'm a detective.'

She dropped the act almost immediately.

'So I'm thinking her family didn't know she was into this nail stuff and, from what I can see, Usma was good at what she did. Earned decent money, too. I'm here to find out what happened to her. The more open and honest you are with me, the better chance I've got of nailing the bastard who did this. No pun intended.'

Kim wrapped her hands around the steaming mug in front of her and looked around the café. There were only two other customers eating their breakfast.

'Think we can take these away? I've got a training centre at the end of the parade. Above the suntan shop. Let's talk there.'

Harry closed the door to Kim's office. They were on the second floor of the end retail unit, which Kim had set up as a training facility for nail technicians.

Kim told Harry she'd met Usma at an exhibition she'd held at the Midland Hotel in Bradford. Kim had gained a reputation online and in the business as one of the best nail technicians around. She'd started her own brand, That Nail Girl, and was keen to franchise it.

'That's some achievement for someone so young.'

'Was brought up poor. Swore I'd give my kids a better start than I had.'

'How many you got?'

'Two.'

'Hard work, isn't it?'

Kim smiled. 'It's worth it though.'

'How's Usma fit into all this?'

'She was shit-hot.'

'Really?'

Kim nodded. 'Don't get many students like her. She just had an eye for it and the steady hands of a surgeon. I've got a good client list but the final nut left to crack for me is the Asian market. Round here, that's a big piece of the pie. When I saw how good Usma was, I gave her a place at the academy for half-price on the proviso she worked for me exclusively and pulled in some Asian clients. Girl was a natural.'

Harry asked her about Usma's job at the bookshop. Apparently it was a job her parents approved of and working there a few hours each week meant Usma could explain a little of the money she was making.

'What did she clear, working for you?'

Kim hesitated.

'Come on, I'm not the tax man.'

'Say, two fifty a week.'

'For working how many hours?'

'Maybe sixteen to twenty. She worked it around college and she'd built up a big client list who were happy to see her whenever she was available.'

'Boyfriend?'

Another hesitation. She shook her head.

'Argh, you were doing so well until then,' said Harry.

Kim stared at him suspiciously.

'Xavier?' said Harry, taking a punt.

'You know about him?'

'I do now.' He smiled at her.

Kim took a sip of her coffee. Harry could tell she was thinking over her response. He tried to make it easy for her.

'Asian girl from a traditional family, loves nails, fashion and dates a white guy. That shit might get you killed in some circles, so if I was her, I'd have done exactly the same. Keep it under the radar and tell no one except my closest friend. It's not stupid. It's smart. But now, the only thing which gets me is, the guy who did this—'

'Xavier didn't do this, he's—'

Harry held his hand up and stopped her. 'The only thing which gets me is, the guy who did this knows everything about Usma. Including who she was dating.'

Kim thought on it. Took another sip of coffee.

'They weren't dating,' she said.

'No?'

'They were fucking.'

'Okay.'

Kim shrugged. 'You go on dates with your boyfriend. Usma and Xavier never went on dates. It was all about the sweat. He got a booty-call. And she got to do what she wanted without repercussions.'

'Modern Asian dating, huh?'

'You can lose the Asian. This is just how it is now; Tinder is all about the action.'

'Glad I'm old-school then. Dinner and romance.'

Kim rolled her eyes.

'Usma is – was – smart. She wanted to earn some money and live a little. There's no harm in that.'

'No,' said Harry. 'Until she was murdered.'

'You have any leads?'

'Enquiries are ongoing. Did she have a locker here?'

Kim hesitated.

'Come on, Kim. We've been doing so well. Shame to stop that now,' said Harry.

'Upstairs. She had a cupboard she kept a few personal things in.'

Harry raised his eyebrows.

Kim shrugged. 'Clothes and stuff.'

'I'll need to take a look.' Harry made to get up.

'Don't you need a warrant or something?'

'I can get one if you need it, Kim, but I don't want to delay this investigation any more than I have to.'

Harry's tone had changed. It wasn't quite threatening but he wanted Kim to know he had a side to him she might not be so comfortable with.

'Come on,' said Kim. 'I'll show you.'

The attic of the academy was bitter: naked bricks, exposed roof and no heating. Kim was standing behind Harry as he put on a pair of gloves and opened Usma's locker, removing the few items in there.

'I can see why she wouldn't have kept this stuff at home,' said Harry, moving some jeans aside to reveal lingerie and a key. Harry waved it at Kim.

'No idea,' she said. Harry believed her. He pulled a plastic evidence bag from his pocket and slipped it inside.

'Anything else?' he asked Kim.

'No.'

'And her boyfriend – Xavier. What can you tell me about him?'

Kim shrugged. 'He's a pig.'

'Not a fan then.'

'You going to see him?'

Harry nodded.

'Then you'll find out for yourself.'

SIXTEEN

HAVING FINISHED THE A&E ward-round, Saima returned to Ranjit's room close to lunchtime and closed the door behind her. Two machines beeped either side of the bed and tubes were connected to both his arms. His turban was resting on the bedside cabinet and his hair had been knotted neatly on top of his head. With his grey beard resting on his naked chest, Saima felt like she had intruded on an intimate moment, she felt the sudden need to run out of the room.

What are you doing here?

She had played the scenarios through her mind. If Ranjit was made aware of who she was and refused to be treated by her, it might be viewed as racially motivated, something the department would not tolerate. Things would kick off, family would get involved and no good could come from that. As far as Saima was concerned, she had the opportunity to prove to Ranjit that he did not need to hate her, even if he hated her religion.

He stirred. Saima braced herself.

'Hello,' said Ranjit in an accent which was more Yorkshire than Indian. He'd been in England for over fifty years and his accent clashed with his appearance.

'That's as strong a Yorkshire accent as mine,' she replied and smiled.

'Forty years I worked in my shop. When I started there, everybody accused me of having a Cockney accent because when I first came from India I lived in London.'

'I didn't know . . .'

Saima stopped herself. She couldn't blow this before it started.

She refocused and removed Ranjit's wallet from her pocket.

'You're stuck here until we get a bed from CCU but here,' she said, handing him his wallet, 'I thought this might cheer you up. It fell out of your pocket when they took you out of the ambulance.'

Ranjit smiled, warm and natural. 'Did you have a look inside?'

Saima nodded. 'I found it when I got home – actually, my husband did.' She laughed, releasing nervous energy, and said, 'He thought I was having an affair. Bringing home a man's wallet.'

Ranjit joined her laughing. The bleating on his cardiac machine quickened. 'Will laughing give me another heart attack?' he said.

'No. Laughing is good for the soul.'

Ranjit nodded, opened his wallet, leafed through a wad of twenty-pound notes and removed them all. 'Here,' he said, offering them to her. 'Please. You take this. God gave me plenty and I'm in your debt.'

'Oh no,' said Saima shaking her head. 'Firstly, it's against the rules and secondly, I did my job. Nothing more. Nothing less.'

Ranjit continued to hold the money in the air. Saima again shook her head.

'I understand,' said Ranjit, replacing the money. 'What's your name, Beti?'

Beti. It was a term of endearment, it meant 'daughter' in Punjabi. It was the word Ranjit would have used had he been accepting of her marriage to Harry.

'Everyone calls me Simmy,' she replied.

A half-truth, no one had called her Simmy since school.

Saima turned away from him and made it appear that she was

checking the drug chart lying at the end of his bed. 'This all looks fine,' she said without reading it.

'The consultant says I need an operation on my heart. Do you think he is right?'

'Yes.'

'It sounded like a major operation.'

'It is. A coronary artery bypass graft.'

'Will it mean I will be okay?'

'It will give you the best chance of leading a healthy life,' Saima answered tactfully.

Ranjit fell silent, his face pained with worry.

Saima hesitated, should she tell him who she was?

'Beti,' said Ranjit, 'could you do me one favour?'

'Of course,' said Saima, regaining her composure and replacing the drug chart.

'I'm sorry to ask but I'm desperate for a cup of tea. This water,' he said, pointing at the jug by his side, 'tastes awful. Could you please help me?'

Saima grinned broadly.

It was all she could do not to laugh, thinking of the number of times she'd asked Harry whether the tea she made was as good as his mother's.

Whether his father would have approved.

Karma.

'It's your lucky day,' she said, reaching into the small bag slung over her shoulder and removing a flask. Saima opened the flask.

'I can't stand English tea,' she said. 'Always bring my own. Fancy an Indian one?'

Ranjit's face softened and he beamed her a warm, almost cheeky grin.

'Fennel and cardamom seeds?' he asked in Punjabi.

'Of course,' replied Saima, pouring him a cup and handing it to him, their hands meeting momentarily.

Ranjit took a sip.

'How is it?' asked Saima.

He smiled again. 'The Indian tea I never forget is the one I first had when I came to England fifty years ago. I had been tasting "English tea" with just a weak teabag for weeks. Finally, when my mother arrived from India, bringing with her everything she needed to make the first Indian tea I ever had in this country, it was like being reborn. I spent an hour drinking it because inside that tea, it felt like she had brought home back with her.'

Ranjit took another sip and closed his eyes. 'Your tea,' he said, 'tastes just like that.'

SEVENTEEN

ON HIS WAY TO meet Xavier Cross, Harry had received a text message from the pathologist, wanting to see him urgently. He'd quickly turned the car around.

Harry parked outside the Bierley mortuary and made his way inside.

At Wendy's office, Harry knocked and waited. When she didn't invite him inside, he knocked again and tried the handle.

Locked.

Harry wandered down to the lab where Ingrid was busy eating her lunch. She told him Wendy was outside having a cigarette.

Harry had never taken her for a smoker. He was usually so good at picking up on that.

Outside, he walked around the back and found Wendy sitting on a bench, a thick brown suede coat wrapped around her, woolly hat pulled down past her ears. A cigarette burned brightly in her hand.

'Thought you would have seen enough tar-filled lungs to avoid cigarettes,' said Harry, taking a seat next to her.

'Everyone needs a guilty pleasure. For Ingrid, it's sugar. I prefer nicotine.'

Wendy offered Harry one from a red packet of Dunhill International.

'No thanks. But glad to see you're not a cheap-and-cheerful Richmond King Size sort of girl.'

'If something's worth doing,' she said and let the statement hang.

'Don't think I've ever shared an informal bench with you, Doc.'

'Doesn't mean I've changed my opinion on you calling me Doc.' Harry smiled.

'When I'm in there, it's always about the victim. Anything. Everything. I don't like to let informality creep in. Too easy for it to become a habit.'

'Fair enough,' said Harry, playing with the packet of Dunhill International in his hand. 'How much do these retail at now.'

'Eleven pounds thirty.'

Harry whistled. 'Damn. Things have changed.'

She looked at him, confused.

Harry put them back on the bench. 'Used to work in my old man's corner shop. We had a guy who bought these. Posh so-and-so, always drove the latest model Jaguar. Always red. I wondered why he bought the Dunhills, always so much more expensive than any other brand.' Harry looked down at his hands.

'Is there an end to that story?' Wendy asked.

He looked up quickly.

'So, you smoke and you're nosy?'

She smiled. 'Don't try your pop-psychology on me. What's next – handing me a stick of gum?'

Harry frowned at her.

'You don't know the gum technique?'

'Should I?'

'Amateur,' she whispered under her breath.

'Go on.' Harry bristled at the word amateur.

She took a drag on her cigarette. 'The chewing-gum technique is offering somebody a stick and, when they refuse, keeping your hand outstretched, the gum hanging between you, until they accept it. If they do, they're more likely to crack under pressure.'

'No shit,' said Harry.

'Try it some time.'

Harry nodded. 'The guy with the Dunhills always bought them because they were red and matched the colour of his car.'

Wendy shrugged. 'Nowhere near as interesting as the gum.'

'Never suggested it was.'

They would have fallen into an easy silence if they hadn't been working a murder case.

'So you wanted to see me?'

'The girl. Usma. It's confirmed, she didn't die of asphyxiation. She died of anaphylactic shock.'

'An allergy? Like you said?'

'Yes. A massive one.'

'To what?'

She narrowed her eyes at him.

'Shit, the wasps?'

'I looked over the body again and, whilst I can't be certain it's a wasp sting, there is a tiny puncture in the skin on her chest. I took a sample of skin and looked at the microscope and found some minor tissue haemorrhage consistent with a syringe puncture or, in this case, a wasp sting. With the swelling of her body, the hives and her bloodwork coming back with massive amounts of mast cell tryptase, it all points to anaphylaxis.'

'Mast-cell-what?' asked Harry.

'Tryptase. It's a specific enzyme elevated when we're allergic to something. Usually, in patients with mild allergies – hay fever, say – we might see slightly elevated levels of it. But in patients with life-threatening allergies – peanuts, wasp and bee stings – the levels are vastly exaggerated.'

She pointed to her throat. 'In Usma's case, her airways closed and that's what killed her.'

'Christ,' said Harry.

'So, the hanging and the barbed wire?'

She shrugged. 'Theatre? Misdirection? Your guess is as good as mine.'

Harry took a breath. 'Which means the killer knew she was allergic to wasps.'

'I'd say so.' She shuddered, and not from the cold.

'How would he know that?'

'Some people wear wristbands if they have a serious allergy.'

'But we didn't find one on her, right?'

'Right. Unless the killer took it with him.'

'Aside from that, who else would have known?'

'Her doctor. Family. Friends.'

'Don't they carry some sort of injection for allergies this severe?'

Wendy took a final puff of her cigarette, put it out on the bench and placed the stub in a bin next to where she was sitting.

'Adrenaline. Did you find one in her belongings?'

'I'll check.'

'An EpiPen, yellow thing, looks like a big felt-tip.'

Harry pulled out his phone and tapped the details into a note. 'Got it.'

Wendy got up to leave.

'One thing,' said Harry, remaining seated. 'Those wasps – you ever seen anything like that before?'

She shuddered again. 'God, no. And seriously, you bring me another body with that sort of stuff going on and I'll be putting in for a pay rise.'

EIGHTEEN

HARRY PULLED ON TO the forecourt of Xtreme Autos on Sticker Lane, wishing he had come here before seeing Wendy. He found the revelation that Usma had been killed by a purposeful wasp sting far more troubling than anything else about the murder. He couldn't stop it swimming around his brain. Such a fucked-up way to die.

But it taught him one valuable thing. The killer had insight.

Harry had phoned the office as soon as he left Wendy, updated them and asked for Usma's medical records to be analysed as a priority.

He also wanted a check on whether Gurpal had any connections to Usma.

He kicked himself for not having requested that earlier.

Who knew about her allergy status? Doctor? Pharmacy? Friends and colleagues?

How was Gurpal connected to this?

The case became more complex with each hour that passed.

Xtreme Autos looked just like any other garage – everything shiny out front and the strong smell of oil suggesting there was a messy bit out back. Beside it was Xtreme Carwash, also part of the business.

Harry entered the office, where an attractive redhead greeted him warmly.

'Are you the two o'clock viewing for the BMW?' she asked presumptively.

Harry shook his head, looking at a picture on the wall, the same one he had seen on the Internet of Xavier standing next to a Bentley in a tight-fitting white T-shirt that showed off his impressive physique. Harry could see the tattoos on his arms were of a dragon. Xavier looked older than Harry had first thought, more mid-thirties than twenties. Harry asked to see him, only to be told that Xavier was in a meeting in the Portakabin next to the carwash and couldn't be disturbed.

Harry didn't have time for that.

Fine spray from a powerful jet-wash splattered Harry's suit as he walked past two men washing a filthy 4x4 Volvo. The men were speaking a foreign language; Polish, Harry thought.

The door of the Portakabin was locked, blinds on the windows drawn. Harry looked at the lock and remembered the key in his pocket from Usma's locker. He removed it. Looked like it might fit. Harry slipped it inside the lock, turned it discreetly but couldn't use it to enter without probable cause.

From inside, Harry could hear an unmistakable sound. He turned to see the Polish guys smirking.

Harry waited.

'Come on,' he whispered. 'Come on.'

Finally, a scream from inside.

'Sounds like a girl's in danger to me,' whispered Harry, smiling, and opened the door.

Harry stepped inside. Xavier was kneeling on a couch behind a naked blonde girl on all fours. The girl screamed again, this time not in pleasure. Xavier stopped what he was doing, almost falling off the couch.

'What the fuck!' he shouted.

'Sorry,' said Harry, putting the key away and removing his gloves. 'I heard a girl in distress. Screaming.'

Harry closed the door and turned the lights on. 'I thought this was a car dealership, not a knocking shop. Come on, Pretty Boy, get your clothes on.'

'Fuck you,' spat Xavier, hands still firm on the girl as she squirmed free.

The girl grabbed her clothes from the floor and covered her body.

Harry pointed at her. 'Get dressed,' he said. 'Then get out.' She didn't hesitate.

Xavier pulled on some jeans, the muscles on his torso flexing angrily. He came at Harry, his face red, sweat still on his temple, ready for an altercation. Harry kept his hands in his pockets as Xavier grabbed him aggressively. 'What's your fucking deal?' he snapped. 'Come on! Before I send you to A&E for an X-ray on that nose.'

'Take your hands off me.'

'You've got five seconds to talk. Or we'll sort this my way.'

Harry let him count to five. Xavier took a step back, withdrew one hand from Harry and threw a punch, exactly what Harry wanted. Harry caught his fist, twisted his hand behind his back and pinned Xavier against the wall.

'That's assault on a police officer,' he said.

Xavier had calmed down, backed into a corner under the threat of being charged. Harry had told him about Usma's death – he didn't seem to care too much.

'Clearly not an exclusive arrangement, then?' said Harry, nodding towards the couch where the blonde girl's underwear lay discarded.

'We had a thing from time to time. No biggie.'

'She think that?'

'She knew the score.'

'How many women know the score?'

Xavier shrugged. 'Why? You jealous?'

'Some piece of work, aren't you,' said Harry.

'Whatever. I like fast cars, fast money and fast women. I ain't married. If an Asian girl wants a bit of rough to show her what a real man can do, what's your beef with that?'

Xavier's shoulders dropped suddenly.

'Shit, you're not, like, her family, are you?'

He looked afraid.

Harry shook his head.

'Thank fuck. She told me her parents would have done her in if they found out. Honour-killing shit.' His eyes widened and he got off the couch. 'Hey, is that what this is about? They kill her cos they found out? Am I in danger? Are they coming for me?'

'Relax,' said Harry and gestured for Xavier to sit down.

'So you're not here to tell me I'm a marked man?'

'You watch too much TV,' said Harry, but he hadn't ruled out the honour-killing angle himself yet.

'How'd you end up in a . . . relationship with Usma?' asked Harry.

'It weren't no relationship.'

'Whatever it was. Tell me how.'

Xavier shrugged. 'I was screwing some girl from that salon. Saw Usma there once. Always had a thing for Asian chicks – it's them scarves around their heads. Kinda kinky sluts, if you ask me.'

Harry leaned forward and slapped him around the side of the head, hard enough that it brought Xavier to his feet. 'Fuck is your problem?'

Harry stood up, now eye to eye with Xavier.

'How about I put a call in to the HMRC? Ask them to investigate your cash-only carwash and the Polish guys you've got working off the books. You see how I can make life difficult for you, X-man?'

Xavier was breathing heavily but he backed off. 'You touch me again, Detective, and I'm bringing it. You got me?'

'Sit your ass down,' said Harry, remaining standing. 'You might think you're God's gift to women because you fuck a different girl every night, but I've got a murdered girl on my hands and the only shit I need to hear from you is the truth or I'm going to get pissed off. And that,' said Harry, crouching now so he was on eye-level with Xavier, 'is not something you want.'

Xavier was grinding his teeth. Harry wanted to knock them out of his mouth.

'Ask what you need. I've got work to do,' said Xavier.

Harry backed off and retook his seat on the couch. 'You can start with your whereabouts on Sunday afternoon.'

NINETEEN

SAIMA MET HER MOTHER-IN-LAW outside the Coronary Care Unit once her shift had ended and together they made their way to the canteen. As they walked, Joyti slipped a hand into the crook of Saima's arm for support. It was a small gesture but it provided a light in the darkness of this situation for Saima. She'd only ever wanted to be accepted by her husband's family.

In the canteen, Saima purchased two coffees and brought them across to the table where Joyti was sitting.

'Here,' said Joyti, trying to give Saima some money as she placed the coffees on the table.

'Oh no,' said Saima sitting down by her side. 'Don't be silly.'

Joyti shook her head. 'I won't sleep tonight if you don't. Where I'm from, mothers-in-law don't take anything from their daughters-in-law.'

'I really couldn't—'

'It's the custom,' Joyti insisted, trying to push the money into Saima's hand.

'I know the customs,' said Saima, closing Joyti's fist around the five-pound note. 'But this has come from Harry's house and since he is your son, no rules are being broken.'

Joyti thought about it, smiled and put her money away. 'I see he has taught you well.'

Saima waved her hand at Joyti. 'And we're both trying to teach Aaron.'

Joyti's expression lifted at the mention of her grandson.

'Is he coming here today, too?' she asked, hopeful.

Saima shook her head. 'Yesterday was an exception. I don't like him in here. I'm always worried he might catch something.'

'Yes. I suppose that is fair.' Joyti looked disappointed.

Both women looked down at their hands, suddenly shy.

Saima opened her mouth to speak, but stopped before she made a sound.

It was only the third time they'd met. The woman opposite her was a stranger really and yet they shared so much. Saima didn't know where to begin.

'Ranjit told me about some tea a nice Indian nurse gave him.'

Saima smiled coyly. 'Ah yes, he's gone far back through my family tree there. I forget that Pakistan was once part of India. My grandparents were born in India. So that makes me . . .' she thought on it, '. . . a quarter Indian?'

Joyti smiled. 'Are you always this . . . happy?'

'I know our whole situation is hard. But right now, I get to sit and have a coffee with you and if anyone saw us, they would just think a mother and daughter were having a drink. That makes me happy.'

Joyti warmed her hands around the cup. 'Did you tell my Hardeep?'

Saima chewed her bottom lip. 'No.'

She told Joyti about the wallet and how she had almost been forced into the truth.

'Is my husband going to die?' asked Joyti suddenly. Bluntly.

Saima paused as she thought of a suitable reply.

'Just tell me the truth,' said Joyti.

'It's a high-risk operation,' said Saima and saw that Joyti understood that she meant there was significant risk.

'When will he have it?'

'This week. I hope.'

Joyti removed a small parcel from her bag and put it on the table in front of Saima.

'I . . . I . . . was looking for some things for my husband last night, packing a bag, and I found these.' Joyti smiled gently. 'I'd forgotten all about them.'

Saima unwrapped the packaging and discovered two delicate gold bangles.

'They're beautiful,' she said, her forehead creasing in confusion.

'I was nineteen when I got married in India. My father had a lot of land and farmed rice and potatoes. We were well off. My mother gave me four gold bangles for my wedding day, two for each arm. I'd always planned to give them to my daughters, but since I had two boys, I decided my daughters-in-law would have them. I gave two to Mundeep on her wedding day and these two were always intended for Hardeep's wife.'

Joyti nodded at them. 'It is time you had them.'

Saima held the weighty bangles in her hand, looking at the intricate, criss-cross pattern etched into the gold. 'I can't accept these. You never thought you would have to hand them to me this way. You never realized Harry would break with tradition.'

The din inside the canteen became louder as a group of children entered, marshalled by two despondent adults. Joyti waited until they had passed through.

'I never realized lots of things. But I want you to have them. I've seen what's inside your heart. I've seen my grandson and I know how Hardeep feels about you. It's all I need, I just wish I could say the same for my husband.'

Joyti reached out to hold Saima's hand. 'We have to alter our traditions. It is time.'

Saima felt her eyes welling up. 'Does Harry know about these?'

Joyti nodded. 'He used to joke with me that if he married a white girl, she wouldn't understand and would sell them to buy shoes.'

'Sounds like him.' Saima laughed, grateful for the distraction from her tears.

'Always joking,' said Joyti. 'Does he still joke like this? About his culture?'

'All the time.'

'Good. It suited him. He never believed in the things we did.'

'He misses you,' said Saima, putting the bangles back inside the drawstring bag and holding it tight in her hand.

'I know. But he is strong.'

Saima wanted to tell her she was wrong. That Harry had buried the hurt somewhere deep so that it couldn't ruin him any more. But that every morning, when he touched his mother's slippers, that hurt rose quickly and sharply and, for the briefest of moments, chipped away at the hope he held on to for better times.

Saima pushed the thought aside. 'What time is Mandy collecting you today?'

'Whenever I call her.'

'My shift's over now.' Saima hesitated and checked the time, three p.m. 'I need to pick Aaron up from nursery.'

Joyti checked her watch.

'Is it far from here?' she asked.

'No, it's just around the corner. Sometimes I walk.'

Joyti placed her hand on Saima's. 'Do you think I might come with you?'

'I couldn't think of anything I would like more,' said Saima.

TWENTY

HARRY WENT STRAIGHT FROM the car garage to Leeds University for his three o'clock appointment with the wasp woman, entomologist Dr Katrina Schultz. Wendy's office had managed to get him in to see her urgently once they'd had the cause of death confirmed.

He was running behind and didn't want to miss this slot he'd been given. Now that he knew they were the murder weapon, Harry needed to know as much as possible about these wasps.

He hurried past the Infirmary towards the medical school. At the bottom of the road, he veered away into the Biological Sciences building and took the lift to the third floor.

From the reception desk, he was taken through to Dr Schultz's lab by a nervous-looking student.

He'd expected some middle-aged, unkempt insect-geek. What he found was a sleek, tall woman in her late thirties, with curly blonde hair, wearing rimless glasses and dressed in dark jeans and expensive-looking black boots.

'DCI Harry Virdee,' he said.

She stood up from the microscope she had been using and offered her hand.

'Dr Schultz, although please, call me Katrina.'

Great smile.

Definitely not what he'd expected.

Katrina offered him a seat on a wooden stool at the lab-bench next to her and walked away to get the sample she'd been sent from Wendy's path lab.

The room was clean and orderly: rows of benches neatly lined with wooden stools and the walls covered in insect posters – it looked like a very tidy school.

One poster in particular caught Harry's eye: a collection of words.

Scary. Horrible. Annoying. Yellow. Nasty. Elegant.

There was a picture of a wasp in each corner.

Katrina returned, carrying a small plastic container. Harry could see one of the wasps they'd found in Usma's eyes inside.

He pointed to the poster. 'What's with that?'

'Oh,' she said, using her fingers to tuck her blonde curls behind her ears, 'we did a data collection from a thousand people asking them what they thought of wasps. Those words were the most commonly used.'

'Right.' Harry looked at it more closely.

'Which would you choose?' she asked.

He took a moment.

'Scary is about right.' He pointed to the container in her hand. 'Especially that thing.'

'This is a spider wasp,' she said, eyes bright. She used a pair of tweezers to remove it from the container and place it on a plastic board on the side.

Harry tensed a fraction.

'It's dead, Harry.'

He smiled weakly.

'The body is somewhat longer than the wasps we routinely see

89

in this country, which are mostly common wasps or German wasps. The sting on this is quite something, much more pronounced and with a far more potent venom.'

'Do we get these in the UK, then?' he asked.

'No. That is, I cannot say they do not exist here definitively, but these are more commonly found in the tropics. The Americas, Asia and Australia. I understand this forms part of an investigation you are leading?'

Harry nodded. He didn't want to tell her exactly how the wasp had been found. That was information they would keep to themselves. If the case spiralled and got media attention and any lunatics wanted to claim credit, that way they would have at least some information that the public couldn't know to help differentiate people of interest from time-wasters.

'Could somebody grow these?'

He regretted his words as soon as he said them and saw Katrina's eyebrow raise.

'I didn't mean grow,' he said, shaking his head. 'Could they be bred? Brought back from somewhere and kept as pets?'

'Oh yes. If you have the right storage, temperature, UV light, it wouldn't be so difficult.'

'Why anyone would want to keep a wasp as a pet is beyond me,' said Harry.

Katrina pointed at the wall chart. 'That's because you chose "scary" as your word. Some people, myself included, think they are fascinating, this species especially.'

'Why this one?'

Katrina, with more enthusiasm than Harry was comfortable with, told him they were called spider wasps because the females hunted spiders and paralysed them with their sting in order to lay their eggs inside the spider's abdomen. That way, the larvae would consume the spider's body as they grew, eventually hatching as adult wasps.

'Would you like to see a video?' she asked, reaching for her iPad.

Harry sighed. 'I'm going to regret saying this, but yes. Go ahead, terrify me.'

'Thank you,' said Harry, handing her back the iPad. 'Sleep will come a little harder tonight, I'm sure.'

'Just nature at its finest, Detective.'

'Tell me,' he said, trying to forget what he'd just seen, 'can you find out how old that wasp is?'

'Old?'

'Yes.'

'Not exactly. I can tell you it's a female, because it has a sting. But beyond that, I can only make an educated guess. It has no wing-wear and its eyes are very dark. I'd say this specimen was recently hatched, but I wouldn't put my life on it.'

'Good enough for me. And if somebody did have these as pets, would they be able to predict, give or take a few hours, when a wasp was going to hatch?'

'Yes. We have wasps and bees in the lab and I'd say we can predict, or I certainly can, within say six-to-eight hours that a wasp is going to hatch.'

Harry looked at the wall chart again.

'Are spider wasps more aggressive than normal wasps?'

'By normal, you mean common wasps?'

'Yes.'

'Their sting is most certainly more painful and delivers more venom.'

Harry couldn't help but think of Wendy's assessment earlier that day: Usma had died of a massive allergic reaction. Perhaps that took more venom than a normal wasp.

'As for aggressive – I'm not comfortable with that word. Because they are larger they are associated with being a more aggressive species, but I think it's more to do with the spider element and how they hunt them,' Katrina concluded.

'Is it labour-intensive, looking after them?'

'Not particularly. They only need sugar-water to survive.'

'One last thing.' Harry held up his index finger.

'Of course.'

'If you had to say where that particular wasp came from, could you?'

'No,' she said, shaking her head and biting her lower lip.

'Educated guess?'

'Statistically speaking, I'd have to say Asia,' she said.

TWENTY-ONE

AT THE PLAYGROUND ADJACENT to the nursery, Saima watched Joyti and Aaron queueing for ice cream. Saima would never normally have allowed it, especially in the cold. But when Aaron had pointed to the van and screamed excitedly, Joyti had been a slave to his demands.

The first thing she had ever bought him. A 99 covered in strawberry syrup. Saima smiled ruefully, wishing Harry were here to share in the creation of the first memory between Joyti and Aaron. The burden of keeping his father's condition from Harry was being compounded by the bitter-sweet scene playing out in front of her, Aaron carefully accepting the ice cream and walking alongside Joyti to a small bench.

Such beautiful innocence.

Such cursed karma.

Harry had phoned to say he'd be home in time to bathe Aaron that evening. Saima had almost hoped he wouldn't make it so that Joyti could come back with her.

Exasperated, she looked towards the sky, as white as Aaron's ice cream, and whispered a prayer.

Can't you make this last for ever?
Can't you make it right?

Saima removed her phone and opened the camera. She zoomed in and snapped a picture, only one. She checked it for clarity.

Perfect.

Aaron was smiling, Joyti was kissing his ice-cream-covered cheek.

It might be the only picture they'd ever have together.

'Look at that face,' said Saima, approaching the bench where her son sat with his grandmother. Aaron's face, hands and clothes were covered in ice cream.

So were Joyti's.

'Mamma, i-cream! I got i-cream!' He waved it at her, spilling more over Joyti's coat. She appeared not to notice.

Saima removed a packet of wet-wipes from Aaron's nursery bag. 'What a mess,' she said dramatically to Aaron, who popped the remaining piece of the wafer-cone into his mouth.

'Mamma, hands,' he said, waving them at her.

'Hands and face, mate,' she replied and quickly wiped them clean. She handed one to Joyti as well.

'Come. Sit down,' Joyti said softly in Punjabi.

Saima sat beside her. Surprisingly, Aaron stayed on Joyti's lap, calm and content.

'He never sits that still with me,' said Saima, laughing.

'Grandmother's touch.'

'Full belly, I think.'

'Tell me,' said Joyti, 'I've never been able to ask you: what did *your* parents make of all this?'

Saima was surprised by the question. And a little unsure how to answer.

She shrugged and blew out her cheeks, watching her breath fog in the winter air.

Her hand went instinctively to the scar on her cheek, the one she kept concealed behind her hair.

Her father dragging her by her hair and throwing her into the middle of the street when she told him about Harry.

Her mother watching, emotionless.

A kick to Saima's side.

The flashing blue lights.

He'd spat in her face as the police arrested him for assault. It was the last time she'd seen him or her mother.

Not quite as dramatic as Harry's father charging at him with a knife, but not far off. She told Joyti all this, keeping her eyes firmly fixed on the paving beneath her feet.

'They moved back to Pakistan. They'd built a house there and since I was the last child to marry, albeit without their consent, they felt no reason to stay here.'

Joyti was silent.

'You both made such a hard choice.'

'It was the right one.'

'What will you tell Aaron when he gets older?' said Joyti.

'The truth.' Saima turned towards Joyti now, determination in her face. 'He's a British boy with parents who love him. He's not Indian. Or Pakistani. Or Muslim. Or Sikh. He's whatever he wants to be when he's old enough to decide what that is.'

Joyti nodded but there was no conviction to it. 'He's going to have it hard,' she said. Saima thought she saw Joyti's arms around Aaron tighten a little.

'Life's hard. We will raise Aaron to be tough enough. Like we were.' Saima corrected herself: 'Like we are.'

Joyti sighed. 'And you have no one?'

'A sister. We've got back in touch over the past year or so. It's not like it was, but it's okay. We're getting there.'

'That's good. It's important to have some family.'

Saima reached to find the bag containing the gold bangles Joyti had given her and waved them at her. 'And I have you now.'

Joyti's smile was full of remorse. 'This is only our third time meeting and even yesterday, when I saw you speaking to my husband, you were positive. I don't know how you do this, with everything you and Harry have been through.'

'I don't focus on what I've lost. Only what I've gained. Together we've overcome our loss and together we will raise Aaron with so much love that he never feels the absence of grandparents or cousins. Many couples have the superfluous stuff without ever having a marriage they can rely on. Whilst we don't have close family relations, we do have the one thing many would envy . . .'

Saima waved the bag at Joyti again. 'A bond stronger than gold.'

Joyti squeezed Aaron tightly, nodding towards a car which had pulled up beside the park. Saima saw Mandy sitting inside.

'My time is up,' said Joyti, kissing Aaron, her face pained at having to leave.

'Don't worry,' said Saima, slipping her arm around Joyti, 'I'm sure there are better times ahead.'

TWENTY-TWO

USMA'S EYES FASCINATED ME. *Seconds after the sting, they were bulging with so much life. Those moments, when her whole world could be seen in her pupils, I felt pure power.*

My doing.

Her eyes faded just as quickly.

A startling transition.

One I've seen before.

At school.

My classmate had died within minutes, by my side.

I hadn't cried like the rest of them.

People thought it was shock.

It wasn't.

How could such a small thing kill? It wasn't a fair fight.

Like tonight.

I'm going to change this completely.

Throw Virdee off his game.

In a place full of hundreds of sinners, my choices will be limitless.

Tonight is all about power. Showing Virdee that I can strike when I want and how I want. I want newspaper headlines and mass hysteria. And in a few hours' time, that is exactly what I am going to get.

He won't catch me tonight.

But he will have another chance tomorrow.

And the day after that.

And when he has failed at every turn and he's broken and desperate, he will realize, this was a fight he was always destined to lose.

TWENTY-THREE

HARRY ARRIVED OUTSIDE INDERJEET Kaur's home, a small terraced house in Hipperholme. Palmer had got him the details and offered to accompany Harry. But this was one meeting he had to do alone.

He waited for the door to be answered, identification to hand. The hallway light came on and a female voice asked who was there. Harry told her and, anticipating her response, slipped his badge through the letterbox. The delay lasted a couple of minutes before the door was opened.

'Long time, Indy,' said Harry.

'About time,' she replied.

The kitchen was simple, sparsely furnished with no personal photographs. Harry hadn't seen any men's shoes by the front door and there was no sign anyone else lived here other than Indy.

He paused by a framed picture of the military symbol of Sikhism on the wall; three swords and a circle.

'Just because the bastard cut off my hair, doesn't make me any less of a Sikh woman,' said Indy, putting the kettle on.

'Couldn't agree more,' said Harry. He was pleased at how well she looked, seemingly having put the past firmly behind her.

A decade before, Harry had attended what at first had appeared to be a domestic incident. Indy had been lying on the floor, unconscious, her long flowing hair cut from her head. Beside her, sprawled in a pool of his own blood, was her white boyfriend Tony, a knife sticking out of his stomach. Harry had called an ambulance for Indy and as uniformed officers attended to the scene he had spied a video camera in the corner of the room.

Red light still blinking.

The sick fuck must have wanted to record Indy's humiliation.

Before anyone else had arrived, Harry had examined the device and played the recent footage which showed Indy's ex-husband Gurpal beating her before cutting her hair from her head in a perverse act of religious punishment. Sikhs were forbidden from cutting their hair, so this was a pointed insult.

Gurpal had been disturbed by Tony and in the ensuing altercation, Tony had charged at Gurpal with a knife. In the struggle, Tony had fallen victim to his own act of aggression, the knife ending up in his own body. He'd died almost instantly.

The footage would have easily got Gurpal off a murder charge on self-defence.

The camera had never made it into evidence.

Amidst a volatile trial, Gurpal had somehow avoided the murder charge but been convicted of Tony's manslaughter and grievous bodily harm for his attack on Indy. Even after his conviction, he had been adamant he had acted in self-defence.

And he knew the footage was there to prove it.

Harry took a seat on a stool by the kitchen counter.

'I'm glad you've got a new life,' he said.

'Had,' she said bitterly.

Harry nodded. 'I've just seen the police reports. Honestly, I didn't know.'

'Because you would have been straight over?'

'Yes.'

'Sugar?' she said, waving the pot at him.

'Just milk.'

'Have you seen Gurpal?'

'No. But I'm going to. After this.'

Her hand shook, just enough to spill the tea she was carrying towards Harry on to the floor. She placed it on the counter and hurriedly cleaned the floor.

'You don't have to be afraid, Indy,' said Harry.

'Nuisance phone calls. A brick through my window with the word "slut" wrapped around it. Police fobbing me off – even when I asked for you personally. What's to be afraid of?'

Harry looked around the room and saw no signs of an alarm.

'Security in this place?'

She shook her head. 'I moved here and left everything behind. Didn't tell anyone I was here, so didn't think I needed some posh alarm. Everything was perfect until Gurpal got out of prison.'

'How soon after did it start?'

'The calls started the very first night. The brick a few weeks later. Yesterday his brother was waiting outside the school I work at.'

'Kashmir? Seriously?'

Indy took a seat opposite Harry. 'I confronted him.'

'And?'

She hesitated.

'And?' said Harry.

Her face twisted into a hatred Harry recalled from years earlier when the case with her husband had exploded. 'I . . . told him that if he or Gurpal came near me, I would kill them.' Indy stared hard at Harry. 'I meant it.'

'I'm sure,' said Harry, understanding the bite to her voice.

Gurpal's family were well known to Bradford police. Rich, out-landish owners of several strip clubs and bars in Leeds, they were frequently in trouble with the law. Fighting, intimidating their work-ers and illegally pimping out some of the girls. Yet Gurpal and his brother Kash had got arranged marriages to girls from India; sub-servient women designed to fulfil traditional roles, trophies they could show off to their community. But they'd misjudged Indy; she hadn't tolerated their bullshit and after four years of abusive mar-riage, she had left Gurpal.

For a white guy.

That was when it had all kicked off.

The video recording of Gurpal cutting off Indy's hair, the high-est insult for a Sikh woman, had been intended to be shared online as a kind of warning to others not to betray their heritage.

During his trial, Gurpal had fiercely protested that a video cam-era he had used to record the attack would prove that he acted in self-defence. He may have been guilty of grievous bodily harm but not murder.

'I can see you playing it back in your mind. What you did with the camera.'

Indy had guessed at what Harry had done. He'd never confirmed it.

Harry focused on the mug of tea in his hand.

'He deserved to die for what he did to Tony,' she said.

Still, Harry stayed silent.

'Do you regret it?' she asked.

Harry had asked himself the same question when he first saw Gurpal's name come up on his case search. At the time, he had been dating Saima, the relationship serious enough that Harry knew he was going to have tough times ahead with his parents. The footage of Gurpal cutting off Indy's hair had only strengthened his hatred of his community's customs and traditions. It had made Harry's blood boil.

Still did.

Did he regret it?

Did he, fuck.

He looked at Indy. He didn't say anything but made sure his eyes said what his lips wouldn't.

She smiled and nodded in agreement.

'I've asked for panic alarms to be installed in the house. They'll be round tomorrow. You good with that?' said Harry.

Indy nodded. 'Thank you.'

Harry removed a pen and a notepad from his pocket and scribbled his number down. 'Anything happens. You call me direct.'

Harry pushed his number into her hands and stood up, his tea untouched.

'What are you going to do?' asked Indy.

'I'm going to pay the son of a bitch a visit. Remind him you've got more friends in this city than he has.'

'But he knows what you did.'

'Exactly,' said Harry.

TWENTY-FOUR

SAIMA ARRIVED AT HER sister Nadia's house, now a Tuesday evening routine.

It had been a chance encounter at a supermarket which had broken the ice. Nadia hadn't been able to have children and had immediately taken to Aaron. Saima ruffled his hair as they walked up the path to the front door. Seemed her boy was able to break down barriers neither she nor Harry had managed to dent.

Nadia opened the door wearing a plain green Asian suit, fully made-up as usual, despite never quite learning how to apply her eyeshadow properly. You'd never have known they were sisters. Nadia had followed the traditional route and had entered into an arranged marriage to Imran, her second cousin from Pakistan, when she had been only nineteen. She had never worked or completed her education. Hers was a small and simple life.

'Hello, hero,' said Nadia, opening the door and beaming a warm smile at Aaron. He immediately left Saima's hand and rushed towards her.

'Sweetie,' he said.

'Not a chance,' said Saima to Nadia, stepping inside and closing the door. 'He's already had an ice cream today. What have you made?'

'Nice to see you too, Sis,' replied Nadia, taking Aaron with her into the kitchen.

'Starving,' said Saima, and again dismissed Aaron's pleas for a sweetie. Her sister was far too generous with them.

'Daal. Chapattis,' said Nadia.

Saima turned her nose up.

'Look at little miss White girl! Too good for Asian food now?' Nadia put Aaron down and he immediately went to the drawer where the sweets were kept. Saima went to intervene but was stopped by Nadia.

'Don't worry, I emptied it. Let him open it. Only way he'll eat his tea.'

Saima relaxed and watched Aaron's disappointed face as he stared into the empty drawer.

'You want this or not?' said Nadia bluntly to Saima.

'Hospitality never was your strong suit.'

'It's that or a bowl of cereal.'

'Charming.'

Nadia picked Aaron up. 'You want Auntie's food, don't you?'

Aaron nodded. 'Then I have sweetie?'

'Deal,' said Nadia.

The sisters were eating their tea in the kitchen, Aaron sitting on Nadia's lap. She stole a kiss every time she put food in his mouth. Saima smiled, momentarily saddened that Nadia would never have children of her own.

'He back here now?' asked Saima, nodding her head towards the living room where the sound of Asian TV was playing loudly. She'd never liked Nadia's husband, even less so now Imran was messing Nadia about through their divorce.

Nadia shrugged. 'He's got the flu. Think his mistress kicked him out. Seems the cow takes him to bed but she won't nurse him.'

'Neither should you,' said Saima bitterly. 'Can't believe you let him live here, knowing that he's got another woman. You're not part of our parents' generation, you know. You don't have to put up with that shit.'

'Divorce will come through soon enough. Then he'll piss off for good.'

'You all right?'

'I just want to be free, now.' She paused then sheepishly added, 'Maybe go out on a date.'

Saima choked momentarily on her chapatti. She took a sip of water and hammered her hand on her chest.

'Date?' she said incredulously. Nadia had never dated anybody.

'Why not? Plenty of guys out there. Might even get another freshie from back home. They'd treat me proper for a green card.'

Saima shook her head. 'You do not want another freshie,' she said fiercely.

'I can't have kids. Doubt anyone here will want me.'

'So? Stay single.'

'Can't afford it.'

'Then get a job. Don't rely on a man.'

'All right for you with your degree and Harry. I need a man like yours. Someone who would do anything for me and look after me.'

Saima smiled, resigned. 'Men like Harry don't come along too often.'

Nadia squeezed Aaron's cheeks. 'Maybe I just keep this little guy then,' she said. 'You want to live with me?'

Aaron nodded his head. 'I live here. With Auntie.'

The mood shifted instantly as Imran entered, wearing traditional Asian attire and dragging his feet on the floor. He grunted some sort of greeting towards Saima, ignored Aaron completely and took a drink from the fridge. He muttered for Nadia to heat him some food up and left.

'I can't believe you put up with him when he's got another woman,' said Saima, scowling.

Her sister had seemed to accept that Imran had found another woman when they'd discovered she couldn't get pregnant. It wasn't uncommon in their community but it made Saima's blood boil.

'It's just how it is, Saima. You get used to it.'

'I wouldn't. Ever.'

'That's why you left. We can't all be like you.'

'Put a tablespoon of chilli in his food. It'll burn the flu out of him and get him out of your house.'

The sisters looked at each other, then at the pan of food on the stove. They burst out laughing, continuing until tears rolled down their faces. Aaron joined in, becoming excitable at the laughter. For the second time that day, Saima felt buoyed; a sense of familial normality, absent ever since she had married Harry.

TWENTY-FIVE

IT WAS RARE FOR Harry not to be home for seven p.m. but tonight he had made the call to finish his day by visiting Gurpal Singh. Harry had collected Palmer from the station en route to Gurpal's house in the Five Lane Ends area of Bradford. It seemed Palmer's meeting with Usma's family had not proved fruitful. They had been alarmed at finding out that Usma had such a large amount of cash in her bedroom, and even more surprised to learn she had been working at the nail salon. But Palmer hadn't discovered anything else they didn't already know.

The tech guys had done a sterling job though. The footage of Burka-man, as they were calling him, had been compared to footage they had of Gurpal Singh. Their height and build were similar and, more importantly, they shared the same shoe size.

'Great work, Simon,' said Harry.

'Thanks, boss. They rushed it through for us. Think this has got everyone on edge. It's the wasps. Who does that shit?' said Palmer, opening a family-sized bar of chocolate that he clearly wasn't planning on sharing.

Harry shook his head slowly; the wasps had been niggling him too.

'And your new best mate, Xavier – he's got an airtight alibi.'

'Enlighten me.'

'Guy was in Amsterdam all weekend at a stag do. He got back into Leeds–Bradford late Sunday night.'

'Didn't fancy him for it,' said Harry. 'Just wanted to give him an uncomfortable day. Guy thinks he's God's gift.'

'Yeah, I heard all about it.'

Harry glanced at Palmer, the two men sharing a smile.

'Right,' said Harry, turning off the main road, 'let's see if we like this prick for Usma's murder.'

Harry drove down the winding driveway, a quarter-mile covered in turquoise glass chippings and white limestone gravel. Ahead, the main house loomed large and overbearing. It was like something from a movie.

Harry pulled up beside a large outbuilding, the size of his own home. Palmer finished the chocolate bar and stuffed the wrapper inside his pocket. He put a firm hand on Harry's arm.

'Let's not start a riot. Eh?'

'Course not,' said Harry.

'You want to let me do the talking?'

'Nope.'

'I'm serious. Conway had a word in my ear. Doesn't want another shitstorm with this lot. Last time was quite enough.'

'That's why you're with me. No more accusations about me tampering with evidence. He was a nasty piece of work and got what he deserved, but this is different.'

'You wait in the car. Let me at least make sure he's here. They see you and they're going to kick off soon as.'

Harry relented. 'Fine.'

He watched as Palmer approached the front door, pushed the electronic keypad and waited. He stooped to show his face to a monitor and a few moments later the door opened, an elderly woman in a sari – Gurpal's mother, Harry assumed – speaking with him.

Harry glanced at the rest of the house for any signs of curtains twitching. The upstairs lights were all on, the house looked warm and welcoming. Harry didn't see any movement at the windows.

The woman pointed to the outbuilding next to Harry's car then closed the door. Palmer returned, opened Harry's door, pointed to the outbuilding and said, 'The boys live in there. Apparently.'

Harry got out of the car. 'Boys?'

'Both sons.'

Harry gave the two-storey building a once-over. 'Bachelor pad for the pricks having a mid-life crisis?'

'Probably.'

'Come on.'

Harry strode past Palmer and hammered on the door, making it shake on its hinges. His heart was racing and he was clenching his teeth, unable to ignore visions of Indy slumped on the kitchen floor, blood pouring from her mouth, hair cut from her head.

The door opened and Kashmir Singh, 'Kash' as he was known, stood there, sweat pouring down his face, dressed in gym-wear. He took a moment to register who Harry was and immediately stepped forward so he was only inches from Harry's face.

'The fuck do you want?' he said, breath stale.

Harry stepped back. 'Need to speak to Gurpal.'

'The hell you do.' Kash moved closer.

Palmer put his arm between the two men and pulled Harry back a little further.

'We need to speak with your brother about an ongoing investigation.'

'He isn't here,' said Kash, never taking his eyes from Harry.

Palmer stepped in front of Harry. 'Do you know where he is?'

'Nope.'

Kash tried to close the door. Palmer placed his foot in the way. 'If you want to do this the hard way, we can. But it only ends one way and you're smart enough to know that. So give us five minutes now or we'll come back with a full patrol and a warrant, and then you're going to have to redecorate.'

'I'll give you five minutes,' said Kash finally. He nodded towards Harry, 'But I ain't talking to him.'

The downstairs was an open-plan kitchen-cum-living-room. By the far window was an impressive range of fitness equipment. Whilst Kash didn't have the intimidating physique of his brother, the weights stacked on the bench-press machine were heavy enough to ensure he wasn't a man to be taken lightly if things kicked off. Posters of *The Godfather* and Al Pacino carrying a machine gun in the movie *Scarface* covered the far wall.

'What do you pigs want?' said Kash.

Harry sighed; everything about Kash pissed him off, especially his arrogance.

'When's Gurpal going to be home?' asked Palmer.

'I'm not his babysitter.'

'We need to speak to him.'

'You got a warrant?'

'Gurpal's on parole. If we process a warrant, that might make his life tricky with his parole officer. We thought we might try this the nice way.'

Kash grunted and pointed at Harry. 'The nice way? Like destroying evidence which would have proved my brother acted in self-defence?'

Harry folded his arms across his chest. 'If the video recording you are referring to *did* exist, it would also have shown him assaulting his wife.'

Kash spat on the floor, phlegm landing inches from Harry's feet.

'She deserved what she got. Fucking slut.'

Harry kept his arms folded but clenched his fists, digging his nails into his skin. He remained quiet.

Palmer pressed Kash again for details about Gurpal and again hit a brick wall.

'Like I said. He left this morning and I don't know when he'll be back.'

'Do you have a mobile number for him?' asked Palmer.

'He hasn't got one.'

Harry sighed. He was going to have to rattle this guy's cage.

'When will he be home?' asked Palmer.

'You deaf? I just told you, I'm not his babysitter.'

'Come on,' said Harry, grabbing Palmer's arm. 'Waste of time. The dumb-bells in this place are smarter than him and his brother put together.'

'Hey,' snapped Kash, stepping aggressively past Palmer towards Harry. A wave of stale breath hit Harry in the face. 'Must be nice having a badge to protect you, huh?'

Harry remained still. He looked Kash up and down.

'You know what happened to my brother in prison?' said Kash.

Harry didn't reply. He didn't know, but something in the way Kash said it made Harry think of the men's shower areas in jail.

'You think you're so fucking smart. But we *know* what you did. We *know*,' said Kash.

'Come on, Harry, we're done here,' said Palmer.

'Man beats his wife. Cuts off her hair in some bullshit masochistic act of honour. I'd say that whatever happened to him in prison, he deserved.'

Harry hesitated but couldn't help himself from adding, 'Karma has a way of returning to be a *pain in the ass.*'

He meant the pun and allowed just the faintest of smiles.

Kash's face broke into a snarl. He backed off, breathing heavily. And smiled.

'Indy used our family. We brought her over here from India, gave her a good life. She didn't want for anything and the moment the bitch got her residency, she fucks off with a white guy. But,' said Kash, smiling a little wider, 'you're like her, aren't you. Don't give a toss about the right way to do things. Heard from the community that you'd shacked up with a Paki slut.'

Palmer stepped hurriedly between both men. 'Harry—'

'Move,' said Harry, glaring at Palmer with a look that made him step aside.

'What's it like, fucking a Paki?' said Kash. 'You got to wash afterwards or what?'

Harry removed his police identification. He stepped closer to Kash, waved it in front of his face then dropped it on the floor.

Kash watched it fall and as soon as his eyes were distracted, Harry brought his elbow into Kash's nose, breaking it. As he fell backwards, Harry grabbed hold of him and pushed him towards the wall.

Kash tried to struggle but Harry held him firm and pushed his nose into the wall, smearing blood across it. He cuffed his hands behind his back, turned him around and shoved him on to the couch.

Kash was screaming, yelling he was going to do Harry in.

'Yeah, yeah,' said Harry, raising his foot and pushing it into Kash's crotch, keeping him pinned in the chair.

'You're done! Fucking done!' shouted Kash.

'Really?' said Harry, waving away Palmer, who had arrived by his side, face drawn.

'I'll have your job for this!' said Kash.

'Funny,' said Harry, keeping his foot firmly between Kash's legs. 'You've got two senior officers whose statements will say you threatened me. Then headbutted the wall to try to pin the blame on me.'

Kash shook his head, blood streaming down his face. 'It'll never wash.'

Harry pointed to the wall. 'There's the blood.'

'He saw what you did,' said Kash, nodding towards Palmer.

'You see anything, Simon?' asked Harry, turning his face to the side.

'Saw him headbutt the wall,' replied Palmer.

Harry pushed his foot a little harder into Kash's crotch, making him wince.

'The thing with you and your brother – the thing which pisses me off the most – is your double standards. Getting girls over from India, treating them like shit and expecting them to conform to some out-of-touch idea of traditional values while you hook up with whichever white girl has taken your fancy.'

Harry leaned a little closer, applying more pressure, his mood darkening. 'Too chicken-shit to just live your life. Too afraid to say no to Mummy, who needs to keep up appearances in the community. You're a pussy and you know it.'

Harry grabbed Kash's face, constricting his cheeks firmly between his fingers. 'You want to cross me? Go right ahead.'

He dropped his voice, whispering now in Kash's ear so Palmer couldn't hear. 'Either of you goes near Indy again, you of all people know I've got no problem crossing the line.'

Harry dug his fingers harder into Kash's face and made sure he was looking at him. 'Unlike you, I'm not all talk. Now, you tell your dipshit brother that we're looking for him.'

Harry let go, backed off and handed Palmer a key to the cuffs. 'We're done here.'

TWENTY-SIX

THE DRIVE BACK TO Trafalgar House was strained.

'Go on. Say it,' said Harry, stopping at a set of traffic lights on Manningham Lane. He lowered the window to let some much-needed air into the car.

'You're my boss. And you know I've always got your back, Harry, but shit, sometimes you take it too far.'

'I know,' said Harry. He didn't regret what he had done to Kash. Truthfully, had Palmer not been there, Harry might have taken it a step further. In his opinion, brown-on-brown racism was as toxic as it got. Harry had suffered enough of that from within his own family. He couldn't tolerate a lowlife like Kash talking shit about his wife.

Palmer shook his head. 'I'll never quite understand it. He's Asian. You're Asian. Yet he feels he can call your wife a Paki and immediately this rage comes over you. It puts everything you've worked for at risk. You want to explain that to me?'

Harry edged the car forwards as the lights changed. 'I wish I could. Just some age-old bullshit. It's not just what he said about Saima. It's the way he reckons he's better than me – a higher class of ethnic because he toes the line when it comes to sticking with your own. He got a freshie—'

'Freshie?'

'Traditional girl from some village back in India. Marriage lasted about as long as he would in a dark alley with me. He ships her back home, screws a different white girl every night and nobody in the community says shit about it. Yet I marry the woman I love, stay loyal to her, raise a family and I'm the social leper. Double standards. Pisses me right off.'

'And if he puts in a complaint? Is it worth the hassle?'

'He won't.'

'Because?'

Harry glanced at Palmer. 'Because he knows I'd make life difficult for him.'

Palmer sighed. 'I'll never understand. In this city, brown versus white is enough hatred for me. Yet from what I've learned working alongside you, there's layers of hate even within that.'

Harry squeezed his hands around the steering wheel, making the leather squeak, his mind taken back to the memory of his father charging at him with a knife after Harry had told him he was marrying Saima.

'Don't try to understand. Not worth the headache.'

Palmer removed another chocolate bar from his pocket and unwrapped it. He offered a piece to Harry, who refused.

'Nice touch, rubbing his nose against the wall,' said Palmer, grinning and popping a double-piece of chocolate into his mouth.

Harry scowled. 'His nose popped like a fucking balloon. Virgin bones. Man hasn't been in a real fight in his life.'

Palmer laughed. 'Virgin bones,' he said, shaking his head.

'I wanted to rattle his cage. If his brother has some sort of sick wasp habit, if he is involved in Usma Khan's murder, he'll be even more pissed off with me now. That's all I need; his composure to slip so that when we do pin him down, he'll break easier than Kash's nose did.'

TWENTY-SEVEN

HARRY ARRIVED HOME AT eight thirty, touched his mother's slippers in the hallway. He silently muttered that Kash had had it coming, imagining his mother's disapproval at how his day had panned out.

Upstairs, Harry found Saima already in bed, reading a book. She peered over the top of it as he entered. Tuesday nights were the only time they broke their rule of always having dinner together. Saima's new relationship with her sister was important to them both. He felt a tad jealous that his own relationship with Ronnie hadn't fared as well.

'Little man out?'

'Like a light,' said Saima, putting the book down. 'We might need to get a fish tank. Aaron is obsessed with the one at Nadia's place.'

'No thanks. A dog I can get on board with. Fish are boring.'

Harry removed his jacket and threw it on to a chair. Saima frowned at him, staring at it.

'Give us a break, woman.'

'I'm not picking it up.'

'I didn't ask you to.'

Harry sat on the side of the bed and dropped his head on to his chest. 'Shit day. Knackered. How was Nadia?'

'The same. Just existing.'

'She hasn't kicked him out yet then?'

'She bloody well should, but it's what happens when you marry your cousin. Pickled politics.'

Saima moved closer to him, kneeling behind his body and draping her arms around his neck. 'Do you want some food?' she said. 'Like a big greasy takeaway? We can veg out and be two little fatties on the couch?'

Harry smiled. 'Let's leave it for Saturday night. Think I'm going to fix myself a Jack and Coke and watch some TV. You want to come down?'

'Bollywood TV?' she said playfully.

'Only if my favourite actress is on. The hot one. What's she called again?'

'Don't you say her name,' said Saima. She hated it when Harry mocked her jealousy.

'Relax. The only woman I would leave you for in the world is—'

He turned his face and kissed her cheek. 'Nobody.'

Saima nuzzled her face into Harry's neck. 'Charmer. You go have your Jack Daniels. But pop into Aaron's room and give him a kiss first. He missed you tonight.'

In the living room, Harry fixed himself a drink and brought it back to his computer. He turned off the television, Saima wouldn't sleep if she could hear it.

He thought of Gurpal Singh. This felt different to his previous crimes. But Harry had witnessed first-hand with his brother how prison could change a man. Harry made a note to get his team to contact Armley prison the following day and see what they could find about Gurpal's time inside.

Harry watched a YouTube video of a spider wasp attacking a tarantula, similar to the one Katrina Schultz had shown him.

Angry little bastards.

He used the Internet to search for shops in Bradford where somebody could buy a tarantula. Since these wasps were obviously being bred, it seemed logical that whoever was doing so would need a supply of spiders. He found six shops, made a note of them and gladly clicked away from the images on his screen.

He picked up his bourbon just as a text message arrived on his phone from an unrecognized number.

Maestro. Bhangra Night. Find what you need there about Usma Khan. Come alone. No drama.

He frowned at the message and tried to call the number but it was switched off. Harry checked the time: 22:10.

He tried to call the number again.

Nothing.

Harry left his Jack Daniels untouched. He phoned Palmer.

'Boss?'

Harry could hear a woman singing badly in the background, the racket deafening. 'Find a quiet spot,' he said.

He waited whilst Palmer moved away from the noise.

'Better?' said Palmer.

'Much. Where the hell are you?'

'Sister's birthday. Karaoke and piss-up in town.'

'You drunk?'

'I'm driving.'

Harry filled him in on the cryptic text. 'Can you get away?'

'Shit, Harry, my sister hates this. I'll have to play it right. Say, forty minutes?'

'Listen, keep alert to your phone. I'm going to head down to Maestro's and see what's what. Put a call in to the duty sergeant and ask if he can get a couple of patrol cars in the vicinity just in case I need it.'

'Sure, Harry. Anything else?'

Harry thought of the spider and the wasps. It was unlikely, but not impossible he was walking into a trap here. 'Tell you what, ask him to get the armed patrol somewhere close by too.'

TWENTY-EIGHT

HARRY PARKED ON A side street off Manningham Lane, opposite Maestro nightclub, feeling like this day was never going to end. He read a text from Palmer confirming his backup. He didn't feel in any danger, the club was going to be crowded, he was hardly going to be ambushed.

Harry remembered the club from his youth. It had closed many years ago but now, under new ownership, it was trying to infuse some much-needed nightlife back into the Bradford scene. Harry had spent his teenage New Year's Eves at the club and, unbeknown to his parents, had his first kiss there, with one of the papergirls who did rounds for his dad.

Tonight, the club was hosting a Bhangra night for students. A queue of Asian kids snaked around the side of the building. Harry got close enough to hear a meaty Asian bouncer shaking his head at a group of four guys.

'Boy/girl only.'

He veered away from the queue and hung back.

Harry checked his phone and re-read the anonymous text message.

No drama.

Harry didn't want to draw too much attention to himself. He figured whoever wanted to speak with him wanted privacy and didn't want the bouncers watching Harry, on edge to see if he was there to check if any laws were being broken.

Yet without a woman on his arm, he was unlikely to get inside without playing the cop-card.

Harry checked the queue.

There were several small groups of young girls.

Too young for Harry to latch on to.

'Shit,' he whispered.

Harry looked up and down Manningham Lane and saw a silhouette hovering in a side street doorway. Most of the hookers had moved on from this area a while ago but a few still remained.

'What's your name?' asked Harry, approaching the scantily dressed prostitute. The orange glow of a cigarette between her lips grew brighter as she took a final drag before throwing the stub to the floor.

'Dawn,' she replied.

'You want to hang out, Dawn?'

'Always, sweets,' she said, and turned to face him. Pink lipstick, blonde hair, textbook blue eyeliner. She was wearing tight leather trousers, black stiletto heels and a cheap imitation fur jacket, zipped low enough to leave her breasts on show; both had a tattoo of a devil on display.

Harry pointed to the club across the road. 'I need to get in there. It's boy/girl only.'

Harry removed his wallet and pinched a twenty-pound note in his fingertips. 'Easiest money you'll make all night.'

'What? You just want me to go in there with you?' she said. The smell of stale smoke on her breath hit Harry like a slap.

'Yeah.'

'Why?'

'I like Bhangra. Can't get in alone.'

She smiled. 'Fuck off.'

'Dawn, you've got the chance to make twenty quid for standing in that queue with me for ten minutes. You prefer some taxi driver's cock in your mouth for that?'

Harry started to put the money away.

Dawn grasped his arm.

'When we're inside – I can go?'

'Yes.'

'Good,' she replied. 'Cos I ain't dancin' to no Bhangra.'

The queue moved slowly. Harry had asked Dawn to zip her fur jacket up over her breasts but she'd left a little on show, enough to give the bouncers a cheap thrill and let them inside.

'What's the deal then?' said Dawn, noticing the rest of the people queuing all looked to be in their late teens or early twenties. 'Daughter inside?'

'Something like that.'

'Honour crap, is it? She hooked up with the wrong sort and you wanna get her an arranged marriage?' She laughed.

Harry shook his head. 'Less dramatic than that.'

When they were near the front, Dawn turned to Harry and asked him for another twenty. They were close enough that, if Harry refused, it might cause a scene and she knew it.

Dawn smiled, then winked at Harry. She leaned closer. 'How bad do you wanna get in there, sweets?'

Harry put his hand in his pocket, removed another twenty and held it in his hand. Dawn tried to take it.

'When we get to the front – you can take it then.'

She shrugged and nodded as the couple in front disappeared inside. They stepped forward and the bouncer didn't even give them a once-over, simply waving them inside. Dawn snatched the twenty-pound note from Harry's hand.

Inside, they stopped at a desk. Harry sighed at the entrance fee. Fifteen quid each.

Harry paid the money. Dawn leaned in close.

'You must really want to get in here,' she said.

The boom of a powerful Bhangra beat reverberated through Harry's feet, as if the floor were shaking. An Asian dance group were onstage, whipping the crowd on the dance floor into a frenzy.

'Mine's a double vodka and Coke,' Dawn shouted over the noise.

'One drink,' replied Harry.

He hated nightclubs. The noise, the sweat, the people. He also hated feeling like a lemon at the edge of the dance floor and queueing for a drink gave him a natural opportunity to scan the room, and with it the crowd.

The club hadn't changed one bit since Harry had last been here twenty years before. The centre of the room was an enormous dance space. A large torch in the ceiling powerfully illuminated a central mirror ball which sent thousands of sparkling lights across the heaving dance floor. Artificial mist obscured the edges of the room.

Harry was served quickly at the bar. He ordered a Coke for himself, and a Coke and double vodka for Dawn. Looking at the crowd inside the club, Harry saw girls in vibrant, multicoloured Asian suits, most of them with drinks in hand. Guys and girls checked each other out; smiles exchanged, prolonged glances and the unsubtle brushing of hands on bodies.

When he returned, Dawn was being chatted up by a slick-looking Asian playboy, clean-shaven, wearing shades and boasting more than one gold chain around his neck.

Harry handed Dawn her drink. The hero smiled at Harry and skulked away. Harry briefly wondered if he might be a person of interest, but when he was welcomed back into a boisterous crowd of other teens, Harry's interest in him waned and he turned back to Dawn.

'He wanted a piece of the white girl,' said Dawn, taking the drink from Harry. She seemed to be enjoying herself, tapping her feet on the floor and moving her head side to side. 'Shagged an Asian fella for a while. He loved this shit.'

Harry sipped his drink and observed the frenetic dance floor. Girls' bodies gyrated against guys' torsos.

Dawn necked her drink, placed the empty glass on a table and turned to Harry. 'We good?'

Harry nodded.

She pointed towards the dance floor. 'When you find her – don't be too hard on her. We were all kids once, remember?'

She winked at Harry, thanked him for the drink and waltzed away.

Harry looked out over the dance floor. It was impossible to make anything out beyond the mass of bodies and the arms waving in the air. There was a raised balcony wrapped around the perimeter of the club. Harry went upstairs and took a slow walk around, looking down on to the dance floor. It was easier to make out the people below him now.

He could see the effortless, gorgeous Asian girls who knew they were desirable and moved their bodies easily with the beat. They were the ones the boys were watching. They were surrounded by an outer ring of wannabes, glad to be included in the cool crew but nowhere near effortless. They were clearly hoping some of the guys might notice them too.

The guys were also split into two camps. Those who had Bhangra in their blood, whose bodies moved like liquid, and the ones who'd got pissed in the hope it might trigger some deep-rooted sense of rhythm, which never surfaced.

But there was nothing out of the ordinary here.

He checked his phone and saw he had a new text message.

Do you see the sinner, Harry?

Harry's heart raced. Keeping the phone in his hand, he glanced around the dance floor. This wasn't someone wanting to give Harry intel about Usma.

The killer was here.

Another text.

Do you see what you started?

Harry started to reply. Then reconsidered.

Who'd I come in with? he replied.

White girl. She's gone.

Harry's breathing quickened.

A new text, this one from Palmer.

I'm here. By the cloakroom. You?

Harry replied urgently.

Killer is in here. LOCK THIS PLACE DOWN. NOW. NOBODY LEAVES. CALL IT IN.

Harry moved quickly towards the exit but stopped in his tracks when he heard a sudden commotion coming from the middle of the dance floor. He paused and moved closer to the edge of the balcony. A group of clubbers were jostling with each other.

With the strobe effects flickering rapidly and artificial mist obscuring his view, Harry could only just make out distressed faces.

Then he saw the blood.

Harry jumped over the balcony just as the dancers on stage lost their rhythm. He landed with a heavy thud on the edge of the dance floor.

The Dhol-player stopped banging the drums and the music petered away, replaced by the sound of screaming.

As clubbers moved towards the exit in a sea of panic, Harry was carried back with them and had to fight his way forward.

He heard a scream for help, then several more.

Harry forced his way through them.

He arrived in the middle of the dance floor to find a group of boys surrounding a girl who had folded to the floor.

'Move!' shouted Harry as he saw the blood rapidly pooling underneath her body. 'Police!' he screamed.

Nobody moved.

'I said move!' he yelled and forcefully pushed some of the crowd out of his way. 'Police!' he repeated, and now he saw the girl, eyes staring up at Harry, panic written across her face, her yellow Asian suit, peppered with sequins, turning steadily brown as it absorbed a stream of fast-flowing blood from her neck.

'Shit,' said Harry and removed his jacket. He crouched next to a boy on the floor who was applying pressure to a wound on the girl's neck. The boy moved aside, clearly relieved someone was here to take over.

From close up, Harry could see she had a deep puncture wound in her neck.

Her artery had been severed, the blood loss was massive.

In the middle of the dance floor, as people continued to scream and run towards the exit, Harry could do nothing but watch as the girl's breathing slowed and she died in his arms.

TWENTY-NINE

HARRY WAS SITTING ON the balcony of the now deserted night-club. SOCO units and HMET officers did their jobs around him, all the usual procedural tasks Harry had seen a thousand times before.

Outside, Harry had left Palmer and a handful of uniformed officers trying to contain four hundred party-goers. Some had fled in the initial panic, others had arrived to see what the fuss was about, further complicating matters. The night grew colder. Here, on Manningham Lane, the setting of two major race-riots in the past two decades, Bradford was once again caught in the middle of a shitstorm.

Harry had two murders on his hands; in all likelihood, they were dealing with a serial killer.

He had contacted the duty inspector at Trafalgar House, who had sent initial responders. Requests for officers from other districts had quickly been put in and patrols from Halifax, Wakefield and Huddersfield had arrived.

It still wasn't enough to control what was happening outside the club.

Media vans were already onsite, social media rapidly spreading the news, most of it inaccurately reported. One thing was certain: controlling the mob outside was a priority. They needed to get details from as many witnesses as possible.

Harry had spoken to the Assistant Chief Constable, who had sent out a 'force request' to North Yorkshire, Humberside and Manchester asking for PSUs, police response units, a van of six constables and a sergeant in full riot gear.

No chances were being taken.

Bradford knew this scene all too well.

Harry wandered outside, still in shock. He saw a sea of blue lights, officers trying to quarantine witnesses into small groups and media vans training their lenses on the unfolding drama. The riot vans were strategically parked to fence the crowd in, ready to be called upon, but nobody wanted to incite anarchy. For now, they simply observed.

The crowd huddled together, all of them dressed for the club, not the cold early morning streets. They'd rushed outside, leaving their jackets in the cloakroom and, unable to re-enter, everyone was shivering, their breath forming clouds of white mist. Girls were crying, boys jumping at the chance to console them. A sea of mobile phones shone bright in the darkness, thumbs tapping furiously, no doubt blasting social media with Chinese whispers.

Girl murdered.

I heard the gunshots.

Terrorism in Bradford.

This was how the wrong stories ended up in the papers. It escalated beyond the facts.

The murder victim, identified by a friend as Jaspreet Mann, was a student out celebrating her twenty-first birthday. She hadn't stood a chance. Whoever had slashed her throat knew exactly what he was doing. He'd gone straight for the carotid artery. Her death had taken only a few minutes.

Harry rubbed his hands together; Jaspreet's blood had dried into the creases of his palms.

Fuck this.

He looked into the crowds of witnesses, thinking only one thing.

Is the bastard here?

Am I looking at him right now?

Harry's phone rang. He pulled it from his pocket and saw it wasn't ringing. Confused, he put his hand in his other jacket pocket and found another device, one he didn't recognize.

A burner. It was ringing.

Unknown number.

Harry thought about the crowd on the dance floor pushing past him, desperate to get out. Dozens of them brushing past his body, any one of them could have slipped a phone into his pocket.

The killer.

Harry pressed the green answer button.

Laughter.

Hysterical laughter.

Harry listened, his patience wearing thin. He scanned the crowds. Dozens of people were on their phones, some recording what was going on. But he couldn't find anyone laughing.

Harry didn't say a word.

Suddenly it stopped.

Still, Harry kept quiet.

'You will catch me, Harry, you know that, don't you?'

Harry didn't recognize the voice.

He stayed mute, desperately scanning the street. If he'd spotted him in the crowd, he'd have marched over and smashed his face into a pulp.

'Why play the games, then? Hand yourself in,' replied Harry.

'Games? I've not even started yet. This is on you, Harry. You ruined my life. And now, I'm going to ruin yours.'

THIRTY

RONNIE VIRDEE ENTERED QUEENSBURY Tunnel, a now abandoned piece of Bradford's history.

He was changing.

But it couldn't happen overnight.

Bradford didn't work that way.

Here, inside a tunnel which connected the world outside to one
of a more hellish nature, Ronnie still had work to do to ensure his
vision for Bradford did not suffer because he had taken his eye off
the ball.

He walked the quarter-mile stretch, accustomed to the stench of
damp and abandonment, using a torch to illuminate the darkness. The
ground was a waterlogged trench, ice starting to form on the surface.
Sections of an ancient rusted train track were glowing orange in the
beam of the torch. Instead of the usual water dripping from the roof,
razor-sharp icicles were hanging ominously from the ceiling.

Ronnie heard screaming as he approached a dry section of the
tunnel, the area lit by several powerful lamps. He found his second-
in-command, Enzo, standing beside a dishevelled man bound to a
rickety chair.

'Anything?' asked Ronnie.

Enzo shook his head, removed his gloves and wiped perspiration from his face. 'Told you these Europeans were tough bastards.'

Ronnie wasn't disheartened. This place broke everybody. Eventually.

He crouched in front of the man, who had blood streaming down his face. Ronnie looked him in the eye and saw only one thing.

Defiance.

He waited a few seconds, staring hard into the man's eyes, as if trying to look into his soul. Then he stood up.

'He's more afraid of his boss than of us,' said Ronnie.

'Give it a few days. He'll break.'

'Maybe.'

Ronnie softened his tone and focused on the man. 'You want out? A new life? Money in your pocket? I can make that happen. Everyone will just think you succumbed to Bradford. No different to any other day for men like you and me. Better way to end this than me putting you to the streets.'

The man spat on the floor and hissed something in Polish.

'That's fine,' replied Ronnie, removing a pair of thick padded gloves from his pocket and slipping them on. 'I like to leave this place knowing that I offered you both sides of the coin. Your choice to go this way.'

Ronnie sighed and grabbed a bag from the floor beside Enzo's feet. Something inside struggled to break free.

'Already?' said Enzo, surprise clear in his voice.

'He's not becoming part of this tunnel. He needs to be found. So they'll know not only are we back but they need to fuck off or they'll end up like this one.'

For the past two years, as Ronnie had slipped back into alcoholism, a European gang, mainly Polish, had aggressively placed their footprint in Bradford. For them, it was simply territory in a city which had one of the largest heroin problems in England.

For Ronnie, it was fucking with a much larger picture.

He was going to change the game in this city but he could only do that if he had *total control*. There were deals going on behind closed doors, none of which could happen if Ronnie allowed the Europeans to continue to increase their profile. They were hard-liners and thought nothing of dropping a body on to the streets of Bradford.

They acted first and thought later, the complete opposite to Ronnie's strategy.

In the past year they had ensured Bradford was second only to Greater London for homicides. Whilst it might have kept Harry busy, it was dragging Bradford back to a place Ronnie had worked hard to raise it from.

'What your boss needs to realize,' said Ronnie, opening the bag in his hand and removing a large, hungry sewer rat, 'is that for him, Bradford is just a piece of currency. He doesn't give a fuck about it. Not like I do. And he and I are nothing alike. You see this guy standing next to you?'

Ronnie pointed at Enzo.

'Best SAS operative of his time. The other guys I employ? Similar. We've a discipline and a code you fuckers will never understand or rise to. It's why you're bound to fail. So, I'm going to send you back to your boss in a way he'll understand. He wants to bring this fight to me – there's only one outcome.'

The man tensed in the chair, eyes glued to the rat squirming in Ronnie's hands, trying to bite its way through his gloves.

'Last chance,' said Ronnie, holding the rat near to the man's face so its fur brushed against his bloody skin. It became immediately animated at the scent of blood.

More Polish gibberish from the man in the chair.

Another gobful of phlegm landed on the ground.

'Have it your way then,' said Ronnie, stepping closer.

He put the bag over the man's head, slipped the rat inside and pulled the drawstring tight around his neck.

The screaming was instant, the man's thrashing in the chair forcing it to topple sideways and hit the ground.

'Come on,' said Ronnie to Enzo. 'We're done here.'

Outside, Ronnie and Enzo lit up cigarettes. In the calm, bitter cold outside the mouth of the tunnel, they stood side by side.

'Only a matter of time before we had to send a message,' said Enzo.

'They don't have the fight in them to take Bradford from us,' replied Ronnie.

'Got some backing though, haven't they.'

'Took my eye off the ball but we'll flush them out.'

Ronnie turned to Enzo, took a deep pull on his cigarette.

'I know that look,' said Enzo.

Ronnie smiled. 'Been two years since we broke ties with Harry. Two years since that night we lost Tara. Time to make things right.'

'He won't turn, Ronnie.'

'He doesn't need to.'

Enzo looked confused.

'You trust me?' Ronnie asked.

'Always.'

'Good. Because I need it more than ever. If we want to flush out these Europeans, put our fist firmly back around Bradford, we're going to need Harry's help. We need someone on the inside to feed us that intel we're missing.'

'We tried that before. Look what happened.'

Ronnie thought about his family situation. His mother wanting to reconnect with Harry and his father's precarious position in the hospital.

Change was coming for the Virdee family.

Change which would put the brothers firmly back on track.

THIRTY-ONE

AT FOUR A.M. HARRY finally entered his home. He checked Saima was asleep, had a brief glance into Aaron's room, then hit the shower, leaving the lights off. He turned the temperature to scalding and sat down in the shower tray. He envisaged Jaspreet's blood washing off his skin, down the plughole.

Do you see the sinner, Harry?

Had he caused this?

If it wasn't Gurpal tormenting him, was it someone else? He struggled to think. Had he pushed it too far, too many times?

He closed his eyes, trying to see what he'd missed.

He sat like that for forty minutes. There was no point going to bed, he had to be at the eight a.m. briefing in a few hours. And he couldn't sleep, there was too much noise inside his head.

The girl had died in his arms.

Eyes wide and disbelieving.

Pleading, panicking.

Harry thought about what he had done to Kash, breaking his nose the way he had.

Was this some sort of knee-jerk reaction?

The bathroom door suddenly opened and Saima stepped inside and turned the light on.

'Harry?' she said, alarmed, barely able to see him in the steam-filled room.

'I'm here,' he said. 'Turn the light off, Saima.'

'Are you okay? Have you only just got in? What happened?'

'Just a really, really, bad night, Saima.'

She opened the shower door, turned the water off and grabbed a towel, handing it to Harry. 'Come on,' she said softly, 'let me help you out of here.'

THIRTY-TWO

HARRY ARRIVED FOR THE eight a.m. HMET briefing having had no sleep. He was pissed off, his mind loaded with questions he didn't have answers to.

Saima had refused to go back to bed and he'd told her all about his night. He'd felt bad that he'd woken her so early and was thankful today was her day off.

Conway caught Harry outside and pulled him aside.

'Some night,' she said.

Harry simply nodded.

'You look like hell.'

'Like you said. Some night.'

'ACC wants a word after the meeting. A sit-down.'

Harry sighed. He knew what that meant. Scrutiny of his decision-making process at Maestro's.

'Did everything I thought was right at the time. If I'd known—'

She put her hand out to stop him. 'ACC wants a word. Not me,' she said.

Harry forced a smile. 'Cheers, boss.'

She nodded for Harry to enter the briefing room. 'Come on. Get up to speed before we make that meeting.'

Harry learned that the riot gear hadn't been required at the night-club and that two dozen constables had managed to take details from over two hundred witnesses. The statements would take weeks to collate.

And then the kicker. The nightclub had only opened three months before and the owners hadn't deemed the installation of CCTV a priority.

There was no footage of the murder.

He must have known that.

After the briefing, Harry accompanied his boss to a sit-down meeting with Assistant Chief Constable Frost, who wanted a personal update from Harry. It felt like walking into the headmaster's office.

Frost wanted to know why the killer was contacting Harry personally.

'Your guess is as good as mine,' Harry had said.

Frost liked the Gurpal Singh angle, the timings worked.

'You've got my full support here, Harry,' he said, holding his gaze.

At Frost's request, they were focusing all their resources on try-ing to find the bastard. The team were in touch with the prison and chasing up a meeting with Gurpal's parole officer.

Frost had pressed Harry hard: was there anything Harry wanted to tell them?

Harry thought about the video camera he had destroyed. The footage which showed Gurpal had acted in self-defence even if he had almost beaten his wife, Indy, to death.

'Nothing, sir.'

It was late morning before Harry managed to grab some time with his team. DI Palmer was at Jaspreet Mann's autopsy, but he'd sent in confirmation that she'd been killed by a puncture to the neck that had severed her carotid artery.

Harry shivered at the memory of her lying dead in his arms, blood soaking through his clothes.

Witness statements provided by Jaspreet's friends revealed she was a dental student at Leeds University, she lived in Pudsey and had been dating a white guy called Roger, also a dental student, who was two years her senior. He'd been at the bar when the attack happened. He was reportedly in bits.

Nobody had reported witnessing the attack. The dance floor had been heaving, mist clouding everybody's view, and the music drowning out all other sounds.

Son of a bitch had picked the perfect location, perfect time and left them with two hundred witness statements to sift through; a fucking needle in a haystack.

For the second morning running, officers had been stationed at Bradford Interchange, canvassing the women using the ladies' toilets as changing rooms, slowly eliminating girls from the CCTV footage they had from Monday morning. Again, it would be weeks not days before they had anything useful.

By lunchtime, Conway had told Harry he looked like hell and sent him home. Thirty-six hours without sleep was most people's limit, and Harry had just passed the thirty-hour mark. He was no exception to the rule. With everything delegated, he phoned Palmer, telling him to stop by his house later that evening to update him on the day.

Sitting in his car in the Trafalgar House car park, Harry closed his eyes and once again ran through events from the night before.

He had missed something.

There was always a tiny detail that got overlooked.

What was it?

He pictured the killer in the club.

Moving through the crowd.

A girl he didn't like the look of.

Dancing with a white guy.

The music, the smoke, the perfect camouflage.

The strike to Jaspreet's neck.

The panic.

Blood.

Everyone rushing for the exit, including the killer.

Outside, amongst the clubbers, he had the perfect opportunity to disappear into the night, unnoticed.

Unnoticed?

Harry opened his eyes.

Unnoticed?

There was something there.

'Got you,' he whispered, and started his car.

THIRTY-THREE

SITTING ALONE IN HER kitchen, Saima turned off the news. She'd heard enough disturbing headlines to last a lifetime. Her horror at what Harry had gone through the night before had not yet abated; he'd given her some of the detail but she'd known there was more to it.

She held her head in her hands.

Tired.

Poor Harry must be a mess at work.

She was grateful she hadn't been on shift today. Usually, on her day off, Saima would take Aaron to her sister's place but, having been awake since four a.m., she had decided against it. She'd hoped Harry would have come home by now – how long could he last without sleep?

The sound of the doorbell made her jump.

She heard Aaron run towards the front door, yelling, 'Postman Pat! Postman Pat!'

Saima hurried after him and opened the door to find Joyti standing there, a Cornetto ice cream in her hand. Standing beside her was Mandy Virdee.

'Hello, Beti,' said Joyti.

Beti. Daughter.

'Three days in a row.' Saima started to smile, then her stomach dropped.

Ranjit.

'Is everythi—' she started.

'Yes, yes. Do not worry. My husband is still waiting for his operation – Friday, they say.'

Relief flooded Saima's mind.

She couldn't stop a nervous laugh escaping from her lips.

'I-cream! I-cream!' Aaron had seen the gift his grandmother had brought him.

'I didn't know what else he liked,' Joyti said.

Saima stepped aside to let her mother-in-law and Mandy inside.

Joyti stopped abruptly in the hallway. She stared down at her slippers. She smiled and touched them gently. Aaron joined her, put his hands over hers.

'Grandma slippers,' he whispered to her solemnly.

Joyti ruffled his hair and crouched beside him.

'Only a grandmother could get away with giving him an ice cream at ten o'clock in the morning,' said Saima.

As Joyti led Aaron into the living room, Mandy reached for Saima, stopping her from following.

'I . . . I . . . need a moment with you,' said Mandy.

'I'm listening,' Saima replied coldly.

'Mum's going to speak with you about a few things. I know she wants change for us all. And whilst I don't know exactly how that might work, I want you to try and move past what I said two years ago. I'd lost my daughter. My marriage to Ronnie was in a bad place and I wasn't thinking straight.'

She couldn't look at Saima. Her eyes were fixed on Joyti's slippers and her voice, when she spoke, was cold.

'Fine,' said Saima. She didn't believe Mandy. She didn't trust her.

'Good. That's really good,' said Mandy awkwardly. 'I'll pick Mum up when she's done here.'

Saima turned towards the living room. 'Close the front door on your way out,' she said.

At the kitchen table, Joyti's face darkened and she reached for her daughter-in-law.

'I cannot miss little Aaron growing up,' she said, surprising Saima with the force in her voice.

'I know, I—'

Joyti held up a hand.

'This morning when I woke up, I could not bear it. I could still smell him. I didn't want to wash my coat with dried ice cream on it because it is the only thing I have which reminds me of him and it made me sad. All of this makes me sad. I am too old to allow this to keep going. I want to see my little Aaron grow up.'

'I was thinking the same thing.'

'I have done what I believed was right, I have stood by my husband despite my own wishes, but I . . . I do not believe I can continue any longer. It will fall to the women to try and save this family.'

Saima swallowed hard. They were words she had never expected to hear, words Harry had almost given up hope of hearing.

She nodded, allowing a smile to spread across her face.

'What can I do?' said Saima.

Joyti nodded at a pan on the stove. 'A long time ago, you made me some tea. It was a dark night for my family when my grand-daughter Tara was taken from us but your tea warmed my heart. So, now, I want you to put water in that pan, put it to boil and sit here whilst I make you *my tea* and then we talk about what needs to be done.'

'Harry always told me my tea was as good as yours. Now I'm tasting it, I can see he was lying,' said Saima.

Joyti smiled. She was sitting on the floor in their living room, cross-legged, Aaron by her side, helping him with a puzzle.

'I have over fifty years' experience,' said Joyti.

'What is the secret?'

Joyti smiled. 'Leave it on the stove on gentle simmer for twenty minutes. Makes the tea thicker and sweeter.'

'I knew there was something I was missing.'

'Can I tell you a story?' Joyti asked.

'Of course,' replied Saima, taking tiny sips of her tea, savouring every mouthful, as Joyti began to talk.

When the Virdees had first taken over their corner shop, it had been hard work, she explained. They had been the first Asian people to move into the estate and were met with huge suspicion.

'My husband never panicked. He would say, "They'll see that we're just like them."'

There was a group of teenagers who used to throw bricks through their windows. They had a regular routine worked out. Ranjit would call the police and one of the boys would be arrested. On their release, the Virdees' window would be smashed again with renewed hostility, and Ranjit would pick up the phone once more.

'One evening, some of them were sitting on the low wall opposite our store, drinking beer. The shop was closed, we were sitting upstairs in our flat, but we could hear them. Shouting. Singing. Threatening. My husband was sick of the games. He told me to stand by the window and watch. If it became violent, I was to call the police. I had Harry on my lap, he must have been about eight years old. I'd begged Ranjit not to go outside but he didn't listen. I kept the phone in my hand, clutching it tight, ready to call the police.'

Aaron had completed his puzzle and wanted to do it again. Joyti broke from the story to help him reset it before continuing.

Ranjit had gone outside, carrying a can of beer he'd taken from the shop. He cracked open the can and asked if one of the boys on the end would move over.

'My window was open, I could hear everything. My husband,

wearing his turban, was sitting in the middle of a group of hooligans. I had never been so frightened.'

'I'm sure,' replied Saima, focused on every word.

Ranjit had chatted with them, swapped his expensive beer for a cheap cider which made him grimace. He made them laugh with a dirty joke.

'Do you know what happened then?' said Joyti.

'What?'

'One of them stood up, told the boys that our shop was okay. He and Ranjit shook hands and the bricks stopped coming through the window.'

Saima sat back on the sofa, unsure what to say.

'He made them see that he was not whatever it was they had assumed him to be. He was just a man. Like them.'

'I can't believe it,' Saima uttered.

'And now, we need to do something similar.'

'What do you mean?'

'You have already done it. When Ranjit was brought in and you saw who he was, you saved his life. And he needs to know this.'

Saima finished her tea and placed the empty mug on a side table, sighing.

'I'm afraid,' she said eventually.

'I know. As am I. All night I was thinking of this story, of all the changes we made when we first came here. Eating meat, my husband drinking alcohol, hiding it always from the religious community. And I realized: with you it is the same. As my husband used to say, we need to adapt.'

Saima came across to Joyti and sat on the floor by her side.

She smiled weakly at her mother-in-law. She wanted to believe they could change things for the better.

'Are you working tomorrow?' Joyti asked.

'Yes.'

'What time do you have your lunch?'

Saima shrugged. 'Depends. We don't really get regulation lunch breaks.'

'Can you meet me at Ranjit's room at one o'clock?'

'I'm sure I can. What are you going to do?'

Joyti reached a hand to Saima's face.

'Not what *I* am going to do. What *we* are going to do.'

THIRTY-FOUR

HARRY COULDN'T GO HOME and sleep now.

Not until he knew what he was dealing with.

He arrived at Cliff Lane in Holme Wood, the largest council estate in the city, run-down, overcrowded and out of the way. More often than not, criminal activity in Bradford was traced back to this area.

Not today, though.

Today, Harry was here for something else entirely.

Help.

He hurried up the steps of the semi-detached house and rang the doorbell. He could hear the TV on loud.

When nobody answered the door, Harry peered through a window and saw a boy, maybe ten years old, watching a Harry Potter movie. He tried the doorbell again and waited.

Nothing. Harry went around the back. In the garden, he found Dawn, the hooker from the previous night, hanging out clothes on her washing line. Harry had contacted his colleagues in Vice and given them Dawn's name, a description and the details which located her on the police database; the devil tattoos on her breasts had helped identify her. Dawn had a record going back two decades. Theft as a

147

teenager, drugs in her twenties and a stint in jail for drunk-driving. Nothing in the last three years, though.

She stared at him, took a moment to register who he was and then came charging towards him, fists clenched.

'What the fuck, yeah,' she said, dropping her voice and nervously glancing up at her back door. 'You some kind of freak? Do you know who I know? Who I can get here like this?'

She clicked her fingers and carried on.

'I get my people here, yeah, and they're gonna knock the brown off you. Time they've finished, you'll be in hospital for weeks.'

She stopped as abruptly as she'd started.

Harry held up his hands, innocent. 'All I was looking for was a little help.'

'You want to get sucked off? Piss off back down Manningham.'

She turned to go back into the house. 'Fucking prick,' she spat.

'Hey!' said Harry, moving towards her.

Dawn slammed the door behind her.

'Christ,' said Harry, hurrying after her. He couldn't have her calling in some lowlife pimp and complicating matters. 'Hey,' he said again and held his police identification up to the glass pane in the door.

Dawn had her phone to her ear. She stepped closer to the window, squinted her eyes and hung up.

Breathing heavily.

Face flushed.

Finally, she opened the door.

'What do you want?' she said, again lowering her voice.

'I want your help,' said Harry.

Dawn had invited him in and closed the door to the living room.

'Can we start over?' asked Harry, extending his hand.

She didn't take it.

'Okay,' he said, retracting it. 'You know what happened at the club last night?'

'Some girl got done in. That's what I heard.'

'Somebody killed her, that's right.'

'So?' she said, crossing her arms defensively across her chest.

'Well, I'm wondering; you'd gone before it all kicked off and everyone ran outside. I'm guessing you went back to your post over the road. Did you see anything?'

'Like what?'

'I don't know. Somebody running away? Leaving in a hurry? Anything that caught your attention?'

She hesitated, then said, 'No.'

She'd seen something.

They always pause before they lie.

'I'm sorry I didn't tell you I was a copper last night,' said Harry.

'Why would I care?'

'I need your help, Dawn. A girl was killed last night.'

'Girls die every day in Bradford,' she said with a scowl. 'This is no different.'

'Actually, this one is. And I reckon you might have seen something.'

'Last night you wanted something and made it worth my while.'

Harry shook his head. 'I'm not a cash machine, Dawn.'

'Then I didn't see nothing.'

Harry pointed to the bruises on her arms. 'Pimp? Or punter?'

'What does it matter to you?'

'Because maybe you help me out here and, in return, I can help you out.' Harry glanced at the bruises again. 'Pimp?'

Dawn nodded.

'You want me to give him a headache?'

Dawn thought on her reply.

'Come on. I'll owe you. And in this city? In this neighbourhood? That's a favour worth having.'

When the chaos had hit and the club had started to empty, Dawn had seen the flood of people leaving, the girls crying, the boys consoling, everyone using their mobile phones.

'And there's this one guy,' she said, 'alone. He walks hard away from the club. Head down. Crosses the road. Walks right past me, moving like the devil's on his ass.'

'Did you get a good look at him?' said Harry, leaning forward.

She shook her head. 'He comes out the club, puts a beanie on his head and just flies right past me.'

'You must have seen something, though?'

'Asian fella. Maybe five eight. Stocky.' She paused. 'I followed him.'

'You what?'

'You work the streets long enough, you know when someone's dodgy. He might as well have had a neon sign above his head.'

Harry wanted to reach out and shake her – for being such an idiot and for being such a genius. If his team had half her initiative, his job would be much easier.

'Go on,' said Harry.

'Damn heels make so much noise. So, I took them off. Walked on the road. I wasn't going to follow him all night. Just wanted to see if he got in a car. I'd add it to the blacklist, let the other girls know. But he didn't. He went into the Lister Mills complex, off Manningham, and I left it at that.'

'Lister Mills? Which part?'

Lister Mills was one of a handful of new developments with over a thousand apartments, shops and office spaces. It was a labyrinth.

'Shit, I don't know. He walked into the complex where all those fancy apartments are. I figured that's where he lived.'

'Anything else you can tell me?'

'No. Swear down, that's all I know.'

Harry's phone rang. A call he needed to take; it was Angus Moore, the senior prison warden at Armley and an old friend of Harry's. He stepped away from Dawn to answer it.

'Angus, tell me,' said Harry.

'Couple of your boys came down here wanting an audience. The governor sent them packing. Paperwork not in order. Is it urgent? They left a message it was.'

'Critical,' said Harry.

'You need a one-to-one with Gurpal Singh's cellmate? That about right?'

'It is.'

'Right. Then get your ass over here. I've got a window for you.'

THIRTY-FIVE

THE LAST THING HARRY needed was to interview Gurpal's cell-mate. His mood was sour, his vision blurry and his head pounding. It was approaching thirty-six hours since he had slept and he didn't have a lot left in him. But Angus had done him a favour and Harry wanted to get this done with; the paperwork would take an age.

He met Angus in the cramped reception area of Armley prison.

'Cheers for this,' said Harry, noticing a glowing red patch on the side of Angus' neck. Another new tattoo; Angus was obsessed with them. Looked like a vampire bat, angry, possibly breathing fire.

'I'll bank the favour for down the line. You okay, Harry? Look ready to drop, mate,' said Angus.

'Did an all-nighter last night. Was planning on getting my ass to bed before you called me.'

'Must be important.'

'It is.'

Harry followed him down a network of dimly lit corridors, heading into the belly of the prison. Eerily quiet, just the men's shoes squeaking on the floor.

'He been a good boy?' asked Harry.

'Pretty much.'

The deeper they walked, the colder the air became. Finally, they arrived at a meeting room, metal door closed.

'Anything I can use?' asked Harry.

Angus handed him a file. 'This is him. Got a parole review in four weeks. Pretty keen to make a good impression.'

Harry patted Angus on the arm. 'Cheers. Like I said, I owe you one.'

The inside of the room had a metal desk and two chairs, all bolted to the floor. Harry remained standing. Fredrick Ashford, Gurpal's long-time cellmate, sat glaring at him across the table.

'Guvnor says it's Freddie. That right?'

He nodded. Shifting in his seat. Uncomfortable.

'We met before?' he asked.

'Nah.'

'You look like you've seen a ghost.'

Freddie shrugged. 'Don't like cops. You always want something.' He looked at Harry, still uncertain. 'Don't you?'

Harry sat down. Placed Freddie's file on the table. 'Just a chat.'

'Got nothing to say to you.'

'You don't know what it's about.'

'Sure, I do.'

'Really?' Harry leaned back in his chair. 'Enlighten me.'

'I know who you are. You set Gurpal up.'

'What do you know about it?'

'He told me everything.'

'And you believed him?'

'One thing you learn in prison. Guys in here bullshit all the time. In the gym. The courtyard. Whose dick is bigger. All that kind of stuff. But between cellmates? That shit doesn't fly. No reason to lie. Too much time to fuck it up and get caught out. Then? If you lose their trust? Who's got your back? No one.'

Harry nodded. Opened the file on the table. 'Makes sense.'

He leafed through the pages. 'What did he tell you?'

'The truth.'

'Which is?'

'You were first copper on the scene. There was a video camera. You got rid of it. Would have shown he acted in self-defence.'

Another nod from Harry. 'I haven't slept in about thirty-six hours, Freddie. You ever done that?'

Freddie nodded.

'Makes you impatient, doesn't it. Body temperature creeps up. Almost feel zoned out.'

Harry fixed Freddie with a cold stare.

'Basically, makes me cranky.'

'What do you want?'

'To know what Gurpal was going to do when he got out. Plans he had. Maybe he spoke about getting even? Revenge? Causing some shit that would get everyone talking.'

'You ruined his life.'

'He beat his wife almost to death; that's what ruined his life.'

'That was between him and her. Man answered for that. Did his time. But you put a sentence on him he didn't deserve.'

Harry stood up and walked across to Freddie, perching on the table by his side. He dropped his voice. 'Maybe I did drop that charge on him. Maybe there was a camera in that room. And maybe when I watched it, I realized a piece of shit like Gurpal Singh deserved everything he got.'

Harry leaned a little closer, his breath caressing Freddie's ear. 'Not going to lie to you, I don't like playing by the rules when lives are at risk. Innocent lives. So, you're going to tell me what I want or this parole meeting you've got in four weeks' time might not go so well for you. Amazing what random searches of your cell can turn up.'

Harry saw Freddie's lip curl. He put his hand on his shoulder and squeezed firmly. 'But I'm sure we are going to get on just fine,' he said, standing up and retaking his seat opposite.

Freddie remained silent.

Seemed the years of camaraderie between the cellmates was stronger than Harry anticipated.

He tried a different approach.

Harry told him what had happened at Maestro's the night before. And about Usma Khan.

The messages for Harry.

'Now, finding shit in your prison cell is one thing. Maybe you do an extra few months. Maybe you don't give a shit about that. But I'm looking at two murders in forty-eight hours. And whoever's doing this knows *me*. Has history with *me*. If it turns out to be Gurpal and later on we discover you knew something about this? That might implicate you as an accessory and, Freddie – that's years.'

Freddie shook his head. 'He was right about you. Some piece of work, aren't you?'

Harry shrugged.

'Maybe I am. But I don't know you. I don't care about what you've done. We've no history. So, you tell me what I want to know and, when I leave this place, it will be like we never met.'

Harry closed the file in front of him. 'Just like that.'

Freddie was thinking on his predicament. Chewing his lip. Sucking his teeth.

'He was pissed off at what you did. Reckons you should have understood where he was coming from, you and him being from the same community an' all. Said you were a coconut, brown on the outside and white on the inside, and that when he got out of here he was going to see you right.'

Harry was watching him closely. He didn't see any signs of a lie. No shifting in the chair, no looking away nervously.

'Which meant what?'

Freddie hesitated.

'He said he was going to see it right.'

'Which means what exactly?'

'He was mad. Fucking crazy with what happened. They put him on pills for it but he never took them. Hid them in his mouth. He spoke about getting even with you every day. But he never said nothing about killing no girls.'

'Getting even?'

'You,' said Freddie, eyes narrowing, brow creasing. 'Said he was going to humiliate you. Make it known what a bent copper you were. Drag your name through the shit. Even if it meant he ended up back in here.'

THIRTY-SIX

HARRY FINALLY ARRIVED HOME at five o'clock, practically delirious from sleep deprivation. He was surprised Saima wasn't home and sent her a text message asking her to wake him in a few hours' time, before collapsing on to his bed without getting changed.

Harry woke to Saima stroking his face. He could hear the sound of the nine o'clock news from downstairs.

'Simon's here, do you want me to get rid of him?' Saima asked gently.

He shook his head, moving to sit up.

He couldn't believe he'd slept for four hours. It felt like he'd blinked.

'You weren't here when I got home,' he said.

'Supermarket. Aaron was getting cranky, cooped up in the house all day.'

She continued to stroke his face. 'You're not going to work tonight are you, Harry?'

'Not a chance,' he replied.

When Saima didn't move from the bed, Harry wiped the sleep

from his eyes and studied her more closely. She looked drawn. Now he thought about it, she'd looked like that for the past few days. Usually by Wednesday evening, after a day off, Saima was full of energy, but something was clearly bothering her.

'What's wrong? Did you go see your sister? Did she upset you?'

'No, no, no, nothing like that. But, we . . . need to talk.'

'Do you need me to send Simon away?'

'No, just promise me you'll make some time for me?'

'Are you pregnant?' Harry took a punt.

She laughed. 'Such a man,' she said.

'That's a no?'

'Save your detective skills for the dead,' she replied, stood up and walked out of the room.

Downstairs, Harry found Palmer drinking a cup of Saima's Indian tea.

'Christ, Saima, you could have made him an English cup,' said Harry.

'He wanted Indian.'

'It's true,' said Palmer, warming his hands around the mug. 'You've been bringing a flask of Saima's tea in for years and never once offered me any. I can see why; this stuff's terrific.'

'Don't get used to it,' said Harry, sitting down on the couch opposite Palmer. 'I'm not the sharing type.'

'I'll leave you boys to it,' said Saima, putting a plate of chocolate digestives on the table for Palmer and handing Harry a plate of chicken and rice.

'Are you sure you don't want anything, Simon?' she asked. 'There really is plenty.'

Palmer waved a biscuit at her. 'This will be fine.'

Saima touched Harry's hand affectionately before she left. He stared after her, bemused. He'd have bet money on the pregnancy card.

'So?' said Harry to Palmer once Saima had closed the door. 'Give me the headlines.'

As Harry wolfed down his food, Palmer briefed him on Jaspreet Mann's autopsy. Carotid artery puncture by a sharp object, nothing else unusual. No wasps, obviously. The family had been told and four of Harry's team were now looking into Jaspreet's life, trying to find a link between her and Usma.

Any link.

There was a delay on getting the footage from Lister Mills which Harry had requested after speaking with Dawn. The managing agent was proving to be a pain over data protection, forcing them to liaise with the landlord, solicitors, all kinds of crap. None of which helped.

'The shops selling tarantulas. Anything there?' asked Harry.

'Nope.'

'How about Gurpal? Any sign?'

'Nothing, Harry. I put four DCs on checking out his old haunts. Clubs he was a bouncer in, ex-girlfriends we know about. After what you did to Kash, pretty certain Gurpal is being extra careful.'

'So, we're up shit creek?'

'Well, except for this,' said Palmer, unlocking his phone, scrolling to a picture and handing it to Harry.

On screen, Harry could see a tattered piece of paper, torn in several places. It was covered in Arabic writing. Apart from one word written across the middle of the page in what appeared to be blood.

Sinner.

'What the fuck?' said Harry, putting his empty plate aside.

Palmer reached for another biscuit. 'I know.'

'Where'd you find it?'

'Inside Jaspreet's pocket.'

'Eh?'

Palmer dunked his biscuit in his tea, waited a few seconds then stuffed it in his mouth. Crumbs fell on to his chest. 'We think the killer put it there before he killed her.'

Brazen bastard.

Harry used his fingers to zoom in on the picture.

'You know what? This isn't Arabic, it's Urdu. Give me a minute,' he said to Palmer and took the phone into the kitchen. Saima was on her iPad, scrolling through eBay pages.

'Here,' said Harry, showing her the picture on screen.

Saima put the iPad aside and took the phone from him.

'Know what that is?' he asked.

Saima used her fingers to zoom and scan the photo.

'Where did you get this?' she asked, puzzled.

'It was found on a victim.'

'Really?'

'Yeah.'

'Was the victim female?'

'Yes.'

'Married?'

'What?'

'Was she married?'

'No.'

Saima frowned. 'This is a Haq Mehr.'

'A what?'

Saima spent a little longer analysing the photo. 'God, how to explain? The girl you found this on was Muslim, right?'

'No, Sikh.'

'That makes no sense.'

A Haq Mehr, Harry learned, was a financial agreement between an Islamic couple, arranged prior to their getting married but signed on the wedding day. Typically, the man would make a sizeable gift of money to his bride-to-be as a token of his commitment to her. It was a safeguard for his bride, a promise that he would not marry her, consummate the marriage and then leave without consequence.

'How much are we talking?' asked Harry.

'Thousands, usually. That picture's not clear but it looks like the amount is in rupees, five lakhs. That's about ten grand.'

'So, why was this found on a Sikh girl?'

Saima shrugged. 'You're the detective.'

Back in the living room, Palmer was as stumped as Harry.

'Nothing so far suggests Jaspreet was married before, never mind to a Muslim.'

Harry frowned at the photo of the Haq Mehr. 'You're sure we didn't miss it?'

'I really don't think so, Harry. I was with the Family Liaison Officer when we broke the news to the family. I spoke to both her brothers and we've got statements from her close friends, nobody mentioned anything about a marriage.'

'This is all wrong. The MO of this guy isn't consistent. Did Conway call in a profiler?'

Palmer nodded. 'He's formulating a report.'

'Wonderful,' said Harry dismissively. 'Usma had wedding mehndi on her hands. Now this marriage certificate. Is this fucker trying to tell us a story or just fucking with our heads?'

'You don't like Gurpal for this, do you?'

'Yes and no. Can't be sure who he mixed with in prison and what it made him into.'

Harry thought again of Ronnie and the dramatic change which prison had had on his life.

'There's just nothing consistent between these two murders. One is planned, perfectly executed, the other is an impulse kill with a massive risk of it going wrong.'

Palmer took his phone back from Harry, helped himself to a third biscuit then pointed at Harry's phone.

'It rang while you were in the kitchen, mate. Couple of times.'

Harry picked it up and saw two voicemails.

Unknown number.

'Shit,' said Harry showing Palmer. 'Just like last night.'

Harry played the first message.

It was twelve seconds of frightened screaming. Harry and Palmer winced in unison.

'It's him,' spat Harry.

'Play the second message,' said Palmer.

This one was shorter.

Flat B, 140 Ashgrove.

THIRTY-SEVEN

RONNIE WAS SITTING IN his conservatory watching the familiar sight of a fox triggering the security light in his back garden.

Joyti had told Ronnie that she planned to speak with Ranjit the following day and introduce him to Saima.

It would end in tears.

Her need to reunite with Harry, now she had spent some time with Aaron, was blinding her to his father's strength of feeling.

The politics of Harry's decision to marry Saima were complicated. Mandy had taken a similar position to Ranjit.

Which was why they needed to speak about it.

A few more minutes passed. The fox circled the perimeter of the garden, continuing to search for food.

Mandy finally entered the conservatory and arrived by Ronnie's side, both of them now watching the fox.

'Almost feel sorry for him when he doesn't find any food. Must have babies to feed,' said Mandy.

'If he's a good enough hunter, they'll do fine.'

'Clinical as ever. What did you want to talk to me about?'

'What do you think?'

'I'm tired of talking about it, Ronnie. What will be, will be.'

Ronnie turned to look at her. 'You know it's not that simple.'

Mandy folded her arms across her chest. 'I'm so tired of this shit. Of this family.'

Ronnie felt as if she had cut him. Which was exactly what she wanted him to feel. Their relationship had suffered after Tara's death and with Ronnie's descent back into alcoholism.

'Mum wants to play nice with Harry and Saima. If Dad survives the operation, that means . . .'

Mandy stepped in front of Ronnie and turned to face him. 'I don't want Harry or Saima to be part of this family. You know that and you know why.'

'Then you had better change your position.'

'Why? Because Aaron looks like Harry and your mother wants a chance to prove that she can raise her grandson the way she couldn't raise Harry and right those wrongs?'

Ronnie didn't like the tone in her voice or the way she spoke so poisonously about Harry. 'You best get a hold of yourself.'

'Fuck off, Ronnie.'

He grabbed her by the arms. Hard.

'What is your problem with this?' he snapped.

He stared into her eyes, searching for the one thing he had never really understood. They had all been so close, yet when Harry had revealed his relationship with Saima, Mandy had turned on him almost as quickly as Ranjit had.

Mandy shrugged herself free. 'My problem?'

'Yes. Your problem. Can't be that Saima is a Muslim. I know I didn't marry someone quite that narrow-minded.'

'Yes. You did.'

'No. I didn't. What is it that you're not telling me?'

Mandy turned away from Ronnie, stepping closer to the conservatory doors. When she spoke, her breath formed a white mist on the glass.

'I have family. Parents. Siblings. Cousins. They know what Harry did and the position we all took. We've raised our children to believe that marrying a Muslim is incompatible with our way of life. Going back on all that . . . the ramifications are huge. And you know this. If your father dies, your mother can be as much a part of Harry's world as she wants to be. And if your father survives, it is for them to decide how they deal with this. But if you think I want any part of it, you're wrong. I'm thinking of the children. Have you considered what happens if they see that we have accepted what Harry did? They can make similar decisions, and that is not something I am willing to entertain.'

Mandy turned to face Ronnie, eyes blazing angrily. 'If you want your brother back as part of this family, that's fine. The price is fixed. It will cost you your marriage.'

Mandy stepped past Ronnie and walked out of the room and slammed the door.

THIRTY-EIGHT

HARRY DROVE WILDLY AS Palmer contacted the duty sergeant from the passenger seat. He demanded two patrol cars and an armed response unit. This time, Harry was taking no chances.

Ashgrove was a couple of miles away, in a densely populated student area right by Bradford University. Harry parked his car in the only available parking space and grabbed a torch and a crowbar from the boot, handing them both to Palmer.

'How long for the patrol cars?' asked Harry, walking at pace.

'Sergeant said they were en route.'

Harry noticed a raucous house-party in progress at number 156, a retro night judging by the noisy Abba anthem and glimpses of the party-goers through the window.

Whatever he was walking into, he didn't like how many people were in the area.

They reached 140 Ashgrove and glanced at the house, then at neighbouring houses. No obvious CCTV.

It was a three-storey Victorian mansion and by the looks of the poor upkeep, had been turned into student accommodation. Council bins overflowing, bin-bags on the floor, most of them torn open,

166

their contents unceremoniously dumped beside a large mound of cigarette ends. Harry left Palmer by the front door and took a quick walk around the perimeter.

No broken windows.

No signs of anything out of the ordinary.

'I don't like this,' said Harry, returning to Palmer, who was spinning the crowbar in his hands. 'Too many people on this street. Too many unknowns. Where the fuck is the armed response?'

'It's only been ten minutes, Harry, they'll be here.'

'Come on.'

Harry climbed the steps and glanced at the electronic keypad from which he could buzz flats A–D. The voicemail had mentioned flat B. Impossible to tell which one that was.

Curtains to his right suddenly twitched and a boy appeared at the window; white, adolescent, scruffy.

Harry removed his police identification, stepped closer to the window and displayed it clearly. He put his finger to his lips and pointed towards the front door.

There was no movement from the fresh-faced student.

Harry tapped on the window and again pointed towards the front door.

The face vanished.

A hallway light came on and Harry told Palmer to lower the crowbar.

The front door opened and the student from the window appeared, wearing only boxer shorts. He looked back over his shoulder nervously but before he could shout to his flatmates about the police at the door, Harry pulled him outside, clamped his palm across his mouth and told him to be quiet.

'I'm DCI Harry Virdee and I need you to be discreet. Understand?'

Harry removed his hand.

'What the fuck, man?' whispered the boy.

'What's your name and which flat are you in?'

The boy held Harry's gaze, his eyes hard with anger. 'Nathan.'

'Flat?'

'A.'

'Which one is B?'

The boy nodded towards the opposite ground-floor window.

'Who lives there?' asked Harry, watching as Palmer had a cursory glance at it and shook his head.

'Curtains drawn,' he said.

'Asian girl,' said Nathan, shivering in the night air in only his boxer shorts.

'What's she called?' asked Harry.

'Leila.'

'You seen her today?'

'Not seen her for ages.'

'What?'

'Shit, we all live here in self-contained flats. Don't see any of the other residents regularly.'

'Last time you did see her?'

'I don't know. Couple of weeks ago.'

Two patrol cars arrived, both coming to a stop outside the house.

Harry kept hold of Nathan but spoke to Palmer. 'Tell them to park at each end of the street. Block it off. And chase up the armed response.'

Palmer headed towards the cars and Harry dragged Nathan into the house, leaving the door wide open. Again, he gesticulated for the boy to be quiet.

'This her door?' whispered Harry.

Nathan nodded. Harry watched his eyes widen as he focused on the door handle. Harry saw what had caused the alarm.

Blood on the handle.

Harry sighed and let the boy go, pushing him towards his flat. 'Get inside. Close the door. Don't come out until I tell you.'

Palmer returned with two uniformed officers. Harry pointed to the blood on the door handle. He pointed to the staircase and whispered orders for the officers to stand guard; ensure nobody came downstairs.

Harry took the crowbar from Palmer.

'Armed response?' he said.

Palmer shrugged. 'Any minute.'

Harry shook his head and again pointed to the blood on the door handle.

They couldn't wait. Preservation of life was the priority.

Palmer nodded.

Both men removed gloves from their pockets, slipped them on and stood in front of the door. Gently, Harry tried the handle, his fingers on the section with no blood.

Locked.

He pounded his fist on the door, rattling it on its hinges.

'Police. Open up!' he shouted.

Nothing.

No sound from inside.

Harry used the crowbar and in two forceful moves broke the door open.

Darkness.

He tried the light switch.

Nothing.

Harry took the torch from Palmer and shone it into the room; difficult to make anything out in the narrow beam. He took an apprehensive step forward.

And then the smell hit him.

Death. Decay. He ran his torch around the room again.

Something crimson shone back at him in the darkness.

Smeared across the wall, still glistening wet, was one word.

Sinner.

THIRTY-NINE

THE HAIR ON THE back of Harry's neck stood on end.

For the first time in a long time, Harry Virdee felt afraid.

He couldn't take his eyes off the wall.

Sinner.

Harry remained in the doorway, Palmer at his shoulder. His feet felt leaden, fear pinning them to the floor.

In the centre of the room, he could just make out what appeared to be the set for an Asian wedding. Four white pillars had been rigged to form a square around what looked like two golden thrones. The first was empty. But on the second was a young woman, slumped back in an exquisite red wedding sari.

Leila.

Her head was bowed, a veil gleaming with diamantés sparkled under the glare of Harry's torch. He inched forward.

Pink rose petals, similar to the ones at Usma Khan's crime scene, lined the floor in a path right up to Leila's feet. There were a dozen or so neatly wrapped gifts on the floor next to a silver tray which held the classic Asian wedding dessert, ladoos.

The room had been cleared; a cheap bedframe had been disman-
tled, the wardrobes pushed up against the windows.

Whoever had done this had gone to a lot of trouble.

'What is all this?' Palmer asked.

'It's a fucking wedding,' Harry whispered.

'Shit.'

'At least we know it's him.'

With no obvious threat in the room and still no sign of the
armed response, Harry approached Leila's body.

He crouched to his knees and shone his torch over her. She had
wedding mehndi on her hands. In her right hand, she held a rolled-
up piece of paper.

Harry shoved the tray of ladoos out of the way, moved a little
closer and pulled a pen from his jacket pocket. He used it to lift the
veil from the girl's face.

It's him all right.

Her eyes were stitched shut. The eyelids twitching.

Wasps.

Harry put down his torch, keeping the beam pointing towards
the ceiling so he could use the light. He felt for a pulse but the girl's
skin was cold.

Nothing.

He lowered the veil and pulled the paper from the girl's hand.

An English marriage certificate.

Blank.

A sudden deafening blare of music made Harry jump. His feet
crashed into the tray, sending the ladoos across the floor.

It was Shenhai, the celebratory wedding music. Harry looked
around the room, nothing.

He stared into the darkness.

A tiny red dot on top of the wardrobe.

A camera.

The killer was watching.

As Harry approached, he saw a laptop connected to two large speakers.

The music stopped.

A pause.

Maybe three seconds.

Then a voice, loud and clear.

'I see you Harry Virdee.'

Harry stopped in his tracks.

'I see all the sinners.'

FORTY

VIRDEE STANDS ALONE OUTSIDE the house as the girl's body is stretchered out.

It is exciting being this close, watching how broken he looks.

Broken?

Not yet.

Wait until he finds the gift I've left him.

It was Leila's eyes, that's how I'd known. It's always there in the eyes.

That's why I remove them.

Sinners, each and every one of them.

No shame. No honour.

Harry's eyes tell a story too.

He carries pain there. Deceit. He's not an honest man.

What does he think, because he carries a badge, that means something?

Not to me.

I know all about him.

This is a fight he was always destined to lose.

I want to see that look in his face. When he loses and realizes this is the end.

And it is coming.

Soon.

The autopsy on Leila's body will be immediate.

And they will find it.

Hidden inside her eyes.

The final piece.

The city of sinners is about to fall.

FORTY-ONE

AN EMERGENCY ONE A.M. autopsy.

Dr Wendy Smith and her assistant, Ingrid, had both been on call. Neither of them looked happy to be dragged from their beds.

But this was a priority.

Leila Amin had been stripped, her expensive, weighty wedding sari carefully bagged, along with the red and gold bangles which matched the outfit.

Three dead girls in three days.

A bona fide serial killer. And a quick worker.

The case would be taken out of Harry's hands in the morning.

Gold Command took over anything this big.

Frost would be taking charge. At least that meant he wouldn't be grilling Harry any more.

But Harry knew he wouldn't be able to shrug the case off that easily.

He had to pin down Gurpal. The elaborate wedding set-up. He was telling Harry a story. *Of betrayal.*

A SOCO snapped dozens of pictures of the naked body. Harry could already see that Leila's body was swollen like Usma's had been.

He was certain that, on closer examination, Wendy would find a puncture wound and they would learn Leila was allergic to wasps.

Bruised ligature marks around Leila's neck, the skin broken in dozens of places, led Harry to assume she'd been strangled post-mortem with barbed wire, similar to Usma, although they hadn't recovered any wire from the scene. What was that about? Once the killer had watched them die, did he just need a release of aggressive energy? There was also bruising around her thighs and blood in the creases where they met her hips.

Wendy was prepared this time. First she placed a scalpel by Leila's head, then she arranged a large plastic bag across Leila's face, tying it tightly around the top of the metal table so it formed a balloon. Anything that crawled or flew out of Leila's eyes would be easily contained without any drama. Harry was impressed.

Wendy then slid her hands under the bag and picked up the scalpel. Carefully she unstitched Leila's left eye. She peeled back the lid and, just as before, a weak, bloodied wasp crawled out of the hollow socket, the eyeball once again removed.

Wendy swiftly tied off the bag before fixing a new one to the table. She repeated the procedure on Leila's second eye and a second wasp was captured. Neither one looked as if it had much life left in it.

'Got you, you little buggers,' Wendy said, and turned to Harry. 'What now?'

'Send them to Entomology, like before,' said Harry.

Ingrid handed the bags to the exhibits officer, who took them at arm's length.

'There's something else here,' said Wendy. She grabbed a pair of tweezers, carefully pinching a small piece of paper from the girl's empty socket.

Harry stepped closer as she unfolded it.

'Not another one,' he whispered.

Apartment 624, Lister Mills.

FORTY-TWO

NINETY MINUTES AFTER LEAVING the mortuary, with the time approaching three a.m., Harry was at Lister Mills. He'd requested an armed response team to meet him there. Two teams had arrived. For now, at least, this was still his case so Harry had briefed the eight armed officers, each one carrying a sidearm and an MP3 machine gun. Once they entered the mill, Harry would have to take a back seat as they took control. This was their speciality.

Lister Mills.

Dawn had tipped them off about this place but the scale of the mill meant scouring the village-sized development would consume weeks not days, and they couldn't simply lock the entire complex down.

Perhaps now, they might have to. Their resources were being stretched like never before.

The red tape around the CCTV and the landlord meant they still hadn't received the footage they needed.

This nutter could be doing anything in there.

With robust orders given, Harry and three of his own officers followed the armed response team into the building.

Inside, they moved quickly and calmly through the foyer. Four men headed for the stairs, three got into a lift and one remained downstairs. As he climbed the stairs, past exposed beams and brickwork, Harry felt his fear solidify in the pit of his stomach. His mind was racing.

They were behind in this game.

And the killer knew it.

They were going in blind and Harry sensed they were about to witness something worse than anything the killer had thrown at them so far.

The men exited the lift on to the roof of the mill where modern penthouse pods sat on top of the building. A bitter chill sliced at Harry's face. He saw pink rose petals on the floor, similar to the ones at the other crime scenes.

Harry and his team secured the area by the lift and the top of the stairs as the armed officers swept the roof, shadows in the night disappearing into the darkness, their torches bouncing off the steel. They returned a few minutes later and led Harry towards the end penthouse.

The wind picked up, screaming across the roof, biting at the men's bodies as they reached the end unit, apartment 624.

Harry couldn't shake his unease.

The windows were dark.

No signs of life at all.

The lead officer buzzed the doorbell. Other officers fanned in behind. Weapons drawn. Harry and his team moved back. He glanced down the walkway but couldn't find a CCTV camera. He did notice a camera just above the door to 624.

There was no response at the door.

Harry gave the order to enter.

The front door was smashed in one fluid blow of a battering ram, the four-man team hurrying inside shouting, 'Armed police!'

Harry gave them a few minutes. Lights were turned on, rooms cleared.

And other lights started to come on. Neighbours had been awoken by the noise.

Harry whispered for one of his team to go and inform any residents stupid enough to come outside to return to their homes.

Armed response called the all-clear and waved Harry inside.

It was like walking into a glossy magazine.

High ceilings, mezzanine floor, grand lighting. The furnishings were entirely gold and purple, like an elegant hotel.

With no obvious threat, Harry stood down the armed officers. They'd wait outside for Harry's team to find whatever they were here to find.

Who lives here?

In the living room, Harry caught sight of a set of wires dangling by the side of a television. A place like this usually tried to hide every wire possible. On closer inspection, Harry saw that they were likely to connect the CCTV to a recording device, now missing. Harry grimaced, the CCTV footage was gone but at least it proved whoever lived here was in trouble.

'Boss! Boss!' he heard one of his officers shout. Harry hurried upstairs and followed the sound of the voice to a master bedroom.

'Who lives here?' asked Harry, marching towards his DC.

Harry was handed a photograph of a young woman with her arms around an older man, presumably her father.

'Found this, boss,' said the officer, and turned a large dressing table mirror which had been facing the wall towards Harry.

Harry's breath caught in his throat.

He thought the scrawl on the mirror was blood at first but, on closer inspection, it looked more like deep red lipstick.

Help me, Harry.

'Who lives here?' he whispered.

The officer pointed to the picture in Harry's hands.

Harry didn't recognize the girl in it.

'Should I know her?' he asked.

'The father. Look at the father.'

Harry focused on the man. Brought the frame closer to his face.

'Fuck me,' he said and shook his head. 'Can't be.'

Harry put the photograph down. 'Find something else!' he snapped. 'I don't believe it.'

Anything else.

Harry hurried to a desk in the corner of the room, his mind awash with chaos. He focused on a box file labelled, *Important.*

Harry opened it and found a tenancy agreement.

Aisha Islam.

Images of the girl in the nightclub, crumpled on the dance floor, came unbidden to Harry's mind.

He turned the page and saw a guarantor's signature, name and address.

Tariq Islam.

The contract quivered in Harry's hand.

'It's true,' he whispered.

Aisha Islam was the daughter of Tariq Islam.

The Home Secretary.

FORTY-THREE

HARRY REMAINED ON THE roof of Lister Mills, his hands resting on the icy perimeter balcony. The wind continued to blow, but he welcomed the cold. Sometimes it was the only thing that could calm his temper.

You're going to lose this one.

He's holding all the cards.

Behind him, Harry could hear the SOCO team ripping apart Aisha Islam's penthouse apartment.

This was the calm before the storm.

And a storm was exactly what it was going to be.

The Home Secretary's daughter.

It didn't get any bigger.

Harry envisaged crews from every major newspaper and TV channel descending on Bradford, the world's media putting his city under their powerful microscopes.

MI5, counter-terrorism, all four HMET teams and almost every uniformed officer would now be working what was looking like the highest profile kidnap case their force had ever encountered.

Yet another change in MO.

This guy was throwing all the rules out of the window. This had meaning. Purpose. It was about more than just the body count.

The killer had three girls on his record.

Why would he spare Aisha? Especially since she was the one girl who guaranteed him column inches?

How was any of this connected to Harry?

It was getting harder and harder to see Gurpal in this. But they had nothing else to go on.

Harry felt sick.

If this was on him . . .

He pushed the thoughts from his mind. He couldn't think about that now.

With only a few hours' sleep in the past forty-eight hours and no let-up in the case, Harry could feel the tiredness creeping in. He was going to nail this bastard. Bradford was not about to let another national headline tarnish its history. At least they'd get the resources now.

Harry's boss, Conway, arrived by his side. Five a.m. was too early for posh heels and a designer suit. She was dressed casually in trainers and a grey fleece jumper.

Conway placed her hands on the stone balcony, looking out over Bradford with Harry. The sleeping city had no idea what it would be waking up to.

'Why don't you go home, Harry? You can't do another all-nighter.'

'What's going on with all this?'

'Frost has organized a GOLD meeting. He's standing you down as SIO and appointing me to take over.'

Harry nodded. Standard operating procedure.

'He's also asked me to remove your team from your command so you can focus on what it is that makes this so specifically about you. We need that puzzle piece, Harry.'

Harry also expected that.

'Don't cut me off completely, Clare.'

'We won't. But this guy has contacted you twice now. We need to look into why. We're pulling Gurpal's brother in. He's lawyered up already. Says you broke his nose and that you are trying to fit his brother up again, just like before. Did you assault him, Harry?'

Harry shook his head. 'It's bollocks.'

They shared a look. Conway didn't look convinced.

'So what happens next?' asked Harry.

'There's a DCI from Greater Manchester being drafted in to look into your ongoing cases and review any previous cases which had any . . . grey areas. Whilst Gurpal Singh is our main focus, we need to look further and harder into anyone you've put away who has recently been released and has a grievance with you.'

'You're going to need more than one DCI team on that,' said Harry cynically.

Conway looked away.

'What you're saying is, you're investigating me,' said Harry, dreading what the next few days held in store. 'Bullshit. You don't trust me any more?' he added bitterly.

'Watch yourself, Harry. I'm here to make sure nothing distracts us from finding Aisha. Her father is the goddamn Home Secretary, in charge of every police force in England, and he's due into Leeds–Bradford this morning. We *need* to be on point. This goes wrong because of something *we've* done? It's everyone's heads.'

'So, my role is what?'

'Assisting.' She paused and added, 'When we need you.'

'You need me. You all know it. This guy likes to play and God knows why he wants to play with me.' Harry stopped for a moment. Took a breath. 'He knows we're going to catch him. He wants attention, to make us look foolish. He wants to make *me* look foolish.'

'You're right. Most likely, he's going to call you again. And we'll be ready. So go home. Get some rest. We've a major incident briefing at ten.' Conway checked her watch. 'Get four hours' sleep. You're going to need it.'

Harry turned to leave. She put a hand on his arm.

'One thing?'

'What?'

She handed him a digital recording device which connected wirelessly to his phone and recorded conversations.

'If he calls again, we need it.'

Harry took the device from her, putting it in his pocket and trying again to leave.

'One more thing,' said Conway, stopping him.

'Yes?' Harry turned, impatient now.

'Let's park the fact I'm your boss, just for a moment.'

'Okay.'

'Off the record.'

Harry nodded.

'Before Bradford wakes up. Before . . . security agencies we don't even know exist turn up and start a wholesale examination of our house, right here, right now, are you sure there's nothing you want to tell me? Nothing that might, say, come to light later and put us all in a difficult situation?'

'About Gurpal?'

'About anything, Harry.'

He smiled and removed her hand from his arm. 'A politician's about to arrive and you're already schooled in the art. Am I dirty? Is this about me? Do I know something which might save that girl's life and I'm withholding?'

He stepped a little closer.

'Since we're off the record? Being mates? Looking out for one another?'

Conway stepped away, clearly taken aback by Harry's tone.

'I've bent rules. You know that. No one who works these streets can afford the luxury of being a straight-line kind of cop. You want to get shit done in Bradford, *you become Bradford*. You learn how to tell a silhouette from a threat. But this?' said Harry, pointing to the penthouse behind them where the SOCOs were working diligently. 'This is not about me bending a rule or pissing off a nutter on the street. Look at the evidence. The wedding stuff. The effort and detail our guy put into that. This has meaning. It's personal. So, let's lose the Harry Virdee angle and put everything into finding Aisha Islam.'

FORTY-FOUR

HARRY GOT HOME AT six a.m.

The house was quiet, cold, the heating hadn't yet cranked into action.

Harry sat down in the dark of the living room.

Another night without sleep.

Was this the plan; to wear him down so he missed something vital?

Usma and Jaspreet had white boyfriends. Something told Harry that they'd soon discover that Leila and Aisha did too.

In the city with the largest ethnic population outside of London, there must have been thousands of girls involved in mixed-race relationships. Was that really what this was all about? It felt so much more than that.

The morning briefing would be intense, all eyes on Harry, wondering the same thing he was.

Why me?

More importantly, how would they save Aisha Islam?

Harry was used to being in control in this city. It was *his* city, one he knew every corner of.

Yet suddenly he was faced with an invasion, power-players from Whitehall and MI5 would descend on Bradford.

For the first time in a long time, Harry felt uncertain.

He heard Aaron's voice from upstairs, loud and delighted to be awake.

'Mamma! Mamma!'

After a minute or so of irritable yelling, Aaron changed his pleas to, 'Daddy! Daddy!'

Upstairs, Harry entered Aaron's room. He heard Saima's voice, speaking to Aaron through the baby monitor.

'Hello, little man,' said Harry, picking Aaron up from his cot.

'Here go,' said Aaron removing his dummy.

'Good boy. Too big for a dummy now.'

'Want get down.'

Harry kissed him, held him close a while and let him go, watching as he ran out of his room, calling for Saima.

Harry sat on the bed and stared at the cot.

Three dead girls.

Three families in a pit they might never recover from.

Aisha Islam, no ordinary victim, missing.

They might get an embargo on press-reporting for twenty-four hours, but ultimately Bradford was about to suffer a hateful trial by media.

Harry saw Saima standing in the hallway, in her pyjamas, Aaron in her arms, looking at him in a way he was used to seeing.

'Another girl?' she asked, walking towards him.

He nodded and told her who.

She sat on the bed beside him and let Aaron wander back into their room.

'At least everyone will be looking for her. Hunting down this . . . creep.'

Saima placed her hand on Harry's and squeezed it. 'Why don't you try and sleep an hour?'

'It'll make me feel worse.'

'What can I do?'

'Nothing,' he said, shaking his head, staring at the cuddly toys in Aaron's bed.

'Don't see you like this often,' said Saima.

'No.'

'Want to share a burden?'

Harry shrugged. 'Always back myself to bring a case home. But this guy? Stuff he's doing? Doesn't care that I'm going to catch him. *He wants that.* Only question is, how much damage is he going to do before that happens? To the girl. To me.'

FORTY-FIVE

TRAFALGAR HOUSE WAS THE busiest Harry had ever seen it. The morning briefing had been pushed back, first to nine o'clock, then ten, and eventually started closer to eleven, allowing time for all the relevant agencies to assemble.

In the largest briefing room, a silence fell over the hundred people gathered as Assistant Chief Constable Stephen Frost entered. Game face on.

All the big names were here, the head of media, external communications, counter-terrorism and rows of other suits Harry didn't recognize. MI5 maybe.

His head was throbbing and he dry-swallowed two paracetamols. Tiredness had given way to a chaotic mind, his thoughts were fuzzy, loud, crowded. But for the moment, he had to focus on the briefing, on how they were going to catch this bastard.

Frost went from the beginning. First, Usma Khan and the discovery of her body in the bookshop. Second, the murder of Jaspreet Mann in Maestro nightclub. Leila Amin at 140 Ashgrove and finally, the abduction of Aisha Islam. When he mentioned Harry's name, he felt the focus of everyone's eyes in the room burning into him.

Scrutiny. His favourite.

As the ACC was assigning officers in the room, acknowledging Harry's boss DSU Conway as SIO, the room fell silent as the doors opened and Tariq Islam entered, along with his close-protection team, four men in dark suits.

Tariq made his way towards the podium, walking at a measured pace, entirely in control. The microphone was moved aside as he shared a few private words with Frost at the front.

Tariq Islam was far from a career politician. He had served in the army and rumour had it he'd headed up a secretive organization called Group 13, a covert paramilitary group whose existence had always been denied by government, though the Internet was awash with rumours. After losing his wife to breast cancer, he had left the military to look after their only daughter, Aisha. A few years later he had entered politics, where rumours had continued to stalk him; apparently he was a hard-liner who wanted to bring back the death penalty and far tougher sentences for criminals. He had built up a loyal following with his right-wing views. Tariq was all about patriotism; his skin colour and religious background remained very much in the periphery. Harry thought, in different circumstances, the two of them might have got on.

He looked remarkably composed for a man whose daughter was at the mercy of a serial killer. He was clean-shaven, wearing a fitted black suit with a navy tie, and his hair was slicked back. Truthfully, Tariq looked as if it were any other day in the office.

Three murdered girls.

Aisha could be the fourth.

Yet, as he took a seat on the front row, his security team staying by the door, Tariq was a man in control.

Frost returned to his briefing but he'd barely begun when the duty officer barrelled into the room, pale-faced, eyes only on Frost. His trembling hand passed a sheet of paper to the ACC.

There was a moment's stillness before everything seemed to happen as if it had been rehearsed.

Frost leaned down towards Conway, whispered in her ear and marched out of the room. Conway, who was sitting right in front of Harry, turned abruptly and ordered him to follow her.

The room broke into anxious whispers as Harry left, the Home Secretary on his heels, his security team in close pursuit.

Harry found Frost and Conway waiting in an adjacent office.

Frost tried to politely ask Tariq Islam to leave but he refused, wanting to know what the emergency was.

'This is my daughter we're talking about, Mr Frost,' he reminded him.

Conway closed the door, ordering the security team to wait outside. She wouldn't accept their refusal.

'He's on the phone. He says he wants to speak to Harry and *only* Harry.'

'What?' said Harry, thinking he must've heard wrong.

'Line one,' said Frost, pointing to the phone. 'Put it on speaker.'

Harry swallowed hard, turning to Tariq.

'Are you sure you want to stay for this?'

Tariq nodded solemnly.

'Okay,' said Harry. 'Here we go.'

He hit line one and the speaker button. 'DCI Virdee.'

They could hear breathing, short and shallow. Worried breathing on the other end.

'Daddy? Are you there?'

Aisha Islam.

'I'm here, baby,' said Tariq before anyone could stop him, desperation suddenly written across his face. 'Are you okay, Aisha?'

She started to cry. 'I'm okay. I'm not . . . hurt.'

There was a noise, a ripping sound, a struggle, a faraway moan.

'Aisha? Aisha?' said Tariq.

Harry raised his hand, glared at Tariq.

'You're on with DCI Harry Virdee.'

'How are you, Detective?' It was the killer.

Harry took a breath.

'I want a peaceful end to this situation. So, you've got my attention. What is it you want?'

'I want to play a game. Do you like games?'

'We'd like to bring Aisha home safely. Her family—'

'Don't play your psychological crap with me, Detective.' The killer's voice changed, irate. 'Do you think I'm stupid?'

'No, I don't. I think you're smarter than anyone in this building and I think you know that.'

A pause.

'That's the first intelligent thing you've said all week.'

'So,' said Harry, glancing at Conway, who was typing frantically on her mobile phone, no doubt trying to get a trace on the number.

'I'd like to see you,' said the killer.

'Name the place.'

'Right now.'

'I'm ready.'

'Tell the father I'm going to Facetime him on his phone.'

Click.

'Hello? Hello? Shit!' said Harry, putting the phone down. 'Your mobile,' he motioned to Tariq. 'Where is it?'

Tariq handed it to Harry, who placed it on the table.

The video-call came in, from Aisha's number.

Harry's heart sank as a video of Aisha, bound and secured in a chair, appeared on the screen. She was wearing a flimsy nightie, her legs exposed and breasts barely covered. She looked as vulnerable as Harry could imagine.

He covered the microphone and turned to Tariq. 'I think you should leave. We're not in control of this.'

Tariq stood firm and refused. Harry looked to Frost and Conway but got nothing. 'Are you sure?' whispered Harry to Tariq, who nodded.

'We're here,' said Harry.

'Show me who is in the room.'

Harry looked to Frost, who shook his head. 'Look, we can—' started Harry.

The killer, standing out of shot, slapped Aisha, the noise piercing through the small speaker.

Tariq cried out in alarm.

'I say. You do. That's how this works,' snapped the killer.

Harry picked up the phone and scanned the room quickly.

'The father. Let me see the father.'

Harry looked at Tariq, who nodded.

'Please,' he said, as calm as he could. 'Don't hurt my Aisha. Please.'

'Harry . . . Do you mind if I call you that?' said the killer.

Harry refocused the camera on himself. Behind him, Conway scribbled a note for Tariq asking him for the phone number Harry was on, his phone number. He wrote it down for her and she left the room. Anything they could do to track Aisha's phone could make the difference here. The longer Harry kept the killer on the line, the better their chances.

'You can call me Harry. What should I call you?'

'Nothing. You call me nothing. Let me look at you. Closely.'

Harry raised the phone so it was level with his face. He saw a shadow off to the left side of the screen.

One wrong move, and I'll get eyes on you.

'Do we know each other?' said Harry.

'Do you think we do?'

Harry took a punt. 'Gurpal,' he said, more of a statement than a question.

Silence.

Just breathing.

Harry wanted to repeat the accusation but he waited.

'Is that who you think I am?' said the killer. He offered nothing more.

'How can I help resolve this?' asked Harry. He felt like the killer had been surprised at the name.

'What are you willing to do, Harry?'

'Anything.' He regretted the word as soon as it left his lips.

'What if I asked you to dance around naked in the middle of City Park?'

Harry hesitated.

'I thought you said "anything"?'

'You let the girl go and I'll dance to any tune you want.'

'I believe you. But what would be the fun in that?'

'Aisha is only twenty-one,' said Harry. 'There's a lot of power in this room. You name your price.'

The killer paused. On screen, Aisha remained still. Harry focused on her, willing her to help him find her.

Come on, kid, give me something.

Anything.

'Let's play a game,' said the killer.

He put the phone down, camera facing the floor so everything went black.

Harry could hear movement.

Suddenly Aisha reappeared on the screen, a close-up of her face. Harry could see where the gag was biting into her lips, the tear tracks down her cheeks.

Tariq shouldn't be seeing this.

'A game. One I think you're going to like.'

The view moved quickly, suddenly. Harry took a breath.

The killer appeared on the screen.

Dressed in a full burka.

Harry let out his breath.

Damn.

Harry's eyes moved quickly, trying desperately to scour for any details about him or their location in this new shot.

Nothing.

'Shall we play?' he asked, his tone now altogether more sinister. He produced a small plastic container.

He removed the lid and placed the container on Aisha's thigh.

She screamed, and Tariq shouted, 'No!'

Aisha's body went stiff, she held herself as still as possible. The killer brought the phone closer towards her so they could see clearly what was happening.

The three of them crowded around the phone as a solitary wasp, looking as if its wings had been removed, crawled on to Aisha's thigh. Harry's stomach dropped. He knew what was coming.

'She's allergic,' Tariq whispered, his voice laced with fear.

The killer spoke up again. 'Fifty-fifty, Harry,' he said. 'What do you think?'

'If she dies, you've got no leverage. Why are you doing this?' Harry said, panicking.

'It's fate, isn't it. Not down to me.'

'Please,' Tariq said suddenly. 'I have money.'

'He speaks again and she dies!' snapped the killer. 'I'm talking to Harry.'

Frost took Tariq to the far side of the room. Harry hoped he could be persuaded to leave the room; they should never have let him stay for the video-call.

'Aisha,' said Harry, 'keep calm, you're doing a brilliant job. Look at me,' he urged, 'stop moving in that chair. It's going to unsettle the wasp. Please, Aisha, you can do this. Block it all out. Just you and me, kid. Just you and me.'

Aisha stared at the screen, straight at Harry.

The wasp paused for a moment. Then crawled further up her thigh, towards her underwear.

Aisha clenched her teeth, her legs started to tremble.

'At me,' said Harry forcefully. 'Eyes on me, Aisha.' Harry softened his voice, even though he wanted to scream. 'Trust me. Just stay still.'

The ordeal lasted another thirty seconds before the killer scooped the wasp back into the container. He loomed large on the screen, putting his hand lovingly on Aisha's head, stroking it gently.

'You ever lost anything you loved, Harry?'

Harry thought about his family.

'Yes,' he said.

'Then we have something in common.'

The killer came towards the screen, his eyes close to the camera.

'We'll play again tomorrow morning, Harry. Ten a.m. Whether she lives or dies is on you. Get some rest. You've had a busy night. You'll need your strength for tomorrow; it's going to be a big day.'

Harry focused on the eyes.

Nothing familiar about them.

'Why me?' he asked.

'Because you started all this. And you want to save this city, don't you? A city of sinners. They don't deserve to be saved.'

FORTY-SIX

BRUISED.

No, broken. Harry felt broken after the phone call.

He and Tariq remained in the room, the silence deafening.

The ACC had left to update the team and Conway was chasing down the mast-cell-site data in the hopes of locating Aisha's phone.

All Harry could hear was the air conditioning unit, ticking over. He didn't know where to begin.

Tariq leaned forward, put his head in his hands and rested it on the table.

'First my wife. And now Aisha. I'm going to lose her,' whispered Tariq. 'Aren't I?'

Harry wanted to say no. But he couldn't give the guy false hope. Tariq Islam might have been the Home Secretary but in this moment, he was simply a father.

Harry stayed silent.

'Do you have kids?' Tariq asked, keeping his head on the table.

'A boy,' said Harry.

'How old?'

'Three.'

'You want to protect them, don't you? From the shit that goes on in the world. As fathers, it's our job.'

Tariq looked up at Harry. 'What am I supposed to do now? She's my little girl. I promised my wife that I would protect her.'

Harry tried to give as much confidence to his voice as possible. He knew the chances of getting to Aisha while she was still alive were slim. But they weren't impossible. 'Don't give in,' he said. 'There are over a hundred dedicated officers in this city fighting for her. Including this one.'

Harry smiled at Tariq. 'Don't give in. We're not.'

Tariq looked around the room. 'Is this place secure?'

Harry frowned. 'Secure?'

'Are we alone?' said Tariq, nodding towards the ceiling.

'Yes. No monitoring in here.'

'You sure?'

'Hundred per cent.'

'Good,' said Tariq and leaned forward, dropping his voice. 'I read your file.'

Harry raised his eyebrows.

'You've been busy.'

'Amazing what you can learn in ninety minutes on a plane from London to Leeds–Bradford.'

'Yeah. I guess you're used to pressurized briefings.'

'I'll say.' His hand went to his forehead, Harry watched him closely.

'Hell of a file you've got. You know I used to be paramilitary?'

'I do, sir.' Harry couldn't help himself, and added, 'Group 13? Right.'

Tariq smiled. 'You shouldn't believe everything you read.'

'I don't. But, if you were involved in anything . . . let's say . . . delicate, might be wise to disclose it now.'

'This isn't about me. It's about you. Why does he contact you?'

'Honestly, sir, I've no idea.'

'Your file is one of constant boundary-pushing. I can read

between the lines.' Tariq paused. 'I know you're the kind of officer who will do anything for a result.'

Harry wasn't sure he liked the implication but didn't say anything. He wasn't sure where this was going.

Tariq drew himself up.

'I want you to know that if this case comes down to you needing to make a call that takes you a little outside of the rules, I'm okay with that. I've got your back, personally. And politically. I can ensure there won't be any repercussions. I want my daughter back. At any cost.'

Harry saw the change in his eyes. Friendly, approachable, to steely. Almost sinister.

'I'm all-in here. There are no half-measures.'

It was the truth.

Tariq nodded, turning to leave the room.

'Since we are off the record here,' Harry said.

Tariq stopped in his tracks, turning back to Harry.

He nodded.

'There is something else I'm working on. Not related to this case. A little . . . personal.'

Harry was thinking about his inevitable future clash with Ronnie. One day, they were destined to collide.

'Go on.'

'Let's just say, if I bring Aisha home. If I put myself on the line – and I mean everything on the line – could I count on you, when the time comes, to put *yourself* on the line? For me?'

'Does it relate to this case?' asked Tariq, immediately suspicious.

'No,' said Harry vehemently. 'It's . . . a personal matter.'

'Any more details you can give me?'

'Do you really need any?'

Tariq shook his head. 'You bring Aisha home and I'm in your debt. You have my word.'

'You know what a kasam is?'

Tariq smiled. 'A sacred promise on my life? Bit old school, Harry.'

'Do you want to give me your kasam?'

Tariq leaned closer. 'Harry, you bring my daughter home and you've got my kasam, my word, my solemn promise that I will owe you one favour – any favour you want.'

FORTY-SEVEN

'FIVE HUNDRED METRES!' SAID Conway bursting into the room, jolting Harry and Tariq from their delicate conversation.

'What?' said Harry, getting to his feet.

'Aisha's phone. It's within five hundred metres of Trafalgar House.'

'Are you sure?'

'Certain.'

Conway left the room, Harry and Tariq followed close behind. They entered a smaller room where the HMET team were crowding around the map of the city centre. DI Palmer had temporary charge of Harry's team whilst he was on restrictive duties.

A perimeter had been drawn on the map where Aisha's phone signal had been recorded.

'Any clues from the Facetime, Harry?' asked one of his colleagues. 'We've been briefed. Anything to add?'

Harry told them the video-call hadn't revealed anything other than a shitty dark room.

The DCIs each took responsibility for searching a quadrant of the circle and left the room, marshalling their respective teams as they went.

'Sir,' Conway said to Tariq.

'Please, it's Tariq.'

'Very well. Can we lose the close-protection unit?' She nodded towards the four burly guards. 'You're as safe here as anywhere and I really need to keep as much of this as possible classified. I'm sure you understand?'

'Of course,' said Tariq and discharged his men to take a break.

'Sir.'

'It's Tariq,' he said again.

'Apologies. Would you be more comfortable in . . . ?' She gestured to a meeting room with a coffee machine.

'I'm fine right here. Please, don't exclude me.'

Conway nodded and turned to Harry.

'When was the last time you slept?' said Conway.

'You expect me to go home?'

'There's a couch in my office. You fry yourself too early, you're no good to anybody.'

'I've had four hours' sleep in the past twenty-four hours. I've got another few in me yet. Let me help.'

Harry glanced at Tariq. Whilst he had no jurisdiction here, Harry was hoping for an olive branch.

'With the new resources we've got, we should apprehend Gurpal Singh very soon. You should go home and get some rest.'

'Everyone's focusing on Gurpal, right?' said Harry, pointing to the circle on the map. 'Let me into Aisha's life. Who's doing victimology? Outside enquiries? All the victims have been students; either the college or the university. Let me help with that.'

Conway told him a team of DCs had been allocated the task and were preparing to leave HMET.

'Let me head that up. If you need me, I'm less than a mile away. I can't just sit here, Clare, having my lunch.'

He used her first name, hoping for a reprieve from being stuck in the office.

Conway nodded.

An officer entered the room and handed Harry's phone to him. They'd cloned it. If the killer called, Trafalgar House would be listening.

Conway stepped out, heading for the operations room.

Harry also made to leave.

Tariq stopped him. Dropped his voice. 'Good luck, Harry. Think on what we spoke about.'

Bradford University's atrium was made entirely out of glass. As Harry approached he could see hundreds of students all having their lunch.

He had sent the two DCs he had been allocated to the main student reception area to see what information they could pull about Aisha – any clubs and societies she was part of.

Harry entered the Richmond Building and waited for one of three lifts to hit the ground floor, observing the students.

A couple stealing a kiss.

Someone reading a book.

Dozens tapping away on their mobile phones.

Harry, you bring my daughter home and I will owe you any favour you want.

Harry rubbed his hand across his face.

More confused than tired.

He needed a break in this case.

Deep down, he didn't believe he was going to catch one.

This guy was taunting them.

He knew he was going to get caught. And he would choose exactly when and how.

The question was, how much damage could he inflict before that happened?

Harry checked the news headlines on his iPhone.

Nothing about Aisha Islam. The press moratorium was holding.

In the main office of the pharmaceutical department, Harry introduced himself to a receptionist and asked to see the head of department. He also asked for a student roster for Aisha Islam's course mates.

The head of department, Professor Norman Bishop, introduced himself to Harry with a firm handshake. They left the reception, headed down the main corridor.

Bishop's office was chaotic. Files, papers and empty cups filled the desk. Bishop offered Harry a drink. He declined and got straight to the point, asking to see a copy of Aisha's timetable, a list of her classmates and who her form-tutor was. Bishop probed about the urgency. Harry told him it was a private matter.

Bishop handed Harry the information he'd asked for. Harry took a quick scan of the papers and saw Aisha's name.

'Any idea who Aisha was friendly with?' asked Harry.

The prof shook his head. 'I've got hundreds of students within this department. Her form-tutor might know, but even then, they only meet with the students once every few months.'

Harry grimaced.

'Her lab partner might know, I suppose,' said Bishop.

'Her what-now?'

'The students are paired up with a lab partner, who they usually work with throughout the course.'

'Do you know whose Aisha's was?'

'It's done alphabetically. So, whoever is above or below her on the student list would be her partner.'

Harry focused on the list and counted down in twos until he hit Aisha's name.

'This girl, Rabeena Akthar. Would this have been her lab partner?'

Bishop took a quick glance.

'Likely, yes.'

'I need to speak with her. Right now.'

FORTY-EIGHT

JOYTI VIRDEE WATCHED AS the doctor left her husband's room at the hospital.

The surgery was scheduled for the following day. It was high risk, apparently. But by the look on the doctor's face, it was also the only thing that would give Ranjit a chance at a proper recovery.

Joyti walked to the window, which gave a wide view across Bradford. She discreetly checked her watch. Nearly one o'clock. Saima would be here soon. Joyti's heart skipped a beat and she looked towards the heavens; white, threatening snow. It made her think of the ice cream Aaron had eaten the day before.

'I-cream,' she whispered and smiled.

From behind, Ranjit's voice sounded tired. As tired as Joyti, who hadn't slept much.

'What?' he said.

'Do you know how long we have been married?' said Joyti, resting her hands on the radiator underneath the window, grateful for its warmth.

There was a delay as Ranjit worked it out.

'Thirty-eight years,' he said.

'Thirty-nine.'

He reconsidered and nodded.

'Back then, I never for one minute thought we would leave India. Never considered we would have to figure out how to live in a country where we were strangers. Do you remember when we took the keys to our shop?'

'Of course.'

'How, on our first day, half of the customers cancelled their newspaper deliveries? Funny to think we were the first Asians on the estate.'

'Worse than that, you remember that old man who died in the shop? Very first morning?' said Ranjit, stifling a laugh. 'He saw the coloured people and dropped dead of a heart attack.'

'I thought the shop was cursed.'

'My mother started chanting prayers and waving around incense to purify the store from the man's death. The ambulance people were still there and word got around she was a voodoo witch.'

Joyti shook her head and smiled. 'The worst opening day we could have had.'

'You wanted to leave.'

'I did. I never thought the white man would allow us to live there. Not after that.' Joyti grimaced at the memory of how tough those early months had been. 'But we did okay. Worked hard. Made them see us as people. Just like them. Even if you did wear a turban and have a beard.'

'I joined their pub. Played snooker and darts with them. Got drunk with them.'

'Wasn't easy, though, was it?'

'I was determined we would make it a success.'

'You never let me wear Asian clothes in the shop. You trimmed your beard. Learned the accent.'

Ranjit switched to English. 'Yes, love,' he said, and laughed.

'We changed. Didn't we?'

'We had to.'

'Do you think we lost some of ourselves? In the change?'

'What do you mean?'

'I mean, if we hadn't taken that shop. If we had stayed in India, how might our lives have been different?'

Ranjit's face took on a serious look.

'I know what this is about,' he said finally. 'Let's not revisit the past.'

'If you have your operation tomorrow and it goes badly, do you want to leave this world without at least trying with Hardeep?'

He sighed and reached for his water.

'I cannot change what he did.'

'You made sacrifices, hard sacrifices to make it work here.'

'I did,' Ranjit nodded firmly.

'We could not change what the customers thought of us back then. Yet, we did.'

'That was different. We *had to* succeed.'

'And we sacrificed some of the things we had been brought up with. Eating meat. Drinking alcohol. Smoking cigarettes. Did you do all those things to fit in?'

'Yes.'

'Was it a hard sacrifice?'

'It was.'

'Yet, for our boy . . .'

'He's not my—'

'Okay,' she snapped, '*my boy*. For my boy, there is no sacrifice?'

'I don't want to talk—'

'We are going to,' said Joyti, determined. 'Today, we are going to.'

Joyti leaned against the radiator, its heat massaging her back. 'What do you think his wife is like?' she asked.

'Like . . . *them*,' replied Ranjit, his voice full of contempt.

'Tell me.'

'A Muslim. They are all the same.'

'You think Hardeep married "one of *them*"?'

'They can twist anybody's mind, these people.'

'Even Hardeep's?'

'If they can brainwash people into killing themselves in the name of their religion, you think our boy is any different? Any more of a challenge?'

Joyti broke into a tried and resigned smile. 'I think our boy could never be brainwashed. I think that, just like us on that estate, in that shop, when the English people got to know us, they realized we were not so different. In fact, we had more in common than we thought.'

'We can adapt. Those . . . those . . . people cannot.'

'And if we met her and she proved us wrong.'

'I don't want to meet her. The breath from her mouth will poison the air.'

'Stop it,' Joyti snapped. Ranjit was too stunned to reply. 'Enough. Three days ago, your heart stopped beating. Tomorrow when they put you to sleep, you might never wake up, and yet still you are prepared to leave this world – to leave me – with such hate in your heart for our boy?'

'I don't want to talk about this any more.'

'We will stop when you tell me what you think she is like.'

Ranjit thought on his answer. 'She will be pretty. Their girls usually are. Kept well. Protected. She will wear a headscarf. Maybe with western clothing. Maybe not. They are not shy about being who they are and what they are. She will speak her language fluently. She won't integrate like we have.'

Joyti nodded, resigned to his rhetoric.

'Do you think she cooks nice food? Makes my boy tea like I used to?'

'Filth. They can't cook.'

'And if you were proved wrong? If you met her and she was . . . normal?'

'Impossible. I know these people. You don't, woman. You haven't seen the world like I have.'

Joyti looked down at the floor. She was suddenly unsure of her plan.

When she eventually looked up, she saw that Saima was waiting outside the door.

Joyti took a deep breath.

'You are going for your operation tomorrow. Would you grant your wife a wish? In case you do not return.'

'I am not forgiving Hardeep.'

'I won't ask that. But could you give me your kasam that whatever else I ask for, you will do.'

Ranjit fixed her with a stare.

'In thirty-nine years I've never asked anything of you.'

Ranjit nodded. Reluctantly.

'Say it,' said Joyti.

Ranjit swore his kasam.

'Thank you,' said Joyti.

She moved towards the door, put her hand on the handle and paused.

'The doctors told you that when you came in, a nurse in A&E saved your life.'

'Yes.'

Joyti opened the door, smiled in hope more than confidence and gently pulled Saima into the room.

'This is the nurse who saved your life,' said Joyti, a quiver to her voice. Ranjit looked over, confused by his wife's tone.

'This nurse is your daughter-in-law, *my* daughter-in-law. She's Harry's wife, Saima.'

FORTY-NINE

HARRY DIDN'T HAVE TIME to wait for half an hour while the students finished their class. Bishop took him down the corridor into the Clinical Skills suite, a large room with dozens of lab-benches, each one accommodating two students, everyone wearing clinical white coats. They passed a mocked-up pharmacy dispensary and Harry was shown to the room next door, a makeshift hospital ward with two beds and baskets full of medical supplies.

He didn't have to wait long before Bishop brought a tall, slim Asian girl into the room, Rabeena Akthar. Bishop confirmed she was Aisha's lab partner and left them to speak.

Harry introduced himself and indicated for her to sit down.

'What's this about?' she asked nervously, eyes darting between Harry and the lab in progress outside.

Harry closed the blinds, which unnerved Rabeena. As he'd hoped it would.

'A sensitive matter,' said Harry. 'Aisha Islam.'

'She wasn't in class today.'

'I know that. Are you two close?'

She hesitated. A twitch in her lips. 'No.'

'Really? I'm told you and Aisha have been lab partners for what? Three years now?'

'Yeah, I know her. Of course I do. But we're not friendly.'

Harry searched her face. Until she felt uncomfortable enough to look away.

'Mind if I see your phone?'

'Why?'

'Humour me.'

'Don't you need a warrant?'

'Only if you have something to hide. Let me tell you how this works. I'm here in a friendly capacity to find a missing girl.'

'Aisha is missing?'

Harry nodded.

'Now, if you lie to me and it turns out something bad has happened to Aisha and you have information which might have helped me, then this,' he said, pointing to the lab behind her, 'all goes up in smoke. You must have worked hard to get into this department. Smart girl. Just tell me the truth and you can go back to your life.'

Rabeena stared at her phone. She unlocked it and handed it to Harry, clearly nervous.

'You know who Aisha Islam is? Right? Who her father is?' asked Harry, accessing her favourite contacts.

Rabeena nodded.

'How many other people do?'

'Not many.'

'But you knew?'

'Yes.'

'Which means she trusted you.'

'I suppose.'

'Even though you weren't close?'

Rabeena shrugged.

'Did she have a boyfriend?'

More hesitation. An involuntary fidget in her hands.

'Not . . . that I know of.'

'Why are you lying to me, Rabeena?'

Harry turned her phone so she could see. 'Aisha is listed third in your favourite numbers. Yet you're not close?'

Rabeena chewed her lip. 'She's my lab partner. We need to speak about—'

Harry suddenly leaned forwards aggressively. Holding her eye contact, he pushed a stern finger into Rabeena's shoulder with every syllable.

'Cut. The. Shit.'

'Hey,' she said, backing away, afraid.

'Your mate is missing.' While he didn't want to divulge anything too sensitive, he needed to know what she knew. 'She didn't come home last night and, bearing in mind who she is – who her father is – your pratting around is making me cross.'

Harry backed off, opening Rabeena's Facebook app on her phone.

'What are you doing?'

'My job,' he said, scrolling through her feed. There were dozens of posts involving her and Aisha.

'BFF for life?' said Harry, showing her the screen.

Rabeena sighed. 'Is she okay?'

'We won't know that until we find her,' said Harry. 'Boyfriend?'

'I . . . I . . . can't.'

'What?'

Rabeena shook her head. 'It's . . . complicated.'

'Tell me who Aisha's boyfriend is,' snapped Harry.

'No,' she said, suddenly forceful.

'Fine. On your damn feet.'

'Why?'

Harry saw she was young enough not to realize that he was bluffing. He removed a pair of handcuffs. 'Rabeena Akthar, I am arresting you for obstructing the course of justice.' He turned her around and pinned her hands behind her back.

'Ow! That hurts!'

'You do not have to say anything. But it may harm your defence if you do not mention when questioned something which you later rely on in court. Anything you do say may be given in evidence.'

Harry cuffed her.

'You cannot do this!' she said, and started to cry.

'I can and I am.'

Harry turned her around. 'Aisha is missing. And you want to play some stupid game of "hide the boyfriend"? Grow up. If she is your best friend, act like it.'

She whimpered.

Harry shook his head.

'I'm going to march you out of here, past all your mates and the professor, and tell him why I'm arresting you. Might ruin your career, I reckon.'

She started to cry harder, trying to stifle it so as to not alert her classmates outside the room.

'You don't know what you're doing!' she said.

'Last chance,' said Harry, pointing to the door. 'Once we leave, there's no turning back. I don't do second chances and I'm shit out of patience with you.'

Rabeena cried harder. Confused. Conflicted.

She was hiding something.

All over her face; the deceit.

He wanted to scare her, get her to confess.

He didn't have the time to actually book her.

Christ, this had better work.

'Ten seconds.'

Rabeena slumped on to her stool, lowered her head, tears dripping on to her knees.

'Time,' said Harry.

She shook her head. 'No!'

'What is it you don't want me to know?'

'Please,' she said. 'Take these off. I'll tell you everything.'

Harry unlocked the handcuffs.

Rabeena looked at Harry with sore eyes. 'He's going to be mad,' she said quietly.

'Who?'

'Her boyfriend.'

Harry raised his eyebrows.

'Andrew Lightfoot.'

'Should I know who that is?'

'*Professor* Andrew Lightfoot,' she said.

Harry's shoulders sagged. He frowned and although he didn't need confirmation, asked anyway. 'In this department?'

Rabeena nodded. 'He's head of Pharmacy Practice.'

FIFTY

RANJIT'S FACE WAS BLANK.

Saima wasn't sure what she had expected.

Something.

Anything.

The monitor by Ranjit's bed continued to bleep. He turned his face away.

Outside, the snow which had threatened all week finally began to fall, turning immediately to sleet as it hit the window.

Joyti grasped Saima's hand.

'Leave us, Joyti,' said Ranjit without looking at the women.

Joyti looked to Saima, concern on her face.

'It's okay,' said Saima, letting go of Joyti's hand and squeezing her arm. 'It's okay. Really.'

Joyti hovered, unsure how to proceed.

'I will say one thing before I go,' she said quietly. 'This might be the one and only time the two of you meet. Nobody knows what will happen tomorrow when they operate. Ask yourself how you want to leave this.'

*

Without Joyti, the room felt cold.

Saima stood by the door, shuffling her feet awkwardly.

She'd imagined this so many times but nothing she'd rehearsed sounded right.

'Say whatever it is you've come to say,' said Ranjit, still turned away from her.

'I . . .'

Suddenly a wave of guilt went through Saima.

For what everyone had suffered.

For marrying Harry.

'I never wanted it to be like this,' she said eventually, her voice ever so shaky.

She didn't know how to say any of this to the back of her father-in-law's head. She crept a little to her right, so she could see his face and saw that his eyes were closed.

He couldn't even look at her.

After everything he had put Harry through, after everything he had put *her* through. He couldn't even look at her?

'Damn you,' she said bitterly, surprising herself.

Ranjit opened his eyes. Turned to face her.

'Is that what I have to do to get your attention?'

'You can say whatever you like. I gave a promise to listen, nothing more.'

He turned away from her again.

Saima felt her temper rising.

'I saved your life. I worked harder than on any patient before you. And . . . I . . . didn't do it so that you would thank me. I didn't do it for you. I did it for Harry. I didn't want you to pass away before the two of you had the opportunity to reconcile and if not, at least to have some final words which might include some sort of forgiveness. I've never had you in my life so there was no loss to replace. Harry's pain is never far from the surface. He did wrong by marrying me? Maybe he did. Maybe I did. We're not perfect. Nobody is.'

Saima inched closer. 'But right here, right now, something perfect can happen. And it's within your power to make it happen. Forgiving is so much harder than carrying hate. But only initially. After that, doors open and with them, memories are created, new ones which replace the darkness.'

Saima's body was now touching the bedframe, she felt hopeful.

'What if I were to show you my respect? Touch your feet like Harry used to touch his mother's,' she said, 'and ask you to forgive me. For any pain I might have caused you.'

She hovered her hands inches above Ranjit's feet.

He opened his eyes, turned to face her and said the one thing which made Saima recoil.

The one thing which *ruined* her.

'If you touch my feet with *your* hands,' he whispered, voice full of malice, eyes narrowing with pure hatred, 'I will be forced to cut them off.'

FIFTY-ONE

SECRETS.

How did the killer know something only two other people knew?

Aisha hadn't told anyone else about her boyfriend.

Harry knocked on the door of Professor Andrew Lightfoot's office.

'Come in!'

He was tall, blond, muscular. Harry thought he must have had Scandinavian blood.

He cast an eye around the room, across the frames on the wall.

A first-class honours degree in Pharmacy from Nottingham University.

A doctorate from King's College London.

He also had a framed picture of himself holding a gold medal, standing on an athletics track.

No wonder Aisha had fallen for him.

'Professor Lightfoot?'

'Sure,' he said, moving around his desk to meet Harry.

'DCI Harry Virdee. Bradford Homicide Major Enquiry Team.'

Andrew's hand paused momentarily on its way towards Harry's.

'Wow,' he said. 'To what do I owe the pleasure?' He shook his head. 'Sorry, pleasure's probably not the right word, considering your department.'

A solid, confident handshake.

'Please,' said Harry, nodding towards Lightfoot's chair.

'Likewise,' he replied.

Harry pointed to the picture of Andrew holding a gold medal. 'What's that in aid of?'

'Argh, ego wall,' said Andrew. 'I tried for the Olympic team while I was at uni. Missed out by a tenth of a second.'

'Which discipline?'

'Hundred metres.'

'What was your personal best?'

'Ten point four.'

Harry whistled. 'Quick.'

'Did ten flat, once. Unofficially.'

'Always the way, isn't it.' Harry liked him immediately, it was a gut feeling.

'How can I help you?'

Harry cut straight to the point, an imaginary clock ticking in his head.

'I'm aware you're in a relationship with one of your students, Aisha Islam.'

Andrew's mouth dropped open. He closed it quickly.

'Sorry?' he said.

His transformation was immediate. Face serious, arms crossed across his chest defensively.

'Andrew,' said Harry smiling, 'don't make me jump through hoops. *I know*. And what I need from you now is the truth. All of it. Every detail. If you do that, it'll go a long way to saving your job when Professor Bishop finds out, which I'm sure he will.'

Andrew wasn't stupid. He simply nodded, uncrossed his arms and leaned them on the desk.

'Can I ask what this has to do with your case?'

'Aisha Islam is missing. And whilst I can't go into specifics, what I can say is that her life might be in danger and no stone is being left unturned. So,' Harry leaned back in the hard chair, 'tell me everything.'

Thirty minutes later, Harry had it all.

It had been love at first sight. They'd been together for a year and they'd been able to keep it a secret. Given Aisha's upbringing with her father in politics, she knew all the tricks. They had never been out together in public, always meeting at Andrew's house. No one would have seen Aisha arriving or leaving.

'Nobody could know,' said Andrew. 'I'd lose my job.'

'That's some risk to take,' replied Harry analysing every inch of Andrew's body language.

'Is she okay?' Andrew asked, genuinely concerned.

'We don't know,' Harry said seriously. 'When was the last time you saw, or heard from her?'

'Tuesday night, here.'

'What happened?'

Andrew looked at Harry then dropped his eyes to the floor.

Harry sighed. 'I'm going to need you to come down to the station. Make a formal statement.'

'Was I the last person to see her?' Andrew asked, colour draining from his face.

He was a smart man, he knew his life was about to be picked apart.

Harry couldn't answer him.

Andrew nodded. 'It wasn't just a fling,' he said earnestly to Harry. 'It wasn't. I love her. I've nothing to hide. Aisha's more important to me than my job.'

Harry believed him.

FIFTY-TWO

'WHAT DID HE SAY to you?' said Joyti, closing the door to the family room where Saima had her back towards her, pouring water from a dispenser into a cup.

Saima steadied herself, determined not to let her exchange with Ranjit sour her new relationship with her mother-in-law. Saima drank the water, feeling it cool and refreshing in her mouth. She turned around and smiled at Joyti, using every bit of strength she had not to show her true emotions.

'I'd like to keep it between us both. It is over. I've made my peace and we move on,' said Saima.

Joyti analysed Saima's face.

A moment of stillness.

'I've been behind the counter of a corner shop over thirty years. Served thousands of people. Caught thieves and liars and have more experience of my husband than you realize.'

Saima refilled her cup. Had another glass.

'I wanted to show him who I really am,' she said. 'And he knows.'

'What did he say?'

'He made a promise to you to listen to me. I made a promise to keep what was said private,' she said, hating the lie but unable to tell Joyti the truth of what her husband had said. Of his utter rejection.

'What will you tell my Hardeep?' said Joyti.

'The truth,' she replied, Ranjit's words still slicing at her.

If you touch my feet, I will be forced to cut them off.

Such anger.

Such resentment.

Saima felt unclean.

Her beeper sounded, her A&E break over.

'I need to get back,' she said.

'Hardeep?' repeated Joyti, arriving at Saima's side and slipping her arm around her waist. It made Saima's lip wobble and her cheek twitch.

'I'll tell him about the operation. The chances. And . . . after that? I think it is up to him to decide whether he comes or not.'

'Don't you think he should?

Saima threw the empty cup in the bin.

'I think he's suffered enough,' she said, then nodded towards the corridor. 'Perhaps they both have.'

Joyti grasped Saima's face in her hands just as Saima's beeper started again.

'What did my husband say to you?' she asked, her face gentle and full of compassion.

Saima could see so much of Harry and a little of Aaron in her. She held Joyti's hands in hers and lowered them. 'Your grandson woke up this morning asking for an "i-cream" and for "Grandma". Let that be the thought that I leave you with.'

Saima embraced Joyti, kissed her forehead and left Joyti alone in the room, her mind immediately turning towards what she was going to tell Harry that evening about his father, about her exchange with him, but more importantly whether she was going to allow Ranjit one last chance to wound him.

FIFTY-THREE

RONNIE WAS STANDING IN the middle of an enormous disused warehouse on the Euroway Trading Estate just off the M606 motorway. Throwing himself into his work distracted his mind from what was happening with his father and the potential fallout from what Joyti was trying to do with Saima. Ronnie was on board with his mother's attempts to reunite the family. He had his own agenda when it came to Harry.

The closest members of his team, seven men Ronnie trusted with his life, were by his side, all of them staring at the far-reaching floor space, exposed metal girders and machinery ghosting in the shadows.

These were men Ronnie had rescued from the bottomless pit of shitty mental-health programmes for disused army personnel, all SAS-patriots who had put their lives on the line for never-ending wars in the Middle East and, when *their* time had come to be looked after, had been discarded like the hundreds of corpses they had racked up defending queen and country. Soldiers whose version of 'norm' was operating at a level most people couldn't fathom. Men who Ronnie had meticulously identified as the perfect partners to help him run Bradford.

'So, this is the future of our organization,' said Enzo, walking around the dilapidated building. The others fanned out to explore the ruin.

'It is. Prime location for transport in and out of Bradford. And at the price I got it, a fucking bargain.'

'Too exposed,' said Enzo.

'That's the point,' replied Ronnie.

The men returned, all of them muttering at how open it felt.

Ronnie listened to their concerns and told them how he planned to change their organization for the better. They needed to trust him.

'We do,' said Enzo finally.

'Good. There's one thing, though, that we all need to get on board with.'

Ronnie stared at the men, each one in turn.

'My brother, Harry. Things are in place to pull him closer to us.'

There were murmurs of discontent.

'I'm going to sell him a vision, the same one I've managed to get you all on board with. You trust me enough to deliver it and so will he. I know Harry. He'll be up for this. We clean out the Eastern Europeans, get Bradford back in our control and then we can change the game in this city. And it's coming, we all know that.'

'Like I told you last night, we've tried to play nice with him before,' said Enzo.

'That was then. This is now. He wants me out of the criminal side of this, and that is where we are heading. No better time to pull him closer to us.'

'You really think you can?' asked one of the others.

'If you guys back me, I can. We've always done things as a team. This, right here, is just as important as Harry.'

Enzo stepped into the centre of the circle, now opposite his boss.

'We're making good money. Why change?'

Murmurs of agreement from the men.

Ronnie removed a wad of fifty-pound notes from his pocket and dropped it on the floor.

'How much is enough? Is it *ever* enough? What if we got back to what you guys signed up for in your army days? Protecting queen and country, all that nostalgic crap.'

'Queen never did anything for me,' replied Enzo. 'Except the promise of a shitty war pension.' More murmurs of agreement from the men.

'Do you know why we've been untouchable so far? Because there's a discipline in this room you cannot manufacture. There are brains you cannot replicate. If you guys want to walk away, live off the money we've all made, I understand that. But Bradford needs us. Now more than ever. And it starts here. We need to change and I need to know if you are with me.'

Ronnie moved away, allowing the men to speak amongst themselves. He watched them further explore the dilapidated warehouse.

Ronnie lit a cigarette and waited.

Confident they would see his vision.

They returned and surrounded him, smiling.

Enzo spoke for them. 'Every cartel was brought down at one point or another because they got lazy and comfortable. Let's be the rulers of our own fate. You want to change the game in Bradford, then we're in. But we need the Europeans out and we need it fast. So far, we've come up short finding out who the boss of this new cartel is. How their distribution happens. If you think getting Harry on board helps with that, then we can look past what's gone on before.'

Ronnie smiled, finally feeling like everything was coming together.

FIFTY-FOUR

WITH ANDREW LIGHTFOOT IN for further questioning, Harry hurried to the briefing room. The CCTV footage from Lister Mills on the night of the murder at Maestro's was in.

Conway, Palmer, the ACC and two other DCIs crowded around a screen as one of the tech guys streamed the footage.

'First run-through?' said Harry, arriving by Conway's side.

'Yeah.' When she looked at him, Conway frowned. 'You look like hell.'

'I'm fine,' he shrugged it off, trying to hide just how jaded he felt.

The footage was in night mode, so it was grainy black-and-white. They ran it from 22:30, at four times normal speed. At 23:38, a man wearing a beanie, head lowered, face away from the camera came into view.

'There,' said Harry, pointing at the screen. 'Timeline fits.'

The footage was reversed and replayed, this time in slow-motion.

'Can't see shit,' said Harry.

'Let's switch to inside,' said the techie, playing around with his screen.

The internal camera caught the side of the man's face.

It was far from clear but certainly better than the exterior footage.

'Do you recognize him, Harry?' asked Conway.

'Can you zoom in?' replied Harry.

The picture distorted.

'That's as good as it gets, I'm afraid.'

'Nothing obvious,' said Harry. 'Christ, that could be anyone.'

'Forward it. See if we can get him leaving. Maybe with Aisha,' said Conway, then she turned to Harry, pulling him out of the room.

'What's the problem?' said Harry as Conway closed the door.

'You need to go home. Get some rest. I need you on point tomorrow, when he calls.'

'*If* he calls.'

'I can't have you burning out and fucking things up tomorrow because you were chasing down leads today that other detectives can sort.'

'I found Aisha Islam's boyfriend,' said Harry defensively.

'I heard. And that's great work. More than we expected. But now, you look like hell. It's approaching four o'clock, Harry, eighteen hours since you took a break, and you're bound to crash at some point. I can't let that happen when we need you the most.'

'You think I can just go home, curl up and sleep?'

'You need to try. If anything changes, I will call you. The ACC is camped out here, watching us all. I need you on your best game when it counts,' she said, digging a finger into his chest. 'And that isn't here, now.'

Harry sighed.

They were interrupted by one of the DCIs opening the door and calling them back into the room. His face said it all: *they had something*.

The same man was now on screen at 00:04 that morning.

Harry had been there only three hours later with the armed response team.

'This is . . . today?' said Harry incredulously, checking the visual time-and-date display was accurate.

'Yeah.'

'Shit,' he said, watching as the man wheeled an enormous suitcase, more like a trunk, out of the lower-ground lift, down the foyer and out of the building.

Head down.

Face covered by a scarf.

Moving slowly.

There was obviously something heavy in the case.

'She's in there,' whispered Harry. 'Got to be.'

There was a murmur of agreement in the room.

'Wait for it,' said the techie.

As the man reached the closest point to the camera, he paused, looked directly at it and waved.

'Son of a bitch,' snapped Harry and banged his fist on the table making everyone in the room jump. 'He's fucking with us,' he snapped.

He felt Conway's hand on his arm, squeezing, the ACC's gaze on Harry.

The techie switched to outside cameras. They watched the man struggle to pull the case up a narrow slope, away from their view, and disappear out of sight.

'Nothing more,' said the techie.

'He's going up Patent Street, tell me we've got cameras there,' said Harry.

The techie looked at him and shook his head.

'What? That's it? We lost him?'

Conway turned to one of the other DCIs in the room. 'Get this information over to Britannia House. See if any cameras pick him up around the area. I want every car in a one-mile radius logged from the time he leaves the mill until sunrise. A suitcase that big; he's got to use a car to move it.'

The DCI hurried from the room.

'Can you play the footage inside again?' Harry said to the techie. 'And pause it as he's waving.'

Harry leaned closer, analysing every inch of the screen.

Nothing.

He backed away and left the room, slamming the door as he went.

FIFTY-FIVE

THE PLACE HAS TWO *rooms.*

One where I house my wasps, the other where darker things occur.

Aisha Islam is crying quietly. Her head is bowed, tears dripping on to her exposed body.

I remove a packaged blood-red sari from the floor and place it in her lap.

'I bought this for my wife. Many years ago, now. A one-of-a-kind piece. Would you like to wear it?'

She shakes her head. Keeps it bowed.

Looking at Aisha's body, legs trembling, I want to know how she will look in it.

'Put it on, Aisha.'

I unfasten her hands.

'I . . . I've never put a sari on before,' she says childishly, a noticeable wobble to her voice.

'Try.'

She doesn't move for a few minutes, the sari in her hands, knuckles white from her grip. Then slowly, she unfolds it and starts to put it over her flimsy chemise.

'No,' I snap. 'Properly. Make it look nice.'

She's trying hard not to cry. Braver than Usma, certainly more fire in this one.

And now, she does it right. Removes her clothes, stifles the tears and starts to dress.

As I watch, I remember the time I bought that sari. The effort it took to find the perfect piece. My mood sours, only for a moment, and I remind myself that in a few hours, I will have my revenge. Virdee and I will meet.

He does not know this yet but he will have his one and only chance to end this.

A choice is coming for Virdee.

Stop me.

Or save Aisha Islam.

He will not be able to do both.

FIFTY-SIX

SAIMA GENTLY STROKED THE side of Harry's face, aggrieved that he'd fallen asleep in his work clothes for the second day running. She'd never seen him like this.

But she couldn't delay telling him about his father any longer. That was not how they did things.

He stirred, then opened his eyes, disorientated.

'Did work call?' he asked, scrambling to sit up. 'What time is it?'

Saima switched the bedside lamp on, forcing Harry to shield his bloodshot eyes. 'After eight. And no, love,' she replied. 'Nobody called.'

'Are you sure? When did you get in?'

'Five.'

Harry reached for his phone.

Saima stopped him.

'No,' she said, a firmness to her voice. She pushed his phone away. 'I've been wanting to speak with you, Harry. I need to speak to you now.'

As she moved her head in the dim light, Harry saw she'd been crying.

'What is it?' he asked, putting his hand on hers.

232

'Get dressed, Harry. Come downstairs. Then we'll talk.'

'No, tell me now. Is it Aaron? Are you okay?'

Saima tried to get off the bed but he pulled her back.

'Damn it, Saima, tell me what it is,' he said, alarmed.

'It's your father, Harry. He's in hospital. And it's serious.'

In the living room, having showered to wake himself up, Harry accepted a cup of Indian tea from Saima. She handed his phone back but told him to leave it on silent. This was a conversation she needed to have with him without interruption. Saima turned the gas fire on, giving the room a cosy warmth, then told Harry everything.

She told him about Ranjit's admission on Monday, how she had helped to save his life. She told him about the flask of tea and the smile on his father's face.

About Joyti, the ice cream and her subsequent visit to the house.

Finally, Saima told Harry that his father was due to undergo a coronary artery bypass graft the following morning and that his chances of survival were, at best, average.

She stopped talking.

'How was Mum with Aaron?'

'She was besotted. Said he looks like you when you were that age. Spitting image. And he just took to her as though he'd always known her. Must be something genetic in it,' she said.

'No. Kids can just sense when someone has a good heart. God, I wish I had seen her.'

'I know. But you will now. I'm certain of it.'

'Don't get your hopes up, Saima,' said Harry. 'My dad can be a cruel son of a bitch.'

'I know,' she said without thinking, immediately regretting it.

With those two words, as her eyes dropped to the table, Harry saw it.

A familiar hurt.

Harry waited until she looked at him.

'Tell me.' He reached out a hand to hold hers.

Saima shook her head, tears in her eyes.

'You've withheld something from me, for the first time ever this week. I understand why. But you don't need to keep anything else from me.'

Harry could see the pain in her face. The creasing of her eyes, the tremble of her lip.

'You know how, whenever you feel upset or have something difficult to tell me, you stand by the window, looking out on to the street, in the dark?' she said.

'Yeah.'

'Why do you do that?'

Harry thought about his answer. He wanted to say that he had learned it from his mother, which was partially true, but it wasn't the main reason.

'I guess, when I stand there, I feel alone. Like the words can't hurt anyone except me. And I'm okay with that. Whilst I watch the world go by, some part of me realizes that life goes on. People go on. That my hurt is just that: *mine*. And since it is *mine*, I have the power to deal with it. Not sure if that makes any sense.'

Saima stood up. 'I . . . want to try it. Do you mind?'

Harry nodded.

Saima turned the lights off, only the gas fire glowing, and walked to the bay window which gave a wide, sweeping view of their street outside. Harry was right. This was the place to say things that hurt.

'I saw it,' she said, resting her hands on the cool ledge underneath the window. 'His hatred. It doesn't matter what I do or what I say. He grew up learning that hatred and it's buried so deep in his soul that he cannot see me for who I am. Only what I am.'

Saima heard Harry get up from the table and told him to stay where he was. She didn't want him close to her. Not right now.

'I look in the mirror and I see just me. A mum. A wife. Sometimes a nurse.' She looked down to the floor briefly. 'What a fool. Seventy years of me being the enemy and I think, just because I'm nice, he's going to welcome me with open arms.'

'What happened, Saima?' asked Harry.

'I honestly believe,' she said, biting her lip but unable to stop the tears, 'that he would rather have died than have me work on him.'

Harry arrived by her side and, although she initially resisted, he put his arms around her.

She cried hard into his shoulder as he tightened his grip, reassuringly.

Then, Saima told him everything.

It took a while for Saima to calm down. Harry thought sharing what she had been hiding must have eased the burden somewhat. But she wasn't finished.

'I want you to do something, for me,' she said.

'Anything,' said Harry wiping tears from her face.

'You won't like it.'

'Won't know until you try me.'

'Promise me you'll do as I ask.'

'As long as it's not apologizing to him for marrying you, I can make you that promise.'

'I wouldn't ask that.'

'Then, shoot.'

Saima put her hands on Harry's chest, where his heart was beating furiously, and told him what she wanted.

'Can you do that? For me?' she said.

Harry removed her hands from his chest and held them, dropping his eyes to the floor. 'Why would you ask that of me?'

'Because, one day, you'll thank me for it.'

'Maybe. But "one day" might be a long time away.'

'So? Could you, do it? For me?'

Before Harry could answer, a ringing noise from the hallway, loud and startling, made them both jump.

'Christ, is that your phone?' said Harry.

Saima shook her head. 'Mine is on the table, over there,' she replied, pointing at it.

'Whose is it, then?'

They moved towards the incessant ringing, pausing in the hall-way where a package lying beside Harry's mother's slippers was vibrating.

'Saima, when did that arrive?' asked Harry.

'It was delivered this morning.'

FIFTY-SEVEN

HARRY STUDIED THE PACKAGE in his hands.

No postmark.

Hand-delivered.

'Harry?' said Saima. 'Is everything okay?'

The fucker had hand-delivered it.

Harry opened it; an iPhone, with a hands-free kit and a piece of paper.

For the sinner.

'Saima,' whispered Harry, concealing the paper in his hands. 'Go pack a bag for you and Aaron. Wake him up. We need to leave.'

'What?' she said.

'Saima, it's this case I'm working on. Now, please.'

Harry made sure his tone got Saima moving. She looked at him hard then ran up the stairs.

He checked his front door was locked and brought the phone into the living room.

The phone had three missed Facetime calls.

It rang again.

Another Facetime request.

Harry wanted to call Trafalgar House so they could monitor it, but he couldn't risk missing the window.

For Aisha's sake, he accepted the call.

The screen was dark but Harry could make out the faint silhouette of a figure.

'You've kept me waiting,' said a familiar voice.

Hand-delivered.

Harry hurried to the window but there was nothing to see. He could hear Saima frantically packing a bag upstairs.

'Why has there been no media response to Aisha's kidnap?'

'Protocol,' replied Harry, in no mood for niceties.

'Your phone.'

'What about it?'

'Show it to me.'

'What for?'

There was a muffled sound on the line. Harry heard a scream. Involuntarily, he looked up to the ceiling, Saima hadn't stopped moving. He attached the hands-free kit and put one headphone in.

'Every time you don't do what I ask, Aisha loses blood.'

'Okay,' said Harry, removing his phone from his pocket.

'Now what?'

'Your wife's too.'

Saima's phone was on the table. Harry held both of them in front of the screen.

'Into the kitchen. Select the forward-facing camera so I can see what you're doing.' Harry followed the instructions, confused.

'Fill the sink. Show me you've turned the phones off.'

Harry did so.

'Now throw them in.'

Harry watched them disappear under water, grimacing.

'Radio 5 live. Within the next fifteen minutes. And Harry, I'm going to keep phoning your landline. If it's engaged at any time before I call back, the girl dies.'

Click.

Hurriedly Harry ran through to the living room and turned on his television. He scrolled until he found the Sky channel broadcasting BBC Radio 5 Live.

The Phil Williams show.

The discussion seemed to be about Brexit.

Harry wanted to call Trafalgar House from his landline. The killer could be bluffing about having his number. But he couldn't risk it. The bastard seemed to know everything else.

Saima entered the living room, her face pained with worry. 'Bags packed. Should I wake Aaron now?'

Harry hurriedly told her what was happening, one ear on the radio.

'Oh God,' said Saima, irrationally looking around their living room.

'He's not going to ambush us, Saima. Can you grab my laptop?' he said. His thoughts were interrupted by the radio and Phil Williams' familiar voice.

'Ahh,' said Phil, 'I'm pleased to say we can now go to Adi from Bradford who we've tried to hear from a couple of times during his breaks on shift at the twenty-four-hour supermarket he's working at. Good to have you on, Adi, and, er . . . you've got a different view to the other Asian callers we've had on tonight, don't you? You believe we should lock down the borders and kick out everyone who doesn't have a job? Explain to us why you have this pretty radical view.'

'Hello, Phil, and good evening everyone, especially my friend Harry, who's a keen listener.'

Shit.

Harry couldn't believe it. His landline rang, the radio reception suddenly crackling. Two rings and it stopped.

The killer wasn't bluffing.

It was him.

Adi? It wasn't a name they'd turned up so far. Likely an alias.

'Holy Christ,' whispered Harry.

'Harry,' said Saima, 'what's wrong?'

He waved her quiet and increased the volume on the TV.

'I just wanted to say something which nobody knows and it's a little strange but bear with me, Phil, because this is worth listening to.'

'Be brief, Adi, cos the eleven o'clock news is only three minutes away.'

The killer dropped the A-bomb.

'Right now, the Home Secretary, Tariq Islam, is holed up at the Midland Hotel in Bradford because his daughter, Aisha, has been kidnapped by a serial killer who's killed three girls, three sinners, in Bradford this week.'

He paused.

'I know this because I killed them. And I've got Aisha Islam.'

Phil killed the line.

The presenter's voice came back on, smooth as you like.

'Right, well, we'll leave that call there for now because we are unable to independently verify that information. Let me apologize if you've been affected or upset by what that caller just said, we're very sorry. We assumed he wanted to give his view on Brexit from what he said to our researcher. Rest assured, we will now be passing the transcript of that call to the police. The news is next . . .'

The radio cut to the news and Harry wondered if, behind the scenes, BBC researchers would be scrabbling to ascertain the story's credibility.

Harry jumped at the noise of the mobile ringing in his hands.

Another Facetime call. Harry answered quickly.

'Now everyone in the UK knows the truth. I want to be *known*, Harry.'

'What now?' said Harry.

'Get in your car.'

'Why?'

'We're going for a drive.'

'What?'

Harry heard Aisha scream again.

'No!' Harry shouted.

'I warned you.'

'Okay, okay,' said Harry, momentarily allowing the phone to slip from his grasp and taking the opportunity to mouth for Saima to go and get Aaron. 'But I'm not leaving my family here,' said Harry, repositioning the phone. 'You need to let me get a squad car here before I—'

Aisha screamed again.

'Shit,' hissed Harry. 'I can't do this with my own family at risk. You know where I live. The game's changed.'

'It has,' he replied. 'Drop them at the police station on your way to meet me. You keep the hands-free kit in and stay on the line. It goes dead? Tariq will be receiving something bloody in the post. If anyone finds out you're coming to meet me, the girl dies. Simple.'

Harry was trying to figure out his best move.

He didn't have any.

'Okay,' he said. 'What if we lose connection while I'm driving?'

'When you're in the car, I will switch this to a voice-call. *Now move.*'

Harry kept the phone's camera on his face, increasingly annoyed that he couldn't see anything on the screen.

He didn't like being watched.

Saima came in holding Aaron, wrapped in his duvet, still asleep in her arms.

Harry took a deep breath.

Just get them to the station.

Harry grabbed his keys, keeping Saima behind him as he opened the front door.

Nothing.

He scanned the street.

Deserted.

He didn't know what he'd expected.

They moved quickly to Harry's car, Saima got in the back with Aaron.

The Facetime was cancelled and the phone rang immediately.

Saima was cuddling Aaron, who now started to cry.

'He's loud, isn't he, Harry,' said Adi.

Enraged, Harry held his tongue.

'You're wise to want to protect your wife and child. Very wise. I'd do the same if mine were still with me.'

He'd slipped up.

This was the first piece of information he'd revealed.

He'd lost a family.

Harry thought fleetingly of Indy.

They reached Trafalgar House in under five minutes. Harry drove right up to the front entrance. He pulled his identification out of his jacket and handed it to Saima.

'Go inside. Tell the duty officer who you are.'

Harry spoke into the hands-free kit now. 'She's going to have to tell them what's happened.'

'She should,' replied the killer. 'As soon as she gets out, you leave. I will hear the car door open. No delays, Harry. Clear?'

'Clear.'

But Saima wouldn't leave him.

'Please,' said Harry. 'You have to. I'm trying to save Aisha Islam's life.'

'I'm scared.'

Aaron reached out his hands for Harry to take him, crying loudly.

Harry couldn't do it. He turned away, urgency in his voice. 'I know, now please: go!'

Saima opened the back door and left the car, stealing one final look at Harry.

He watched her enter Trafalgar House, put the car in gear and drove away.

FIFTY-EIGHT

'WHERE AM I GOING?'

'Head towards Saltaire. Take the route which takes you past Mumtaz restaurant.'

Harry drove the route, arriving just a few minutes later.

'I'm here,' he said. 'It's closed.'

'I had my first date with my wife in that place. You can keep driving. I just thought you'd like to know. Relive it with me.'

Harry made a note to check the detail with Indy as soon as this was over. If this was connected to her, if this was Gurpal, he might have just slipped up.

'How long ago?' asked Harry.

'Twenty years. Almost to the day.'

'What happened to her?'

'What makes you think anything has happened to her?'

'A feeling.'

Harry stopped at a red light.

The killer laughed. 'I had to go away for a while. She left me.'

'Were you in jail?'

No response.

'She left you for a white guy? Is that what this is all about?'

'She was a sinner,' he spat. 'People should stick to their own kind. When they do not, there have to be consequences. When promises are broken? Vows? We let it lie. We've got used to being shamed.'

'How so?'

'I told you, Harry. You don't get to psychoanalyse me.'

'I'm sorry,' said Harry, pulling away again.

'No. You're not. People are not sorry any more unless they have something to lose. It is being proved every day – all over the world, people with no voice are doing things which will forever be remembered in history, things that make people sorry.'

'Like this?'

'Yes. Where are you now?'

'Just passed Frizinghall.'

'Head towards the Salts Mill Art Gallery. You're nearly there, you've nearly got me.'

'I'm going to bring you in?'

'Yes. Tonight, if you wish. You will get to decide. We are always caught in the end.'

Harry arrived at the art gallery. 'I'm here.'

'Park the car. Walk down Victoria Road. Towards the canal.'

Harry hesitated.

'I can see you, Detective. Are you really going to stop now?'

'Am I going to put my life on the line? Walk into a blind alley? I'm playing your game but I'm not stupid.'

'Of course you're not. Do you have weapons in the car? Anything you can use if I ambush you?' The killer laughed.

'Yes,' said Harry.

'Bring it. Whatever you need to feel better about this. You're not at risk.'

Harry got out of the car, he glanced around the darkness.

Nothing.

Again.

What was he walking into?

Harry opened his boot, found his torch and crowbar.

He walked cautiously down Victoria Road and reached the Leeds–Liverpool Canal, the water still and peaceful. A hard frost glistened on the banks as Harry walked along the path. The wind sharpened, the temperature plummeting.

'Turn right. Down the path. In a half mile or so, there's a bridge.'

With adrenaline flooding his body, Harry hurried on, alert for any surprises.

'Over here,' said the killer.

The canal was a straight route and Harry could make out a bridge in the distance.

On it, bang in the centre under the glare of an adjacent street-light, Harry saw a figure, dressed all in black, face covered.

He wasn't alone.

There was a girl in front of him, his arm around her neck. Below them the water of the canal glistened in the moonlight.

The wind whipped fiercely, cutting into Harry's ears, slicing through his clothes.

'Don't run, Harry.'

He hadn't realized he'd quickened his pace.

'I told you, you were safe,' the familiar voice said. 'As for her . . .'

Harry arrived on the bridge, now only twenty feet between them. 'Look, you know who her father is. He . . . he . . .'

'You want to cuff me? Or save the girl? She's injured, Harry. You'll need to decide quickly.'

'The girl,' said Harry.

'If you let me go, I'm bound to kill again. Are you sure about your choice?'

Harry stopped.

'Throw the phone into the canal.'

Harry pulled the headphones out and threw them into the canal with the phone.

There was a moment's peace as the wind died down.

The killer moved, fast and efficient, lifting the girl and throwing her into the canal before running away.

Harry charged, arriving where the killer had been, torn between wanting to go after him but unable to leave Aisha in the canal. He peered over the edge of the bridge. Aisha was thrashing in the water.

'Shit!' he screamed and he jumped in.

The freezing water momentarily shocked Harry into inaction. But he regained himself, looking desperately around.

Where are you?

He took a breath and submersed himself, forcing his eyes open in the murky water.

Harry searched desperately.

He came up for air.

'Aisha!' he shouted. Nothing.

He disappeared under the surface again.

Still nothing.

But he kept going.

Searching.

Something brushed against his hand. He shook off the weeds.

Not weeds.

Hair.

Harry turned back. An arm. A wrist. Something sharp.

Got her.

Harry pulled her close, and swam to the bank.

He dragged the girl to dry land, hurriedly removed the hood from her face and tore the gag around her mouth.

It wasn't Aisha Islam.

He felt for a pulse.

Nothing.

Harry tried to free her hands but they were bound with barbed wire.

Harry tore open her shirt to commence CPR and recoiled, crying out in despair.

She'd never stood a chance; a devastating terminal wound in her chest.

Next to it, carved into her skin:

SINNER.

FIFTY-NINE

THE BLUE LIGHTS OF two squad cars, an ambulance and a SOCO support unit turned the usually peaceful canal-side into a frenetic crime scene.

Harry was sitting by the bridge, on the cold, hard grassy bank. He'd dried off as best he could and wrapped himself in a blanket from the ambulance.

Another dead Asian girl on their hands.

Conway arrived. She was putting in as many late nights as he was at the moment. She sat down next to him.

'That . . . was really something,' she said.

'I thought it was Aisha.'

'You'd have done it even if you knew it wasn't her.'

'I would.'

Conway paused.

'I'm sorry, Harry.'

'So am I.'

'No, about your father. I dropped Saima home. She told me everything. How are you even functioning with all this going on?'

'What?' Harry snapped round to look at her. 'You left her there?'

'There's armed officers outside and a DS in with her.' Conway laid a hand on his arm. 'She was terrified, Harry.'

'I know. I . . . didn't know what else to do. Bastard had me by the balls.'

'You did the right thing.'

'He said his wife had left him. That he no longer has his family. I tried to get more from him but he wouldn't give it up. Can I use your phone? He let something slip. I need to call Gurpal's ex-wife Indy and verify it.'

Conway handed her phone to him.

'Shit, I don't have the number. Can you call the station and get it? But let me make the call.'

Conway nodded and moved away from Harry, dialling as she went.

Harry watched as the victim, identified by a credit card in her pocket as Sabrina Salem, was loaded on to a stretcher.

Did she have a white boyfriend too? Or was the bastard just binge-killing anyone now?

Conway returned and handed Harry her phone, the number already punched in.

Harry hit the call button, registering the time as he did so: 03:00.

She'd probably think it was another prank-call and not answer.

'Hello?' said an alert voice, a hint of panic to it.

'Indy, it's Harry.'

'Hey, I thought . . . it was another prank.'

'Is it still happening?'

'Nothing for the past couple of nights. I think maybe having the squad car passing my house so frequently and the obvious police-alarm stickers on the windows might have scared him off.'

She sounded hopeful. Harry glanced at the girl's body being loaded into the ambulance and wished he were.

He asked her about her first date with Gurpal but she couldn't remember.

'Might it have been at Mumtaz restaurant?' he asked, thinking back to what the caller had said.

'You know what, it might have been. Poshest place in Bradford for a curry. He definitely would have been trying to impress me.'

'How likely is it that you went there?' he asked, seeing Conway step closer, hope in her face.

'I'm not sure, Harry, but we went there a lot.'

Harry thanked her, didn't answer her questions about why he wanted the information at such an inhospitable hour, and hung up.

He told Conway what he'd learned.

'It's something,' she said.

'Perhaps,' said Harry. 'Thing is, a lot of first dates happen in that place. Like Indy said, you want to impress an Asian girl, you take her there.'

'I'll pass it on to the team. Get them to visit her tomorrow and get a statement. Good work, Harry. Now, let me arrange a squad car to take you home.'

'I'm fine driving.'

She shrugged.

'I'll brief the ACC, but he's going to want to hear about tonight first-hand.'

'I'll be at the eight o'clock briefing.'

Harry could tell she wanted him there but she had to ask, 'Are you sure you're up to it?'

'We'll get him in the next twenty-four hours, Clare. Tonight, we must have got some footage of him. He has to have snatched that girl as an impulse.'

'I don't think so, Harry. The whole set-up – sending you the phone? I think he's been planning every step of this for a long time.'

Harry stood up. 'Need to get home. Explain to Saima what the hell happened tonight.'

'Not before a medic checks you over.'

'She is a medic.'

'A doctor, Harry.'

'I will. Tomorrow. Right now, I need to see my family.'

Clare stood up. 'Your father, Harry. Do you need some time?'

'No,' he replied. 'How could I take time right now? Anyway, we aren't that close.'

'I'm going to keep officers at your house, Harry. Until this is over.'

'I'm sorry, that's not enough for me.'

'You want a safe house?'

Harry shook his head. 'Saima will hate that. I'll think of something else.'

'I'm still posting officers outside your home. This . . . is personal, Harry. Somehow.'

He looked over to the bridge.

'Just wish I'd saved her.'

'I know.'

'All this mess he's making? I've got a horrible feeling he's got something planned, some sort of apocalyptic finale. How we prepare for that, I don't know.'

At home, Harry discharged the officer who had been staying with Saima.

He found his wife upstairs, sitting next to Aaron's cot.

Harry entered, guilt assaulting him like the bitter chill of the canal water.

'How's he doing?' said Harry.

'Shattered. You could play a drum in here and he wouldn't wake up.' She didn't turn around.

Harry reached for her hand.

'Don't,' she said.

'I had no choice, Saima. You *must* know that.'

'My husband goes to meet with a serial killer and thinks that's okay?' Saima glared at him.

'Did they tell you everything at the station?'

'No. I was looking after a frightened, hysterical child – unless you'd forgotten.'

'Please don't do that. You think it was easy? I did what I had to, so you and Aaron would be safe.'

'What about you?' she hissed, slapping him on the arm.

Aaron stirred. Rolled over and stayed asleep.

'Let's go downstairs, Saima.'

They sat in the kitchen, all four gas hobs burning to heat up the room.

'Wow,' she said, after Harry had told her everything.

'I know.'

'How has this not got out yet?'

'Media blackout. Although now? That's blown. The Home Office will put out a statement first thing then the ACC will do a press conference. It's about to go viral.'

'So, it's somebody you know?' Saima asked.

Harry shrugged. He didn't want to get into it. 'Maybe. There's a team looking into my previous cases.' He shook his head. 'This guy is something else. He's . . . angry.'

'At what?'

'I don't know. But he keeps coming back to the word "sinner".'

'Well, what sin have you committed?'

Scissors. Blood. Michael King dying at Harry's feet. Ronnie going to jail.

'Unpaid parking ticket?' he said.

'Be serious, Harry. What does he want?'

'To be remembered. That's what he said to me.'

'What's next in the investigation?'

'He's got twenty-four hours before we nail him. Thirty-six at most.'

'How do you know?'

'He's binge-killing, spiralling towards something.'

'And Aisha?'

Harry shrugged.

'Are you happy here with police protection outside?'

Saima shook her head. 'He knows where we live. I . . . can't stay here until you've got him.' She pointed at him. 'You can't either.'

'I have to, Saima. He has to be able to contact me.'

'What if he tries something?'

'There's two armed police outside with machine guns.'

'What if he takes them out?'

'He's not Rambo.'

Harry was thinking of where Saima could go.

'What about your sister?' said Harry. 'Can you stay with her tonight? If this doesn't wrap up before tomorrow, we'll reassess.'

'I'll call her in a few hours when Aaron gets up. I'm not sending him to nursery, I'm not letting him out of my sight until this is over.'

'Honestly, I don't think you or him are part of this guy's plan. He let me drop you guys at the station, it's not about *my* family. It's about me.'

Harry was about to embrace her when their landline rang. Startled, he grabbed the phone.

'Hello?'

'Harry? It's Tariq Islam.'

'Oh,' replied Harry, pulling away from Saima and giving her the thumbs-up, displacing the look of panic on her face.

'Can we talk, Harry?'

'Sure. How can I help?'

'Face to face?'

Harry checked his watch: 04:30.

'I can see you after the eight a.m. briefing?'

'I was thinking about right now?'

'Now?'

'Yes. I'm outside your front door.'

SIXTY

HARRY POURED GENEROUS MEASURES of Jack Daniels into two tumblers and handed one to Tariq Islam.

'Voters knew about this? I'd lose my ethnic holding,' said Tariq, spinning the glass of whisky in his hand. 'Damned if I do. Damned if I don't.'

'Diversity in action. Do what everyone in Bradford does. Absolve your sins during Ramadan.'

Tariq smiled weakly and tipped his glass towards Harry before taking a sip.

'I'm surprised,' said Harry, sitting opposite Tariq at his dining table, 'that you'd trust me enough to share a whisky with me. Political careers have ended on less.'

'Don't give a damn,' said Tariq.

Harry analysed him carefully. Tariq looked like he was struggling with something, playing with the glass, unsure whether to offload what he had come here to say.

Harry took a punt. 'Why are you here? Really?'

'Shrewd,' said Tariq, smiling to himself. 'You've heard the rumours about me?'

'You've already told me that Group 13 doesn't exist, but then again lots of things which don't exist actually do,' replied Harry, intrigued.

'Paramilitary background means I've taken lives. And on my way to becoming Home Secretary, I cut some corners. Used my . . . influence.'

Harry felt like they had reached the edge of a precarious tipping point. 'This isn't a protected conversation. Don't tell me anything I don't want to know,' he said, not wanting to become entrenched in Tariq's political darkness.

'This guy,' said Tariq, continuing to play with his glass. 'Do you think it's about me?'

Harry sighed. 'The world isn't that black and white. I'm sure you have done stuff to get where you are. I've viewed the Internet chatter about you. You're either a coconut or a Jihadi in disguise. But this thing? Not on you.'

'He's smart, though. Isn't he? Not just some loon who woke up and thought, "Shit, I want to create a legacy."'

'Yes. He is. And planned this well.'

There was a pause as both men let the other think on their words.

'I heard what you did tonight,' said Tariq.

Harry grimaced. 'Pretty stupid, according to my wife.'

'She might not be far wrong. But I'm still grateful. You jumped into that canal thinking it was Aisha. For that, I'll always be in your debt. No matter how this . . . ends.'

Harry sipped his whisky.

Tariq finished his drink. One aggressive gulp.

'Refill?' asked Harry, reaching for the bottle.

Tariq shook his head. 'When I walk out that door, trial by media starts. They're all over the hotel. Which is why I came tonight. Tomorrow, we lose control.'

'He's creating as much noise as possible. Trying to throw us off our game.'

Tariq grimaced. 'It's working.'

'What did you come here for? Really?'

'I . . . heard your father is ill. In hospital.'

'He is.'

'Yet, you're still fighting for my daughter.'

'I don't like to lose.'

'Are you close to him?'

Harry stared at his wedding ring, playing with it in his hands. 'Since you've trusted me with your drinking habits, I'll tell you that we haven't spoken for some time. Because of the woman I chose to marry.'

'Saw the Islamic painting on the wall in the hallway. Your wife is Muslim?'

Harry nodded.

'Brown-on-brown racism. Worst kind.'

'Exactly.'

Harry finished his drink, put the glass on the table and asked Tariq again why he was here.

'I want you to level with me, Harry,' said Tariq.

'Okay.'

'Aisha. She's not coming back, is she?'

Harry chose his words carefully.

'You came here to ask me whether tonight was our last shot?'

'Yes.'

Looking at Tariq, Harry saw a widowed father in the worst of *all* situations and couldn't deliver the usual soundbite.

'Having seen the son of a bitch in action tonight. The effort he went to? The sheer audacity of what he pulled off?' said Harry, putting his hand on Tariq's shoulder, one father trying his hardest not to lie to another.

'I think you should prepare yourself for the worst,' he said.

SIXTY-ONE

SAIMA PLACED TWO LARGE bags on the floor of Nadia's living room. Harry had dropped her outside, impatient to get to work. He looked shocking and Saima worried his midnight swim in the filthy canal water might have given him a bug.

'Thanks for this, Sis,' she said.

'How bad is the damage?' asked Nadia, immediately picking Aaron up and taking him to the fish tank in the corner of her living room.

'Could have been worse,' said Saima. She had told Nadia they had suffered a burst water-pipe which had badly damaged their home and that she needed to stay for one night while it was repaired. She hadn't wanted to worry Nadia with the truth. Saima couldn't quite believe it herself.

Saima started unpacking the bag she had made up for Aaron, who was mesmerized by the fish.

'I feed them!' he said, concerned Nadia was going to do it.

'Okay, okay,' replied Nadia, handing him a small tub of fish-food.

'Careful,' said Saima. 'Last time he threw the whole lot in.'

'There's not a lot left,' said Nadia, helping Aaron to shower the water in the tank with food.

'Mamma, look!' he cried as the fish swam for the surface.

Nadia put him on the floor. Aaron pushed his nose up to the tank, practically hypnotized by the dozen or so fish.

'Imran here?' asked Saima, nervously.

'Upstairs. Still got the flu.'

'Did you tell him we are staying?'

'I did.'

'And?'

'You're *his* cousin too.'

'I don't want to cause a scene.'

'You're not. Anyway, he owes me. I've been waiting on him hand and foot for three days solid. Bloody man-flu. Can't you give him something?'

'I'd give him a kick out of this house.'

'Yeah, well, we're not all as feisty as you.'

'When is he leaving?'

'Once his bit-on-the-side gets pregnant, he'll leave. Until then, he'll drag his heels on the divorce.'

'And you're okay with that?'

'Saima,' snapped Nadia, loud enough that it startled Aaron, 'will you just let it be? You're here for one night, can we just enjoy that? Hasn't happened in years.'

Saima nodded. She hated that her sister wasn't as headstrong as she was.

'Do you want some breakfast? I was going to make samosas,' said Nadia.

'This early?'

'It's Shabraat tonight. I'm making it for the mosque. Hey, why don't you come?' said Nadia excitedly. 'Be like old times.'

Shabraat happened every year a couple of weeks before Ramadan. Women would get together at the mosque for an all-night praying session. It was a religious occasion but, for the women gathered, it was also a chance to catch up and spend some time together.

Saima had always loved Shabraat. As a teenager, spending a whole night at the mosque had felt so secretive.

'I . . . can't,' she said, nodding at Aaron.

'He'll be asleep. Imran will be home. Oh, come on, you'll see all the old lot there!'

'Yeah, and what am I going to say to them?'

'Nothing. We told everyone you got married and pissed off somewhere. Nobody cares. Everyone's done worse than you, anyway.'

'Worse than me?'

Nadia shrugged. 'Black guys. Gays. Affairs. Divorce. It's all happening.'

'In the open?' said Saima incredulously.

'Don't be stupid. Come on, let's go.' Nadia smiled conspiratorially.

Saima shared so little with her sister and was working hard to rebuild their relationship. Perhaps this could make a difference for them?

But there would be questions.

And Saima couldn't leave Aaron with Imran.

'No,' said Saima. 'I can't. But I'll help you cook.'

Nadia nodded, frustration clear on her face. Saima hated to disappoint her.

'Tell you what,' said Saima smiling.

'What?'

'Once the samosas are done, you and I can pick out an outfit for you to wear this evening. Just like we used to do. A full-on fashion show!'

A grin Saima had not seen for years appeared on Nadia's face, her eyes sparkled and she looked genuinely excited.

SIXTY-TWO

ANOTHER MORNING IN THE overloaded briefing room on the top floor of Trafalgar House. The floor was alive with activity; phones rang incessantly and officers moved quickly through the hallways.

They had one hour until the killer was supposedly calling back for another game of wasp kill.

Harry focused on the television screen at the front of the briefing room, he increased the volume and leaned forward as the press conference started downstairs.

Harry had seen the vans arriving all morning: BBC, ITV, C4, Sky, CNN.

As the ACC spoke on screen with Conway and Tariq Islam either side of him, Harry wondered if the killer was watching.

Of course he was.

The ACC had advised Tariq not to attend but some of the suits from the Home Office had thought differently.

Show the world you're a father first, a politician second.

Show the killer your human side.

Bullshit, as far as Harry was concerned.

It all was.

None of this was going to make a difference.

Gurpal Singh's name was going to be made public today, as a 'person of interest'. Aside from that case, Harry had a dozen more files on his desk of recently released prisoners or perpetrators he'd put away who might have held a grudge. He'd had a quick nosy. None of them interested him. His team had looked for any intel on 'Adi', the name the killer had used on the radio. Nothing had turned up.

Harry had seen this guy. Spoken with him and watched as he'd thrown his latest victim off the bridge.

Whilst many clues pointed towards Gurpal Singh, Harry was no longer sure he was their guy. Harry knew him – he wasn't smart enough to pull this off. No matter how much prison might have changed him.

Harry sighed.

All *Asian* victims.

The *Asian* Home Secretary.

This was a clash of cultures, about those traditional values that had little place in the modern world they lived in.

Harry knew it all too well. His mind drifted to his father.

He'd be going in for his operation in the next few hours.

Harry wasn't sure whether he wanted him to survive it or not.

Neither outcome felt right for him.

Harry had been blocked from attending the conference. They didn't want the personal connection to be made public. Since the killer had mentioned his name on the radio, journalists were already speculating about who his friend Harry might be. As yet, they hadn't identified him.

As yet.

The ACC was talking on the screen. A carefully written script intended to get the wider public on high alert.

It would only drive the killer further underground.

Harry focused on Tariq Islam as Frost handed over to him. He appeared calm.

He stepped forward, looked into the media scrum and put his hands in his pocket.

'I'm not the Home Secretary. Not a politician. Just a father, who loves his little girl, Aisha, very much and wants her home. Aisha, I want you to know we're all thinking of you and, like you, we're being brave and strong.'

A pause.

Dozens of camera shutters clicking.

Flashes going off.

'To whoever is holding Aisha. Talk to her. Ask her to tell you the joke about the Englishman, the Irishman and the Chinese man. It's her favourite. It'll make you laugh. She makes everyone laugh. Try it. I promise you, you will see a very special young woman.'

He looked down at his hands.

'Please,' said Tariq. 'My wife died young and I have only Aisha. She means everything to me. Somebody out there must know something.'

He paused.

'I'm putting up a 50,000-pound reward for information which leads to the safe return of Aisha. So, please, if anybody knows *anything*, get in touch with the police.'

Tariq stepped away.

The media erupted with questions but Tariq filed off stage, flanked by the ACC and Conway, and the cameras diverted back to the news studios.

Harry, Conway and Frost met Tariq Islam in a small meeting room to await the phone call they'd been promised. They had two technical support officers with them. They'd rigged Tariq's phone, so they could record it and, more importantly, track the killer's location in real time.

With everything set, Tariq backed quietly out of the room.

At first, he'd objected to the idea that he wouldn't be present for this second call.

But ultimately, Harry felt as though he had secretly been relieved to stand down.

Trauma a father didn't need to witness.

Harry checked his watch: 09:56.

They waited in the room, blinds drawn.

Harry felt uncomfortable. Once again on the back foot in this twisted game.

The nerves in the room were palpable.

10:00.

Nothing.

10:20.

Still nothing.

'He's fucking us around,' said Harry.

When still no call had come in by 11:00, they stood down. Frost left the room but Conway held Harry back.

'You look knackered, Harry. Hell of a few days you've had.' He wasn't sure whether she was talking about the case or the situation with his father.

'Midnight swims aren't exactly my idea of a good night's rest. Third night in a row this guy's kept me awake. Maybe that's his plan. Disorientate me, so I miss any clues.'

'I'd love to send you home, Harry, but I need you here. In case the bastard does call. You want to take a load off in my office?'

Harry shook his head. 'I'm fine. What can I do from here? I can't sit here sipping coffee all day, making nice with him –' he nodded towards Tariq, who was loitering outside with his close-protection team.

'Frost's going to ask him to leave. He's drawing too much attention being here and, Home Secretary or not, this isn't his house to oversee. We need to be allowed to do our jobs.'

'Good. Do we have anything from the CCTV surveillance from last night around the canal?'

She shook her head.

'How's that possible?'

She shrugged. 'My guess is he ran hell for leather, went as far as Thackley then into Dawson's Wood. It makes good cover. After that? He could have gone anywhere. We're looking, Harry. Once he pings on a camera, we can track him.'

Harry watched as the ACC put his arm around Tariq Islam and led him away. 'What can I do?'

Conway pointed outside, where a large board displayed pictures of the victims.

'Find out what links those girls and how he chose them. That's how we end this.'

SIXTY-THREE

HARRY CALLED THE FIVE victims' boyfriends in.

He chose a meeting room rather than an interrogation room, he wanted to keep it informal. There was a chance that one of these men knew more than they thought they did and it was easier to coax that type of information to the surface when someone didn't feel under the pressure of an interrogation.

He'd met Xavier Cross and Andrew Lightfoot, but he'd not yet come across Jaspreet, Leila or Sabrina's boyfriends.

'What's the crack, yeah? We can't be suspects all in the same room like this?' said Xavier.

'I'm sure you won't mind sitting here in a room like this if it leads to you providing the kind of information that gets you a fifty-grand reward. Or have I got that wrong?' Harry said.

'Mate, for fifty grand I wish I did know something.'

What the fuck did Usma Khan ever see in this prick?

Xavier was uncomfortable but the others were more patient.

Harry held his hands out passively. 'None of you guys are under suspicion,' he said honestly. 'But you might be the guys who can

solve this and help us save Aisha Islam's life. Claim that reward.'
He nodded at Xavier, who held his stare.

'This killer targeted the five girls you were dating. But here's the thing,' said Harry, sitting down, 'all of you were dating secretly. None of you ever stepped out in public. I've read all your statements. You dated these girls in secret because of all the cultural bullshit that came along with it.'

Xavier had clearly assigned himself the role of group leader.

'How's it work then?' he said. 'If we figure something out in this room and it saves the girl, we split the fifty-k five ways?'

'Christ,' snapped Aisha's boyfriend, Andrew, 'is that all you care about? I know you've all lost someone but my girlfriend's still out there and all you give a shit about is lining your pockets?'

Andrew turned to Harry. 'Seriously, one of the girls was seeing this dumbass?'

'Who you calling "dumbass"?' snapped Xavier, getting angrily to his feet. Harry got there first, stepping between the two men. 'Hey! This isn't helping.'

Harry pushed them apart, back to their chairs.

The other three remained quiet, their loss clear on their faces.

'The six of us in this room can save Aisha Islam. I'm certain of it. There is something that connects these girls, a common thread that enabled our killer to learn about your secret relationships. And you guys could help me find the answer. Maybe there's a place you all have in common. A takeaway you all used? A restaurant? Clothes you bought the girls from the same shop? It could be anything.'

Harry moved his seat forwards a little.

'This guy hates that these Asian girls were dating white guys, that's pretty clear.'

'Racist,' one of the boyfriends that Harry hadn't met before muttered under his breath.

'Absolutely. Question is, how did he know? What is it that connects you all? There *has* to be something. And,' said Harry, trying his hardest to hammer this home, 'yes, there's fifty-k on offer, but park that for a moment. You guys,' he turned away from Andrew Lightfoot, 'have lost your girlfriends and I can't imagine how that feels. But we could stop Andrew losing his. We could find the thing that saves Aisha Islam's life.'

SIXTY-FOUR

NOTHING.

Absolutely nothing.

After three hours delving into the clandestine dating histories of all five couples, Harry didn't have anything to link them.

Tired, irritated and unable to see the wood for the trees, he let them all go.

Harry walked into the incident room, still heaving with officers, and stopped in front of the case board. Across the top was a large photograph of each of the five victims. He folded his arms across his chest, and stared at it, trying to connect the scraps of information he'd just had from their boyfriends.

So many dead ends.

Andrew Lightfoot had been Harry's best hope, easily the brightest of the bunch and the only boyfriend who needed to hide his relationship as much as the girls had to.

Andrew and Aisha had gone to a lot of trouble to keep their affair a secret. None of his colleagues knew a thing about them and Aisha's friends were just as ignorant. Rabeena had been interviewed three times now and hadn't yet told them anything helpful.

Harry remembered the killer's words,

'*People should stick to their own kind. When they do not, there have to be consequences. When promises are broken? Vows? We let it lie. We've got used to being shamed.*'

Harry's head was starting to hurt. The tiredness creeping in.

'There's something here I'm not seeing,' he whispered.

He tried to block out the noise of the room, the phones ringing, the chatter, the tapping at computer keyboards and the pairs of eyes staring at him, all wondering why the killer had chosen to play this game with him.

Five girls.

Five separate universes.

Nothing in common except the boyfriends.

Harry closed his eyes.

What were they all doing?

Keeping secrets.

And?

Something shifted in his mind.

Almost there.

What were they all doing?

'Harry!'

He was jarred from his thoughts suddenly by Conway who put her thumb and little finger to her ear, phone call. She pointed to the conference room, urgency written across her face.

It was him.

Harry sprinted to the conference room.

'Where's Frost?' Harry asked.

'No time, line one,' she said and switched on the recording device.

Harry hit the speaker button.

The blinds hadn't been lowered and from outside he could see dozens of eyes looking his way as he spoke. Harry turned his back to them.

'DCI Virdee,' he said.

'It's time,' said the killer, his tone immediately different. Irate. 'You want to end this? Then tell them what you did?'

Conway looked at Harry in shock.

'What?' said Harry, confused.

'I'm tired of this. It needs to end. So, tell everyone what you did!'

Harry frowned at Conway, who was monitoring the recording device, looking to the tech guys just outside for a trace.

'Tell them your secret. You killed a man. You ruined a family.'

Harry's heart started to race, his hands prickling with sweat.

Blood.

Scissors.

'I don't know what you're talking about.'

He could feel Clare's eyes on him.

'Did you think you would get away with it? What did I tell you last night? There have to be consequences to people's actions.'

Harry's mouth went dry.

How was this possible?

Only Harry and his brother knew the truth.

'You think this was about the girls? Come on, Harry. I wanted *your* attention. I wanted everyone's attention. To shame you. To ruin you.'

'Let me speak to Aisha,' said Harry.

'Say it.'

'Say what?'

'That you're a sinner. I want to hear you say it.'

His voice was rising.

Angry.

Bitter.

'Say you took a life. That you thought you'd got away with it. Say it, Harry, or I will kill her.'

Aisha's voice mumbled from somewhere in the background.

'No, please, not again.'

Scared. Weak. Worn down.

'Okay,' said Harry desperately. 'I . . . I'm a sinner. I took a life and I thought I'd got away with it.'

Silence.

'Tomorrow night. We end this, Harry. I will phone again tomorrow at six p.m. In return for Aisha's safety, I want something from you.'

'What?' asked Harry.

'Your life,' spat the killer and hung up the phone.

SIXTY-FIVE

'I'VE NEVER SEEN THAT look on your face before, Harry,' said Conway.

Harry dropped hard into a chair, his mind a mess.

I took a life and I thought I'd got away with it.

How could the killer know something only he and Ronnie were privy to?

Scissors. Michael King. Blood pooling at Harry's feet.

And how did it tie into this investigation?

'Harry?' repeated Conway.

'No idea what that was about,' he replied without looking at her.

Christ, had Ronnie told anyone about their secret?

Conway perched on the table. 'Harry, look out there,' she said, pointing to the incident room where people were still staring at them both. 'There's a hundred officers working this case, around the clock.'

'I know.'

'Don't bullshit me, Harry. Do you know what he was talking about?'

'No.'

'We've all made mistakes, Harry, innocent ones.'

'Clare,' said Harry looking at her, 'I'm serious. I've no idea what he was on about.'

It was true. Harry didn't. He was confident the only people who knew were he and Ronnie. His mother had been unconscious on the floor.

Case closed.

Ronnie served his time.

Harry couldn't believe he would have told anyone the truth.

Harry ran his hand across his face, scratching at thick angry stubble, and glanced at the clock on the wall. Two p.m.

'I'm tired, Clare, he said. 'Going home. If things change? Call me? One of the PCSOs got me a cheap burner. Number's on the noticeboard.'

Before Harry got up, she grabbed his arm.

'When I play this tape to the ACC, he's going to wonder just what this guy is talking about.'

'Then the ACC and I will have something in common,' said Harry, and got up to leave.

Harry dialled Ronnie's number.

They hadn't spoken about their father yet, but that wasn't why he was calling.

That wasn't right.

Not a lot was right in this family.

They might have been at loggerheads over Ronnie's drug-dealing, but they were still family.

Twenty-four months of silence and now in the space of twenty-four hours, two tumultuous events had thrown them back together.

Harry called him. He didn't answer. He tried again and got the same response.

'Shit,' he whispered.

Ronnie had a habit of not taking calls from numbers he didn't recognize. Harry texted him.

Lost my phone. Call me back. Harry.

As he waited for Ronnie to call, he phoned Saima at her sister's place. She was well but Aaron had got sick. Saima suspected it was the bitter cold of leaving the house in a rush late the night before that had given him a bad chest. She sounded happy enough, though.

One less thing to worry about.

Harry ended the call just as another was incoming.

Ronnie.

'Hey,' said Harry, answering it.

'Little brother. Long time.'

Harry hadn't realized just how much he'd missed Ronnie's voice until he heard it.

'You want to meet?' Ronnie ventured into the silence.

'Shall I come to the house?'

'I'm not there, kid.'

'Warehouse?'

'No, I needed a time-out. I'm at Fulneck golf course.'

Harry found Ronnie leaning against a stone pillar marking the beginning of the course. He had a golf club across his shoulders, an arm draped over each end.

'Hey,' said Harry. He wanted to embrace his brother, yet now, being here, it felt so awkward.

A handshake at least?

Ronnie didn't move.

Harry stared down the hill of the first tee, at the grass glistening with frost.

'Ball's going to slip and slide.'

'Might give me a few extra yards on the drive.'

Ronnie pulled a golf ball from his pocket and placed it on the tee he'd already stuck in the ground.

'Hurts. Doesn't it?' said Ronnie.

'What?'

'Being here. Feeling how normal it is. Realizing what we threw away, how it could have been.'

Harry nodded.

'After two years' radio silence, you're either here to take me down – in which case, I think we ought to play a round together first – or you need my help. I'm hoping it's the latter.'

'Could be about Dad.'

Ronnie smiled. 'I knew she'd tell you. It isn't about that. That's just . . . what it is.'

'You're in luck: I need your help,' said Harry.

Ronnie waved his club at Harry. 'I'm still here, little brother. Always will be when it comes to you. You know that.'

The words stung.

Harry felt small.

'You're just . . . here for me? No questions asked?' said Harry.

'Yeah,' said Ronnie. 'What do you need?'

'I don't believe you.'

Ronnie smiled.

He moved past Harry, unzipped the golf bag, removed a plastic tee and another golf ball. He crouched, pushed the tee into the ground and placed the golf ball on it.

'Christ,' he said stretching. 'Feels like old times. Feels, I don't know, like we never fell out.' He paused, looked at Harry and added, 'No?'

Harry stared at the ball by his feet. 'You never change,' he said.

'Got to earn it, Harry.' Ronnie pointed behind, where the school building rose steeply. 'Taught you that, then. Twenty years later, with everything we've been through, that rule still applies.'

'After you,' said Harry.

Ronnie nodded. 'So, it's like this. One shot. Really, we should be hitting the green from here. You get closest to the flag, I'll help you. If I do, you answer one question of mine. With the truth.'

Harry looked down the fairway. He visited a driving range every month with some of the guys from work. He didn't play off a handicap and hadn't played a round of golf in years but when it came to hitting a clean strike, he was sure of himself.

'Got it,' he said. 'When we were younger, Ron, you let me go first. I always thought it was so you could see what you had to beat.'

Ronnie squinted at Harry. 'It was.'

Harry shook his head. 'No, it wasn't. It was so, if you felt kind, you could botch your shot. Make me feel good.'

Ronnie smiled. 'How long did it take you to figure that out? Once you made detective?'

'Something like that. Which is why, today, *you're* going first.'

Ronnie removed a white golf glove from his pocket and slipped it over his hand. 'As you wish, little brother.'

Ronnie lined himself up. He positioned the club, performed a few routine twitches, then stopped. He backed off, sat on the low stone wall and put the golf club down.

'You want to know how many times I picked up the phone to call you, Harry?'

When Harry didn't reply, Ronnie continued. 'Maybe twice a week. Sometimes more. Never could hit call.'

Harry didn't know what to say.

'I'm giving it all up.'

Harry stared at Ronnie. Eyes narrowing. 'You couldn't.'

There was something in the way Ronnie was looking at Harry which sent a shiver down Harry's spine. 'What are you saying?'

'I'm saying,' said Ronnie, getting back to his feet, 'that people change.'

Ronnie retook his position by the golf ball. This time there was little preparation. He lined it up, paused a few seconds, then took a measured swing. The golf ball flew straight and high. On its descent, it veered left and landed in a patch of rough, about ten yards off the fairway and about thirty yards from the green. Could have been worse.

'About one fifty,' said Ronnie. 'Yeah?'

'You measured that swing,' said Harry.

'Sure, I did. I don't need to hammer it on to the green and risk overshooting. I just need to whop your ass. And I reckon one fifty is enough.'

Harry took the three-wood from Ronnie, the rubber grip warm from Ronnie's hands.

'Glove?' asked Ronnie.

'Nope.'

'Same old Harry.'

'Style over substance. You don't change.'

Harry lined up the shot. He removed the ball from the tee, adjusted it a little and replaced it. He looked down the fairway. Behind, Ronnie started a mock-commentary which made Harry smile; they'd always done that as children.

'Cut it out,' said Harry.

'Wouldn't be the same, though, would it?'

Ronnie continued, his voice a whisper. As Harry lined up the shot, he felt overwhelmed with sadness and gritted his teeth.

Ronnie fell silent. Harry focused, just the noise of the breeze in his ears, and swung. He heard the sweet sound of the golf ball ping off the tee which went soaring after the ball.

'Shit,' said Harry, dismayed as his shot veered sharply right and flew out of bounds. 'Shit,' he repeated.

Ronnie whistled. 'Shanked it.'

'Shit three-wood,' said Harry, dropping the club on the ground.

'Nothing wrong with the club. You had your feet all wrong. Moved your head before you hit the ball. Looked like a damn rag-doll. Golf is about stillness.'

'Get fucked,' said Harry.

'So, it looks like I get to ask you one question and only the truth will do.'

Harry faced Ronnie, dismayed he wasn't in the driving seat.

Dismayed at just how comfortable this all felt, in spite of a two-year hiatus.

Ronnie stepped closer to Harry and looked him straight in the eye.

'My question is,' he said solemnly, prodding Harry firmly in the chest, 'what the fuck does a big brother have to do to get a hug around here?'

SIXTY-SIX

THE BROTHERS WERE THE only people inside the Fulneck club-house, which closed at four o'clock but the caretaker had given Ronnie the keys and told him to drop them through the letterbox. Ronnie brought them over a couple of coffees and took a seat oppos-ite Harry at the corner table.

'You look like shit, kid.'

'I feel like it,' replied Harry, adding more milk to his coffee.

'Home Secretary's daughter?'

'Yeah. As fucked up as it gets. He's a serial killer who wants max-imum exposure before I nail him.'

'And you're going to?'

'Only a matter of time. He's binge-killing.'

'Let's talk about the old man first. Get it out the way.'

'Nothing to say about it.'

'He had his op this morning. He'll be in recovery now, Mandy's there with Mum.'

'Prognosis?'

'Won't know till later.'

Harry couldn't bury his anger at the way his father had spoken to his wife the day before.

'You want to know a secret?'

'What?'

'I've been visiting Tara's grave every day. Straight after AA meetings. Remember them?'

Harry scoffed.

'Place hasn't changed much. Similar crowd. Few new faces.'

'How's the wagon?'

'Still on it.'

'Good.'

'I . . . visit her grave. Sit next to her and try to show her that I'm changing. That . . . I've learned. That's the thing with loss, you don't realize until it's too late.'

Ronnie fell silent for a moment.

'What do you need my help with?' asked Ronnie.

Harry didn't want to talk about it. It felt good to just sit here with his brother, out of the way of the case. He stared out of the window across the greenery of Fulneck valley.

I know what you did, Harry. The life you took.

There wasn't a day that went by when Harry didn't question why he'd allowed Ronnie to take the blame for Michael King's murder. Maybe things would have turned out differently if he hadn't let it happen. He couldn't remember the conversation which led to that decision being made. He couldn't even remember switching clothes with Ronnie.

'Kid?' said Ronnie.

Harry stopped reminiscing and told Ronnie what had happened with the murder victims and the cryptic notes. Finally, about the threat, *Tell them your secret. You killed a man. You ruined a family.*

When he'd finished, he looked at Ronnie for a response.

'Have you told anyone what happened, Ron?'

'What?'

'You heard.'

Ronnie took a deep breath.

'Can't believe I'm about to say this,' said Ronnie shaking his head. 'Especially with the old man at death's door. I did what I did with Michael King because I'd got used to being both your brother and a father figure to you. He was a *shit* dad. Spent ninety per cent of his time in the shop obsessing over the pennies and the other ten per cent down the Temple. Community, honour, tradition. All that bullshit. He was never really a dad to us. Sure, we didn't want for anything; we had food, clothes, a roof, education – but none of the big stuff. He didn't know how to help us grow into men in this world we called home, a world he only knew as a choice.'

Ronnie got up and stood by the window. Sleet began falling outside, a slow rhythmic patter on the roof of the clubhouse.

'I did what I did because I'd got so used to protecting you that it was second nature. I was hard on you when we were young. Yeah?'

Harry nodded.

'Dad just dished out religion and tradition, so I tried to give you something else. That night, when Michael fucking King chose to try to rob our shop, it was instinct to take the blame and protect you. I never thought twice about it.'

Somehow the brothers had never really spoken about this. It was too big.

Ronnie continued. For years, he had blamed their father for that night because *he* should have been the one to be there to take responsibility and protect his boys. But Ranjit had been at the Temple.

'I don't regret it,' said Ronnie. 'Jail opened my eyes. It's a shit world we live in. With shit rules.'

'It's always been shit, Ron,' said Harry, still unsure where Ronnie was going with this.

'I know,' said Ronnie. 'But what you don't realize is, amongst all this shit we contend with, one rule *always* reigns supreme.'

Ronnie retook his seat at the table, his face serious, his eyes focused on Harry like lasers.

'Family first. I can't say the whole family sticks to it, but I certainly do. You want to know if I ever told anyone the truth about that night?'

Harry nodded.

'I told two people. The first was my business partner, but he's no longer with us.'

'We don't know if he told anyone.'

'He didn't have anyone else to tell.'

'How do you know?'

'He was completely alone, Harry, which is why I trusted him.'

'Who's the other person?'

For the first time, Ronnie looked uncertain.

'Who did you tell?' asked Harry, eyes narrowing at his brother.

'I told Dad.'

SIXTY-SEVEN

ANOTHER NIGHT WITHOUT SLEEP was starting to affect Harry; his head felt leaden, fogginess clouding his thought-process.

His father knew?

'What did he say?' whispered Harry. 'That I was toxic? Ruined your life? That everything I touch turns to poison?'

Ronnie had moved back to the window, standing by the side of it, as sleet continued to spatter against the pane. 'No. He said nothing.'

'Nothing?'

'That's right. For some reason, we never spoke about it again. Just . . . buried it.'

'When did you tell him?'

'Same week you left home. Mum was a mess. Dad equally so. We were arguing,' said Ronnie, reliving the exchange and closing his eyes. 'He shouted at Mum that you should have died in her womb.'

Harry grimaced.

'It was ugly. For some reason, I thought telling him that you had saved Mum from Michael King would help. Show him that you had defended the honour of our family. There you have it. I told two people. So, whatever game this killer is playing, he didn't get the intel through me.'

'Then how does he know?'

'No idea.'

'What about Mum or Mandy?'

'They weren't in the room when I told Dad.'

'I don't get it.'

'Have you told anyone?' asked Ronnie.

'Don't be daft,' said Harry.

He received a text on his phone from Saima.

Aaron's not well. Doc at work's written him a prescription. Can you pick it up? Please?

'I've got to go, Ron,' said Harry, standing up.

'Everything with Dad has made me think, we need to sort things between us, Harry.'

'Yeah,' he replied, sheepish.

'I've got things to discuss with you. Stuff you need to hear.'

'I'll make time. Once we've got this guy, I'm all yours,' said Harry, stepping past the table and embracing his brother.

'Promise?' said Ronnie.

Harry held him tight. 'I promise.'

SIXTY-EIGHT

HARRY PULLED INTO THE car park at Bradford Royal Infirmary. A phone call from the car had brought him up to speed on developments at Trafalgar House.

Nothing significant on the tip line yet, but with Gurpal's name now public knowledge, intel was streaming in about possible sightings of him. Two in particular stood out – he'd been seen with an Asian girl the day before.

Harry sat in his car, tired, head full of noise. His thoughts were scrambling: killer, Saima, Ronnie, Dad, Aaron, Mum. How had he not called his mother? She must have been sick with worry for her husband. But Saima had been there for her.

Saima.

He couldn't take that on right now. Not while he still didn't know which way was up.

Harry made his way to A&E and collected the prescription for Aaron from Balraj, his long-time friend and Saima's boss in A&E, who informed Harry that whilst his father's surgery had gone well, his heart was struggling to recover and the next few hours would prove critical. Balraj didn't sound hopeful, adding to the noise in Harry's mind.

Harry also learned the matron was desperate to see him but he had no time for that. He thanked Balraj for the update and headed towards the pharmacy.

'Mr Virdee!'

He turned to see the hospital matron, carrying a large bag, waving at him from down the hall. She beckoned him into a side room and made a point of closing the door fully.

'We've been trying to contact your mother and your older brother – Ronnie, is it?'

'That's right. What's this about?'

The matron was taller than Harry with a pronounced jaw and broad shoulders. Harry had the distinct impression he was in trouble and he didn't like the feeling one bit.

She frowned. 'It's a little delicate. While I appreciate your father is in a very serious condition and, in times like this, religious symbols and icons can be of great help, I'm afraid,' she said, removing a large parcel wrapped in a stiff orange cloth from the bag she was holding, 'he cannot keep this here with him.'

She unwrapped the parcel. Harry's father's kirpan.

He didn't move.

The same dagger his father had charged at him with.

He hadn't seen it since the night he left.

'It was in a bag in his locker. The ward sister found it whilst looking for a list of medications he usually takes. I'm really very sorry, Mr Virdee, but this is a serious health and safety violation. It *cannot* stay here.'

Harry couldn't believe it. The image of it flashing at his body etched on his mind as his mother threw herself in the way.

'I . . . I . . . can't take it,' he said quietly.

'I have to insist.'

'My brother. He'll be here later.'

'That won't work. I can't have it here a moment longer. It's more than my job is worth if, God forbid, something were to happen . . . If you're unwilling to take it, I'll be forced to submit it to the police for safekeeping.'

Harry stepped away from her and opened the door. 'Then I suggest you do just that,' he said.

Harry got to the hospital pharmacy at 17:32. The shutters were already down.

Two minutes past their closing time.

Harry rattled the shutters in anger.

Nothing.

'Fuck's sake,' he said hunting for his temporary phone.

No Internet on this brick. He couldn't search for the nearest late-night pharmacy.

Harry left in a hurry to get to the closest one and hoped it was still open.

He arrived at Sahara Pharmacy on Duckworth Lane a few minutes later and joined the queue waiting to be served by an Asian woman wearing a headscarf.

It was moving slowly, mostly old people, except for two young Asian girls in front of him. They were nervously whispering to each other. Eventually it was their turn to approach the counter.

'Can I speak to a lady pharmacist?' said one of the girls.

The counter assistant shook her head. 'I'm sorry, there's only a male pharmacist,' she said, pointing behind her towards an Asian man in a tunic and skullcap.

'Can I speak with you instead?' said the girl to the assistant.

'What about?'

The girl dropped her voice. 'I need the morning-after pill,' she whispered.

The counter assistant's reply was also discreet but Harry heard it. 'I'm sorry, but only the pharmacist can help you with that.'

The girls left the store, muttering in annoyance.

Harry stepped forward.

'Does that happen often? Girls not wanting to buy the morning-after pill from a male pharmacist?'

'Asian girls rarely want to speak to the men about anything,' said the assistant, taking the prescription from him, placing it in a red basket and passing it behind to a second counter.

'It'll take five minutes,' she said.

Harry took a seat. He was thinking about the girls who'd left the store.

What was it that was irking him?

Were the girls worried about being judged? Found out?

In the Asian community, sex was strictly an after-marriage sort of deal.

What connects these girls, Harry?

They were all having sex.

They were all . . . *sinning.*

Harry knew the murder victims' medical records had been checked; a routine, first-line enquiry. None of them had visited the student medical practice since they'd been enrolled.

No contraceptives.

Nothing on file anyway.

'Virdee?'

Harry approached the counter, his mind racing. The pharmacist handed over Aaron's antibiotics, providing instructions on how to administer them.

'Great,' said Harry, and pointed to a consultation room. 'Could I have a word?'

'Sure.'

The two men entered the privacy of the side room.

Harry showed his identification.

Sinner.

The word was playing loudly in his mind.

'Two girls just came in here. They left because they didn't want to speak to a bloke. Is that common?' asked Harry.

'Very.' He nodded solemnly.

'So what do they do now? Keep trying pharmacies until they find a woman on shift?'

'Pretty much. I work across a few pharmacies and I've seen women travel miles from their local pharmacy to get the pill. I'm guessing they're afraid they'll be found out or recognized if they go too close to home.'

'Really?'

'Yeah. It's not just Asian women, but it's more common with them. There are a lot of Asian pharmacists in this area and it's a small community. I'm sure you don't need me to tell you that. So, they go elsewhere. Look for a white pharmacist, preferably a woman.'

'Can't the boyfriends buy it for them?'

'No. The pharmacist has to speak to the person taking it.'

'Always?'

'Absolutely. It's illegal to supply it otherwise.'

'Do the girls get it for free or have to buy it?'

'If they're under twenty-five, it's free – but only in selected pharmacies.'

'Right.'

Harry's mind was racing.

'Is there a trail? Paperwork?' asked Harry.

'Only if they've got it for free from one of the pharmacies on that scheme. If they pay, there's nothing on record.'

'Computer or paper?'

'Both.'

'If I wanted to know if a girl had taken the morning-after pill, could you tell me? Even if it wasn't supplied at this pharmacy?'

'No.'

'In your experience, what's the split of girls who get it for free and those who pay?'

'It's twenty-five quid. Under twenty-fives usually find a pharmacy where it's free, in my experience.'

'Do you have a list of pharmacies on the scheme?'

'I can print one.'

'Perfect. One other thing,' said Harry, waving the prescription bag at him. 'Says on the door you do free deliveries here? Could you get this to my kid? I've got an urgent case I need to attend to.'

The pharmacist took it from him and smiled. 'Sure.'

While he waited for the list of pharmacies on the scheme, Harry called each of the victims' boyfriends in turn.

One by one they confirmed that their girlfriends had all sought the morning-after pill.

Each girl had insisted on visiting a pharmacy out of town, one which provided it for free.

Crucially, they'd all visited the same one.

Harry gripped his hand into a fist.

He'd found it.

The clue that linked them all.

SIXTY-NINE

HARRY PULLED UP OUTSIDE Pudsey Midnight Pharmacy, dismayed that the heavy snow which had been threatening all week had finally started to fall.

The pharmacy was only a couple of miles from where he had met with Ronnie earlier, in a predominantly white area on the border between Leeds and Bradford.

Inside, one elderly patient was waiting for her prescription. The retail section was small, the usual array of goods. Bang in the centre of the wall behind the counter was a black-and-pink poster highlighting free sexual health services in the pharmacy: chlamydia and pregnancy testing and free morning-after pill for under twenty-fives.

There was nobody serving at the counter but Harry could see two staff in the back, a girl dressed casually standing next to a professional-looking white guy in his late thirties.

'Can I speak to the pharmacist, please? In a private room,' Harry asked when the assistant had come out and given the old woman her prescription.

The girl disappeared into the back and returned with the pharmacist, who was wearing a name badge that said 'Peter'.

In the consultation room, Peter explained what Harry already knew about the scheme, but was reluctant to share any paperwork.

'Data-protection laws. You'd need a warrant,' he said.

Harry sighed.

'Are you the manager here?'

Peter nodded. 'The manager and the owner.'

'Are you aware a major murder and abduction investigation is happening in Bradford, right now?'

'The politician's daughter?'

'Exactly. I'm working on that case, which is why I need to see your paperwork urgently. I'd love to do this by the book but I don't have the time to get you a warrant. I need to find Aisha before anything happens to her.'

Peter didn't know where to look.

'I already know that she obtained the morning-after pill in this pharmacy, along with four other girls, all of whom are now dead. This is the only thing which links them. That's weird, Peter. It's the kind of thing that gets alarm bells ringing.' Harry left the threat hanging in the air between them. The last thing Peter needed was for his business to suffer at the hands of the media.

'I need to see that paperwork and a list of all your staff. Noticed you've got CCTV cameras outside. How far do they go back?'

'A month.'

'I might need that data too but, for now – just the paperwork for these pills.'

Peter took a second, panic clear on his face, mulling over his options.

Eventually, he turned around and hunted on the shelf behind him. He took a tired-looking blue box-file off the shelf and handed it to Harry.

'This it?'

Peter nodded. 'All emergency contraception paperwork has to be kept together. That's a record of everyone we've given the morning-after pill to since I bought this place.'

'You keep confidential paperwork in here? Where staff have their lunches?' said Harry pointing to a bin in the corner where the remains of a microwave meal were evident.

'They're all bound by confidentiality agreements,' replied Peter defensively.

'So, a girl wants to buy the pill discreetly but it's not so discreet?'

'It is. I do the consultation and fill out the paperwork.'

'Then who sells it to them?'

'Whoever is on the counter. I have to approve the sale, but they process it.'

'You don't do it yourself?'

'Sometimes I do.'

Harry rolled his eyes.

'I'll need a list of all your staff,' said Harry again, sitting down and opening the file.

Peter left the room, quicker than he'd entered. Harry didn't allow the door to close, instead holding it open by using a heavy box of what appeared to be pharmacy bags lying on the floor. He didn't want to miss anything Peter might say to his assistant.

Harry sat at a small table, opened the file and started leafing through an enormous batch of paperwork which contained the names, addresses, GP details, current medications and allergy status of the women wanting the pill. It didn't take long for Harry to find a form which listed bee stings.

It was all here. In this blue box.

Peter returned with a list of staff employees.

'Can I have some privacy?' Peter turned to go when Harry spoke again. 'And a coffee?'

*

Nothing.

None of the victims' names were on any of the forms in the box.

'Explanation?' Peter had once again joined Harry in the side room.

'Are you sure they got it here?'

'Positive.'

'Then . . . I . . . don't know. Maybe . . . the paperwork got misplaced.'

'Are you kidding me? That's a bit convenient, isn't it?'

'I always complete the paperwork. I . . . I . . . don't get paid otherwise.'

'So, where is it?'

'I don't know.'

Had the killer removed the paperwork?

Harry grabbed the list of staff names.

One Asian name.

Adnan Aziz.

'This guy,' said Harry, pointing at the name. 'Who is he?'

'My driver. He delivers prescriptions.'

'How long's he worked for you?'

'Since the start.'

'Full time?'

'Yeah.'

'Does he have his lunch in here?'

Peter nodded.

'What's he like, Adnan?'

'Adi's a good worker; quiet, keeps himself to himself.'

Adi, the name the killer had given on the radio.

'He been at work today?' asked Harry.

'No. He's been off sick all week.'

Harry's eyes widened.

'Really? Usual for him?'

'No. First time.'

'What's he like?'

Peter shrugged. Harry could sense he'd alerted him to the fact Adnan was a person of interest. 'He's quiet. Works hard.'

'Get on with everyone?'

'Keeps himself to himself.'

'Anything unusual about him? Extreme views?'

'Like terrorism?'

'Anything that strikes you as odd.'

'No. He . . . he's just a regular bloke. He listens to music, he's into gardening.'

Harry started to collect the papers he'd looked through.

'I guess there's one . . .'

'What?' Harry asked, alert.

'Well, he has a strange hobby.'

Harry waited, expectant.

'He keeps wasps as pets.'

SEVENTY

EN ROUTE TO ADNAN'S address, Harry called Conway. When she didn't answer, he tried Palmer.

'Harry?'

'We've got him!' said Harry, focusing hard on the road where snow was starting to set. He informed Palmer of what he had discovered.

'Get armed police there, liaise with—'

'Whoa, whoa, Harry, we're on our way to pick up Gurpal Singh. Got concrete intel where he is. Conway has everyone on it.'

'She's wrong! Is she there?'

There was a muffled noise on the phone, then Conway's voice.

Harry repeated what he had just told Palmer.

'You need to pull it, Clare. This is our guy. I need armed—'

'Harry, you know that we need Gurpal. We *have* to make this arrest.'

'Fine,' snapped Harry, 'but send me a squad too. I'm telling you, this is our guy. I'm certain.'

Conway dropped her voice, steely as ever. 'I cannot pull an operation like this when we've been looking for this guy for ninety-six hours, Harry. You know that. If you're wrong—'

'Goddamn it, Clare, I'm not!' shouted Harry and slammed his hand on the steering wheel, the car losing traction in the snow.

'Both armed response teams are in Keighley, Harry. Even if I dispatched one to you now, in this weather it would take them easily over an hour. We're all set to take Gurpal down.'

'Send me my team at least then,' said Harry. 'I'm going after this guy, with or without backup.'

Another muffled noise on the phone, then Palmer's voice, strained, under duress.

'Harry?'

'Leave. She's got enough men on this.'

Harry gave Palmer the address.

'How quick can you make it?'

'Shit, I don't know. In this weather? I'm on my way to you, Conway's released me. But it's just me, Harry.'

Harry gave him the address, told him to get a couple of squad cars there too and hung up the phone.

Harry parked two hundred yards from Adnan's home, the snow now blizzard-like. He was on Folkestone Street, off Killinghall Road, a densely populated Asian area of the city. Opposite the house, the grand Madni Jamia mosque's towering green dome watched over Harry as he exited the car, opened his boot and grabbed his crowbar.

Harry slipped the crowbar up his sleeve, the curve of the metal U-bend concealed in his palm.

He paused.

Don't do this alone.

Wait for Palmer.

Four dead girls.

Aisha's life at stake.

Harry walked towards the house.

It was an end-of-terrace with a snicket running down the side. Harry went around the back. All the curtains were drawn.

He lifted the lid on a black council bin and pulled out the one black bag inside. He carried it down the side of the house, tore it open and emptied the contents on to the floor, spoiling the unbroken snow.

Charred paper. Torn to shreds, only partially burned.

BT phone bills.

Only one number, called repeatedly.

He sifted through usual household shit, a repugnant mix of eggs, onions and takeaway curries, and found a scrunched-up DIY receipt.

Harry unravelled it.

Tornado 2-ply 2mm high tensile barbed wire. 200m. £34.99.

Harry held his breath.

He put the scrap of paper in his pocket and hurried to the rear of the property. He texted Palmer what he had found, urged him again to get Conway to send reinforcements and informed him he was going in.

If Aisha Islam was inside, Harry needed to get to her as soon as he could.

Harry knocked loudly on the rickety wooden door, both panes of glass were cracked.

He closed his fist around the crowbar.

Harry kept looking at the windows, looking for any movement.

He knocked again.

When there was still no response, he placed his elbow on to the pane and pushed firmly. The glass crumbled. He slipped his hand carefully into the gap and unlocked the door.

Inside, Harry crept through the ground floor, crowbar now in hand.

Empty.

Nothing remarkable.

Upstairs was the same.

Three doors, all open.

Harry cleared the rooms quickly, two bedrooms and a bathroom.

Nothing sinister.

He was alone.

It didn't look like Adnan had been here for a few days. He had time.

Harry hurriedly searched both rooms. The first appeared to belong to Adnan's mother, although it was heavy with dust. She might have died recently. Had that been the catalyst for all this?

The other bedroom was Adnan's. Harry turned it upside down. *Wardrobes, desk, bed.*

On the inside of the wardrobe door, Harry was shocked to find photos of an Asian wedding. Two empty bride-and-groom thrones.

A large marquee in a picturesque garden.

It didn't look like England.

Harry plucked a wedding invitation from among the photos.

Adnan Aziz & . . .

The bride's name had been torn out.

The rest of the photos showed hundreds of people in and around the marquee.

The other side of the door had large stencil-drawings of wasps, their larvae, some calm, others frightening. Looking at them, Harry felt afraid. There was so much anger in them, a dormant rage which was clearly now being explored.

At the back of the wardrobe, Harry found a key attached to a metal fob.

All. 18. Spare.

An allotment key.

Harry breathed a sigh of relief.

If found, please return to the warden at Lister Mills allotments.

Harry closed the wardrobe and hurried back downstairs.

He knew where Aisha Islam was.

SEVENTY-ONE

HARRY PARKED HIS CAR at the allotments. The journey had been frustrating, traffic backed up for miles, accidents in their dozens, the snow causing chaos.

He glanced at the thickening layer of snow on the ground.

Harry couldn't go charging in, he needed to know as much as possible about this guy first.

He called Palmer but he was still a good forty minutes away, thanks to the gridlock on the roads.

Harry phoned the duty sergeant at Trafalgar House demanding two squad cars urgently. Between the major operation to apprehend Gurpal Singh and dozens of accidents dotted around the city, resources were stretched. Yet he heard the urgency in Harry's voice and told him he would get patrols there as a priority.

For now, Harry waited. He needed backup. He removed the BT bill from his pocket and dialled the only number Adnan seemed to call.

'Golden Age Care Home, how can I help you?' said a female voice.

It caught Harry off-guard.

'Hello?' repeated the voice.

'Hi,' said Harry, searching for his best opening to get information without policy and procedure weighing him down.

'This is Adnan Aziz calling,' said Harry, trying his best to imitate how Adnan spoke.

'Mr Aziz,' said the voice firmly, and clearly exacerbated, 'as I have told you several times today, your mother is fine. She ate the food you left for her and as usual, we have washed her, given her some milk and she is ready for bed.'

Whoever was speaking was not a fan of Adnan's.

'Thanks,' said Harry, searching for something else which might give him more information.

'I'm sorry I call you so much.'

'You do need to trust us, Mr Aziz. We are a specialist dementia care home and know exactly how to care for your mother.'

Harry thanked her for her time and hung up. He thought of the second dusty bedroom in Adnan's house. Seemed he was having some detachment issues. Harry called Palmer and Trafalgar House again, and again was given the same information.

He hung up.

'I can't fucking wait,' he hissed. 'Aisha might be dead by then.'

Harry took the crowbar with him and left the car, one final text to Palmer telling him where he was heading.

Lister Mills overlooked the allotments. Even as the snow blizzarded around him, he could see the penthouse pods on top of the mill and the balcony where he'd stood only two nights ago once they'd realized Aisha Islam was missing. They'd been *so* close, if only they'd known.

Harry passed through a set of stone pillars, into an overgrown wasteland, wishing he had proper walking boots on. The path was treacherous, snow causing his feet to slide. He kept his torch off, not wanting to announce his arrival.

The falling snow created an absence of noise, a tranquillity which seemed out of place in the clear abandonment of the allotment.

Harry reached a row of ramshackle wooden sheds at the bottom of the field. They appeared desolate; ruins of a once thriving allotment community. Hanging on the doorways, decaying numbers marked each one.

Harry stopped outside number eighteen.

Something was wrong.

Something was off.

He'd been so confident he'd find Aisha here, but now he wasn't so sure.

He pushed at the door, feeling the snow icy on his hands. Flakes of snow dropped on to his neck, icy water now sliding down his back, a welcome relief from the burning sensation in his mind. Harry slipped the key he'd taken from Adnan's house inside the lock. He backed off, raised the crowbar and pushed the door open. He swung his torch over the room.

Nothing.

It was empty.

Harry had been holding his breath and now let it out.

This had to be it.

Had to be.

Harry took another scan around the allotment, then stepped inside, keeping the crowbar in front of him.

Completely empty.

Cobwebs, broken plant-pots, two bags of soil and a large metal pole.

Dead end.

Harry noticed the shiny tip of the metal pole. The rest was crusted in orange rust but the tip glistened like new.

Harry shone his torch along the floor.

There.

A slab, maybe a metre square. He moved towards it and tried to push his fingers into the crevices surrounding it but couldn't.

He glanced around the room.

Harry grabbed the pole and pushed the shiny end into one of the corners and leaned on it, using his weight to lift one side several inches. He pushed the pole further, wedging it between the slab and the ground, then used his hands to move it aside.

Damn thing was heavy.

Harry stared down into a dark black pit.

He thought about where he was.

Lister Mills.

The most impressive mill in Bradford. Back in the war, it had an underground network of air-raid shelters built to protect the workers.

He removed his phone, the cheap Nokia burner, to update Conway and force her to pull the bullshit operation in Keighley.

No reception.

Harry turned to go back outside.

That's when he heard it.

A scream.

Agonized and frightened.

He froze.

Harry shone his torch down into the hole.

He could just make out a passageway.

Another scream.

Harry moved quickly, unthinkingly. He lowered himself into the bunker. Once inside, he raised the crowbar and used the torch to illuminate the way, creeping forwards. He could hear water running down the cracks in the walls and the damp stuck to his skin.

He was more afraid then he had ever been.

He reached a bend in the passageway and suddenly saw Aisha Islam, strapped to a chair, her gag lowered. Harry moved towards her just as she screamed,

'No!'

Harry hardly had time to register the punishing blow of a steel bar.

He thundered to the ground, unconscious before he hit it.

SEVENTY-TWO

HARRY CAME TO, LYING on the floor in the dark, the deafening sound of buzzing in his ears.

Wasps.

The sound was unmistakable. He fucking hated wasps.

In the distance, he could hear a voice, calling his name.

Palmer?

Harry didn't move, head on the ground, eyes towards the floor. He still held the torch in one hand, crowbar in the other.

The wasps were noisily circling his body. Every so often, he felt one of them brush past the back of his head.

Was he bleeding?

Were they drawn to the blood?

Harry wanted to panic.

Was the bastard here? Watching, waiting for him to make a move so he could pounce?

He felt one land on the back of his neck.

Harry froze. Held his breath.

The tickle of its tiny legs.

He thought about what the entomologist had said: *'Once they're born, Harry, they only eat nectar.'*

Harry didn't feel reassured. He stayed perfectly still for as long as he could, relieved when it flew away.

He had to get out of here.

Harry started crawling in the dark, but he had no idea where he was or which direction he'd come from.

He had to use the torch.

Even if this wasn't a trap, he'd never get out without the torch.

The buzzing was constant, how many of the little bastards were in here?

He could hear shouting from somewhere.

Keeping his face to the floor, Harry let go of the crowbar and covered the torch lens with his free hand. He switched it on, his hand absorbing the light but providing just enough illumination to give him a fleeting glance ahead.

The corridor was there.

Nothing else.

Harry switched the torch off, got on his hands and knees and went for it.

He crawled quicker than he thought possible, eating up the ground, turning right when he hit a wall.

The sound of wasps didn't stop.

Claustrophobia started its treacherous assault as Harry hurried down the passageway, he could now clearly hear Palmer's voice.

At the end of the corridor, Harry looked up to see Palmer, crouching above the hatch, face pained with concern.

A wasp flew towards him. Startled, Palmer moved away, cursing.

Harry got to his feet and hurried up the ladder.

Palmer helped him out of the hatch.

'Christ, Harry, are you okay?'

Harry pointed to the hatch. 'Close it,' he said, patting his body down, paranoid a wasp had become trapped within his clothing. He spied a couple on the snow-covered windows of the hut.

'Shit, you're bleeding,' said Palmer, lowering the hatch.

Harry touched the back of his head and felt warm, sticky blood. The world was spinning in front of his eyes.

He dropped to one knee.

'Bastard was here. With Aisha. Did you see anything?'

'Are you all right, boss?'

'Did you see anything?' snapped Harry.

'Just two sets of footprints in the snow, leading away from here to the road.'

Harry checked the time. He'd been out of it for thirty minutes.

'When did you arrive?'

'Few minutes ago. Bloody snow played havoc with the roads.'

'Armed police?' asked Harry looking up at Palmer.

He shook his head. 'Still in Keighley. One unit is now en route.'

'Too fucking late. They got Gurpal?'

Palmer nodded.

'Wrong guy. I told Conway!'

'She had to make that call, Harry.'

'Yeah, she made the wrong one.'

Harry stood up, touching the back of his head again. 'Have a look, will you?'

Palmer moved behind Harry. 'Skin's broken. Wound doesn't look deep. How's your head?'

'Like there's a fucking wasp inside, attacking my brain.'

Harry headed for the door. 'Come on, we don't have much time.'

Inside his car, Harry let Palmer drive. He called Conway, who sounded sheepish and concerned in equal measure.

'He's called us, Harry.'

'What? When?'

'Few minutes ago. Spoke with me. Told me what happened.'

'And?'

'Adnan wants to give himself up and end this. He knows his

time is up. It's happening in the next ninety minutes. In City Park. By the fountains.'

'What?' said Harry utterly perplexed.

'Get down to Trafalgar House. We've a briefing set up. It's all in play, but we need you.'

Harry checked his watch: 21:00.

'You're telling me he wants to end all this? Just like that?'

'Yes. With two specific instructions.'

Harry waited for the sting in the tail.

'Go on.'

'He'll only hand the girl over to you.'

Harry thought about his clash with the killer: *he'd been at his mercy.*

It didn't make sense.

'What's the second?' said Harry.

Conway paused. Harry heard her take a breath. 'He wants the handover televised.'

SEVENTY-THREE

GOLDEN AGE CARE HOME is not the place I envisaged my mother spending her last days. The dementia she has developed is a result of the shame and dishonour we all suffered. Ever since that fateful day, her mind has tried to erase what happened. For years, I thought of doing what I have done this week. But she would have suffered even more. Now, with her time close to an end, she will not have to endure the consequences of my actions. Her descent into the final stages of this disease has finally released me to unleash a plan years in the making. I am grateful she cannot remember the night which started all this. The night when the guests whispered about what had happened, their tongues like knives, slicing at our misfortune.

We thought when we arrived in this country, things would change. They did not.

I've left the girl bound in the car. In an hour's time, once I leave, the finale will be in sight.

It won't be forgotten, as I was.

Instead, my message will be whispered in homes throughout

the city: 'This is what happens to sinners when they stray from the path . . .'

Fear will replace complacency.

She likes me to put her to bed and I have done so every night since she was admitted.

Tomorrow, I will not.

'Ma,' I whisper, lifting her from the wheelchair and placing her into bed, 'I must go now.'

My grief at leaving is real.

I make sure my mother is comfortable, the pillow behind her head, the duvet underneath her chin and a second bedsheet tucked around her feet so they do not get cold in the middle of the night, because here, unlike when she lived with me, nobody will come to check.

I kiss her forehead, squeeze her hand, knowing it will never happen again, and turn to leave.

The time has arrived.

I am coming for you, Harry.

SEVENTY-FOUR

HARRY HAD NEVER KNOWN chaos like it.

The briefing room was in disarray, dozens of micro-conversations taking place.

Harry was outside, speaking discreetly with Conway. With the Chief Constable, the top officer in Yorkshire and all three assistant chief constables now in the building, her decisions were being scrutinized, but she stood firm. She'd made a call based on the intel available to her. And they had been searching for Gurpal Singh as their primary focus of interest.

'What was his story?' asked Harry.

'Gurpal had been with one of the strippers who worked in his brother's club. An old flame. They were off the grid, coked-up for a few days of debauchery. When she saw the news alert, she contacted us, afraid. Plain sailing after that.'

Harry sighed, observing the drama unfolding in the briefing room. Men in suits flapping around Tariq Islam.

Eyes darting towards him, everyone wondering the same thing: *What linked Adnan to Harry?* Now they had his details, Adnan's life was being torn apart.

Nothing – absolutely nothing – linked him to Harry.

'Nothing triggers with you?' asked Conway.

Harry shook his head. 'Never met the guy. Don't know him.'

Conway kicked at the door of the briefing room, frustrated. Harry could see her remorse at not following his lead. 'He knows you,' she said.

'At least, he thinks he does.' Harry nodded towards the briefing room. 'Come on, let's see what Whitehall and the BBC have agreed.'

'City Park is being cleared at the moment,' said Conway to Harry. 'Armed crime tactical team, complete with snipers, standing by.'

'So, we're all set,' said Harry accepting a blister pack of paracetamol from one of the suits. His head was banging.

'No,' said Conway. 'Whitehall is still in discussion with the BBC.'

'We cannot televise this exchange,' said Harry glancing at the power-players in the room. 'Guy's a nutjob. Since when has it been policy to allow the kidnapper, or killer in this case, to dictate the terms of a handover?'

'Since he took my daughter,' said Tariq.

'Look,' said Harry, dry-swallowing two tablets, 'I know what is at stake. We all do. But there's no way he gets a global TV audience. It's unheard of.'

'It's not. There is a precedent.'

Harry stared at Tariq, incredulous. 'This is a serial killer.'

'Who might kill again, if we don't comply with his request,' said Conway.

Harry stared at her in disbelief. 'Request? Or demand?'

The Chief Constable looked like he'd aged a year in the space of a few hours. He didn't say a word. Beside him, men in suits – MI5, Harry assumed – remained silent, watching the discussion.

'Whitehall and the BBC will make the call,' said Conway.

'It's not happening,' said Harry shaking his head.

'They're suggesting a six-second delay. We block the broadcast to the rest of the UK. Only West Yorkshire gets the live transmission,' said Conway.

They were actually considering this.

'You're kidding? Right?' said Harry.

'These are extraordinary circumstances, Harry,' said Tariq. 'The question is, if we get the green light, are you willing to do this?'

Harry looked at the glib faces in the room.

He couldn't believe this.

'Run me through it,' said Harry.

'Adnan wants Manchester Road cleared. He'll be driving a white Volvo Estate, approaching via Jacobs Well and taking the right into Hallings, by City Park. If we stop the car, he'll kill the girl. He said he'll be streaming BBC iPlayer to check we are live – which is good for us because it makes the transmission delay easier, should Whitehall get the BBC on board. We'll have snipers at five strategic locations: Town Hall, the court building, the Wool Exchange, Bradford Hotel and St George's Hall. Armed police units yards from you and two surveillance teams in the vicinity. The exchange is set for ten p.m.'

Harry closed his eyes and massaged his temple.

'God, you're really serious,' he said.

'We've a chance to end this. With no further loss of life,' said Conway.

'He said that?'

'Yes.'

'And you believe him? After what just happened with me?'

'Especially after what just happened with you. It sounds like he had his chance to kill you and Aisha. Yet, he didn't. Perhaps you've finally made him see his only way out of this is to surrender.'

'You don't believe that any more than I do, Clare. We're handing him a huge card to play here. A sensationalist murder on live TV.'

Tariq came across and put his hands on Harry's shoulders. 'I've said my piece to the people who will ultimately make this decision. With a six-second delay, snipers and armed police, we have a chance.'

He put his hands together, as if in prayer. 'If we walk away from this and my daughter dies, we will always ask ourselves . . .' Tariq turned and spoke to the whole room: 'Might we have saved her if we had done what he asked? What if? That is not something I want to live with. Do you?'

Harry closed his eyes, trying to find some clarity in the madness.

The look of terror on Aisha's face in the moment Harry had seen her.

'Okay,' he said, knowing Tariq was right. Harry didn't want to live with the 'What if'.

'I'm in,' he said.

SEVENTY-FIVE

HARRY WAS STANDING ON the top floor of Trafalgar House, staring into the distance where an enormous police presence was clearing City Park and a radius of half a kilometre around it. Flashing lights, barricades, the sweep of a police helicopter, all that activity made a stark contrast to the beautiful, calming allure of snowfall. The ground was white in all directions, now at least half an inch thick.

Harry imagined the two-man sniper teams, positioning themselves on the roof of the five buildings Conway had spoken of. Going through their briefings, all of them wondering if they might have to pull the trigger.

The horrifying splatter of red blood on crisp unbroken snow.

Who'd be making the call to shoot?

The door to the corner office opened and Tariq Islam stepped into the room, closing the door behind.

'Keep the lights off,' said Harry, turning back to the window.

Tariq arrived by his side, both of them staring at the snowfall.

'First snowfall of the year,' said Tariq. 'Beautiful.'

'It should be. But tonight, it isn't.'

'How's your head?'

'Doc says I'll live. If I start throwing up or feeling faint, I'm in trouble. Concussion. A&E job.'

'We're on. BBC director general has spoken with Whitehall. Eight-second delay, any more and the killer might realize we're buffering. Transmission only goes to West Yorkshire. No warnings to the public.'

'What about all the mess down there?' Harry nodded towards the park.

'They're being told it's a gas leak. No real panic. Just to leave the area.'

Harry checked his watch. 'Thirty minutes to go. I'll need to get to the incident room. Get wired up.'

'Conway tells me you'll be carrying a weapon.'

'That's *my* condition. Bastard got the better of me once. Likelihood is I won't need it. We've enough snipers and armed police in the area. But it makes me feel like I've an added advantage.'

'It was brave what you did tonight. For Aisha.'

'Brave or stupid, not so sure.'

'Does your wife know what you're about to do?' asked Tariq.

Harry nodded slightly. 'It's being broadcast in West Yorkshire. If she saw it and I hadn't told her, she'd kill me herself.'

'How did she take it?'

'Not well. She's probably praying as we speak.'

'Harry, can I ask you something?'

Tariq turned to face him, leaning against the office window.

'Adnan Aziz; nothing shows up on any databases. He's been in the UK ten years, got married to a local Bradford girl who died in a car accident . . .'

'I know,' said Harry who had seen the file. 'I don't know him, Tariq.'

'So why pick *you* to do this?'

'No fucking idea,' said Harry. 'Maybe we're about to find out.'

SEVENTY-SIX

THE SNOW WAS FALLING heavier now, perfectly blanketing City Park.

Unbroken.

The white unblemished landscape all around Harry was calming. All that purity, along with the deafening silence only falling snow could bring. Harry closed his eyes. The snow reminded him of Saima.

Lister Park.

Arms around each other.

Dancing in the snow.

Cold faces, warm lips.

One of their earliest dates.

Harry opened his eyes and checked his watch: 22:00.

Showtime.

He closed his eyes and slowed his breathing. He hoped Saima wasn't watching, but knew she would be. Any nerves he felt were really for her, it was hard not to feel safe with ten snipers watching his back.

His hand was drawn to the firearm holstered at his waist, tucked beside his bulletproof vest.

Even though he was weapons trained, he had never fired an active round in his career. All the same, he felt more secure with the gun at his side.

City Park was deserted. The water fountains were still. There was a peace to the scene, just the quiet, cool breeze and the falling snow. On any other night, it would have been spellbinding.

Harry had a microphone in his ear, the surveillance team giving him real-time updates, everyone wondering if the killer was going to show or if they'd been played for fools.

'Harry,' said Conway, her voice clear in his ear. 'He's on the line. I'm patching you in.'

There was a brief delay, then the killer's voice.

'Detective Virdee?' he asked.

'I'm here,' said Harry.

The line went dead.

'He's gone, Harry.'

'Got that, cheers. How's everything your end? As peachy as mine?'

'What's got you so chipper?' said Conway.

'This guy got me once. Won't happen a second time. Not on live TV anyway. We're not on yet? Right?'

'No. If he arrives, the BBC will change their regular feed in West Yorkshire with the delay. Cameraman is on the roof behind you.'

Eight seconds to pull the transmission if it all went sour.

Harry was aware senior politicians in Westminster were viewing the footage, watching it live, without the delay.

What a goddamn situation to become a celebrity in, he thought.

'Stations, everyone,' Harry heard in his ear. 'We've got him on Manchester Road. A mile and closing.'

Harry took a breath. For the second time that evening, Adnan had Harry in unfamiliar territory.

Afraid.

'He's at the roundabout, Harry. Turning right.'

Harry was trying to calm his heart rate.

'Car approaching, Harry,' said Conway.

'Got him.'

'BBC transmission is now up.'

Harry focused on the car. Calmly, serenely, the snow continued to fall.

His earpiece fell silent.

They would have switched to another channel.

Leaving him to focus on the exchange.

He waited, hand nervously twitching near his firearm.

The Volvo pulled up, killed its engine.

It stayed where it was, snow continuing to fall on the windscreen.

Slowly, the passenger-side door opened.

Harry braced himself, ready.

Aisha got out wearing a flimsy red sari, her arms, stomach and chest exposed to the snow which quickly chequered her body. Harry could see she was gagged, blindfolded and wearing ear-protectors.

She hesitated by the car, unable to move.

Adnan climbed out of the passenger door behind her.

He wore a traditional Asian tunic, thin against the wind, and a beanie.

No thick jacket or obvious explosive belt.

Adnan kept close to Aisha, holding a knife up near her throat but not across it.

'I've got eyes on Aisha and Adnan,' said Harry, his hands shaking with adrenaline. 'No obvious threat. Be prepared for anything now. This guy is not to be underestimated.'

They began a slow walk towards Harry, mindful of slipping on the snow.

From all four corners of City Park, Harry envisaged the scope of rifles fixed on Adnan's head.

Harry started walking, closing the gap.

They met halfway, by the dormant water fountains, stopping a few metres apart.

Adnan smiled. Aisha was holding an iPhone, streaming live BBC iPlayer.

With the eight-second delay.

Adnan seemed unfazed.

'You really don't know who I am, do you?'

'No,' said Harry. 'I just want the girl. Nobody needs to get hurt here.'

'There are armed police, here? Right? Snipers on the roof? The whole business?' said Adnan, excited.

'This can all end peacefully,' Harry said carefully.

'You're carrying a gun,' said Adnan, nodding towards it. 'Point it at me.'

'There's no need,' said Harry, but his hand twitched for it.

Slowly, Adnan waved the knife at Harry. Very slowly. He wasn't stupid. Knew the snipers would have itchy fingers.

'I say. You do. Now point your gun at me.'

Harry breathed out deeply, his breath white in the freezing air.

'Do it, Harry,' said Conway's voice in his ear.

Harry unholstered his pistol and pointed it at Adnan's head.

'Now that microphone on your chest,' said Adnan. 'Throw it in the fountain.'

'Aisha,' said Harry. 'First, let me get her to safety.'

Adnan shook his head. The knife wavered again in his hands.

Harry braced for a shot from a sniper. He tensed his own hand around the gun, finger on the trigger.

If he fired now, he'd save the girl.

But Adnan had always been one step ahead. Harry couldn't shoot him now, there was no way to know what contingency plan he might have in place.

'Do as I say, Harry.'

'Why?'

'Because I want to tell you something. Just between us.'

'If I remove the microphone, you need to release Aisha.'

'Okay.'

Harry tried to figure out if Adnan was bluffing. Slowly, he reached his left hand up to his chest, keeping his gun trained on Adnan.

'There,' said Harry. 'Now let her go.'

As promised, Adnan dropped the knife, released Aisha into Harry's arms and raised his hands in surrender. Harry grabbed Aisha with his free hand, never letting his gun drop.

Quickly, eyes darting between her and Adnan, he tugged at her blindfold and removed the ear protectors from her head.

It was her, she appeared fine. He pushed her behind him.

'On the ground,' shouted Harry, turning back to Adnan. 'Now!'

Officers rushed forward from their lookout spots, weapons raised.

This was too easy.

Harry felt a creeping sense of dread at the back of his neck.

Adnan stepped forward, closer to Harry's gun.

'Back down!' shouted Harry. 'On the ground! Now!'

Adnan smiled. 'Harry, this is all I wanted.'

Harry put a hand behind him, reaching for Aisha, pushing her away.

'Walk away, Aisha, slowly. Someone will come for you.'

She didn't hesitate.

'You really don't know who I am, do you?' said Adnan.

Armed officers were getting closer, guns trained on Adnan. Fifteen feet away.

Adnan looked around, bemused at the activity, a helicopter now swooping overhead, police at every corner of City Park.

'The snow is beautiful,' said Adnan, blinking it out of his eyes. 'I couldn't have asked for a better setting.'

Harry didn't like the look on his face.

'What for?' Harry asked.

'Tell me,' said Adnan, smiling now, 'do you know where your wife and child are?'

Harry's hand tightened on the pistol. His eyes narrowed and he searched Adnan's face.

'I know exactly where they are,' said Harry.

Adnan nodded. 'At Nadia's house.'

He smiled again.

Harry's eyes widened involuntarily.

'Bullshit,' he said, but his stomach clenched in fear.

'You see,' said Adnan, getting on his knees, holding his hands up in surrender. 'Nadia's husband is my brother. And that wife of yours was never yours to have. She was mine. She should have been mine.'

Harry heard a shout from an officer behind him but he couldn't make out the words.

He could only hear Adnan.

'If you tell your police friends that I have them, that my brother has them, they'll die. So, you see,' said Adnan, finally lying on the ground, 'Saima and Aaron's only hope is *me*. What are you prepared to do to see them again?'

SEVENTY-SEVEN

ON THE TELEVISION SCREEN, the camera zoomed for a close-up.

Unmistakable.

Adnan Aziz.

Saima would have known him anywhere.

The transmission cut.

This was personal.

Harry had known all along that it was, but she'd never thought it was about them.

Saima stood quickly, needing to check on Aaron. She needed to get to the police station. But she found Imran standing in the living room doorway, Aaron slung over his shoulder, half-asleep, drowsy, his face flushed where the fever from his chest infection was raging.

'What are you doing?' she snapped, stepping forward to take her son into her arms.

She stopped when she saw the blade in Imran's hand.

Nadia was out at the mosque at the all-night prayers. Saima was alone with Imran.

'Did you think you could do this to us?' he hissed. 'Ruin my brother, my family, dishonour us all and there would be no consequences?'

'What? Please, give me my son, look at him, he's not well.'

Imran placed Aaron on the couch, gently laying him down. Saima lunged for the knife but Imran struck her hard, the back of his hand like a rock against her cheek.

Saima flew across the room, tripped over the coffee table and hit the floor clumsily.

Pain in her side.

Blood in her mouth.

She raised her head to see Aaron asleep on the couch and searched the room desperately for a weapon.

Imran grabbed her by the hair, dragging her across the room and into the kitchen. Saima didn't scream, she wouldn't wake Aaron, he would not witness whatever was about to happen.

In the kitchen, Imran tried to bind her hands together. Saima resisted, trying to claw at his face with her nails.

Imran slapped her again.

'You bitch, you stay still or I'll go in there and hurt your boy.'

Imran grabbed her by the neck, squeezing her throat.

'You understand?' he hissed, eyes wide, lips curling.

Saima immediately went limp, afraid more for Aaron than for herself.

Imran roughly taped her hands together and yanked Saima to her feet.

'Now, we go for a drive. If you make a sound, do anything stupid, then it is not you but the boy who gets hurt.'

He grabbed her by the throat again, 'You understand?'

Saima nodded, the edges of her vision blurring.

Again, she tasted blood in her mouth.

Imran raised the knife to her throat. 'One wrong move and I slit the boy's throat. Then I'll leave you alive so you'll always know it was *your* fault.'

'Please,' she said. 'Don't hurt him. I'll do anything you want.'

'Good,' said Imran, shoving her towards the door. 'Now, move.'

SEVENTY-EIGHT

HARRY WATCHED ADNAN BEING escorted to a police van, his hands forensically bagged, surrounded by armed officers.

He had to be bluffing.

Aisha Islam had been taken away. Harry was sure that her reunion with her father would have been an emotional one.

Overhead, the helicopter continued to circle City Park.

Conway was rushing around, unable to keep the smile off her face. This was the biggest thing they'd faced in their careers. And as far as Conway was concerned, they'd nailed it.

Do you know where your wife and child are?

Harry dialled Nadia's home.

Six rings.

Eleven.

Conway reached him and Harry put out his hand,

'Just phoning Saima. Telling her I'm all right. Give me two?'

She nodded, put her arm on Harry's shoulder and squeezed it tightly. 'Great job, Harry,' she said, beaming.

Harry turned away.

'Fuck,' he muttered to himself.

How was this possible?

The confidence in Adnan's voice.

Harry dialled again.

Nothing.

He looked towards Adnan being escorted into custody.

Safe from Harry.

'Holy shit, this isn't happening,' whispered Harry, running his hand across his face, wiping the snow clear. He observed the high-fives of his team, the embraces, the jubilation of an operation carried out well.

Do you know where your wife and child are?

If he told Conway what Adnan had said, Harry would never get close enough to him to find out what the fuck was happening. He was under police protection now, and Adnan's lawyer would never let Harry get in front of him.

He hurried towards Conway.

'Listen, just got a call from the hospital. Old man's surgery didn't go so well. I need to get there. Fast. Can you deal with things here?'

'Of course, Harry,' she said, still clearly elated their operation had gone so smoothly and Tariq Islam had his daughter back safely.

He started to walk away.

'Harry?' she said, walking quickly towards him.

He stopped.

'Your firearm? I'll take it back in,' she said.

Fifteen frantic minutes of hazardous driving, losing his traction on the snowy roads several times, and Harry finally arrived at Nadia's house on Great Horton Road.

He tore up the footpath and went straight for the door.

Unlocked.

Harry stepped inside.

'Saima!' he called out, rushing through the house. He cleared all the rooms in under a minute.

Empty.

'This isn't happening,' he said, unable to think, unable to breathe.

In the living room, on an old coffee table, the only thing in the room was a plain white envelope.

Harry snatched it.

A wedding invitation.

Adnan Aziz & Saima Hayat.

An invitation to a wedding eighteen years ago.

Saima would have been only seventeen.

It had to be a mistake.

Saima would have told Harry.

He looked around the empty house.

He'd spoken to Saima only an hour and a half before. Whatever happened here had happened recently, they couldn't be that far ahead of him.

He couldn't tell the powers that be. He wouldn't take the risk that Adnan had been bluffing about that.

He needed Adnan out of prison.

Fuck.

He was in custody in Trafalgar House and there was simply no way Harry was going to get him out of there.

'Shit,' said Harry, trying hard not to panic.

Nothing made sense.

Only one thing Harry was certain of.

He had to get to Adnan.

SEVENTY-NINE

ADNAN HAD BEEN PROCESSED, fingerprints and photos taken. His clothes had been removed and bagged and a doctor had examined him before he'd been sent into the basement prison cells of Trafalgar House.

The station was still buzzing in the wake of bringing him in and rescuing Aisha. On the upper floors, statements were being drafted, officers debriefed. Tariq and Aisha were at Bradford Royal Infirmary where she would spend the night, no doubt surrounded by Tariq's close-protection unit.

Harry approached the duty sergeant, Kevin.

'People are talking about a big promotion for you after tonight, mate. You really held it all together. Especially after what that animal put you through this week.'

'Tell me about it,' said Harry. 'Listen, before the lawyers get here and we get into due-process, I want a few minutes with him. Just the two of us.'

Kevin frowned. 'Shit, Harry, I don't know. There's breaking procedure and there's doing that.'

'Five minutes. Ten at the most, mate. Come on. Like you said, after what he's put me through this week? I just need to know, why me? Help me sleep a bit easier.'

Kevin nodded slowly.

'I'm trusting you, Harry, yeah?'

'Relax, I'm not about to give the most high-profile prick we've ever caught a reason to file a claim against us.'

Harry set off, then paused. 'One thing – is Gurpal down there too?'

Kevin shook his head. 'We let him go, Harry.'

In the gloom of the basement, Harry walked along the row of prison cells until he reached the last one. Adnan was sitting cross-legged on the floor, his back against the wall. He smiled when he saw Harry.

'I've been waiting for you,' he said.

Harry unlocked the cell and charged at him, grabbing him by the scruff of the neck and yanking him to his feet.

'Harry, you're so predictable,' Adnan laughed.

'Where are they?' hissed Harry. 'I'll fucking nail you to this wall.'

'No. You can't.'

Harry let him go and threw the wedding invitation after him.

'You've got the wrong girl. The wrong guy.'

Adnan let the invitation fall to the ground.

'Where are they?' said Harry. 'You think I won't kill you?'

'Not in here, you won't. You'd never get away with it. Why do you think I handed myself in? I'm in the safest place in the world.'

He smiled again.

Harry wanted to rip his face off, anger boiling in every part of his body.

'What the fuck are you?' he said, taking a step back, looking for an angle, knowing he had none.

'What do you want? Money? A way out of here?'

'I want to ruin you.'

'Why?'

'You took something from me.'

Harry pointed to the invitation on the floor.

'Explain it.'

'The marriage was agreed the moment Saima was born, between *our* families. She is my second cousin. *It is our way.* As it has always been. You know that, Harry.'

'Bullshit.'

'We exchanged our vows over the phone when she was seventeen. But she never got on the plane to come to the ceremony.'

Harry thought about the pictures he'd seen at Adnan's house. The wedding venue. The empty thrones.

He thought about the victims killed this week.

The clues.

'If she never got on the plane then the marriage never took place,' spat Harry, entertaining the sick fantasy.

Adnan smiled again. 'You are so foolish. We said our vows, Harry. Our Nikah. I don't care about the formalities, she made a commitment to me. She married me and then she left. She ruined my family. My father died. When I told you earlier that you had killed somebody, I was referring to him. The shame you and Saima caused. He could not take it. My mother fell ill. I came here to make things right but I found a world of sin. I realized you were the real problem. You took something which belonged to me.'

'You depraved prick! I didn't even know Saima when she was seventeen.'

'As if I would believe anything you say.'

'Where is she?'

'You'll never find her.'

Harry grabbed him again, pinned him against the wall, desperate to inflict as much damage as he could on him.

'Do it,' said Adnan. 'Kill me, *ruin yourself.* Because I'm not going to say any of this until I'm in court. Until I've got the media where I want them, and then I'm going to tell them the whole story and lay the blame at *your* feet. And people will talk about it for *years*. The warning will go out to girls that they cannot act this way. And every time people hear the name *Harry Virdee*, they will think of me and what I did and how it all started with *you*.'

Harry let him go but Adnan wasn't done.

'We are just like the spider and the wasp. Here you are, paralysed from my sting with nowhere to go whilst the seeds of my actions start to consume your life. You lost, Harry.'

Harry so badly wanted to smash his face in. He was way behind in the game.

'Is she alive?' he said.

'That depends.'

'On what?'

'What I say when I make my phone call.'

Harry left him, walking purposefully away, face burning with a heat he knew well.

But he had one card yet to play.

Upstairs, Harry returned the cell keys to Kevin.

'Thanks,' said Harry.

'Shit, you okay? Look like hell.'

'Just, you know, speaking with that psychopath. Proper piece of work. One more thing?'

'Sure.'

'You called a lawyer for him yet?'

'Next on my list.'

'Don't, not yet. Let him think on the shit he's done? Get used to that cell before the fucking suits arrive and give him rights he doesn't deserve.'

'Sure, Harry.'

'And hold off on his phone call too. I want him to stew as long as we can. Can you do that?'

'Sure,' said Kevin. 'After tonight, it's the least I can do for you.'

Harry exited Trafalgar House without attending the debrief.
One chance to stop Adnan.
One chance to save Saima.
One chance to save his boy.

EIGHTY

MIDNIGHT CRISIS MEETINGS WITH Ronnie were something Harry had hoped were confined to the past; yet here he was right now, standing inside his cash-and-carry, with Enzo also present. Ronnie had a look of disbelief on his face as Harry told him everything.

'I need your help, Ron, and I need it now,' said Harry desperately. He turned towards Enzo, and swallowed his pride. 'You too.'

'How long ago were they taken?' asked Ronnie. His expression had changed to one Harry was all too familiar with.

The darkness.

'Two hours ago,' said Harry, his every word laced with urgency.

'Enzo, you mind giving us a moment.'

Harry saw the look of disapproval on Enzo's face.

'I'm not excluding you, friend,' said Ronnie. 'I just need a moment alone with my brother.'

Enzo nodded and left, walking away into the gloom of the cash-and-carry.

'There's fucked up and then there is this,' said Ronnie removing his phone and hurriedly typing a text message.

'Will you help?' said Harry.

'Of course I fucking will,' replied Ronnie. The landline rang and Ronnie answered it. He held a hand up to Harry.

'No, I'm not kidding,' said Ronnie, speaking authoritatively into the phone. 'Couldn't give a toss about the snow. Get everyone here, ready to work within thirty minutes.'

He hung up.

'You've got a plan?' asked Ronnie.

Harry nodded and told him.

Ronnie shook his head, chewed his bottom lip. 'That's audacious, to say the least.'

'I can pull it off. I know I can. My family is on the line.'

'*Our* family,' said Ronnie, coming across to Harry and putting his hand reassuringly on his shoulder. 'Harry, I'm going to need something from you in return.'

'Anything.'

'A promise. That once this is over, you'll owe me one favour; any favour I want. No questions asked.'

'You've got it. Just help me get Saima and Aaron back.'

'I will. First, give me your kasam.'

Harry sighed. 'At this moment in time, I'd chop off my right arm if you asked. You have it. I swear a kasam, on my life, that I will owe you.'

Ronnie nodded outside, in Enzo's direction. 'Going to need his expertise. Which means you playing nice with him. Got it?'

'Yes.'

'Right. Now let's run through this one more time. Frame by frame. Because if we get this wrong, Harry, we're all going to burn.'

EIGHTY-ONE

HARRY RETURNED TO TRAFALGAR House at half past midnight, heart pumping, adrenaline flooding his body. He hurried to the top floor where Conway was getting ready to leave. Only an hour before, the briefing room had been buzzing with officers wrapping up the kidnap case. Their resources had been stretched to maximum capacity but that was done now, there were less than a dozen officers present – just another night shift.

In the kitchen, Harry hurriedly moved the toaster, grateful Conway hadn't got around to having the faulty thing replaced. This time it wouldn't be toast that burned. He balanced a large pack of kitchen-roll on top and pushed the whole thing under one of the wooden cabinets. He turned the toaster on, cranked up the power to full and left the room, wedging the fire door slightly ajar.

Outside, he waited a few minutes, until it started to smoke, then hurried down the corridor to Conway's office.

She was packing up for the night and looked as tired as Harry felt, now entering his twentieth hour without sleep.

'Christ, I wasn't expecting to see you back here,' said Conway.

'Too wired to go home.'

'How's your father?'

'Stable but serious. We'll know if he's going to make it by morning.'

'Wow. I'm sorry, Harry. Some week it's been, huh?'

'Did I miss anything at the debrief?'

'Nothing that can't wait until the morning. Go home, Harry. Sleep for a couple of days.'

'Is the chief okay with how it all went down?'

'Are you kidding? You're his new go-to guy. How did it feel out there in the middle of it all?'

Harry shrugged. 'Tough. Had some nerves.'

'Some nerves? You held it together like it was just any other day. Look, Harry, about not backing you up when you made the call. I was—'

'Already forgotten,' said Harry, smiling and using every ounce of energy to make this all appear as normal as possible.

'Thanks. Now, go on,' she said, grabbing her coat and her briefcase. 'We're done here. All in all, a good night's work.'

The fire alarm hadn't sounded yet and Harry didn't want her to leave until smoke was filling the corridor.

'Hang on,' he said. 'You . . . er, got anything to drink in here? I could use a hit of something to bring me back down to earth.'

She smiled. 'It's sure been one of those—'

The fire alarm sounded.

'Oh Christ, what now?' she said turning back to Harry. 'Have a look, will you?'

'Sure,' he said and stepped out, closing the door behind him.

Harry rushed down the corridor to see black fumes now wafting from the kitchen. He watched as several officers arrived in the hallway at the same time.

'Shit!' shouted Harry. 'Everyone out! Now. Full evac!'

They nodded and backed away towards the stairs.

Harry ran towards Conway's office and saw her rushing towards him.

'Jesus! It's real?'

Harry nodded, 'Bloody kitchen's on fire. Did you replace that damn toaster?'

'Shit,' she said, looking horrified at her error. 'Come on,' she said, pulling him towards the stairs.

They hurried downstairs until they hit ground level.

The duty-officer, Kevin, was gathering officers to assist in clearing the cells so they could all exit into the backyard.

Harry rushed over to Kevin. 'How many prisoners?'

'Eight,' he said.

'Let me help.'

Conway came with Harry as they followed another six officers downstairs into the cells. 'Give me cell eight's keys,' said Harry, taking them from Kevin. 'Clare, you and me take Adnan? At least with two of us, the bastard won't get any ideas.'

She nodded, anxious.

'Fire,' said Harry, staring Adnan straight in the eye.

For the first time, Adnan looked nervous.

Unsure of himself.

'Come on,' said Harry.

Adnan looked reassured when he saw Conway by Harry's side.

Harry cuffed Adnan's hands and pushed him out of the cells.

They moved quickly. Harry had his hand firmly on Adnan's arm, digging his fingers in, letting him know he was there.

Outside, the cold air sliced across their faces as they all hurried into the rear yard, a perfect picture of white, unbroken snow which continued to fall. Perimeter walls, fifteen feet high, were a serious warning against any thoughts of escape.

The prisoners lined up.

'On your fucking knees,' said Harry.

He kicked out at Adnan, who duly obeyed, glancing nervously around.

Conway stood the other side of him.

'Is this day ever going to end?' she said to Harry.

'Brigade will be here any minute. Get this shit sorted.'

'Better do,' she replied, shuddering, 'it's bloody freezing.'

'Murder. Kidnap. Snow. Now a fire. Throw in thunder and lightning and we'll have a real-life horror movie.'

Harry glanced behind him at the rear wall.

Movement.

Ropes.

He watched out the corner of his eye as two men came over the top. Both hidden behind balaclavas.

Ronnie's team.

They hit the ground silently and came running towards the prisoners.

A gunshot rang out.

High in the air.

Conway instinctively dropped to the floor.

Harry turned to find the men only feet away.

They were quick.

'Down, down, down,' one of the men shouted.

Another shot.

A scream.

'Don't make me ask again.'

Everyone dropped to the ground.

Except Harry.

'You deaf?'

'What do you want?' he asked.

'Just him. Nobody needs to die here. Just him.'

He pointed at Adnan.

'Not a fucking chance,' said Harry.

'Listen, pig, if you get in my way I'm gonna have to go right through you,' one of the balaclavas yelled.

Harry didn't move.

There was a flash of movement and one of the intruders suddenly lunged at Harry, slashing a blade at his arm.

It cut hard.

And deep.

Harry yelled out in pain and fell to the ground.

Blood splattered the snow.

He rolled over, clenching his teeth as the pain detonated through his body. He watched the two men drag Adnan towards the rear wall. One kept his gun trained on the yard. Nobody else moved.

A taser to the neck saw Adnan collapse to the floor. He was thrown over a broad shoulder, secured with a rope and hoisted over the wall. In under four minutes the whole operation was over. The team had disappeared, taking their ropes and their target with them.

Harry tried to get to his feet, groaning at the gash in his arm.

'Shit, Harry, are you okay?' said Conway, rushing towards him.

'Stabbed me,' he whispered.

'Stay where you are. Here,' she said, removing her jacket, tearing the sleeve off and using it to wrap around his wound. She pulled it tight and Harry yelled again.

'What the hell just happened?' he asked her.

Conway glanced at the rear wall in disbelief. 'We just lost the most wanted man in England,' she said.

EIGHTY-TWO

SAIMA VIRDEE HAD FAILED her son.

She was tied to a chair, mouth taped, hands in her lap, bound with barbed wire. From an adjacent room, she could hear Aaron crying.

Her little boy.

Saima winced at the noise, sadness quickly turning to rage deep in the pit of her stomach.

How long had he been crying?

How long had she been here?

She tried to struggle free of the barbed wire but it sliced at her skin. If she could have freed herself by shredding every inch of her wrists, Saima would have done so, but it was tied too tight.

Please stop crying, Aaron.

Mummy needs to focus.

She was in a warehouse of sorts.

She could just make out large metal containers outside of the small, dank side room she was being kept in. Other than that, nothing that gave her any clue.

Saima closed her eyes.

This was all her fault. She should have seen this coming.

But how?

She'd certainly never meant for this to happen.

Her marriage to Adnan had been arranged for as long as Saima could remember. She'd never really thought about it, it was just how things were done. But on the morning of the flight to Pakistan, she had unpacked the heavy red sari Adnan's mother had sent her.

Up until that point, the wedding had been something people spoke about, an idea. Yet now, holding the sari in her hands, Saima had started to feel rotten inside.

She couldn't explain it any other way.

Rotten.

She had unwrapped the sari and tried it on. Standing in front of the mirror, Saima saw nothing more than a child in adult clothing. She panicked.

It was to be a joint wedding, her parents and her sister had flown out early to help with the preparations but Saima had had to stay to take her exams. She was going to college to become a nurse, she couldn't miss her A levels.

When the morning of the flight had arrived, she had spoken to Nadia.

'Don't worry, it will all be okay once we are married. Come, Saima. I need you to share this burden with me.'

Burden.

Is that what being married was about?

Saima had not gone to the airport.

She had remained at home, growing increasingly afraid of what her parents would do.

Her parents had made a list of improbable excuses; missed planes, passport issues, everything. Nadia's wedding had gone ahead. When the family returned, her parents clearly considered the matter simply postponed. Saima had exchanged her Islamic vows over the phone already, according to her parents she was married. It just wasn't recognized by UK law yet.

But the more Saima thought about it, the more she knew, she was *not* married, and moreover she didn't *want* to be married in this way.

She refused her parents' request to sign the papers that would allow Adnan into the country as her husband.

She knew she'd been right when, aged twenty-two, she'd patched up the detective who'd come into A&E after a fight. That meeting with Harry had changed everything.

The fall-out had been severe.

The scar on her face, a result of telling her family about Harry and standing firm that she would not marry Adnan.

Shame.

Dishonour.

One day, Saima had simply left home.

Her family had tried to make her see sense. Hassled her at work. Saima had threatened them by pointing out Harry was a policeman and that if they continued to harass her, Harry would make sure his colleagues arrested them.

Finally, they had left her alone.

Saima had never told Harry about Adnan.

She hadn't seen the point. The marriage, as far as she was concerned, was no more than a telephone exchange. She had met him only once as a fifteen-year-old at Mumtaz restaurant. Even then the families had spoken about their future union. Now that she had retracted her paperwork to allow him into the country, she had simply thought nothing more of it.

Saima had learned that Adnan had finally made it into the country and married another girl from their community. She had believed the matter closed.

When she had rekindled her relationship with Nadia and seemingly cleared the air with Imran, she had been buoyed by the weight of knowing everybody had moved on.

Water under the bridge.

Darker times giving way to light.

Imran entered the room, his face twisted into a hatred Saima now understood.

She tried to talk but the tape over her mouth was strong.

Aaron was still crying.

He's in pain, she thought.

Imran closed the door and came close to her, Old Spice aftershave poorly masking the smell of sweat.

He kneeled by her side, eyes dark as stone.

'Now you will learn that those words you whispered down the phone were not just words.'

'I—'

Imran raised his hand for her to be quiet.

'Enough! You were so pure, so perfect. There was no need for you to sin as you did. Everyone in this city has forgotten their values, *our* values. But no more.'

Imran placed his hand on Saima's. 'My brother will fall tonight. And when he does, what is his *will become mine.'*

EIGHTY-THREE

BRADFORD ROYAL INFIRMARY WAS fast becoming a place Harry never wanted to return to. He'd been here too much recently for his liking.

One eye on the clock, he was in desperate need of treatment. He saw one of Saima's friends bustle past, gave her a wave, and she returned moments later to call him through. He identified himself to the night sister, Linda, who was friendly with Saima, and she saw to it that he was treated without delay.

'Saw Balraj earlier for a prescription for Aaron. Said he was working a six-six?' said Harry, trying to sound calm when he was anything but.

'He is. In a piss-bad mood. Always is, on his first night shift,' she said, looking at Harry's arm. The injury was just below his left shoulder.

'You're lucky,' said Linda. 'It's only a flesh wound, but it is going to need stitches.'

'How long?'

'I'll get straight on to it. Gonna need a clean, a tetanus shot and maybe two dozen stitches.'

'How long?' said Harry again, impatient.

'Thirty minutes.'

He nodded, checked his mobile and read the message his brother had sent him.

Don't stress about the old man. He's right where he needs to be.

So Ronnie had Adnan. He could afford to take a breath.

But not for long.

Harry's mind raced as Linda treated the wound. He didn't feel the pain, the fear of what Saima and Aaron were going through was far worse.

He sent Ronnie a hurried text.

Any news from the old man since I saw him?

No change.

Ronnie could be a sadistic bastard when he put his mind to it. Harry wasn't sure how Adnan would fare under Ronnie's scrutiny.

'How do you feel?' Linda asked when she was done.

'Light-headed,' said Harry. 'A little sick.'

'Did you bang your head when you fell?'

Harry nodded, he knew everything she needed to hear.

'Should have mentioned that earlier. I'm going to have to keep you in for observation.'

Harry nodded, here was the risky bit. 'Get me five minutes with Balraj, will you.'

'I did page him.'

'Try it again. Tell him Harry's here.'

'Come on, come on,' whispered Harry checking his watch again: 01:35.

By his estimation, four hours since Saima had been taken. When Harry had spoken to her at nine thirty, she'd sounded normal.

What the hell had happened in the hour between that call and Adnan surrendering to Harry?

Saima was leverage for Adnan, leverage he had intended to use.

'Harry?' said Balraj, coming into the side room, stethoscope bouncing around his neck, shirt hanging out of his trousers.

343

'Hey,' said Harry sitting up on the bed.

'Shit, are you okay?'

'Flesh wound,' said Harry. 'Listen, I need a favour.'

'Linda was saying you were feeling light-headed? A little sick?'

Harry told him he had made that up so they would admit him for a few hours.

'Why?' asked Balraj, confused.

'I've got to leave, mate, but I need an alibi in case what I've got to do goes bad.'

Balraj shook his head, more confused than ever.

'Look, I've got a massive case about to break and two people's lives are at risk. I'm the only one with the intel to save them, but I need to do it off the books – and for that I need an airtight alibi. We've been brothers since the corner shop days and you've *never* let me down.'

Balraj nodded, having never seen Harry so panic-stricken before.

'Sure. Whatever you need.'

'I need to be here "in spirit" for the next six-to-eight hours. Can you sort that?'

Balraj nodded. 'I'll document I'm keeping you in. Possible concussion.'

'Where's the CCTV in this place? How do I get out without being seen?'

'Out of here. Left and straight down the corridor leading to the ambulance bays. There's cameras out there, though.'

'On the left, or right?'

'Right.'

'Can you give me a towel? Make it look like I'm holding an ice pack?'

'I can get you an ice pack if you want?'

'No time,' said Harry.

Balraj stepped out and returned a few seconds later with a folded towel.

'Perfect.'

'Harry, what's going on?'

Harry didn't answer and got off the bed, grabbed an unopened packet of cheap hospital paper towels and wrapped the towel around them, making it look like an ice pack.

'Just buy me a window to leave without one of your colleagues seeing, and make sure you document that I was here until six and left soon after.'

Balraj stepped outside and after a couple of minutes gave Harry the all-clear to leave.

Outside, holding the towel against his cheek to prevent his face from being seen and keeping his head down, Harry hurried towards the exit, on to Duckworth Lane. He saw Ronnie's Range Rover parked on the other side of the road, covered in snow, and walked cautiously on the footpath.

'We good?' said Harry, getting into the passenger seat.

Enzo pulled away, accelerating quickly.

'We good?' asked Harry more forcefully.

Enzo nodded. 'Piece of cake,' he said amicably. 'My boys didn't cut you too hard, did they?'

'No. It was perfect. Serious enough to need treatment, not so serious they put me out of commission. Is he talking yet?'

'No.' Enzo's eyes stayed glued to the road ahead. 'We don't have the luxury of time if we're going to end this with a good result, Harry.'

'Don't worry. I only need five minutes with him.'

Enzo glanced at Harry, uncertain.

'Everyone has a weakness,' said Harry. 'And I know his.'

EIGHTY-FOUR

HARRY ENTERED QUEENSBURY TUNNEL alone having dispatched Enzo to the other side of Bradford. He needed a backup in case Adnan proved tougher to crack than Harry anticipated.

Serial killers were always after the same thing: control.

If Harry took that away from him, he'd have the best shot of saving his family.

Harry heard screaming in the distance.

As he got closer to it, he realized it wasn't screaming.

It was laughter.

Harry turned his torch off as he arrived beside Ronnie, who put down the blowtorch. Sweat was dripping down his face and he had blood spattered across his hands.

Adnan was kneeling on the ground, bloodied and bruised, burn-marks on his chest.

'Won't talk,' said Ronnie. 'Not yet anyway. If we had a couple of days, we'd do it. But time's the one thing we don't have. How's the arm?'

'I'll live,' said Harry, kneeling beside Adnan. 'What is it that you want, you sick fuck?'

Adnan spat a mouthful of blood at Harry which fell short. He wiped his face with the back of his hand.

'What are you?' said Adnan. 'A police officer? Or a criminal? It's hard to keep track of you, Harry.'

'I'm a lot of different things. Right now? I'm a husband looking for his family.'

Adnan stared at Ronnie. 'And you?'

'I'm here to get the job done.'

'I won't tell you where they are. It's time for you to suffer like I have.'

Harry got to his feet and told Ronnie to bring Adnan to the mouth of the tunnel and leave the tools he was using to torture him with.

Ronnie pulled Harry aside.

'Why?' he said. 'Clock's ticking.'

'Pain isn't going to work with him, I'm going to show him he's not the only one with something to lose.'

Outside, Harry threw Adnan on the ground.

Adnan's blood soiled the snow and he grimaced as the cold sliced through his wounds.

'Your phone,' said Harry to Ronnie. 'Facetime Enzo.'

Ronnie stared at Harry, puzzled. 'Say again?'

'Do it.' Harry kicked out at Adnan. 'You like the video-call thing, don't you? Let's see how you like being on the receiving end this time.'

Enzo answered quickly, Ronnie immediately passing the phone to Harry.

'Show me,' he said, then crouched by Adnan's side and showed him the screen.

Adnan stared at Harry with intense hatred. Then he looked at the phone and slowly his smirk faded.

'Thing is, those guys who bust you out of prison? They're now outside that care home your darling mother is in. I don't like to take advantage of an elderly woman, but if you don't tell me where my wife and son are? I'm going drag her from that place, bring her here, put her in the tunnel and make sure she lives the next year in darkness. With the rats. And the cold.'

Adnan's jaw tensed.

'I don't care about her. It's why I put her there.'

Harry laughed.

'I've seen your phone records. You call the home on average six times a day. You visit her twice daily. You take her food in. Even this week, when you've been killing innocent girls and fucking with my city, you still had time for Mummy, didn't you?'

Harry stood up and kicked Adnan, who no longer looked so pleased with himself.

'Typical little Asian boy, pandering to his mum even when he's a grown man. You're pathetic.'

'You leave her alone,' spat Adnan, every word now laced with panic.

'Enzo,' said Harry, turning the phone towards him. 'Lift her. Strip her naked and put her in the boot.'

'No!' screamed Adnan, and stood up suddenly, lunging for Harry. He knocked the phone from Harry's hands and got his bloodstained hands around his neck, his grip powerful in spite of the injuries Ronnie had inflicted.

Ronnie pulled him away and threw him on the ground.

'Got you,' whispered Harry, wiping Adnan's blood from his neck.

Harry picked up the iPhone. The screen showed Enzo, walking towards the care home.

'You want to watch?' he said to Adnan, who was back on his feet. Harry turned the phone so Adnan could see.

'Your choice. Either I take the only thing you care about and stick her in a place worse than any hell you're going to,' said Harry, pointing behind him at the tunnel, 'or we end this now.'

Adnan was breathing heavily, his eyes shifting from the phone to Harry.

On screen, Enzo reached the front entrance of the care home and rang the doorbell.

'Okay!' shouted Adnan. 'You tell him to back away. You tell him to leave her!'

'Stand down, Enzo,' said Harry, speaking into the phone and showing it to Adnan, who watched Enzo retreat to his car.

Harry ended the call.

'Now,' he said stepping closer to Adnan. 'I'm not going to ask again. Where are Saima and Aaron?'

'If I help you here, you'll kill me. Take me back to the police station and I will tell you everything.'

'No, you fucked that up already,' said Harry. 'You'll come with us now. I take my family back and your brother takes you. An exchange. After that? It's on you. You can try running from the police if you like but I'm sure they'll find you.'

'How do I know you'll leave my mother alone?'

'Because, unlike you, I'm not a sociopath. I'll do whatever it takes to get Saima and Aaron back, but once I have them, this ends.'

Harry dialled Enzo again, the rings audible for Adnan to hear.

'You've got until he answers. You haven't told me by then, nothing saves your mother,' said Harry, coolly using every last bit of patience he had.

First ring.

Second.

'They're at a warehouse at Leeds – Bradford Airport,' said Adnan.

EIGHTY-FIVE

THEY ARRIVED AT THE airport forty minutes later, Ronnie's Range Rover easily cutting through the snow.

Harry sat in the back wringing his hands, eyes staring out the window.

Ronnie pulled off the A58 and away from the main terminal building, under instruction from Adnan. Behind, Enzo was following in another vehicle.

They drove a mile and pulled into a large industrial estate; it looked like a new cargo area was being built.

'Where now?' said Ronnie, slowing down.

'If we give you what you want, you will kill us,' said Adnan.

Harry wanted to put his head through a window.

'Nothing would give me more pleasure. But you're forgetting one thing. My son's in there. I'm not putting him through that. We're doing this by the book.'

Harry leaned forward and spoke to Ronnie. 'You hear that?'

'Yeah,' said Ronnie. He didn't sound convinced.

Harry could see Adnan weighing up his options.

'When we make the exchange,' he said, 'before my brother hands

Saima over, you'll need to call the police – 999. I want them on their way, so we know you will not kill us.'

'Absolutely not, no police. Let's get one thing straight, when this is over, you go back to your cage with no idea of what happened to you. You were taken, you were tortured and then you were set free. You mention me or my wife and your mother ends up in the tunnel.'

Harry grabbed at Adnan, gripping his face with one hand. 'Are you starting to realize you fucked with the wrong man?' He let go, leaving Adnan's eyes blazing with fury.

'Now, which warehouse is it?' asked Harry, pointing in the distance at dozens of them at different stages of completion.

'End one. Green shutter,' said Adnan.

'What's inside?'

'Shipping containers.'

'Heading where?' asked Harry.

Adnan didn't reply.

'You were going to try and get them back to Pakistan? For what? An honour-based homecoming?'

Harry grabbed Adnan by the throat, pulling him close.

'You're damn lucky I *can't* kill you. Because if I could, I'd do it a thousand times over.'

Enzo went round the back as Harry and Ronnie approached the side door to the warehouse. keeping in the shadows, ghosting past pallets of cement, breeze-blocks and timber all covered with a thick layer of snow. They'd left Adnan in the car, handcuffed, gagged and locked in the boot. Ronnie offered Harry a gun. He didn't want one, but had his crowbar with him.

Harry snapped the lock, there was a sharp crack of metal.

The men kept in the shadows of the mammoth storage facility, exposed steel and towering girders. They headed towards a small office at the back, where a dull light was on.

Harry heard Aaron crying and started to rush towards the sound. Ronnie's grip on his arm pulled him back.

'Not so fast,' he hissed.

They were halfway across the depot when Harry saw Aaron, lying on the cold, dirty floor crying.

Ronnie held up a hand.

They heard glass shattering.

Enzo.

Loud.

Too loud.

Aaron sat up, afraid.

From inside the office, Harry saw a dark shadow stand and make for the door.

In that moment, with only twenty yards between them, Aaron saw Harry.

'Daddy!' he yelled.

'Shit,' hissed Ronnie. 'Go!'

Harry was already running for his son.

Harry reached Aaron just as Imran stepped outside, brandishing a knife. Seeing Harry scooping Aaron up in his arms, his eyes widened and he retreated quickly back inside the office.

'Hey, little man,' said Harry, hugging him tightly, tears spilling from his eyes.

Imran re-emerged, pulling Saima by her hair. He had the knife at her throat.

'Stay back!' he yelled.

Keeping hold of Aaron, Harry moved towards them. Saima had bruises on her face. Her eyes were red, there was dirt smeared across her cheeks and her wrists were bound with wire.

Harry handed Aaron to Ronnie, who struggled to take him.

'No! No! No!' screamed Aaron, the wail echoing around the warehouse.

'Get him out of here,' said Harry.

'Where?'

'I don't know, just get him out!'

Ronnie retreated with Aaron back towards the entrance; Aaron's screeching was deafening.

'I don't know how you found me,' spat Imran. 'But I'm glad you're here. Now you get to watch as I take something from you that was never yours to begin with.'

Harry inched forward, hands out passively, desperately looking for a way out of this.

'It's over, Imran. Just . . . let Saima go and we all walk away. If you do this, yes, you will take Saima from me but I'll also take something from you. You'll go to jail, you won't be able to be with your family. *We'll both lose.*'

'She destroyed my family the day she broke with tradition. The day she chose you over my brother.'

'That's not how it happened. We . . . we . . . hadn't even met, then.'

'Bullshit!'

'It's the truth, Imran,' said Harry, continuing to creep forward. 'I just want this to end with no more bloodshed.'

'How did you find us?' spat Imran.

'I'm a police officer.'

'No . . . What did you do to my brother to make him tell you?'

'I offered him a deal. And he took it.'

'I don't believe you. Is he dead?'

'No,' said Harry. 'You want to talk to him? I can make that happen.'

'No. I want to see you suffer. I want you to watch your wife die. I want to regain my family's honour.'

Imran's veins were bulging on his neck.

'Okay!' said Harry, eyes searching desperately for Enzo in the shadows, 'I understand we've got to pay. Just . . . let me have a final few words. At least give me that.'

Imran nodded. 'Say what you have to.'

Keeping his hands outstretched, Harry took a few precarious steps towards Saima.

Only a few feet now between them.

'Try anything smart and I'll kill you too,' snapped Imran.

'Saima,' said Harry and smiled, 'listen to me.'

She blinked back tears, mouth still taped shut.

'Just lower the knife, Imran. An inch, that's all. She can't focus on me with the blade against her skin.'

Harry dropped to one knee and laid his crowbar down on the floor beside him. 'Look, I'm not going to try anything. I'm surrendering the only weapon I brought with me. You can see that.'

Imran lowered the knife, only an inch.

'Saima, before this happens, I want you to think back to Tuesday morning.' Harry laughed. 'Remember when we were in the bathroom with Aaron. You were getting ready, brushing his teeth. Remember what he did?' Harry smiled, really selling the family memory bit. 'Before you're taken from me, think about that. It will help you.'

Saima's eyes were on Harry's.

'Please,' he said. 'Don't be afraid.'

Saima dropped her head on to her chest, the blade now again in contact with her skin.

Harry watched her, fists clenched, tense against the barbed wire. Then, with a strength he had never seen in her before, she sent her head backwards, the back of her skull thundering into Imran's nose.

It shattered on impact.

Aaron had given Saima a nose bleed.

At the same time, Harry leapt forwards, shoving Saima out of harm's way.

Imran didn't hesitate, he came forward with a mad fury. Blood dripped down his face.

The men struggled and Imran dropped the knife, which clattered to the floor. He raised a knee into Harry's stomach, knocking the wind from him. As Harry crumpled to the floor, he lashed out, sending his palm into Imran's nose to compound the damage.

Imran fell backwards, toppled over and hit the floor, blinded by his own blood.

Harry struggled for breath as Imran got urgently to his feet.

This guy was unstoppable.

Harry watched in horror as he picked up the knife.

Before he could use it, Harry heard Saima scream as she swung Harry's crowbar at Imran's head, striking him across the temple.

Imran froze and crumpled to the floor.

Saima's face was as dark as rotten fruit, eyes narrow, face contorted like she was possessed. She gripped the crowbar in her hands, barbed wire cutting into her wrists, making them bleed. She stood over Imran and struck his head again.

'You don't get to live after what you did,' she screamed as blood started to pool around his head.

Imran didn't move.

Harry froze, pure disbelief at what Saima had done.

History repeating, Harry with a body at his feet, blood all over the floor, weapon in hand.

'Saima,' whispered Harry, gently putting his hands on hers.

She gritted her teeth, stared at Imran's lifeless body, jaw muscles tensing.

Harry put his arms around her and tried to pull her towards him.

He heard footsteps and turned to see Ronnie rushing into the room, gun drawn. As soon as he saw Imran's body he put it away.

'Shit,' said Ronnie, stopping by Harry. 'Did you?'

Harry shook his head. Danced his eyes towards Saima.

Ronnie sighed. 'Oh, Jesus,' he whispered.

'Where's Aaron?' asked Harry.

'With Enzo. He . . . couldn't get in the back. Window was too small.'

Harry nodded.

'How is the little guy?'

'Wants his daddy.'

'I know.'

Harry pulled Saima away from the scene, back towards the office.

'Are you okay?' he asked. She still looked possessed by fury.

'I want to go home,' she whispered coldly.

'We're going,' said Harry.

'I'm not going to jail,' she replied. 'Not for him.'

'You're not,' said Harry forcefully. 'I will sort this.'

'How can you—'

'Nobody will ever know.'

She nodded firmly. 'They don't get to win. You hear me?'

'They won't. I . . . I . . . just need a minute with Ronnie. Let me take you to Aaron. Enzo is a good guy. He's one of us, a police offi-cer,' lied Harry. 'I need you to be with Aaron. Calm him down and leave me for a few minutes to arrange this. Can you do that, Saima?' asked Harry, holding her face in his hands.

'I can,' she said, the defiance of what she had done clear in her face.

'Good. Come on,' he said, 'let's get your hands free of this damn wire and get you to Aaron.'

Harry and Ronnie stood by the side of Imran's body.

'I've got a crew on the way,' said Ronnie.

'Good,' replied Harry. 'His body needs to disappear.'

'It will.'

'Bury it deep in the tunnel, Ron.'

'Not the tunnel. Too good for this piece of shit. I'm going to torch it. Make his brother watch.'

Harry grabbed Ronnie. 'Not Adnan. You know what needs to happen to him!'

'Don't worry.'

'Tornado 2-ply barbed wire. Make sure,' said Harry.

'I've got it from here.'

'I don't know what to say, Ron.'

'You don't need to. Whenever this settles down – next week? Next month? You remember you promised me something.'

Harry embraced his brother.

'I owe you, Ron,' he said. 'More than you'll ever know.'

EIGHTY-SIX

THE NEXT TWO DAYS were a blur.

Dog walkers had found Adnan's body the following morning, hanging from a lamppost near the Leeds–Liverpool Canal. Whoever had done it had used the same barbed wire which Adnan had used to strangle his victims.

With his reputation for violence and intimidation, Tariq Islam had become the prime suspect. He'd denied any knowledge of it. Far from being enraged and actively pushing out a campaign to deny his involvement, Harry had watched as he addressed the media, repeatedly saying,

'I've given my statement to the police and I'm happy to cooperate with their investigation as fully as possible until this matter is resolved.'

The man was a national hero, the ex-military politician who had used his connections to enact his own revenge on a twisted ethnic serial killer.

He was gathering an *enormous* online following, the public having a real appetite for the street justice handed down to the killer.

Truthfully, *it had done his reputation no harm.*

*

Ronnie had covered his tracks.

In the moments following Adnan's abduction, CCTV showed three armed men racing away from Trafalgar House. Whilst Bradford had a robust camera network, there were black holes. Each and every one of which had been exploited by Ronnie's men, on direction from Harry. Harry heard someone say it looked like an inside job.

The car used to abduct Adnan had been dumped and burned.

The police had no leads.

No one at Trafalgar House was crying over Adnan's murder.

A somewhat muted investigation into the fire had been launched, but since there were no CCTV cameras in that area, it had simply been put down to mechanical error.

Harry had been signed off work for a month with the injury to his arm. He was keeping a low profile and hadn't left the house. No one was pressing for an alibi, but the hospital records were airtight, Balraj having signed him out at six a.m.

Harry had nothing to worry about.

Apart from Saima.

Aaron had done as only a three-year-old could and got back into his routine quickly, unaware of what had really happened.

But Saima was a different matter.

She'd gladly nudged her sister into believing that Imran had finally left her for his other woman. But when it came to her own recovery, she wasn't doing so well. She had slept for almost two days, content to let Harry look after Aaron. Harry had let her be but she knew she couldn't hide for ever.

Seventy-two hours later, Saima was sitting at the dining table, having showered and finally changed out of her pyjamas. Harry saw it as progress but her face was drawn and she had large bags under her eyes.

'Hey,' said Harry, pouring himself a Jack Daniels and bringing it to the table.

Saima looked at his glass.

'I could absolutely understand if the last few days made you want to finally have your first alcoholic drink,' he said.

She smiled weakly. It faded just as soon as it had appeared.

'Where to begin?' whispered Saima.

'For you? Or me?'

She shook her head, smiling ruefully. 'Who has the greatest secret to tell? That was some heist to pull . . .' she hesitated to say his name, 'that bastard out of jail. Balaclavas? Ropes? Guns?' she said, swallowing a lump in her throat.

She finally looked at Harry. 'Just *who* did I marry?'

Harry looked down at the table.

'I know what happened between you and Adnan,' said Harry. 'What I don't understand is why you didn't tell me?'

She shrugged. 'I was a kid. I erased it from my mind. The Saima who didn't get on that plane as a naïve girl died the day she took that stance.'

She pointed to Harry's drink. 'Does it help? With the lies?'

Harry sighed. 'No,' he said, pushing it aside.

'What we put that little guy through?' Her hand went straight to her throat, guilt clear on her face.

'Hey,' said Harry, moving across to her and kneeling by her side. 'Aaron's fine. He doesn't even know what happened. You should have seen him tonight in the bath. Honest, he won't ever remember it.'

'I will.'

Harry paused. Held his breath for a moment.

'Did he hurt you, Saima?'

She shook her head. 'No. He said he was going to. But he didn't get the chance, the twisted fuck.'

Saima swore so rarely, Harry was a little stunned.

'I killed someone,' she said, turning to face him. 'I'm a *murderer.*'

'No,' said Harry. 'You can't think that way.'

She raised her hand to silence him. 'You know the worst part?'

'What?'

'I don't even regret it. When I did it, the release of rage it gave me— God, what am I saying?'

'He got what he deserved. It was him or you.'

'I'm glad it was him. What I don't understand is how I'm still sitting here. Why I'm not in prison? How . . . how . . . I got away with it? How you found me? How . . .' she again refrained from using Adnan's name, '. . . *he* was found hanging from a lamppost after being broken out of jail. He was the only one who knew where we were. That means . . . you? You did this? But how?'

Harry stood up, picked up his drink and turned away from Saima.

'Don't stand by the window, Harry. Not this time. You've got something to tell me, then you do it right here at this table. Face to face.'

Harry sipped his whisky.

He wanted to stand in the bay window, he wanted to feel safe.

But Saima was right.

Not tonight.

Harry sat opposite Saima and put his drink on the table.

'My brother, Ronnie,' he said. 'There's something about him you need to know. Something about *me* you need to know. Something that started nineteen years ago, in our corner shop, when *I* killed someone.'

EIGHTY-SEVEN

FRIDAY NIGHT, A WEEK after the trauma of what had occurred with Saima, Harry arrived at the Leeds–Liverpool Canal, where Ronnie had left Adnan hanging from a lamppost.

The snow had melted, leaving the ground waterlogged and glistening under the glare of streetlights. Harry walked the route he had done when Adnan had killed his fourth victim, throwing her from the bridge.

Why here?

Why now?

He saw the silhouette of a man sitting on a bench. Harry scanned the area. He couldn't see Tariq Islam's personal protection detail anywhere but assumed they were close by.

'Thought you would have had enough of this city by now,' said Harry, taking a seat next to Tariq.

'I've had enough to last me a lifetime,' replied Tariq, offering Harry a plastic cup of coffee.

'Thoughtful,' said Harry taking it.

'Least I could do.'

'You surprised the hell out of me with your call.'

It was a lie.

Harry had been expecting it but hoping the call would never come.

Tariq was staring at Harry, smiling.

Harry sipped his coffee, waiting for the inevitable.

'And people thought my history was murky,' said Tariq finally.

There it was. As loaded a statement as Tariq could have delivered.

'Don't follow,' said Harry, staring at a bridge he had jumped from a few days before. He shuddered at the memory of how cold the water had been.

Tariq told Harry that he had looked into Adnan's history at the Home Office. The visa application submitted by Imran, who just happened to be married to Nadia.

'Took a little digging to bring this thing back to you,' said Tariq. 'Figured out Nadia and Saima are sisters.'

Harry sighed. 'Who else knows?'

'Nobody yet. I've sealed the papers. Perhaps they'll go missing.'

Harry stared at Tariq. 'Why would you do that?'

He waited for an answer.

'Some heist you pulled off. No idea how you did it. Looked into you. Nothing stands out. Brother's got a record. But nothing there to link to this. So how did you do it?'

Harry tightened his grip around the coffee.

'Don't follow,' he said quietly.

'Group 13. People have been hounding me with that shit for years. Covert ops. Whispers of assassinations. All that stuff people love to speculate about.'

Harry let him speak.

'That's what it would have taken to pull off what you did. That kind of discipline,' said Tariq.

He put a hand on Harry's shoulder and squeezed it. 'Out-fucking-standing,' he said.

Their eyes met. Harry saw that Tariq was beaming.

'Tell me how. And I'll kill the investigation from my end. Burn the papers. Make Adnan just another illegal who wanted to do this country harm. But I want to know how you did it. I need to know.'

Harry sipped his coffee.

How much could he trust Tariq?

'You told me that if I saved Aisha – put myself on the line – you would owe me a favour.'

'Yes. And I seem to recall getting the distinct impression there was a favour down the line to be had.'

Harry nodded.

'He deserved what happened to him – Adnan.'

'Agreed.'

'Can't we just leave it at that? Call that my favour.'

'We could. Except, that makes us even. No more favours down the line.'

Harry sighed. Thought about the pact he had made with Ronnie and how badly they needed someone like Tariq Islam for what their future might hold.

'Are we off the record here?' asked Harry.

'Yes.'

'You want me to trust you with this, I need something in return.'

'Such as?'

'I don't know. A secret I could bury you with. Something which makes us even.'

'You don't need that. We are alike, you and I. We get shit done. Sometimes at the expense of how things should be done. I don't know what I would have done had I lost Aisha, she's all I've got. For saving her life, you have my allegiance. The fact you managed to string that son of a bitch up to that lamppost,' said Tariq, nodding in the distance to where Adnan had been found, 'simply makes me admire you.'

Harry grinned. 'You wouldn't believe me if I told you.'

'Try me.'

'I will. But when the time is right. Can we leave it at that?'

Tariq thought about it. 'I don't like not knowing. Makes me wonder just what else you are capable of.'

'Do you know Bradford? I mean, before this shit happened?'

'Every Asian man knows Bradford. Doesn't take long to find a relative or family friends in this city.'

'It's not like anywhere else. It's . . . I don't know, sort of like Gotham. You've got to stay in the shadows sometimes, become the city. Understand its energy, the good and the bad. And there's some dark times to come, maybe darker than we've ever known. But after that – it's all about moving forwards. Winning. And that's when we'll revisit this conversation. Can you live with that?'

Tariq stood up, put his hands in his pocket and looked around the canal. 'I guess I'll have to, Harry.'

He turned and put his hand out.

Harry stood up and shook it.

'I've got you covered,' said Tariq. 'Adnan's history won't ever get connected to Saima or to you.'

'You're a good man,' replied Harry.

'No. I'm not. At least, not in the conventional sense. I'm aiming for the top position in politics and I'm pretty certain this . . . bond, let's call it, that we have forming here, is the start of something useful.'

Harry's eyes narrowed, both men analysing each other hard.

'Have a safe trip back to London,' said Harry.

Tariq let go of his hand and smiled.

'So long, Harry Virdee. Till we meet again.'

Harry watched him leave.

Had he just made a powerful ally or was he now a pawn in something he was yet to fully understand?

Time, it seemed, would tell.

EIGHTY-EIGHT

SITTING IN THE QUIET of Ronnie's cash-and-carry, Harry was on edge. The workers had left for the evening, leaving the brothers alone in the office.

'How's Saima?' asked Ronnie. 'Is she coping?'

You'll owe me, Harry.

That's why they were here. The favour Harry had committed to. One he had to keep.

'She's doing okay. It'll take time. I had to tell her about us.'

Ronnie raised an eyebrow. 'Everything?'

Harry smiled ruefully. 'If I told her everything, she'd never believe it. She knows about what happened in the corner shop and about your real business interests.'

Ronnie sighed and chewed his lip. 'Complicates things, Harry.'

'You helped save her life and Aaron's. As far as she's concerned, you're a hero. We spoke about the truth and then, as Mum used to say, poured dirt in the grave.'

'So, she knows what? That I distribute drugs?'

'Yes. And that's all.'

'At least you don't have to hide it from her now. Because the

366

family is going to unite, Harry. And it starts right here. Right now.'

Ronnie handed Harry a detailed folder, full of official-looking articles and statistics. He sat down in a large, executive leather chair and beckoned for Harry to do the same.

'Government's broke. Cuts to policing, NHS and every area of spending,' said Ronnie.

Harry was confused. 'What's this got to do with us?' he said, only giving the file a cursory glance.

'There's six months of work in your hands. A blueprint for the future.'

Harry rested the file in his lap and waited for Ronnie to explain.

'Drug crime is at an all-time high. Politicians cannot hide it any more. Ninety per cent of the services for addiction have closed, leaving addicts with nowhere to go except back to the streets. Crime pays for them to use the drugs and round and round we go. Puts a strain on everything. Finally, Whitehall is about to give the green-light to a trial, starting in Bradford. Legalizing heroin through registered outlets. I've been working with some people high up the food chain, all very hush-hush. Sensitive matters.'

Harry stared at Ronnie in disbelief.

'Don't look at me like that. You know what I'm saying is true. We legalize it, make the supply pure and remove the criminal element. Everybody wins. Pressures on policing, health and social mobility all ease. We're looking nationally at overall savings of billions and it starts here. In Bradford.'

Harry knew that, for some time now, conversations had been spiking about the legalization of drugs. It was a war the government was never going to win.

'Pure heroin isn't any more dangerous than booze,' said Ronnie, pointing behind Harry towards the shadows of the cash-and-carry. 'At least with alcohol, the government coffers are lined.'

Harry placed the file on the desk. 'What does it have to do with me?'

'The trial needs to work and it will, but there's one problem. The Europeans making inroads into this city. Darker animals than me. Those boys drop bodies like confetti. You know what I'm talking about. HMET's body count was at an all-time high last year.'

'Argh, shit, I know what's coming,' Harry said, resigned.

He grimaced and scratched the stubble on his face.

Ronnie took the file from the desk, opened it and removed the very first page, a large colourful graph. He held it up for Harry to see.

'We're looking at a seventy per cent reduction in crime. A twenty per cent reduction in the strain on NHS services. Fuck me, that's a lottery win for this city. But I need to flush these European bastards out of Bradford and, so far, I'm struggling to find out who they are. We remove them – we win. I get out of the illegal drug trade, into a legal supply route and we create history. As long as I can prove it works, the rest of the UK will follow. Might take years, but it will happen. We create a legacy which will never be forgotten. It's what Tara wanted – change for this city and to make a difference. And it's what you wanted – me out of the game. This way we all win.'

Harry stood up and turned to stare into the gloom of the cash-and-carry. He approached the window and stood, hands in pockets, head bowed.

'Still like to stand by the window to think?' asked Ronnie.

'Mmm,' replied Harry.

He'd promised Ronnie and couldn't renege.

Yet this was far from simple.

Harry had dealt with over a dozen murders in the past eighteen months, all connected to a new breed of European criminal. Like Ronnie had said, these guys thought nothing of dropping a body.

Harry heard Ronnie come towards him, both brothers now side by side, looking into the shadows of the warehouse.

'Once they realize Bradford is going to legalize a trial of heroin, they'll want to come for the guy arranging the supply. Ensure it never happens. They'll put everyone I care about in danger. It's how they work. No boundaries. I want us all back together and this way, it can happen. We take out the garbage, get our hands dirty one last time and after that, we go legit.'

Ronnie put his arm around Harry. 'That's what I want from you. One final time. Help me and Enzo take these guys out. You work from the top, us from the bottom and, in a year's time, we'll change this city and our family's futures for ever.'

Harry looked at Ronnie now, eyes narrowed, jaw tense.

'I want you out of this life once and for all. I want my family back together. And you know I always repay my debts. I'll do this with you. One last time,' he said quietly, now turning to face his brother. 'Like you said: once it's done, Bradford will finally turn that corner.'

Harry embraced Ronnie tightly, feeling both hopeful and at the same time, apprehensive.

One year. One team. *One fight they had to win.*

EPILOGUE

STANDING ALONE BY HIS father's body, Harry stared at the monitors bleeping by the hospital bed.

Blood pressure: 100/55.

Pulse: fifty.

It was late, there was nobody else around.

Another day where Ranjit Virdee had neither woken up nor passed on.

Limbo.

Harry knew what Limbo felt like.

He paced the room.

He'd made a promise to his wife.

'If you touch my feet, I will be forced to cut them off,' whispered Harry. He wasn't sure he could keep it.

Looking over at his father, anger burned deep in his chest. But there was something else too, something softer.

He took off his jacket, hung it over the door to the room, blocking the view through the small square window so that no one passing would see what was about to happen. Harry rolled up his sleeves and took a cushion from behind his father's head.

370

'That is some poison you have in your heart for me, Dad,' he said, shaking his head.

Holding the pillow in his hand, Harry squeezed it hard. 'But these things need to be done.'

Harry ran the tap in the sink, filling a plastic jug with warm water. He grabbed a towel, stood by the foot of the bed and pulled the bedsheet back from his father's feet. He lifted them and placed the cushion underneath.

'I came here to say so many things, Dad. Now I'm here, there doesn't seem much point.'

Harry poured a little water over his father's feet, grabbed a bar of soap from the sink and gently washed them.

He took his time, making sure they were fully lathered before pouring warm water from the jug over them, the pillow absorbing the water, stopping it from soaking the mattress.

Harry dried his father's feet, again taking his time, and left them exposed.

'When a son loses a father, he's supposed to wash the body. Purify it before it is cremated. And whilst we might not be there yet, if it does happen, you wouldn't want me to honour you that way.'

Harry backed off, stood by the wall, looking at his father and not retreating to the window which is where he wanted to be.

'I didn't do this off my own back,' said Harry. 'Saima asked me to. My way – no, our way of saying we forgive you. *We get it.* You can't change. It's too late in the day, you're too long in the tooth – you pick your cliché.'

Harry stepped forward and put his hands on his father's feet. 'Never did touch yours every morning.' Harry shook his head slowly. 'Dad, I've spent all this time hating you for what you did to me but I realize . . . I did it to you, too. To us all. For that – only for that, mind – I am sorry,' said Harry, squeezing his father's feet gently. 'But I'll never be sorry for marrying Saima. She came in here to try to show you how good she is. That she is worthy of your love. You gave her your poison. Yet, still, she asked me to do this. Because if you don't recover, she doesn't want me to feel the pain of knowing that the last thing I should have done for you, washing your body, I couldn't.'

Harry removed the pillow from under his father's feet and placed it on the floor under the bed. He grabbed his jacket, pulling it on slowly over his wounded arm.

'If you do die tonight, I'm certain that wherever you go, you will see that I made the right choice.'

Harry dimmed the light in the room.

'But if you decide to wake up, that's okay too. Because I'm done with the pain, Dad. I'm done with the past. I'm done with you.'

ACKNOWLEDGEMENTS

Huge thanks to former DCI Stephen Snow for his time and help in assisting with the procedural aspects of this novel. Any errors are mine, sacrificing protocol for drama! Seriously, mate, you really supported me on this and I'm massively grateful.

Dr Louise Mulcahy, for some pointers with the finer details of post-mortems. Once again, any errors are solely mine in the pursuit of pace and drama.

Dr Seirian Sumner (@waspwomen) for entertaining my (many) bizarre queries to do with wasps. Your knowledge of these fascinating insects is incredible and I will admit to shifting my views from 'uneasy' to 'interested'. I am really very thankful for your input.

Phil Williams for allowing me to fuse reality with fiction. I do hope you are never faced with such a scenario as happens in the book, but you can always call on Harry!

To my brilliant editor, Darcy Nicholson, for your passionate support. We've worked really hard on this and I'm proud to have you on my team. You are my secret weapon in a fiercely competitive market. To the Transworld family – every link in the chain is vital and as important as the writing itself. I'm privileged to have such a talented unit on my side.

To my agent, Simon Trewin and WME, for their continual support and encouragement.

To writing friends who have become a second family: Ayisha Malik, Abir Mukherjee, Vaseem Khan, Imran Mahmood and Alex Caàn for being 'there' and championing everything we are all trying to achieve; there isn't a cliché in sight and long may it continue!

To my friend Vinod Lalji, for the constant encouragement. You never, ever allow me to waver from the objective and keep me on-point.

To my family, for their continued understanding and support when I am stressed, busy, unsociable, late, moody and all the other things you've become accustomed to when I'm in 'writing-mode'.

Final words (as always) for my wife; we started this together and we continue it together. I write the books for you; a dream which became reality and a reality which transcended our expectations. So, keep doing what you do; it makes me do what I do.

A. A. Dhand was raised in Bradford and spent his youth observing the city from behind the counter of a small convenience store. After qualifying as a pharmacist, he worked in London and travelled extensively before returning to Bradford to start his own business and begin writing. The history, diversity and darkness of the city have inspired his Harry Virdee novels.